The Orphan and the Sea

Julie Lesch

Contents

Chapter 1

London, England

December 1813

Twilight had fallen yet the beauty of the subtle, diffused sky went unnoticed for it revealed the ominous stretch of darkness with its betraying shadows concealing predators of intended violence and misfortune. These blackened streets of London were the foreboding domain for society's most corrupt and bloodthirsty criminals. The inclement weather was as disagreeable as the morbid region. It was the period of decay with a bitter cold that enveloped the body in a frigid shroud, sinking deep to the bone, bringing forth a state of numbness.

A small, distinct shadow cautiously made its way through the desolate streets that would be teeming with life on the morrow. Hovering deep into the ragged overcoat that swallowed the child's tiny frame, beneath it was a tunic consisting of various holes and rips; torn trousers that barely provided any warmth against the arctic bite of winter.

Ginelle Hayes fled to the shadows, seeking concealment that would provide obscurity against imposing threats. Her fears heightened, she could smell stale fear in the air and hear the frantic beat of her heart, its rhythm like a persistent drum in her ears. Her body trembled violently, seeking what warmth her dilapidated attire could offer.

She stiffened as a deep rumble surfaced from her empty stomach. She closed her eyes against a sudden wave of vertigo. The thought of a hot meal sent her senses reeling. Her body screamed for nourishment, anything to appease her ravenous hunger and fill that deep hollowness in her belly. The sheer lack of strength rendered her weak and prone to illness. She couldn't remember the last time she had tasted a bountiful meal. It had been nearly a sennight since she had escaped Pierino, her supposed guardian.

Continuously, his burly fists and unstable temperament had reminded her of her unworthiness. Her body still bore the marks of his rage and drunkenness as she unknowingly pressed a small hand against the bruise that darkened the underside of her jaw. She resisted tears as she slipped into a dark alley, her boots moving swiftly over the roughened, damp cobblestone slick with ice.

She settled into a dark corner, sinking to the ground in defeat as she was overcome with tears and a heart-wrenching sorrow.

She was an impoverished child; alone in a dark and merciful world with no one to love or be loved. She was forced to live on the bleak and forsaken streets of London. She felt a swift tightening in her chest at the memory of her father, her dear sweet father; a blacksmith who had worked tirelessly into the night. Her hands reached to the silver locket around her neck and gripped the chain with shaky fingers. The locket had belonged to her mother, who had died while giving birth to her only child.

Ginelle curled into a ball as a horrific image emerged. She had found her father collapsed on the floor, clutching at his chest as though his stiffened fingers sought his pained heart. She had been too little to fathom the horror of the situation and the depth of her father's agony and grief of losing his beloved that it eventually led to taking his own life. How could she have not known the weight of his sorrow? How could she have not noticed the signs of his pain, pain so severe that he would end his own life and abandon her, his only child? Had he not loved her enough to live life with her? The grotesque image would forever plague her mind; taint her dreams.

She had no family that her father ever spoke of; it had always been just the two of them. The day after her father's death, she found herself on the streets and straight into the hands of Pierino Basilotta. At her fragile state and age she welcomed anyone who was willing to cradle her, protect her from harms way and at the time, he appeared to be a genuine man quite concerned for her. Pierino was her means of security for the impending void of loneliness was ever present.

The years to follow would only bring more pain and sorrow, expanding the black void of isolation and fear. She knew with each passing year brought on unraveling horrors. Her guardian praised his chivalrous act in taking in an orphaned child and claimed a debt was to be paid for his valiant deed. Therefore, she was forced to pick-pocket and provide what little income she could for her 'charitable guardian' and whenever he disapproved of her findings, she faced the brunt of his anger and the blow of his fist. Food was given based on obedience and many nights she curled onto her pallet, listening to the deep rumble of her empty stomach.

It wasn't until she reached fourteen summers that Pierino approached her, claiming she had poor techniques for thievery and therefore must provide another method of payment. A fear unlike any other settled in the pit of her stomach as he described in explicit detail of another way of getting coin from the adequate rank of society.

"Just a bit o'polishin' yer look-" he paused as he reached across the table to touch her face and she reared back, immediately regretting the impulse as his black eyes narrowed to slits of fury. "Ye best be gettin' use to a man touchin' ye." He growled venomously.

That night she fled. She would not fall prey to his malicious intentions and violent outbursts any longer. She welcomed the dark, empty streets to that small corner with a pallet conjured of hay. She would not become accustomed to men for they were vile creatures who lusted for coin and women. Her instincts warned her that Pierino would not give her up so easily for he had announced many times that she was his 'prized possession'. She never truly understood the meaning behind his words but knew that what he had in mind for her was intolerable, causing her stomach to churn at the mere thought of it.

As she sank deeper into the corner of her newfound pallet, she closed her eyes and gripped her mother's locket, seeking sleep. Sleep eluded her for in the past sennight, a new fear surfaced; darkness. She trembled as she sank deeper into her coat, her eyes darting warily around the alley in fear of large, bruising hands to snake out and grab her.

The first break of dawn was a remedy as ripples of sunlight cast over the boisterous streets of London. Ginelle surfaced from the alley, pulling the edges of a brown linen cap down around her face to conceal the tedious strands of flaxen hair and the unusual large eyes that attracted unwanted attention. She studied the array of London's inhabitants that included those of peasantry to those equipped in the latest customs that tossed coin carelessly to merchants alongside the cobblestone street.

She pressed a small hand as her stomach groaned, protesting against that hollow emptiness. Ginelle surveyed a nearby vendor with an exuberance of fresh fruits and vegetables. Her mouth watered instantaneously as she imagined the sweet juices along her tongue as she savored a bite of an apple or pear.

The vendor was a short man with a protruding belly and a distinct, crooked nose and a disarrayed mane of thin, copper hair. He appeared to be a man not to be trifled with. She had stalked similar streets to this one and was familiar with the vast center of marketing. London was known for its dainty shops, supplying heaps of rich fabric and lavish materials that only those of comfortable wealth could afford. She imagined what it would be like to enjoy the simple pleasures that London had to offer with its lush gardens and magnificent spectacles that beckoned bystanders to mingle.

Ginelle's eyes focused on a fresh, red apple, jarring her from her thoughts. She slipped effortlessly through the cluster of patrons; a skill she acquired from pick-pocketing, her fingers twitched with anticipation in the pockets of her woolen coat as she approached the cart.

She cast a wary glance in the vendor's direction just as he turned and caught sight of her extended hand reaching for a fruit. His pudgy face turned red with rage as he spun widely about and seized her wrist with grueling fingers. She squealed in alarm, stunned that she had been caught as he jerked her forward and she dropped the apple in a sudden panic.

"Ye petty pilferer!" her eyes widened as his grip tightened around the bone of her wrist, forcing a whimper from her throat. "Ye will not cheat me!" she watched in profound horror as he reached within the folds of his withered vest and withdrew a dirk with a sharp intended blade.

She felt a flood of terror wash over her as the sun glinted off the acute blade poised above her wrist entangled in the vendor's iron-grasp.

Suddenly, a firm feminine voice rang out from the crowd and the vendor's body stiffened as his hand gripping the ugly knife paused in his vengeance. Ginelle remained riveted with terror, her eyes barely leaving the blade hovering above her delicate bone.

"Sir!" that solid, methodic voice called again, catching Ginelle's attention and she cautiously turned her wary gaze from the blade to survey a woman approaching with an elderly maid trailing at her heels.

She was tall for a woman with dark, raven curls piled high atop her head with several wayward strands framing her oval face. Her eyes were a deep azure blue, darkened from the obvious display of anger etched into her refined, graceful features. The woman was beautiful draped in a thick, velvet cloak as she stood proud, her gaze unwavering as she studied the vendor in evident disapproval. She was equipped in a lovely gown of sapphire satin, the color enhancing the dark, smoky gaze glaring relentlessly at her captor.

"Milady-" the vendor started only to be abruptly dismissed as the woman's resolute voice interrupted.

"Unhand the child." She stated firmly, her unyielding voice catching the attention of spectators nearby.

The vendor's grip tightened a fraction and Ginelle winced as she peered helplessly up at the woman, the only civilized being to ever show a smidge of kindness to her well being since her father. She saw a sudden realization form in the deep-set of the blue eyes staring back at her but it quickly disappeared as she turned her full attention back to the merchant.

"Tis but a mere child that takes an apple from your stand." She said, "Whatever the cost of your precious fruit, I'll gladly bear the expense."

"I grow weary of these streets rats!" the man hissed through clenched teeth as he jerked on Ginelle's wrist, forcing another cry from her throat.

Ginelle watched as the woman reached within a soft, leather pouch and withdrew several gold coins and extended the generous pile to the merchant's ravenous gaze. "I believe this is a sufficient amount to compensate for the lack of one apple and a satchel of your fruit." The man hesitated and she added, "If the amount is not agreeable to your acquisitive taste than I shall find a more willing peddler." She slowly began to turn away and any hope that had flared within Ginelle's chest suddenly diminished.

"Wait!" cried the vendor and the woman turned back to him, a quizzical brow arching as her hand hovered between them.

The merchant shoved Ginelle away and she stumbled roughly before falling to the cobblestone.

Lady Eloise Ashford stiffened as the small child hit the ground, painfully scraping her palms along the roughened street as she attempted to catch her fall. Her eyes narrowed on the short man staring vigorously at the coin in her hand. She thrust the money into his greedy hands and he turned to bag a portion of fruit. Eloise handed the fruit to Lucile and moved to kneel before the child as she slowly collected herself.

Instantly, the child tensed as her attentive gaze swept over Eloise. She sensed a flight-or-fight state and sought quickly to ease her fears. "You need not be afraid." She said soothingly, reaching out to push a strand of hair aside that had fallen free from the cap. The skittish child jerked beneath her tender gesture and eased back onto her haunches, ready to flee if necessary.

When she had first set eyes on the child entangled in the vendor's grip, she had mistaken the child for a lad that is until she had stared into a pair of haunting, brown eyes, eyes so large and beautiful that they couldn't possibly be thought of a young boy. She could see such heart-wrenching sorrow in those eyes that it had nearly stolen the very air from her lungs, a sorrow so deep that it matched the capacity of her own suffering.

The child was donned in nothing but rags and filth, the linen cap concealing a mass of tangled hair. She couldn't be more than nine summers; mayhap younger for the clothes nearly engulfed her petite frame. It was than she noticed the ugly bruise just below her jaw line where a large hand had struck her.

Her chest ached with concern at the child's vulnerability and innocence. One so young should never endure a life of poverty and hardship. The child belonged to someone and she of all people knew the extreme of heartache when losing a loved one. She couldn't bear the thought of leaving her to the streets, to fall prey to those like the merchant, or worse, forced to deal with the ugliness that surely waited among these dangerous streets at night.

"Are you hungry?" she asked softly, simultaneously catching a spark of light in her soft eyes. Yet, the child remained cautious, her stance indicating her reluctance. Evidently the child had been through many hardships and was understandably guarded.

She smiled at the child and motioned to the bag of fruit cradled in Lucile's arms, a disgruntled look plastered to the older woman's face as she observed her mistress. "I have plenty of fruit to share." Eloise paused as those brown eyes glanced at the bundle. A dark brow lifted as Eloise continued, "Or mayhap you would prefer a warm meal?"

As if on cue, her treacherous stomach growled nosily and Ginelle cringed on the inside. She wanted desperately to trust this woman whose kindness struck her nonplussed. Why would a woman of her stature show any concern to an orphan such as herself unless she had ulterior motives? She wanted willingly to go with this gentle woman with her beautiful smile and glinting blue eyes, but years of neglect and abuse forced her to be cautious. She had made the mistake of trusting a stranger once; never would she make that mistake twice. Yet, it had been days since she had eaten and she didn't know how much longer she could continue without putting something in her belly.

Those deep, azure eyes softened as the woman continued, "My name is Eloise. What is your name, little one?"

Ginelle bit down on her lower lip for she was unable to resist the gentle lilt of that voice and her name slipped out. "Ginelle." She said it so faintly, fearful that someone passing by might hear of it and inform Pierino of her whereabouts. Immediately she regretted giving her name for it would be a grave mistake to give out her name so carelessly.

Eloise face broadened with a triumphant smile as she said, "That is a beautiful name. I would really appreciate your company for luncheon, Ginelle. Would you be so kind as to oblige my wish and have tea with me?"

Ginelle bit down on the automatic 'aye' that surfaced in her throat and studied the woman kneeling before her and then cast a wary glance at the elderly woman standing a few feet behind, clearly displeased by her pinched expression.

She felt a deep, sinking feeling in her chest as her eyes averted to the bag of fruit in the maid's hands and she turned tearfully back to Eloise. "I c-cannot repay ye for the fruit." She said solemnly.

Eloise features contorted in disbelief that the child would concern herself with such a petty matter that was of no significance to her. "Can we be friends?" she asked gently.

Ginelle was hesitant but the possibility of befriending this compassionate, enchanting woman, even for a brief moment forced an automatic nod. Eloise smiled, "Than as companions can I not favor you with apples?"

Ginelle smiled tentatively.

Eloise smile widened, "Now, will you come with me so that we may get that warm meal?"

Ginelle struggled with impulse as she contemplated her rising fears. Surely it wouldn't hurt to spend just a little time with this woman whom she wanted desperately to trust but her instincts warned her to be cautious.

Eloise extended a hand to her and said reassuringly, "You can trust me, Ginelle."

Ginelle hesitantly lifted a small hand to that larger one and froze as she turned her palm over to inspect the gush of blood seeping from a deep gash along the inside of her hand. She gasped and wrenched her hand back, pressing the wound against her chest, in fear that she would ruin Eloise's beautiful gown.

Sensing her inward thoughts, Eloise reached out and pried open her small fist to inspect the ugly gash. "I can apply a little salve to heal that right up." Her hand moved to Ginelle's elbow and pulled her gently to her feet.

Eloise reached within her cloak and withdrew a cream handkerchief and gently dabbed away the blood. "I've ruined it." Ginelle said morosely.

Eloise laughed softly, "Do not fret, sweeting. I've plenty." She wrapped the delicate cloth around her wounded hand and got to her feet. "Come, let us get out of this dreadful weather."

Ginelle timidly accepted her offered hand, her fears warning her that she was making a mistake, yet this woman had rescued her from a fate that could have left her with a severed hand. She sensed a maternal nature and a lasting sadness buried behind the depths of her blue eyes. Ginelle had suffered many hardships to recognize another grieving soul and as much as her fears advised her to be mindful of the consequences of her carelessness in trusting a stranger, she was intrigued to know more about Lady Eloise Ashford.

It wasn't until they left the outskirts of the city behind that she began to panic. Ginelle gripped the leather seat as the carriage rocked precariously from side to side, heightening her fears.

Sensing her unease, Eloise said reassuringly, "You need not be afraid, Ginelle. The carriage is perfectly safe." Then another thought occurred, "You've never been to the country, have you?"

"We're going to the country?" Ginelle questioned nervously.

Eloise nodded, "Yes, to my manor."

"Tis the Ashford plantation." The elderly maid added her voice stern and quite direct.

Ginelle frowned for she knew there was some significance to the older woman's statement but the thought quickly diminished as the carriage turned onto a winding, dirt road leading up to the most magnificent structure enclosed in a valley of oak trees. The white manor was built in brilliant sophisticated construction, laid out along the northern boundaries. The massive plantation house was surrounded in thick vegetation and outlined in lush greenery that stretched for miles.

"Ye live here?" she asked in awe.

Eloise nodded, "I am the Lady of the manor."

"Lord Ashford is master here." The maid stated and Ginelle sensed a warning beneath the older woman's somber tone.

Ginelle turned to study the maid just as Eloise cast the elderly woman a look of exasperation. "Is he yer husband?"

Eloise suddenly laughed, "Dear no, he is my brother."

"Master Dorian is a prominent businessman." The elderly maid said.

"What does he do?" Ginelle asked, curious to know more about Eloise and her family. Was he anything like his sister? She couldn't imagine a man, any man for that matter to be as kind and gentle-natured as Lady Eloise.

"He grows and exports tobacco. I do not particularly approve all that which it entails but it is a profitable business." Eloise stated.

Ginelle frowned, "Entails?"

"Our plantation is one of the largest with the finest crops among the region. My brother is gone for several months, even years at a time, tending to business. Even as we speak he is away on a transatlantic trade. The business is quite demanding."

They rolled to an abrupt halt and Eloise descended from the carriage with the assistance of a footman, followed by her dutiful, sour maid. Eloise extended a hand to Ginelle, mindful that she would not accept the footman's assistance. Ginelle gingerly allowed Eloise to assist her from the carriage and fell in at her side as the two older women made their way inside, Eloise tugged lightly on Ginelle, keenly aware of her reluctance to follow. Inside they were greeted by the steward, a tall slender man with sharp inquisitive eyes that swept over Ginelle intently.

"Good evening, Bogart. My guest and I will take our luncheon in my room, if you will have Noelle send us a tray, please."

"Aye, milady." Bogart replied, tipping his head with considerable courtesy.

Eloise led Ginelle upstairs, laughing softly as Ginelle lingered behind to study the enormous manor with its rich, mahogany furniture and beautifully polished floors. She caught several displays of art lining the corridors and thick tapestries along the walls.

Ginelle never imagined that she would come in contact with such a lavish home made of fine material and admirable collections of certain wealth.

They made their way up a winding stairway and down several corridors until they finally came to a door. Ginelle gasped as Eloise opened the door and stepped into the room. The chamber itself was larger than the mere shack she and Pierino had shared. The balcony drapes had been pulled aside so that the evening sun could paint gentle hues of gold across the charming cream, canopy bed with a wide headboard done in intricate detail of vines and leaves. Four posts supported a sheer white material to drape around the extravagant bed supporting a high mattress with a number of feather-stuffed pillows and thick white coverlets. Beautiful white furniture was dispersed throughout the room which too displayed the same design of vines and leaves etched into the smooth wood. A marble mantel took up most of the right wall where a maid had already stoked a fire, the flames crackling in defiance to warm the slightly chilled room.

Eloise crossed the room and removed her velvet cloak and placed it on the bed. Ginelle remained in the doorway, unable to move, fearful that she would ruin the beautiful carpet that covered a large portion of the floor.

"Come, warm yourself by the fire." Eloise said, motioning to the hearth.

Ginelle stiffened as impulse urged her to do just that. Her bones ached for the warmth of a fire and the plush cushions of the white sofa occupying the center of the room. She peered down at her bedraggled attire and retreated a few paces.

Eloise frowned, "Will you not come and sit with me? I would like very much to enjoy your company for the evening."

Ginelle's hand entwined nervously as she stared down at her sooty boots. "I am unclean." She stated, embarrassed.

Eloise moved to stand above her and gently lifted her downcast face. "Do not concern yourself with materialistic items." She stepped away and moved to sit on the sofa and patted the cushion next to her.

Reluctantly, Ginelle crossed the spacious room to the vacant spot beside Eloise and lowered herself to the edge of the seat. Immediately warmth began to seep into her weary bones and she felt the tension slightly ease from her muscles.

"How many summers are you, Ginelle?"

Ginelle bit down on her lower lip, hesitating before replying. "I am fourteen." A sudden perplexed expression contorted Eloise's face.

"When was the last time you have eaten?"

Ginelle paused and that alone answered Eloise's question as she studied the thin child sitting at her side. She was emaciated, her cheeks sunken with black circles beneath her haunting eyes. Due to her obvious fragile and thin state, she had estimated the child to be at least eight summers but fourteen? The evident lack of nutrition and warmth had taken its toll on the girl.

"Can you remove your hat?" Eloise asked gently.

Ginelle waited, contemplating whether she should really remove it. It was her security blanket, her disguise. Slowly, she reached up and removed the hat. It unleashed a long tangled mass of silver-blond hair. The lack of nourishment had done some damage for her hair was thin but it had potential to be radiant. Eloise studied the garments that covered her little frame and wondered what horrid display of protruding bones awaited beneath her swallowing attire.

"Why do you hide your beautiful hair?"

Ginelle worried her lower lip with her teeth as she looked away. Should she really confide in Eloise? Her heart ached painfully, wanting desperately to trust someone, anyone. She ached for companionship and a sense of security. Before she could help herself, against her self-discipline, the words began to spill freely.

"My guardian forced me to pick-pocket." She fell silent, expecting Eloise to scold her but she remained silent, listening intently and so Ginelle slowly continued. "He claimed that I was to amend his good deed in taking me in off the streets."

"Did he hit you?" Eloise asked, studying the ugly bruise just below Ginelle's jaw.

Ginelle lifted a shaky hand to the tender, purple abrasion where he had struck her so forcefully that the blow had sent her reeling backwards. "Aye, many times."

"And you ran away?"

Ginelle met that azure gaze filled with such compassion and sympathy that she nearly burst into tears. "He had others plans for me."

Eloise stiffened, realizing why the child concealed her hair. Even she had mistaken her at first glance for a lad and that had been the purpose of the hat.

"And this man-" Eloise asked, "Is he dangerous?"

Ginelle dropped her head knowing that her answer would surely send her on her way. What gentle bred woman would trouble herself with a street rat? "Aye, milady." She said softly, her eyes transfixed on the floor.

Eloise reached out and lifted Ginelle's head so that their eyes interlocked. "I am sorry that this has happened to you. No child should have to endure such cruelty." Her hand fell away from Ginelle's face and Eloise turned her head away as if struggling internally with conflicting emotions and troubling thoughts.

She stood and Ginelle watched her pace curiously back and forth, the deep blue of her sapphire skirts in such bold contrast to the lush white carpet beneath her feet. Her abrupt pacing came to a quick halt as she turned and stared down at Ginelle; her gentle eyes wide with an assertive notion. "I want you to live here." She said, "With me."

Struck silent, Ginelle peered up at her as if she didn't quite fathom what she had just said. She couldn't possibly be suggesting that she, an impoverished child live among the prosperous? It wasn't proper. Was Eloise being cruel? Was she jesting or simply mocking her pain? Had she made another mistake in confiding in Eloise?

"I d-don't understand."

Eloise returned to her seat and reached out to grasp Ginelle's hands in her own. "Please hear me out, sweeting." She said firmly, "I was once irrevocably happy. I was married to the most charming, handsome man and he and I were deeply in love." She paused and when she spoke next, her voice cracked with a sudden dispiritedness, "I was to have his child." She became quiet before adding, "I am widowed." A heavy silence descended and than she said with a heart-wrenching declaration, "And I am childless."

Ginelle paled as the deep sadness she had sensed earlier that day was fully displayed on Eloise's beautiful face. She had lost both her husband and child. Though they both had known complete and utter different worlds, they shared alike in their anguish.

Eloise fingers tightened around Ginelle's hand as she said, "You were robbed of a childhood by a cruel man. You deserve an education and a chance at life."

"And ye the chance to be a mother?" Ginelle asked softly.

Eloise straightened a corner of her mouth lifting as she attempted a smile that didn't reach her blue eyes. "You and I are alike in our sorrows and I believe together we can mend our sufferings. I know that I can never be your mother but I would like very much for you to stay."

"I am-" Ginelle started and than paused as a sturdy knock sounded at the door.

Eloise bid them entry and remained silent as a young girl entered carrying a tray laden with food. Instantly, Ginelle's stomach rumbled noisily and she eyed the food with a ravenous stare.

After the maid had left, Eloise said, "Stay for some time, Ginelle. At least until the wintry season has passed. Please, consider it?"

Ginelle bit down on her lower lip, suddenly aware of the bad habit. She dreaded the thought of returning to the dreaded cold and darkened streets of London and most importantly, Pierino. What would it hurt to stay for awhile? To warm herself and eat aplenty and allow herself just a smidge of companionship that she so desperately yearned for? She studied the woman sitting across from her. How could she deny Eloise this request when she had done so much for her in just a mere day? Eloise had truly suffered a terrible loss yet she still had compassion to show upon a mere peasant such as herself?

Hesitantly, she nodded. She would consider it for a time because for now, she was safe from the frigid weather and the threat of Pierino. He would not think to look for her here.

Eloise smiled with a look of certainty and motioned to the food displayed before them. Within the next hour, Ginelle listened intently as Eloise talked endlessly. She hadn't quite realized how famished she truly was until she peered down to find the tray completely depleted. She realized than that Eloise had not touched a single thing and she resisted tears for the tray had been sent up specifically for her.

Lucile paced nervously in the corridor as her mistress appeared, closing the chamber door quietly behind her. Immediately, the elderly woman turned to Eloise, her withered face pinched with distress. "Milady, I do not think it wise to bring the child here. Master Dorian will not be pleased."

"Lucile." That stern voice halted any further disapproval from the older woman as Eloise said, "I am the Lady of the manor. The child stays. It is not up for discussion." She gathered her flowing skirts of her sapphire gown and descended down the hall with Lucile at her hem.

"I know it is not my place, mon cher but you and I both know that his tolerance has its limits. He will not permit that child-"

Eloise whirled, causing Lucile to stiffen with bewilderment at Eloise's apparent dismay. "That child will die if she spends another night on the street." Eloise quickly gathered her composure, straightening her spine as her eyes softened, "Forgive me, Lucile but you cannot expect me to sit by and allow an innocent child to die at the hands of winter."

Lucile reached out and grasped Eloise's shoulder and squeezed gently. "Your grief is understandable, but you cannot continue to burden yourself with their loss, twas out of your hands."

Eloise lifted her chin, quickly concealing the distress in her eyes as an exact resolve settled across her graceful features. "The child stays."

Ginelle stared at the empty silver tray sitting before her and pressed a small hand to her full stomach. She felt herself on the verge of tears but knew it was ridiculous to cry over a meal. Eloise Ashford was a beautiful, gracious woman. Should she really consider her proposition? As she thought this, she stared around at the lovely, white room and wondered what it would be like to wake every morning with a heated hearth at your feet and feathers beneath your head and servants assisting your every need without having to endure the bitterness of winter and the impending dangers that the eerie streets of London presented. Could she possibly be free of Pierino Basilotta, at least for the time being?

The door suddenly opened, jarring Ginelle to awareness and she immediately tensed as she met those deep, azure eyes but they were always soft and full of warmth. Eloise smiled as she approached; her posture impeccable as she carried a bundle in her arms.

"This shall be sufficient enough until we can get you attire that is more fitting." Ginelle hesitated before gingerly accepting the nightshirt from Eloise's extended hand. She held the garment to her chest and gently traced the delicate ruffles.

"I shall send Ingrid up shortly to assist you." She turned to leave.

"I cannot repay ye-"

Eloise turned and held up her hand and shook her head, relinquishing any more words from Ginelle as she said, "You need not repay me." She smiled. A light touched her blue eyes as she continued, "On the morrow we will visit a seamstress in town and select from many beautiful collections of color and fabric for your gowns to be made. You would like that wouldn't you?" she reached out and touched the rim of Ginelle's nose.

Despite her objections, Ginelle's mouth curved into a smile at Eloise's tender display of motherly affection.

Her happiness was short as Eloise departed and left Ginelle standing in the center of the room, clutching the delicate piece of cotton to her chest. She suddenly felt that pressing loneliness and ached for Eloise's presence. She struggled to breathe; finding it difficult to bring air into her lungs. Her eyes moved warily around the room, studying the dark corners as the sun slowly began to slide from the sky, pulling the blue canopy in its fall and slowly creeping up behind was an ominous black shroud.

She felt as if the walls were enclosing her in and the spacious room began to grow smaller and smaller.

She turned to study the window, wondering how difficult it would be to climb from it when an abrupt knock sounded at the door.

Ginelle pivoted, uncertain as of what to do as she stared helplessly at the door. The latch lifted and the door parted as a young girl stuck her head inside and sneered sharply at her.

"Milady claimed you were a bit bashful." The girl chimed as she pushed open the door and stepped in, crossing the room to close the thick drapes covering the window she had been pondering only a moment ago.

The slender girl turned to study her more intensely with curious, green eyes and a pale face full of freckles. Thick, red curls framed her oval face and she reached up to tuck a lone strand behind her ear. "I am Ingrid." She said pointedly, her eyes suddenly accusing as they settled on the garment in her hands. "Do you need my assistance?"

Ginelle sensed that the red-haired maid was not pleased that she was here, assisting her. Those green eyes lingered on the nightshirt, indicating the garment belonged to her and she was not exceptionally thrilled about it. Ginelle shook her head, quite wary of the maid and her cold demeanor.

Ingrid snorted, "Vera' well." The maid took a few moments to check the fire before leaving, subjugating her once again to the dreaded enclosure of the room. Darkness overpowered her, trapping her in a terrifying cloud of paranoia. Her body began to tremble as her fingers tightened around the cotton in her hands. She looked helplessly towards the fire, instantly seeking its warmth in hopes that it would chase away the cold that had seeped into her bones along with a sense of foreboding.

She sank to the floor before the hearth and began to rock back and forth, clutching the silver locket dangling from around her neck as she whispered a melody her father use to sing to her whenever she was scared.

Why father? Why did you abandon me? She thought to herself. Tears glided from beneath her lashes and she quickly brushed them away for Pierino had always said tears were a form of weakness. She should be happy shouldn't she? She was warm and her stomach was full, so why this sudden deep sorrow?

With that last thought in mind, she settled onto the carpet below the mantel and curled into a ball as the heat from the fire caressed her face with warmth, coaxing the remedy of sleep to come.

Chapter 2

Eloise greeted the morning with a new outlook on life and a small ball of hope unfurling within her chest. At first glance she had thought Ginelle a mere child but at fourteen summers she was practically on the brink of womanhood; with no guidance, she thought solemnly.

She would never be the child's mother for in fact she was but a few years older than the girl herself, but she could be her mentor, teach her the things a mother should teach a daughter, she thought as she made her way down the hall towards the chamber where the girl slept. Immediately she stiffened at the abrupt chill of the room and she shivered as her eyes widened to find the bed unstirred.

Instinctively, her heart dropped. Had Ginelle run away? She stood frozen, gripping the latch as she searched the remnants of the room until she felt a wave of relief seize her as she spotted the curled, sleeping body on the floor near the hearth.

Her relief was quickly overcome with extreme displeasure at the evident chill in the room. Why had Ingrid not returned to rekindle the fire?

Eloise crossed the room and knelt next to Ginelle, gently rousing the child until those eyes of soft brown fluttered open and peered up at her, widening for a brief moment until recognition settled. She quickly sat up, turning her face away in slight embarrassment as she smoothed the wrinkles from the nightshirt she had been clutching through the night.

"Why did you not sleep in the bed?" Eloise questioned gently, "You could have caught a chill sleeping on the floor." Eloise helped Ginelle to her feet and immediately moved to the door where she and a maid exchanged hushed words unclear to Ginelle.

Eloise turned and smiled yet Ginelle sensed she was displeased, "I am sorry." She said, "I did not mean to upset ye, tis just that I-" she fell silent as the older maid Lucile came marching in the room, tugging a reluctant Ingrid in tow.

Ingrid barely cast a glance in her direction as she stood before Eloise, her hands tucked nervously in the apron of her gown. She kept her green eyes leveled to the floor as Eloise started, "Ingrid, you will have a breakfast tray prepared and brought to our guest and when you return I want a full explanation to why you lacked in your duties this morning and as for your idleness, you can see that the grand stairway is washed and scrubbed."

Ingrid curtly nodded, "Aye milady." She hesitated as if she wanted to say something in return but refrained and hastened from the room.

Ginelle stiffened; had she been the reason to why Ingrid had disregarded her duties? She felt the intense urge to speak in Ingrid's defense. "Milady, if I have troubled ye-"

Eloise composed her displeasure as both she and Lucile turned to peer at Ginelle. Eloise stopped her mid-sentence. "Do not fault yourself for Ingrid's mistake. She lacked in her duty this morning, therefore she is entirely at fault and it is not acceptable."

"Lady Eloise was lenient with Ingrid, far more than Master Dorian would have been." Lucile stated, the undertone of her voice relaying a clear message.

Ginelle averted her eyes to the older woman. She was a handsome woman, with austere features that indicated her proud disposition. Her gray hair was pulled tight into a chignon at the nape of her neck, not a single strand out of place. Her unwavering, dark stare made Ginelle uneasy as the older woman studied her return. Somehow, sensing from her rigid stance and bold stare, she felt as though this woman disapproved of her presence just as much as Ingrid but for an entirely different reason that was unknown to her.

Lady Eloise was lenient. Far more than Master Dorian would have been. Trepidation snaked down her spine at the older woman's words. She was certain that the older woman continued to warn her and every warning seem to focus around the Laird. She trembled on the inside at the thought of the man. Would he have beaten Ingrid for her disobedience?

A servant suddenly appeared in the doorway, "Forgive my intrusion, milady. A missive has just arrived for you."

Ginelle caught the flare of anticipation in those bright, blue eyes as Eloise motioned for Ginelle to take a seat. She settled into a chair as Eloise turned to say something to her dutiful Lucile. She stared at her retreating back before Lucile retrieved the nightshirt and placed it gently on the bed as Eloise left the room.

Instantly, Ginelle felt her departure and resisted the urge to follow Eloise. "Mistress has taken quite a liking to you." Lucile said standing across from Ginelle with her arms folded firmly in front of her.

Ginelle did not sense any animosity from the woman as she had from Ingrid but she sensed a protective layer that was unbreakable.

"Lucile." Eloise called from the door. "May I have a word with you?" Ginelle could sense the utter excitement in the lilt of her voice and wondered for a brief moment what sort of news she had received to bring on this sudden happiness.

Lucile stepped into the hall to observe her mistress' obvious cheerfulness and a dark brow rose as she asked, "I suspect the missive brought good news, than?"

"Yes, indeed." She cried with glee, "Dorian will be returning shortly. The missive was written nearly a sennight ago and his letter claims he would be arriving home in seven days, that day is tomorrow."

Lucile stiffened with anticipation as well as apprehension for their small guest. "Shall I inform the servants of his arrival?"

Eloise nodded, "Yes. I had not anticipated on an early homecoming. There is much that needs to be done."

A bath was prepared and Ginelle eagerly obliged as she stripped away her rags and stepped into the steaming water. Eloise was there at her side to wash her hair and help scrub her back. She couldn't remember the last time she had, had such a luxury. She was not unnerved by Eloise's presence and in fact, welcomed it as her new found guardian described the entails of becoming a civilized, well-educated woman.

"A formal education is customary. You will be taught the basics in reading and writing. You will study arithmetic and the art of music and dance. You will learn many languages. You will grow accustomed to polished manners that will prove accessible when you manage your husband's estate once you are married."

Ginelle stiffened at the mention of matrimony.

A husband?

She had not given much thought to marriage and the thought of it made her stomach churn on the inside. What woman would submit herself to such imprisonment?

A man merely sought to control your every whim and thought. Nay, marriage was out of the question. She would never marry. She would not fall prey to another man so he could use his fist to silence her.

She quickly sought to change the subject. "How were ye taught to read and write?"

"I was sent to boarding school." Eloise fell silent as though she wanted to say more but turned away to retrieve a garment dispersed across the arm of the sofa. "I borrowed this from Ingrid until we can provide you with more suitable attire. She is not quite as small as you but will be adequate for the time being."

Ginelle reached out with hesitant hands to accept the gown. The cotton print dress was suitable considering her rank but immediately Eloise hastened as if to explain. "I could not find anything else that would fit your frame."

Ginelle knew it must have pained Ingrid terribly to have loan the gown to her. She must remember to thank her later though she was quite certain the maid wouldn't accept her gratitude.

"Let us not dally any longer than necessary. We have much to accomplish. We must find you a seamstress so that we may start on a wardrobe more fitting."

Ginelle wanted to tell Eloise that it wasn't necessary because she was not planning on staying for too long but she found that she seemingly enjoyed Eloise's presence. She enjoyed their conversations and most importantly, she never felt the need to tense when Eloise was near. She was devoid of her fears with Eloise at her side.

The dress was a smidge to big on her small frame but it offered warmth that her body had been denied from the rags that now lay discarded along the polished floor. The gown also provided a disguise from Pierino. He would not recognize her in a servant gown. Her disheveled hair now clean and combed had been pulled back into a plait, several strands slipping from their restraint to frame her face.

Eloise left the room momentarily and when she reappeared, she presented Ginelle with a velvet blue cloak and draped it around her shoulders. Ginelle lightly touched the material, marveling at its beautiful texture as they made their way down the hall. Ginelle was quick to notice the distaste etched into Ingrid's face and the scowl that deepened as the maid slipped by them.

She dropped her head, her hands entwining nervously against the skirt of Ingrid's dress. What had she done to displease Ingrid so? She pondered this as they made their way into the frigid air where they were greeted by an elderly coachman. He assisted them into the waiting carriage where Ginelle quickly settled into the leather seat and Eloise followed.

It wasn't until she realized their journey was leading them straight back into town that she felt that impending fear of Pierino rise. She suddenly had a shortness of breath and quickly turned her face to the window at her side. She closed her eyes against the sudden numbness seeping into her bones as her fingers curled painfully in her lap; her knuckles turning white from gripping them so tightly. What if he spotted her? Would he steal her from Eloise in broad daylight? The thought nearly made her choke on a sob at the dreaded fate that surely waited if she fell into Pierino's clutches.

A gentle hand fell on her shoulder, jarring her to awareness. "There is nothing to fear." Eloise said softly, her eyes large and blue, revealing the deep sincerity there.

Ginelle smiled in hopes of convincing Eloise that she believed her, but as she turned to peer out the window and the familiar perimeter of town came into view, she felt her heart thrust inside her chest along with a deep sense of foreboding dread.

Eloise spent the next several hours skimming through yards of fabric. She selected various materials that included muslin and silk and beautiful ribbons to adorn her hair. Before she knew it, she had everything she would have never dreamed of possessing. After getting her measurements, the seamstress started on a gown that fastened in the back and was made to fall around her ankles. Eloise explained that the cotton garment was a bed gown and Ginelle was relieved to know that she would not have to borrow Ingrid's any longer.

The seamstress described several printed and colored gowns with vertical bodices as Eloise listened intently while Ginelle remained cautious, careful to watch the passing bystanders outside the large window, fearful that she would see a frightening, familiar silhouette.

She was amazed that Eloise would go to such lengths to provide her with such a wardrobe. This list consisted of shifts and stays, gowns and petticoats including hats, shoes and all sorts of accessories, things she never imagined wearing.

When they left the seamstress with her extremely long list of needlework, Eloise took Ginelle's hand and they proceeded down the street. Somehow holding that larger hand in her own, she had a sense of belonging, self-worth. Eloise would never replace the mother she never knew, but Eloise had stepped in to care for an impoverished child, taking her under her care as if they were the dearest of kin. Just as quickly as that warmth spread through her chest, it rapidly diminished as a quick and rational thought came to mind. She would never rightfully belong with Eloise. She didn't belong in her world. She had been fearful of trusting a complete stranger yet somehow Eloise had quickly earned her trust and devotion, she had welcomed her into her aristocratic life without as much as a second thought.

Just as the merchant had called the previous day, she was naught but a street rat. A blacksmith's daughter abandoned to the streets. Her veins were not of an aristocratic blood and she was naught but an imposture at the Ashford manor. She now fully understood Ingrid's distaste and hatred. She was naught but a fraud to the maid and could she blame her? Why should Ingrid a maid, serve a lowly street rat?

Sensing something amiss, Eloise tugged lightly on Ginelle's hand, "What troubles you, sweeting?"

Ginelle paused, chewing on her lower lip before finally spilling her thoughts. "Ye have given me so much. I am not of privileged blood. I am not worthy of yer kindness."

"Is that what troubles you?" Eloise asked, perplexed. "Haven't you noticed that social rank is not of any importance to me? You tell me that it isn't right to dote on a child deprived of clothing and food, of shelter?" Eloise face altered with that all too familiar pain dwelling beneath the surface and she quickly concealed it from Ginelle's observant stare.

Ginelle remained silent as Eloise took her hand once more and they continued down the boisterous street teeming with life. She slipped closer to Eloise's side, seeking her protection as Eloise walked proud and unfettered by the utter chaos of the townsfolk.

The sun was beginning to descend, casting subtle hues of dusk across the sky as they made their way back to the plantation. Ginelle's body felt heavy with exhaustion from the earlier happenings of the day and eagerly sought sleep. She peered over at Eloise who sat straight in the leather seat, staring out the window, her eyes staring past the line of trees as if deep in thought.

As they pulled to a halt in front of the house and the coachman assisted them from the carriage, Ginelle tensed as Lucile came bounding from the house towards her mistress, her face pinched with anxiety.

"Milady." She called, casting a fearful glance in Ginelle's direction. "I must speak with you."

Eloise rushed forward to intercept the older woman and they exchanged a few words. "What is wrong, Lucile?"

"Tis Master Dorian, he's here." Ginelle's heart dropped at the older woman's apparent distress in her somber tone.

"Already?" Ginelle turned to look at Eloise who appeared far more excited than her worried maid. "Lucile, help Ginelle to her room and assist her to bed. We have had a trying day."

Lucile stood concerned as she stared at her mistress retreating back, than slowly turned to look at Ginelle, "Come child." She said and as Ginelle moved forward she caught the glint of alarm in the woman's dark eyes.

Ginelle settled onto the large bed and stared at the door where moments ago, the elderly maid, Lucile had departed. A heaviness settled in her chest and her heart beat to the rhythm of fear. Master Dorian had returned home. Though Lucile had tried to conceal her obvious distress, it was quite clear that the older woman was frantic on the inside. She peered down at her hand that had been cleaned of all blood and bandaged. She flexed her fingers across the cotton of her nightshirt and sighed, struggling against tears. Eloise had been so kind but she didn't belong here. She had willingly agreed to consider Eloise's proposition, but the reality of it was simple. Now that the Laird had returned, she had to leave.

She got to her feet and turned to admire the lovely canopied-bed. For a moment, she fancied it her own. She moved to the window and leaned against the frame, staring out into the vast approaching darkness. She gripped her mother's necklace and shuddered at the thought of returning to those dark, desolate streets where the threat of Pierino was consistent. For a short time, she had thought herself safe from him for he would have never thought to look for her here.

A single tear slipped from beneath her lashes. Eloise had done so much for her; had catered to her as though they were kindred. She couldn't continue this farce pretense. Eloise had given her silks and ribbons and filled her stomach and warmed her blood but most importantly, she had given her a moment of true happiness, even if it were for a short period of time. But what could she give Eloise in return? A street rat such as herself had naught to offer. Eloise's generosity knew no bounds and she couldn't allow herself to willingly accept her charity any longer.

She would leave.

Tonight.

Her chest felt heavy with the loss already. She would lose Eloise. She had only known Eloise for a short time and was accustomed to loss, and yet it still pained her deeply. She quickly swiped at the tears and stepped away from the window. She turned to survey the room, realizing her peasantry clothes were gone. She found Ingrid's dress lying across the arm of the sofa. Knowing the maid had reluctantly agreed to lend it to her; she decided she had no other option but to keep the gown, for the time being. She would return it once she found a set of garments for herself.

Ginelle lifted her head and studied the room one last time. None of this was real to her but the limitless pain, that deep hollowness in her chest. She quickly dressed and made her way to the door. She paused as her eyes settled on the cloak dispersed across the bed. The thought of having to endure the unforgiving winter sent a tremor through her. She scooped the garment in her arms and slipped out of the room, vowing she would return it as she stepped into the darkened hall.

Eloise stopped abruptly as she came to the open study, immediately her eyes fell on the tall, formidable frame standing by the window. Her heart somersaulted as an image of their father rushed to mind for the man cast in shadow was a sheer replica of Clayton Ashford. As if sensing her presence, he turned and those piercing blue eyes regarded her with sudden warmth, quickly casting aside the frightening image.

"Dorian." She gathered her skirts and crossed the room to her elder brother, easing into his comforting embrace. Those strong, secure arms wrapped protectively around her, holding her tenderly as he had done when she was younger.

He planted a kiss atop her head as he said, "I have missed you." His deep resonant voice soothed her soul. Only she knew her brother's gentle nature for he rarely displayed it to others. To many, he was the dangerous and dark laird. His word was law, yet he could not resist anything when it came to his little sister.

She stepped away to peer up at him, taking note of the lines of fatigue around his eyes and mouth. "Was the trade successful?" she inquired.

He smirked, "Do you suddenly have an interest in my profession, soeur?"

Eloise smiled as she stepped back, "Tis no secret that I disapprove of it."

"Indeed." He said, watching her curiously. "You are hiding something." It wasn't a question but an assertion as those distinct, inquisitive blue eyes studied her intensely.

She moved to put space between them, bracing herself for his anger for she was certain he would disfavor the idea of their house guest. "I went to the market yesterday."

A dark brow arched as he said, "Alone? That does not please me." His voice dropped to a dangerous lilt.

Dorian would never hurt her of that she was certain but his temper was to be feared. Cautiously, she continued. "I came upon a child." She lifted her azure gaze to stare more firmly at her brother as realization settled in those lucid eyes.

"Eloise-" he began earnestly, "Pray tell that you did not bring a stranger into my house." There it was, she thought, that simmering rage just beneath the surface.

She stood her ground, determined to do what she could for Ginelle, even daring to challenge the Laird. "She needs a home, Dorian." She stated firmly, lifting her chin defiantly. "And I am willing to provide her a home. She is my concern."

"In what sense?" Dorian growled.

She forced herself to not flinch against his sudden rising anger. "She needs me."

His hands curled into fists at his sides, his jaw set into a dangerous line. "Damn it, I will not permit it and you will not defy me in this."

"Dorian please-"

"What do you know of this stranger?" he waited and than said. "It is out of the question."

Eloise narrowed her eyes at her brother, "You speak nonsense. What of the criminals and thieves you purchase to work in your fields? They are far more of a threat than that of a mere child."

"Those criminals and thieves sleep outside these walls a field away and are heavily guarded."

She fell silent as she regarded her brother with smoky, blue eyes. She had expected his imperious manner but the girl was merely a child. "Dorian." She said more softly, her eyes blurring with unshed tears. "Please grant me this request."

A heavy silence settled between them and she feared he was certain in his decree.

"The child may stay under certain circumstances." He paused so she could absorb his words. "The child is your responsibility. She is to stay clear of the fields and my men. She is not to interfere, is that understood?"

Eloise nodded, resisting the urge to smile.

"One more thing." His face darkened before adding, "She is to stay clear of me."

After his sister had left the study, Dorian Don Ashford turned to poor himself a healthy glass of brandy. He drowned the distilled liquid in one swallow and slammed the glass down with enough force to shatter it. He swept a hand through his dark tresses as he pondered over their 'house-guest'.

He could not deny his beloved sister anything and blast the wee brat for she knew it. His hardened heart was guarded against everyone and everything except his younger sister. He loved her more than life itself and couldn't imagine life without her. He had not been accepting of her betrothal to Philip Sussman but her apparent happiness slowly encouraged him to allow the young lad to marry his sister.

It wasn't until the death of her husband and that of her unborn child that she succumbed to sorrow and grief, becoming a mere shadow of herself. It tore him apart to see her suffer. On that reason alone, he agreed to allow the child to stay for he could see a change in Eloise, a spark of life that had not been there when he left seven months ago. Though he disapproved greatly of it, mayhap it would be a healing remedy for his sister.

Eloise was indeed a beauty, a spitting image of their docile mother but nothing like her in spirit. Their mother had been timid and meek, where as Eloise was willful and resolute. He admired her bravado for only she could walk away unscathed after their exchange of heated words.

He settled into the leather seat at his desk and leaned back to stretch his long legs as his thoughts darkened. Just as quickly as they surfaced, he dismissed them, not wanting to dwell on the past. His mind turned to more important matters such as business. The weather had proved to be dreadful on his voyage, prohibiting his efforts in trading. Gratefully, the wintry season was almost at an end. In the duration of several weeks, he could return to sea. In the meantime, he would have his laborers in preparation for planting season.

As Eloise made her way down the corridor, seemingly pleased, she came to a sudden halt as Mirabelle, a chambermaid hurried towards her, clearly frantic. "Milady!"

"What is wrong, Belle?" she asked, a fear settling in the pit of her stomach.

"The girl has run away." The young maid cried, turning to point to the abandoned room. "Tis empty."

"What?" the blood drained from her face as she rushed by Belle and pushed open the door to find a vacant room. She whirled back around to grab Belle's shoulders. "Do you know where she went? Did you see her?"

The maid shook her head helplessly, "Nay milady, but her cloak is missin'."

Gathering her skirts, Eloise fled down the corridor, rushing to the study. She didn't bother to knock as she pushed open the door, her abrupt arrival instantly bringing Dorian to his feet. "What is wrong?" Dorian demanded, coming around the desk to his sister.

"Ginelle has run away."

He frowned and than mumbled a stream of curses. "Damn it, I should not have agreed to this." He said as he swept pass his sister and out of the room.

Eloise was close at his heels as he snatched up his discarded cloak and proceeded out the front door. He bellowed for the stable boy to bring him his horse and whirled to intercept his sister, his eyes narrowing as he commanded, "You are to stay here."

Immediately she shook her head, "No, I will come with you."

"Bloody hell Eloise, do not argue with me."

She grabbed his arm as he started to turn towards the stable boy who approached with his horse. "You don't understand, Dorian. She is very skittish. She will only run when she sees you."

He pondered this for a moment before violently hissing under his breath as he swung up into the saddle and extended a hand to her. He grabbed the reins and spun the thoroughbred around as Eloise slipped her arms around his midriff, he stared towards town.

"No!" Eloise cried from behind, "She would not go to town."

He frowned as he growled, "Where then?"

She pointed to the dark foliage behind their estate. "There!"

She had been a complete and utter fool, Ginelle thought as she trembled violently in her cloak. Somehow, she had thought the dense forest would prove to be a safe refuge compared to the dangers of town. The darkness here was far more threatening. A sudden wind forced scattered leaves astray, bringing forth a bitter cold. Trees swayed in warning, their entangled limbs appeared like extended arms beneath the ghost moon. She felt the anxiety surfacing and she spun widely about, whimpering as distinct growls emerged from the blackness. Had she imagined them?

The fierce wind whipped at the hood of her cloak, tearing her hair free of its bound. Her eyes jumped warily from side to side as she backed away in haste, her fears heightening with each strangled breath. Despite the cold air, she felt beads of perspiration bathe her back beneath the cloak as she forced down a panicked cry.

It was then she heard a hoarse cry before a thundering black beast erupted from the darkness. Her eyes widened in stark alarm and she gasped in terror as she stumbled backwards; a root catching her heel before tumbling to the ground as those powerful hooves came thundering towards her.

She released a scream and brought her arm up above her face to take the brunt of the attack. Her heart hastened within her chest and she clenched her eyes shut, waiting for the impact, only to stiffen as gentle hands grasped her shoulders, shaking her.

"Ginelle!" Eloise voice penetrated her fear and she was overcome with a wave of relief to that familiar, soft voice and she opened her eyes to peer into that worried, azure gaze.

She said nothing as she bolted upright into Eloise's arms. She clenched her eyes closed against the tears as those comforting arms wrapped securely around her shivering frame.

Eloise simply held her, rocking her gently as though she were a babe. She reached up to push tangled strands of hair from her face as she whispered gentle words to ease her fear.

As Ginelle eased back to look at Eloise, it was than she spotted Death sitting atop the ominous black beast snorting in protest and she was unable to tear her gaze away from those eyes of steel. That cold, calculating look regarded her in bold assessment. The man's domineering disposition made her tremble as panic seized her as an urging impulse insisted she flee.

"What possessed you to run?" Eloise's anxious voice forced her eyes from the menacing figure as she searched for a plausible answer. Eloise didn't wait for a reply as she got to her feet and helped Ginelle up. As she started towards the horse and the dangerous looking man with his unwavering stare, she stiffened and backed away.

"It's okay." Eloise quickly sought to appease her fear, "Dorian will not hurt you."

Dorian? This dark, menacing stranger was her brother? At that thought, she watched as the man called Dorian dismounted and extended a hand to Eloise.

Eloise hesitated, "Come back to the manor with me, Ginelle."

As silence carried out, the towering stranger moved towards her with a grunt of impatience. She released a squeak of alarm as she backed away, Eloise protesting in alarm as her brother scooped Ginelle up and deposited her into the saddle. She didn't have time to deal with the sudden rush of fear or the swift urge to faint as the man called Dorian turned to do the same with Eloise.

The man seized the reins and turned the massive beast around, urging the horse back towards the plantation on foot. Her heart pounded within her chest as she stared at that rigid back and the mane of black hair falling to broad shoulders. This man was dangerous. Each stride bore that of authority and an aggressiveness that she dare not test. As the estate came into view, she wondered if she would have to face Eloise's immediate words of distress or this man's tyrannical fist.

Ginelle studied Eloise's pacing frame as she sat on the bed, wrapped in a thick coverlet. The evident dismay contorting the fine lines of her agile face made Ginelle uneasy as Eloise tugged at her cloak and tossed it carelessly aside. She stopped her anxious pacing to stare down at her, planting her hands on her hips as if to scold a misbehaved child.

"What were you thinking?" she demanded, her voice was soft but stern.

Ginelle lowered her gaze, uncertain as to what to say. How could she tell Eloise that she didn't belong with the affluent society, with her?

"Do you understand the danger that awaited you? A child unattended is simply an invitation to brigands."

Ginelle stiffened, her eyes widening in immediate alarm. She had not given much thought to other threats. Her thoughts had focused strictly on the darkness and Pierino. Eloise stepped forward and gently grasped her shoulders. "I'm sorry. I did not mean to frighten you, but you must understand that you are susceptible to many risks."

Ginelle nodded soberly and yet was not comforted for the image of a dark and imposing man came to mind. What danger did the Lord Dorian present?

After Eloise had retired from the room, Ginelle forced herself to bed. As the fire beneath the mantle crackled, Ginelle tossed and turned beneath the blankets, her thoughts were racing and the feeling of trepidation rising. When she finally fell asleep, her dreams were plagued with terrifying images.

She was running. The ground beneath her was soft but tiny pebbles pierced the soles of her feet. Her face was wet but there was no rain, she must be crying. She was crying. She pressed a shaky hand to her chest and felt the frantic beat of her heart, pulsing violently.

Ginelle!

She gasped as she came to a sudden halt. That voice! She knew that voice and dreaded it! Her feet wouldn't budge. She demanded her body to move but she remained frozen as she watched the trees sway in warning. He was upon her.

Ginelle.

The voice was closer. She heard the distinct sound of boots crushing decayed leaves. She turned as a shadow emerged, the silhouette revealing naught of its features but sharp, black eyes; eyes of a predator.

Ginelle bolted upright in bed and inhaled sharply. Her eyes moved instantly around the room, taking in her surroundings, reassuring herself she was safe and far from Pierino. She fell back against the headboard and pulled the coverlet to her chin as she cast a wary glance to the window where the vivid moon taunted her, silver rivulets of moonlight slipping pass the parted drapes to flow across the bed. She could find no comfort in its ethereal beauty.

A child unattended is simply an invitation to brigands. She closed her eyes as she focused on each labored breath. Eloise words came rushing back in a grip of terror. What would have happened if she had fallen into the wrong hands? Her logical decision from earlier now seemed reckless and foolish. The weather was terrible and she had no means of shelter. Where else could she go but back into the hands of Pierino? She shuddered at the thought as she reached up and gripped her mother's locket.

The silence of the room was deafening. She could not seem to shake the tremors from her body and it seemed as if the darkness that clung to the room had grown even darker.

Ginelle closed her eyes and struggled to keep her anxiety at bay. She could hear a sudden gust of wind outside her window and that sent her heart reeling against her chest.

She shoved the heavy quilts aside and stepped down from the bed. Her borrowed nightshirt fell low around her ankles as she made her way towards the door. She gripped the latch with unsteady hands as she quietly parted the door and peered out into the abandoned hall.

She could hear naught but the gentle patter of her feet as she slipped through the shadows. She pushed a stubborn strand of hair from her face as she turned a corner and came to the top of the winding stairway. Slowly, she made her descent, her eyes straining against the heavy darkness. Her heart began a rhythmic pounding within her chest as she came to the bottom and paused, her eyes settling on a door slightly ajar and the floor below it illuminating a flickering light.

Ginelle approached the door and pushed it open. Immediately, her eyes settled on the stoked fire beneath a mantle in exact replica to the one in her room. She moved with hesitant steps towards the fire, somehow drawn to the large, spacious room.

"What are you doing here?" she stiffened at the great, harsh voice coming from the right side of the room and she whirled to study the solid silhouette staring back at her with those glacial eyes of steel.

Dorian leaned comfortably into the overstuffed chair, taking pleasure in the warmth and comfort it provided when a distinct noise brought him alert. His hand moved to the blade hidden beneath his tunic, his eyes narrowing in speculation. His fingers paused around the hilt as a small, distinguishable shadow made its way discreetly into the room.

The warm, radiant glow cast from the fire encased her in a shroud of deep, flickering gold. Shadows danced across the delicate features of the child's pensive face as she took small overt steps to stand before the hearth.

The nightshirt swallowed her little frame and Dorian contemplated the child's age. Her bone structure was painfully fragile; her petite frame naught but a thin, feeble body beneath the cotton shift. Her pale tresses had been pulled back into a plait, several tedious strands escaping their restraint to frame her ethereal face.

A disturbing notion occurred to him. She was a pretty child.

His scowl deepened and he promptly banished the disquieting thought. "What are you doing here?" the words were released on a deep growl, indicating his sudden shift in mood.

The child pivoted, those large brown eyes widening in abrupt panic. As he leaned forward to better examine the sudden rush of blood that fled her face, she retreated a few paces, her limbs trembling as though he were going to pounce on her at any moment.

"I-I'm s-sorry." She fumbled with words as a profound fear paralyzed her.

"You shouldn't be here." He warned; his anger evident in the baritone of his voice. He stiffened as the sudden glint of tears surfaced in those wide, soft eyes and yet he could see her struggle to hold them back. Without another word, she turned and fled the room.

The next morning, Ginelle was seated at a beautifully long, trestle table laden with food. A brilliant chandelier hung above; heavily adorned with glass crystals glinting in the morning light emitting through the heavy drapes, but its beauty went unnoticed as her thoughts were disturbed with an assertive pair of cold, blue eyes. After her encounter with the dark laird last night, sleep had eluded her. She feared what the break of day would bring, fearful that the domineering lord would scold and berate her inquisitive actions the previous night, but he man was vacant from the breakfast table and as she spared a glance at Eloise at her side, she appeared unaware of what transpired.

The servants scurried in haste around the table, each carrying a tray exhibiting an assortment of food from boiled eggs to blocks of cheese. Her mouth watered as her eyes settled on fresh baked biscuits and a bowl of steaming oatmeal that a maid carried her way. As soon as the porridge was placed in front of her, she wasted no time in devouring the tasty meal.

A gentle laugh erupted at her hearty appetite and Ginelle paused with the spoon just inches from her mouth to peer at Eloise grinning with amusement flickering in the blue of her eyes. Eloise reached over and gently patted her hand gripping the utensil. "We will have to work on your etiquette."

Ginelle smiled sheepishly as she watched Eloise take a modest bite of the porridge and than slowly, Ginelle mirrored the gesture. Almost immediately, her stomach protested, growling nosily to force a deep blush into her cheeks.

Suddenly, the steward, Bogart appeared in the dining hall, his slender frame garbed in his usual black waist-coat and cotton trousers. "Milady?" he inquired, catching Eloise attention. "Lieutenant Stefan Cummings is here to see Master Dorian."

Eloise smiled as she gathered to her feet and Ginelle quickly did the same as a tall, slender man followed in behind the cynical Bogart. Lieutenant Cummings was a young and handsome man with an abundance of unruly, wheat hair. He produced a charming smile as his russet eyes met Eloise from across the room. "Lady Ashford, tis always a pleasure." He moved to accept her hand and gently caressed her knuckles with a kiss.

"Lieutenant, we are pass formality. Please, call me Eloise." Ginelle watched their exchange from beneath her lashes.

"As much pleasure as it would bring me, Lady Ashford, I must refrain for my gentleman reverence would not permit it." He replied with a dazzling smile.

His eyes than rested on Ginelle and immediately she dropped her head to avoid his stare as her fingers entwined nervously against the skirt of her dress. She felt someone step in beside her and the tension slightly eased from her body as Eloise said, "This is my ward, Miss Ginelle Pattinson."

Ginelle was quick to notice that Eloise had not mentioned her real last name and for that she was grateful. If someone were to learn of her whereabouts, she would never be safe for Pierino would not give up in finding her.

A look of interest brightened the man's eyes as he turned to fully address her but still spoke to Eloise. "I was not aware that you had taken in a protégé, milady. Is the young miss kin to the Ashford line? It is a pleasure to make your acquaintance, Miss Pattinson."

Ginelle was relieved that the Lieutenant had not repeated the same custom of kissing her hand as he had done with Eloise.

Those observant, russet eyes averted back to Eloise. "Where might I find your troublesome brother?"

Eloise smiled, "He is in the study. May I inquire of your visit, Lieutenant?" she paused for a moment before adding, "I assume you bring unfortunate news?"

Reluctantly, he nodded. "Aye, milady." His voice lacked in exuberance.

Eloise quickly sought to conceal the disappointment, offering a smile that didn't quite reach her eyes. "Very well, Lieutenant. I will not keep you from business."

Ginelle watched as the Lieutenant took her hand once more and softly kissed her knuckles. His hand lingered for a moment and than he straightened and left the room. Ginelle peered up at Eloise but her expression revealed naught of her displeasure.

As Dorian studied the engraved map dispersed across the mahogany desk, a knock jarred him to awareness. Lieutenant Cummings didn't wait for an invitation and instead pushed open the door and strolled into the room.

A dark brow arched, "Lieutenant? What brings you to my estate?" his eyes narrowed as his old and trusty companion slid comfortably into the leather seat across from him. "I see you find no difficulty in making yourself comfortable, lad."

Cummings smirked, "Aye." He leaned back into the seat and surveyed the study, pausing to admire the marvelous collection of leather-bound books lining the walls of the room. "This room is smothering." he tossed one leg over the other as he turned back to peer at Dorian who merely scowled deeply.

"Surely you did not come all this way to criticize my study? What brings you here, Lieutenant?"

All amusement fled Cummings' face as he dropped his leg and leaned forward, "There is trouble brewing at sea. That bastard Reyes has captured another of our vessels, this one containing valuable cargo."

"Which vessel?" Dorian demanded his voice dropping precariously to a dangerous tone.

"The Silver Wind. He seized the shipment of barrels containing cash crops, the expensive furs-"

Dorian abruptly stood, flexing his hands along the smooth surface of his desk as he asked, "What of the crew?"

Cummings stiffened his face paling beneath that intense, blue scrutiny. "They were seized, Captain."

Dorian gritted his teeth, his jaw flexing as the muscle ticked dangerously; his temper flaring. He swept a hand through his disorderly mane of black hair and turned to the window. Two vessels had been seized by the self-proclaimed Spaniard King, stealing him of profitable cargo, not to mention the lives of his men.

He released a string of curses before turning back to his Lieutenant. "Is there a ship docked?"

Cummings nodded, "Aye, The Lady Charlotte."

Dorian's thoughts instantly turned to Eloise. He had just returned only to be forced back to sea once again, but this time he would not know when he would return. "Inform the crew and prepare the vessel."

Cummings nodded briefly, "Aye, Captain."

Dorian watched his retreating back before sweeping an arm across the effects adorning his escritoire. He cursed violently beneath his breath as he turned and braced his hands against the wall, his temper rising to dangerous measures.

"Dorian?"

He turned as Eloise stepped into the study, her blue eyes assessing the broken clutter along the elegant rug. "What news did Lieutenant Cummings bring?" she gently closed the door and stepped towards him, the deep-set of her eyes daunting as she approached him.

Dorian straightened and inhaled deeply to brace his sister's verbal attack that was surely to come. "Another vessel has been claimed." He said sharply, "A Spaniard has laid siege on my crew and cargo."

Eloise stiffened, "You are leaving?" she asked, perplexed.

He nodded.

"So soon? You have just returned."

"I leave tonight."

She blanched as the blood hastened from her face and she advanced towards him in outrage. "This is absurd!"

"Eloise-"

"No." she said firmly, her eyes stormy with affliction. "You haven't even settled and already your obligations are calling you."

His face darkened, "I have responsibilities that I cannot disregard."

She lifted her chin and glared definitely up at him, "What of your responsibilities here, Dorian?"

His fists clenched at his sides as he glared down at her, resisting the urge to throttle her. "Several of my men will remain behind to see that the fields are tended and the laborers are guarded. I have far more important matters to attend. The fate of my crew depends entirely on me, Eloise."

His sudden flare of anger was quickly extinguished as those blue eyes glistened with tears. He reached out and gently cupped her chin, "What is it that you fear soeur?"

Eloise peered up at him as she fought back her tears. "I fear the day you will not return."

Dorian pulled her gently into his embrace, holding her tenderly as he had done when she was little before she had gone to boarding school. He placed his chin atop her head and said, "You need not fear for my wellbeing." He said to reassure her.

"You are not immune to death, dear brother." She stepped back to look up at him, "How long will you be gone?"

He hesitated, "I know not. There is much that needs to be done. Tracking the Spaniard will be my biggest challenge as well as finding my crew. The cargo can be replaced but the lives of my men cannot. Much time will be needed to find them."

"I understand your responsibility." Eloise said gently struggling internally to conceal her dismay. Dorian was all she had left of her family; she couldn't bare the thought of losing him.

Ginelle knew something was amiss once Eloise returned to the parlor. Her raven curls were slightly disarranged, her ivory complexion revealing a faint blush and there was a dull redness in her blue eyes. Had she been crying?

She cleared her throat as she moved to the far side of the room to peer out the window. She was quiet for a moment before turning to a rather large, black object sitting in the corner before the mantelpiece. Eloise reached out and touched the sleek black surface before asking, "Do you know what this is, Ginelle?"

Ginelle stepped forward in curiosity as she studied the magnificent piece in all its ebony glory. Eloise settled onto a leather bench and lifted the heavy lid to reveal a row of black and white keys. Ginelle settled in beside Eloise as she continued, "It is a piano."

"A piano?" her face brightened with genuine interest.

Eloise smiled, "Have you heard of it?"

She nodded, "Aye, but I have never seen one until now."

She fell silent as Eloise began to play a soft melody. Her fingers danced delicately over the black and white keys, creating a structured flow of musical notes and gentle cords. The sound was alluring to Ginelle. The combination of notes blended together in a perfect cadence created a beautiful rhythmical harmony. Ginelle smiled despite the doubt clouding her thoughts. Would she ever learn to play such a magnificent instrument?

"Music is a necessary skill." Eloise started, "You will have both music and dance lessons. You will also learn to cook and sew. You will have a wide expanse of domestic skills in a few years time."

She stopped playing and turned to smile down at Ginelle, but Ginelle was quick to notice that her eyes lacked happiness and revealed a dull light, as though something deeply troubled her.

"That is lovely." Eloise said, pointing to the locket around her neck.

She glanced down, not realizing she had been gripping the chain all along. "Twas my mother's." she said softly reaching up to open the small case concealing a miniature portrait of her mother.

"She is beautiful." Eloise said, studying the small picture of the blond haired woman. "You resemble her."

Ginelle's heart fluttered within her chest as she lifted her head to peer at Eloise. "You think so?" she asked gleefully.

Eloise straightened; her smile widening. "You have her eyes."

Ginelle lowered her head as she reached up and touched the delicate picture. She smiled to herself. She resembled her mother.

She had not realized that Eloise had slipped from the room until she lifted her head and found herself alone. She focused her attention on the beautiful stretch of black and white keys and felt her fingers twitch with curiosity and anticipation. She reached up and gently pressed down on a key; the note sharp and intricate. She smiled as she pressed down on two other keys, both producing a different tune. Her smile broadened as she tested the others, each individual sound heightening her eagerness to learn and explore music.

She caught a looming shadow in her peripheral. Her gaze jerked from the keyboard to the imposing frame watching her through cold, observant eyes. She wrenched her hands from the piano as if the instrument had burned to the touch. Ginelle wondered now if he would scold her because of last night or worse, beat her. She remained unmoving, fearful as of what to do as he continued to stare at her, making her consciously aware that they were alone. It was obvious the dark laird disapproved of her presence. Did he too disagree with her staying here because of her lowly rank? This was after all his estate. If he commanded that she leave, there was naught Eloise could prevent.

"I will not tolerate thievery while I am away. Is that understood?" his declaration shocked her. Did he really believe she would steal from Eloise? "Is that understood?" his voice dropped to a dangerous pitch and she stiffened.

"Aye, milord." She answered sorely. It pained her deeply that someone would think so poorly of her, but what else was she to expect? She was after all a street rat prone to pick-pocketing but he knew naught of her circumstances. She had done it in order to survive. Ginelle blinked away her tears, not wanting to show a sign of weakness before this towering beast of a man.

It wasn't until he left the room that she allowed the tears to come. She brushed them away with shaky hands and moved to stand by the window as tiny snowflakes fluttered from the sky, falling gently to the moist terrain below. She shuddered with grief as an image of her papa came to mind, the two of them playing in the snow. A sob lodged in her throat and she turned from the window, pressing her back against it as she closed her eyes against the intense pain surfacing in her chest.

Her papa was gone.

Forever lost to her.

Later that evening, Ginelle noticed once again that the dark Lord was absent from the table. As the servants scurried around the room, going about their tasks, she was keenly aware that Eloise appeared withdrawn, her usual manner of buoyancy all but dissolute. Ginelle toyed with her utensils as a thought occurred to her.

She remembered something he had said earlier to her in the parlor. I will not tolerate thievery while I am away. That would explain Eloise's sudden change in mood. Her brother was leaving again? She didn't realize how disturbing his presence truly was until she felt sudden relief at the thought of him leaving. He was a formidable man that unnerved her. Although it was a welcoming remedy her heart ached for Eloise for it was evident she adored her elder brother and wanted him home.

"How long will he be gone?"

Eloise stiffened as if suddenly jarred to awareness. She turned those deep, azure eyes to Ginelle and she wondered if she had made a mistake by meddling when it was none of her concern, but it pained her to see Eloise distraught.

"I do not know." Eloise replied, her voice barely revealing the sadness that was clearly there in the blue of her eyes. She smiled than as she reached over and patted Ginelle's hand. "No need to fret. He is quite capable of taking care of himself." Though she spoke the words to Ginelle, she was certain they were said aloud as if to reassure herself.

Chapter 3

The next few months passed in a blur of eagerness and excitement for Ginelle. It was almost as if she and Eloise were beloved kindred for they spent every minute of every day together. They spent hours on her lessons, Eloise claiming that she should have had an education at the early age of six or seven. There was much to be learned and Eloise was as ardently to teach as Ginelle was to learn.

Eloise had started with the basics. Ginelle was taught to read and write and than eventually when she mastered that, they moved on to reading. She began with simple material until she accomplished it and moved on to more difficult text. Eloise was amused by Ginelle's appetite for knowledge and impressed by how quickly she adapted to her schooling. She had an absolute desire to learn and study new and exciting things despite beginning at a later age.

She became well equipped in the knowledge of a domesticated gentlewoman and that in which was required. She excelled in arithmetic and literacy and grew accustomed to polished manners. She had an innate capacity to learn, absorbing all the skills taught to her. She relished in the art of dance and took immense delight in music; she was taught needlework and despite pricking her fingers numerous times she was fascinated in learning something new.

Time all but ceased to exist as the months passed in haste and soon a year was upon them. Along with her wide varieties of education, she was instructed on etiquette and the proper apparel for certain occasions. Eloise kept her well informed on housewifery skills and managing her own estate one day. Secretly, Ginelle vowed that, that day would not come. She vowed never to belong to a man who would control and possess her. The very thought disturbed and frightened her.

They spent much time in the garden, reading poetry and discussing art and music. They attended the opera and when the weather was warm and inviting, they went horse back riding.

Ginelle valued all the knowledge given to her, including every moment she and Eloise shared, delighting in the happiness they shared. Even Lucile was beginning to show signs of warmth, occasionally her thin mouth would lift in a reluctant smile despite her impassive manner. Ginelle had learned much of the older woman who protectively followed in Eloise's shadow. Lucile cared for Eloise as if she were own.

Pierino was still a consistent fear in the back of her mind, always a shadow, haunting her dreams, reminding her of her self-worth and at times dragging her back to the bottomless pit of oblivion. Every night, her dreams were plagued with sharp, black eyes and large hands, reaching to steal her from Eloise. She eagerly learned as much as she could in hopes that one day she could defeat her demon and be relieved of her nightmares.

20 November, 1814

My dear Dorian-

I pray that you are safe, dear brother and that my letter reaches you in good time. I fear the day that I will no longer receive your letters, though they are a great comfort to my heart but a distinct reminder that you are away. A year has already transpired and much has happened. Ginelle is excelling exceptionally in her studies, her eagerness for knowledge is limitless. She and I have grown inseparable. I find myself adoring her more each day; I dare say we have become much like sisters.

I pray the weather at sea isn't too dreadful. I have yet to hear of the wellbeing of your crew and if you have found your vessel. I know that the good Lord keeps you safe and guides your path but I am anxious for the day of your return.

With love,

Eloise

5 June, 1815

My dear Dorian-

It is good to hear that the weather is pleasant at sea. Though I have never been fond of traveling, I'm sure the Atlantic is a beautiful sight beneath the sun. I am relieved to hear that you have retrieved your vessel but terribly disturbed that you have yet to hear of your crews' whereabouts. I will continue to remind you that I greatly disapprove of your journey and I am in constant fear for your safety. Your letters put me at ease if only for a short period of time until I am anxious for the next. I insist you put an end to this frivolous pursuit. I know your pride would not allow it but I'm asking you to allow the authorities to handle the man that which you hunt. I fear the day that you are forever lost to me.

With love,

Eloise

25 October, 1815

My dear Dorian-

The weather here has changed along with the trees. Ives has purchased new laborers for the fields; he keeps me well informed. Ginelle and I went riding yesterday. There was a slight chill in the air but the ride was pleasant nonetheless. Lady Margaret Bennett hosted a ball in honor of Elizabeth's coming of age. I would like very much to do the same for Ginelle. There has been much gossip about my 'ward'. I keep her status very discreet. Neither she nor I are concerned with the loquacious ton.

Having her here brings much assuagement of my worry for your well-being. I pray every day that your journey is a safe one.

With love,

Eloise

24 January, 1816

My dear Dorian-

Ginelle continues to excel in her studies. I know that you were against the idea of her staying here with us but she has brought much light into my life. You do not know the happiness she gives me.

I've seem to have caught a mild cough. It is nothing to concern you with but at times I find it extremely bothersome. Though there has been much frost on the land and I believe I might have caught a slight chill. I am anxious for your return, dearest brother.

With love,

Eloise

14 March, 1817

My dear Dorian-

This will be my last letter to you and it bears unfortunate news. I have kept this from you for some time and please do not be angry with me for doing so but I know the extreme guilt that weighs heavily upon your shoulders and the lives that depend on you, but I'm afraid my condition has worsen and there is not much that can be done. I am very ill and have been for some time. It appears my health has been deteriorating without my knowledge and only recently has plunged for the worst. I struggle now in writing you this letter. I have just recently been bedridden, ordered by the doctor to remain as I am. We are at a loss to the sudden mysterious illness that has claimed my health. Ginelle reads to me every day, her presence is a comfort beyond means but my heart aches for your return.

Please, return to me in haste, so that I may spend my numbered days with those I love. I fear time is of essence.

Love always,

Eloise

Nearly three years have passed since she had been brought to the plantation and much has changed. She had been given a formal schooling and taught the essentials of managing a household and the basics of etiquette. She learned to understand novels, plays and even complex literature that she never dreamed of understanding let alone read. She took a keen interest in music and had become quite adapt to the piano. She felt as though she had no limit as she accepted and viewed each task as a challenge to be accomplished. But nothing had prepared her for the devastation of heartache.

Her body was numb and she felt a distinct wetness on her cheeks as she stared at the woman sleeping in the large bed. Lucile stood in one corner, the elderly maid struggling to hold her distraught at bay. Ginelle reached out and gently brushed a strand of hair from Eloise's face. She felt her heart splitting within her chest, a definite crack that was deafening to her ears. She was unaware that she wept for her eyes remained fixated on the woman who had given her so much within three years. She had grown to love Eloise, despite her mistrust of strangers. Eloise was the mother and sister she never had. She was her mentor; her beloved companion.

A sob erupted from her throat and she choked back the tears that stole the breath from her lungs. Her hands trembled as she brought the coverlet up to Eloise's chin. She appeared serene and yet, it wasn't Eloise. She was frail and frighteningly gaunt. Her cheeks were pale and sunken, the faint blush that enhanced her ivory beauty all but gone. Her hair no longer pinned in defiant curls now lay dispersed in disarray across her pillow. Her labored breathing indicated that the chest pains had returned. The suffering her beloved friend endured left Ginelle feeling utterly and hopelessly helpless. How could she show Eloise the same compassion and care she had shown her?

A sudden moan of pain jarred her alert and she stiffened as she reached out to clasp Eloise's hand as those blue eyes fluttered open, the glint of life fading from those azure depths.

"I am here, Eloise." Ginelle said softly, her voice cracking with despair as Eloise's face contorted with pain.

Despite her suffering, Eloise smiled gently as her eyes shuddered closed for a brief moment before opening to rest on Ginelle. "Do not weep for me, sweeting." Her voice was faint, barely audible for the illness was there in her weakened tone. She reached up with a frail, trembling pale hand and tenderly brushed the tears from Ginelle's cheek.

"What s-should I do?" Ginelle cried painfully, "Tell me what I can do?" Ginelle gripped those frail hands in her own, clinging to Eloise as though to prevent death itself from stealing her friend away. "Please Eloise." She felt her chest tightening with desperation.

Eloise took a moment to bring air into her lungs before speaking, "You have mend me in ways that I thought could not be healed." She cupped Ginelle's face with her trembling, clammy hand, "You have brought me much love and happiness. You are my sister." Her arm grew heavy and she lowered it back to the mattress.

There was a shuffle outside the door and Lucile rushed from the corner to stand at her mistress side. Ginelle continued to grip that frail hand in her own, her eyes resting on Eloise, unaware of anything but her beloved sister.

Belle, the chambermaid suddenly appeared, her eyes glistening with tears for fear that her mistress has already passed. She spared a desperate glance at the bed. "What is it, Belle?" Lucile demanded.

"Master Dorian." She said anxiously, "He's arrived!"

Lucile pressed a shaky hand to her ample bosom and ushered the frantic maid from the chamber. "Go now and find the doctor."

Ginelle heard nothing as she struggled to control the flood of emotions consuming her.

As the abrupt sound of footsteps ascended from the hall, Eloise whispered, "Do not be afraid to give your heart away, Ginelle."

Lucile moved forward, gently placing her hands around Ginelle's shoulders and pulled her to her feet. Ginelle grasped Eloise's hands until they were wrenched away.

The door suddenly crashed open, jarring her back to the severity of the situation and the hands gripping her trembling shoulders. Her vision blurred as a man enclosed the space from the door to the bed with abrupt haste, instantly falling to his knees to grab the hands that she had been holding moments ago. The doctor, a short and small man with a peaked nose shortly followed, carrying the leather bag that contained the tools he had examined Eloise with earlier.

"Come, my pet." Lucile said softly as she gently urged Ginelle from the room where the servants huddled, some weeping softly on the shoulders of others while several stood frozen, their faces pale and fearing the worst.

The image of Eloise lying lifeless with eyes no longer blue as the sky struck her with such force that her knees gave way as she released a heart-wrenching sob and tears flooded uncontrollably. She heard a number of gasps erupt around her and Lucile's voice as they scrambled to catch her falling body. A man appeared at her side and as the hall spun widely out of place she was able to catch a glimpse of his face but his name would not register as she slipped into darkness.

"You are here." The words were released on a strained gasp as Eloise attempted a smile and studied the man kneeling at her side, gripping her hand tightly. A strong, callused hand reached up and gently brushed her cheek as beads of perspiration dotted her forehead and trickled down her throat. She swallowed as a severe dryness lingered in her throat, fearing it would bring on a fit of coughs that had plagued her for several months. Her chest rose and fell with increasing difficulty for each breath brought pain as her body trembled violently. She forced a smile to her lips, wanting to ease the fear that dwelled in the depths of those glacial, blue eyes.

"Nothing would keep me from you." His voice strained against the rising storm of affliction. His face darkened with intense wretchedness as his body stiffened with anguish and the room around him seems to grow dull and colorless, his vision suddenly gray.

Eloise reached out and gently tugged a strand of black hair from Dorian's face. "Do not grieve for me, frère." She paused as she struggled to bring air back into her lungs. Dorian tensed, his heart pitching in his chest but those blue eyes turned back to him, "This is a bittersweet blessing."

His body went rigid and his dark features contorted as he was seized with maddening grief. "I will be reunited with Philip and my child." She smiled as her eyes became distant as if peering upon those very faces.

"Eloise-"

"Promise me that you will abandon your reckless ways." Tears trickled from the corners of her eyes and fell to wet the pillow. Her voice broke as her fingers tightened around Dorian's. "Promise me that." She pleaded.

"I promise." He leaned forward and kissed her forehead, closing his eyes against a wave of despair threatening to consume him. He leaned back to peer down at her as she whispered one last request as a haze of pain clouded her eyes. Her fingers tightened a fraction as her plea was released on a painful breath. "Take care of Ginelle. For me, please Dorian."

Dorian went numb as the smaller hand in his own went limp, the passion for life slowly fading from her eyes as her head lolled to one side and she breathed her last breath.

A swift and unexpected pain seized his chest as the blood rushed from his face. He was gripped with an insensibility that seeped to the bone and he sat frozen, holding that still hand as if compelling her back to life. His body shuddered with an overwhelming darkness, a swallowing blackness that came from deep within. He loosened her hand and stood to his feet, his conscience barely assessing the grieved faces surrounding him as someone, a maid, released a cry of anguish.

It wasn't until strong, reassuring fingers gripped his shoulder that he was pulled from desolation. He averted his gaze from the bed to Lieutenant Cummings and allowed the man to take him from the room as the doctor paused at the door to examine Dorian if only for a brief moment before entering the room.

Once in the hall, he wrenched away from Cummings as a dark and ominous cloud enveloped him in a shroud of raw pain. Cummings stepped aside as his gaze followed Dorian's rigid back down the hall, a minatory darkness following in his wake.

Chapter 4

The household had fallen into a state of robotic depression. The servants carried on with their daily tasks seemingly aware of the desolated cloud that had fallen on the plantation. Several dispirited days had passed since their mistress was claimed from illness and a heaviness settled.

The servants grew fearful of their dark laird who barricaded himself behind closed doors and took to the bottle. He rarely ventured from the study, not even to the fields that he neglected so carelessly. Many knew to stay clear for his demeanor had blackened dangerously and they feared he would succumb to the dreaded fate that which his father before him suffered. The servants whispered that the bottle would be his undoing, if not the brandy than surely the frightening darkness that slowly encased his soul. They feared all was lost for their lord.

Sleep was peaceful. Sleep eluded the feelings that all but threatened to drain her of life. Her eyes fluttered open and instantly Ginelle felt the sudden blow of heartache. She rolled from the window where rivulets of sunlight filtered in through the drapes. She clenched her eyes against the tears that she refused to shed. How many times must she cry for another loved one lost to her?

Someone was stoking the fire within the hearth. She didn't bother to open her eyes, having adjusted to the servants but simply gripped the coverlet more firmly and pulled it to her chin.

An unseen force jerked the blanket away and her eyes opened on their own accord. She studied the older woman standing at the end of the bed, signs of depression clearly written on her pinched face. The woman had once been intimidating with her assertive, dark stare and the firm set of her mouth but over the years the two of them had established a genuine relationship and here lately, Lucile was her only means of comfort.

"I cannot allow you to waste away in this room." Lucile stated firmly, moving to stand at Ginelle's side. "Tis been nearly a fortnight and you continue to wallow in bed." Her stern expression revealing nothing of the grief that she endured on the inside but Ginelle could see an indication that she had not slept well or eaten much since Eloise's passing. Despite her solemn disposition Ginelle had always admired the older woman for she had an unrelenting maternal nature, just as her mistress.

She pulled herself upright and leaned against the headboard, instinctively raising her hand to block the sun from her weary eyes. She felt the immediate heaviness settle in her chest and the urge to lie back down. "Lucile-" she blinked away tears as she looked up at the older woman. "What should I do?" her voice shook as she released the tears and a sob lodged in her throat.

Lucile settled on the bed and gently grasped Ginelle's shoulders, "You will remain here, at Ashford."

Ginelle shook her head, her eyes doubtful. "You and I both know that I do not belong here."

Lucile reached out and gently grabbed her chin, "And you and I both know that here is where Eloise would want you to be."

Ginelle wanted to believe Lucile for her old fears had resurfaced with Eloise's death. Foolishly, she had allowed herself to become attached to these people, even this austere woman sitting before her who had been against her arrival from the beginning. She had grown to love them as they loved her. She had established many friends but she was not of noble birth and this home was not her own. She was an imposter; always have been. There was no denying her rank.

As if sensing her thoughts, Lucile said, "Why would you want to leave, after all that Eloise has done? It would all be for naught."

Ginelle lowered her head as she was seized with a pang of guilt. She wanted nothing more than to remain with the people she had begun to call her own but could she really open her heart again? She had lost her parents and now Eloise? Was she destined to lose every person she loved? Was she to live a life of loneliness? She couldn't bare the thought of more anguish. The dreaded thoughts made her heart constrict and than a fearful image came to mind. She would have no choice but to return to the streets. With Eloise's death, Pierino had returned.

"I want to stay." She said with great longing. She wanted desperately to remain at Ashford; with the memories of Eloise.

"We will have no more talk of you leaving." Lucile said sternly as she gathered to her feet. "I will have Ingrid bring up your breakfast and then mayhap you can go to the garden for some fresh air?"

Ginelle nodded but her heart sank deeper when the older woman left, leaving her alone to face the burden of her sorrows. She knew in her broken heart that remaining at Ashford was not an option. There were too many reminders of the happiness she and Eloise shared. Gripping the locket around her neck, she leaned back against the headboard and shut her eyes, her chest rising with a stifled sob.

The door suddenly opened and Ginelle stiffened abruptly as Ingrid entered, carrying a tray that contained her breakfast as she crossed the room to deposit it on the table. In three years time, Ingrid had grown a little taller and curvier and her animosity towards Ginelle had intensified.

Ingrid turned her venomous glare on Ginelle, her mouth thinning with a deep scowl of distaste as she curtsied in mockery. "Your breakfast, milady." Her sneer widened before she left the chamber, leaving Ginelle all the more convinced that here was not where she belonged.

His days were bleak and slurred. Through the many preparations and the ceremony, he had been in a darkened haze, oblivious to all but the closed casket containing Eloise's lifeless body. Could he really continue without the little warmth in his soul? Could he roam the halls knowing Eloise would not be in the next room, laughing and smiling? That the piano would never again play a soft, gentle tune at the tips of her fingers? He stared at the empty brandy bottle he had drained the previous night where sleep had banished him, forcing him to brace the brunt of his sister's devoid existence.

With a violent sweep of his hand, he knocked the empty bottle from his desk. It fell to the carpet with a silent thud. He stood from the chair where he had spent the dark hours of the night wallowing in despair, thinking on memories that now lay in his past. He swept an unsteady hand through his tousled hair as he moved to the window. Eloise had been his purpose in life. She had been his only light and now that light was forever diminished.

His eyes strained against the sharp, morning light as he studied the vast expanse of land that had once belong to his father and now belonged to him. Below the window was the flourishing garden that both Eloise and their mother had loved.

His thoughts came to a breaching halt as his eyes settled on a small woman sitting just below the window. Streams of sunlight cast her in brilliant hues of yellow, capturing the vibrant silver of hair pulled back at the nape of her neck. She had donned a gown of black, strictly for mourning, her skirts flowing over the bench that which she sat upon. Cradled in her lap was an open book. He studied her intensely as his face darkened with uncertainty to the woman's identity. He took keen notice to her quivering form as she struggled to keep her posture straight as she clutched a handkerchief in her hand.

There was a sudden quick knock at the door and he jerked to awareness as he turned to glare dangerously at the intruder. Bogart cautiously cracked the door and peered inside until he spotted his Lord's whereabouts. "Forgive my intrusion, milord-"

"Come here, Bogart." He was unaware of the old man's alert expression as he cautiously moved to stand at his laird's side. "Who is that woman?" he demanded, his eyes never straying from the mysterious girl.

Bogart frowned as he dared a glance at his laird's dark face. "Tis Miss Ginelle, milord." He replied tentatively.

Dorian stiffened. He had not given any thought to the child his sister had taken in three years ago. Bogart slipped quietly from the room as Dorian continued to stare at the woman as something his sister said came rushing back to memory.

Take care of Ginelle. For me, please Dorian.

As if suddenly aware that she was not alone, the woman looked up and Dorian was struck a blow that nearly rendered him of breath. She had been a pretty child when he remembered her last but the vision before him was naught as he had imagined. Her complexion was that of porcelain, with large, unguarded eyes that revealed a storm of pain. For some reason unknown to him, he felt a slight twinge of intrigue as he continued to watch her. This small woman had brought Eloise much happiness?

The spell was broken when she leapt to her feet and fled the garden. His features hardened as he stared at the empty bench where she had been moments ago. She had every reason to fear him and fear him she should. Clenching his jaw he stalked from the window and moved towards the door. He had enough of drinking away his sorrows. It was best he got away from these enclosed walls and seek the tedious labor of his well-neglected fields; anything to keep his thoughts from straying towards unwarranted distractions.

Once she was safely within her room, Ginelle released the breath she had been holding. She pressed a shaky hand to her chest as she struggled to bring her frantic heart to a steady pace. How could she have forgotten?

That cold, calculating stare had unsettled her feeble bravado, forcing her fears to the surface. Having been so absorbed in her mourning over Eloise, she had forgotten the dark laird who struck a terrifying fear within her. Though her heart yearned for nothing more than to stay here with her memory of Eloise, her fear of the menacing Lord overshadowed it.

She was adamant about her decision. She would leave and what were the chances that Pierino would still be searching for her? Mayhap is interest in her was no longer? Did he think her dead? She prayed for the latter in hopes that he would end his pursuit in finding her.

There was a shuffle outside her door and she stepped back, her heart thrusting against her chest at the thought of that imposing frame looming on the other side. Her eyes widened in alarm as the latch lifted and the door parted.

"Ginelle?" Lucile's voice brought on a flood of relief and her shoulders sagged. The woman came up short as she found Ginelle standing a foot away, clearly distressed. "What troubles you, child?"

Ginelle shook her head and offered a small smile for the older woman. "Nothing, Lucile. You startled me is all." She pressed a hand against the throbbing pulse at her breast.

Lucile frowned but didn't question the notion that something was wrong. "You haven't touched your breakfast." It wasn't a question but an indication of her disapproval.

"I wasn't hungry." Ginelle replied softly, turning from the older woman to stand at the window. She studied the region surrounding the manor and pondered over which direction would be best to take. The city was furthest from her mind.

"You are far too thin to discard food." Lucile scolded, moving to gather the untouched tray. "I will have Cook brew you some tea and mayhap a bowl of porridge?"

Ginelle continued to stare out the window. She nodded but said nothing. Her fingers gripped the window sill as a deep sadness lodged in her chest. Once she heard the click of the latch, she dropped her head and wept.

The remainder of the day, Dorian sought the fields to keep all disturbing thoughts at bay. His men were startled to find their lord sober but were not oblivious to the silent storm that simmered within. He bellowed commands to the unfortunate laborers who were subjected to his temper as he suspected their work, taking immediate notice that several lacked in their efforts. His men stood aside, casting wary glances amongst each other, but none dared approach their dangerously tempered Lord as he demanded penance for their negligence. Several laborers were ordered to be lashed.

Dorian was unaware that he was causing a stir of questions of uncertainty to his sanity. His crops lacked in abundance due to his carelessness but the criminals that worked his fields were held responsible for their own workmanship. It would take a great deal of time to get his fields back to a satisfying result and he welcomed the challenge, anything to keep him occupied.

He would also need to send word to Cummings on the whereabouts of his missing crew. Cummings had obligingly taken his place at sea when he had returned to Ashford and he had yet to hear any information concerning his vessel and the bastard, Reyes. How he would like to drive a rapier through the Spaniard's heart. He had stolen the lives of many men; men who had trusted their Captain.

As the day continued brining the slow approach of dusk, he worked tediously until his body was weary with exhaustion and could no longer stand. He ordered the laborers back to their quarters and his men to their hall as he retired for the night. He brushed the sweat from his brow and mounted his horse. As he made his way back towards the manor he paused as his eyes averted to one of the windows that proclaimed a dim glow.

His thoughts instantly turned towards the girl from the garden. It unnerved him that he did not find her presence at Ashford unwelcoming; was it simply because he was honor bound? Twas apparent that Eloise had taken the child in to appease her grief but in her letters to him, she had described with much enthusiasm of the child that brought her much happiness. His sister had been proud and her affection for the impoverished child evident. Could he really banish the girl without the feeling of betrayal at his sister's request?

A feeling of anger washed over him at the thought of this sudden burden thrust upon him. Why should he care for an impoverished girl who meant nothing to him when he had more and important matters to attend?

What of your responsibilities here, Dorian? Those daunting words that his sister had last said to him the night he left came back to haunt him, plaguing him with guilt. Eloise had been his responsibility, and now she was dead.

His fingers curled around the leather reins as he jerked his horse around and dug his heels into the mare's side as he fled in the opposite direction of the house. Whether he approved of it or not, he knowingly made a vow to Eloise. There was never a moment that he could deny her anything and even after death, he could not deny her this last request.

Ginelle had risen early to greet the break of dawn. She had tossed and turned through out the night, her thoughts tormented with the ultimate decision that she had no other option but to leave Ashford. The memories here were far too painful. The happiness she had once shared now seemed all but a dream.

She was angry. How could Eloise abandon her, just as her father had done? She had said from the very beginning that she didn't want any of it, and now here she was, destined to be, alone and forced to endure the infinite pain of loss.

She reached up and gripped her mother's locket, clinging to the silver chain that was a comfort. She had considered selling the gowns that Eloise had, had made for her and than quickly dismissed the terrible thought. She couldn't bare the thought. They had been made specifically for her, out of the kindness of Eloise's heart but they didn't really belong to her. None of this did. The only rightful item that did was the precious trinket around her neck. She couldn't contemplate parting with it, but her options were limited. She would have no other choice but to barter the necklace in means of travel. She would get as far away as she could, possibly even travel to America and find work.

Ginelle stiffened as the door to her room opened. She remained as she was, standing before the window as Lucile stepped quietly into the room. The older maid straightened, her expression altering to one of surprise to find Ginelle awake and fully dressed.

"You are awake?"

Ginelle nodded as she turned away from the window, still gripping the locket between her fingers as she moved to stand beside Lucile. "Lucile-"

"Master Dorian has asked to speak with you."

She stiffened with alarm as everything she had been prepared to tell Lucile fled as apprehension caused her stomach to churn. "W-what does he want?"

"I know not but simply that he sent me to find you and bring you to his study."

"You will have to tell him that I cannot."

"I am sorry my dear but I cannot do that. Master Dorian expects you in his study as we speak. If I return without you, he will not be pleased."

The last thing Ginelle wanted to do was face that menacing man with his glacial stare. His obvious distaste of her not only angered but frightened her. She was well aware of the gossip whispered among the servants. They feared their own Lord and the dreadful tales that were muttered of the man were frightening. Would he now demand that she leave Ashford immediately? What other reason did he have to summon her?

Reluctantly, she followed Lucile from the room and down the hall, all the while her heart beating an irregular pulse that had her nerves scattered.

He had not slept at all that night, his mind continuously contemplating the unwelcoming burden that he unknowingly agreed to care for. He had not given the girl much thought since she had come to live with Eloise but now the girl was his responsibility, whether he liked it or not. The thought suddenly made him furious. Why would his sister do such a careless thing as to bring a complete stranger to his home?

His anger vanished as abruptly as it had come for he couldn't be angry with his sister who had put others before herself, who cared nothing for the standards of society but for the welfare of those less fortunate. As much as he disapproved of it, he had made a vow to his sister and he was one never to break his word. Besides, how difficult could a docile chit be? Was she not at an agreeable age for marriage? She could remain here at Ashford until a suitable suitor came along to take this excess baggage off his hands.

At that thought, a knock sounded at his study door and he stood as Lucile entered followed by the object of his thoughts. The older woman stepped aside to allow the girl to enter and immediately he was struck by how lovely the morning light placed across her delicate face.

Annoyed, he dismissed Lucile with a wave of his hand and the woman hesitated before closing the door behind her, leaving the two of them.

Dorian frowned as he caught a tiny flicker of fear in those soft, brown eyes but as quickly as it came, a sudden resolve settled to conceal any emotion that lay within. He felt a slight twinge of admiration as he studied her rigid frame. She was small and childlike, her ethereal beauty stirring him in a way that was unsettling and most disturbing.

His face darkened and his mood blackened as he quickly sought the words he had prepared to say. "Do you have any immediate kin?" he was keen to notice the sudden stiffening of her frame yet her eyes remained unyielding and her small hands entwined in front of her.

"I do not, milord." He jerked at her reply. Her voice was soft and sweet and his irritation increased for that gentle tone did something strange to him.

"There is no one?" Ginelle tensed at the harshness of his words. It took every ounce of control to keep her knees from buckling and her legs from giving beneath her. She kept her hands entwined to keep her fingers from trembling as those piercing blue eyes studied her in bold observation.

He was much larger than she remembered. In fact, he was by the far the largest man she had ever encountered. The sheer size of his frame brought on the sudden impulse to take a step back even though the desk stood between them. His skin was a golden bronze, having darkened from spending several years at sea. His chiseled features sharp and define, revealing a rugged exterior. His jet-black hair had been tamed at the nape of his neck by a leather thong where several stubborn strands escape to caress the firm-set of his jaw.

His presence indicated authority and a threatening manner that she dare not test. His ice-blue eyes watched her in cold assessment. She couldn't allow his domineering presence to unravel her bravado. After today, she would never lay eyes on this man again.

"I am indebted to you and your family." She said; her voice shaking as those blue eyes darkened. "I thank you for allowing me to stay here, at your home. I shall leave as soon as possible. I simply ask to loan a carriage for my departure. I'll gladly repay when I am able."

She forced herself to meet that intense stare and almost lost control of her swaggering display of confidence. Silence settled between them and she feared he would decline her request. Was he truly so merciless that he would deny her a means of transportation?

"It is simply out of the question." He said his voice hard and absolute.

She felt a sudden sinking feeling in her chest. Had she truly expected that he would show her any generosity? "You will remain here, at Ashford."

She blanched as she met those glacial depths watching her intensely. Had she heard him clearly? "I-I beg your pardon, milord?"

His gaze did not waver as he said, "Here is where you will stay."

Ginelle frowned, clearly perplexed as to why this man would want her to remain in his home. As much as she wanted to remain at Ashford, it was clearly not acceptable especially having to endure his presence along with the immense sorrow of Eloise's memory. She knew absolutely nothing about this man but the rumors whispered among the servants only heightened her fears. It had been quite evident from their first encounter that he did not particularly like her, so why than would he insist she remain at Ashford? At least with Pierino, she knew what to expect.

She shook her head, "I cannot."

A dark brow lifted and his blue eyes narrowed as he said, "You cannot?"

"I am very grateful but I-"

"It is not up for discussion." He growled darkly, clearly annoyed.

She stiffened at his abruptness and felt a sudden anger seize her. What right did he have to make demands of her? "You are saying that I do not have a choice?" she felt her heart quicken within her chest.

"That is what I am saying." She dropped her hands and they curled into fists at his maddeningly, relaxed manner.

"I do not understand."

He leaned forward to flatten his hands on his desk as he said, "What is there not to understand? You are to remain here at the manor."

"By what right-"she felt the heat rush to her face, her fear all but forgotten as she took an angry step closer to the desk, "-do you have to make such demands?"

His features darkened as he said, "By rights of guardianship."

Her sharp intake of breath went unnoticed as she stared nonplussed into that face of implacable resolve. "You are not my guardian." She stated as though to assure herself.

His jaw tightened as he said, "Unfortunately miss, I am."

He straightened to his full height and she was keenly aware of how close they were and it set her heart at a frantic pace as she found herself unable to avoid those cold eyes. It wasn't so. This man did not have rights over her. She had made a vow that no man would control her.

She frowned at something he had said, "Unfortunately?" she narrowed her eyes at him, "If you do not wish to willingly be my guardian, than why do so?"

She refused to back down at the evident display of anger etched into his hard face. She was not the skittish, fearful child cowering in the corner that she had once been. Eloise had taught her much over the past three years, bestowing a courage she thought she had not possessed; though she found her newfound confidence wavering beneath those icy depths staring boldly back at her.

A thought suddenly struck her, "Was it Eloise that asked of this unfortunate burden?"

His expression revealed nothing but the muscle at his jaw tightened, "I made a vow that I intend to keep. You will remain at Ashford until I can further consider your future."

Ginelle almost laughed at the irony of the situation. Here she had expected that the dark Lord would gladly see her on her way when in fact he had commanded she stay. Her anger returned as she closed the study door, resisting the urge to slam it.

He was mistaken if he thought to make demands of her. He most certainly was not her guardian and never would she allow another man especially one so dictating as this one to have any means of control in her decision making or her future.

Her thoughts instinctively turned to Eloise. Had she truly given this menacing man incapable of warmth and compassion control over her wellbeing? The thought made her tremble on the inside. Why would Eloise do this to her? She had known of her fears, why would she place her life in the hands of another man? Something about Dorian Ashford unraveled her senses in a frightening way. She was suddenly struck anew with an astonishing realization. It was apparent that a man like Dorian Ashford was to be feared from the sheer size of him and authoritative demeanor but she had stood her ground if only for a brief moment. The thought was a remedy for if she could stand against a man like Dorian Ashford than surely her fear of Pierino was in the past?

As she returned to her room and closed the door firmly behind her she released the breath she had been holding. She felt her anger return full-circle as their conversation replayed over in her head. It mattered not for she would be gone before tomorrow.

She pushed herself away from the door and moved to gather her bundle of belongings she had stuffed under the bed earlier that morning. She had given much thought over the past couple of days and as much as her heart yearned to stay at Ashford simply to hold onto the memories of Eloise and their short life of happiness together, it was clearly out of the question. There was nothing here for her. If she could reach America than she would never again set eyes on Pierino and Dorian Ashford.

The day had steadily progressed and with it, Ginelle had learned that several of the laborers had been ordered to be whipped. Ginelle trembled at the thought. Dorian Ashford had exacted these brutal lashings. What man would harm the flesh of another unless they were cold and merciless? She knew too well the severity of many punishments and shuddered at the thought of the violent lashings they would receive. How could she possibly remain at Ashford knowing a man such as Dorian would harm the hands that tend his fields?

As dusk approached, she felt that confidence she had earlier commended herself slowly break off into little fragments of apprehension and uncertainty. Remembering her last happening when she had tried to leave, she found herself terrified beyond her imagining. Could she attempt the foliage without being swept away by her fears? Was she making a grave mistake? She and Eloise had ventured to the forest many times on occasion but they had not traveled far, only to a familiar spot by the river. She knew that fear of Pierino would always be in the back of her mind, though she convinced herself that she was not a child anymore that could allow a man to intimidate her, but could she really survive on her own? These walls had protected her for some time but she couldn't continue to hide any more.

Eventually, she would have to face the impending dangers lurking on the outside.

She quickly dismissed any disturbing thoughts from her mind for she refused to allow her fears to deter her from her decision.

Ginelle waited until darkness had fallen and the house fell silent, indicating the servants had gone to bed. She gathered what little belongings she possessed and started for the door. She paused as her hand touched the latch to turn and survey the room that she had almost claimed for her own. She felt the sudden rush of tears and quickly turned away from the beautiful chamber. She would not think of Eloise for the pain encircling her heart was agonizing.

She made her way into the hall and was relieved to find it empty. She slipped cautiously through the shadows, continuously glancing over her shoulder in fear that Lucile would be lurking somewhere nearby. Nothing went unnoticed to the older woman.

It wasn't until she stepped out into the night that she allowed herself to take in a sharp breath of air. She pressed a shaky hand over the pulse that throbbed beneath her palm and quickly surveyed her surroundings. She was relieved that the tobacco fields were on the opposite side of the plantation and she wouldn't have to encounter any of the men that guarded the region but she couldn't allow herself to feel any triumph just yet because she had yet to get a horse.

A sudden chill caused her to stiffen and she realized she had forgotten her cloak. She bit down on her lower lip as she considered returning for it and than quickly decided against it. She had come too far to turn around and risk everything. Gathering her skirts in one hand and cradling her possessions in the other, she slipped effortlessly towards the stables. She felt an immediate wave of guilt for stealing a horse but she vowed silently that she would send money for the stolen mare.

The stable door creaked on the hinges as she slipped inside. The horses stirred in theirs stalls at her presence as she quickly assessed them. She paused as she spotted a massive black beast at the far end of the stable. She shivered as she studied the magnificent creature, recognizing it as the one that had nearly trampled her that night in the forest. She most certainly could not ride an animal as large and fearsome as that one.

Ginelle turned to find a much smaller and docile mare. The horse watched her warily through dark, beady eyes as she approached the stall. It took her an excessive amount of precious time to saddle the mare but she managed after a few struggled attempts. Her heart pounding and hope flaring within her chest that she nearly accomplished her escape, she led the horse from its stall and out the barn. Just outside the doors, she allowed herself enough time to mount the horse but her skirts prevented her from mounting properly. She paused as she reached down to gather skirts and it was then a looming shadow fell over her and a large arm clamped around her waist.

Ginelle didn't have time to comprehend the situation as panic gripped her in an icy shroud. She felt a scream in her throat as her arms instinctively came up to attack the face of her attacker. The arm around her waist tightened as her struggles forced both she and her assailant to lose their balance and stumble back into the stable. She felt her throat closing in as she struggled to bring air into her lungs. Her eyes burned with tears as that large arm around her waist refused to budge. She kicked her legs out but to no avail.

Suddenly, she heard a distinct rip and gasped when her attacker's foot caught her skirts and they both went tumbling.

She stiffened for the impact and the large body to crush her but in a sudden swiftness, her attacker shifted his body to take the brunt of the fall as she landed softly on top of him. She felt immediate fear as her hands encountered sheer muscle beneath a thin tunic. She lifted her head and her eyes clashed with a pair of icy blue depths. She inhaled sharply, her eyes widening in sudden alarm.

Dorian had known from their heated conversation and Lucile's warning earlier that day that the little chit would attempt to leave. He was no fool for she had foolishly tried once before and had failed. So he waited patiently all evening, and wasn't surprised to find her small shadow slipping through the halls, oblivious to his presence. She was impossible and his instincts demanded that he let her go but his vow to Eloise forced him to continue his pursuit.

He had thought to stop her before she got to the horses but he amused himself by allowing her to struggle with the task of saddling the horse and he couldn't seem to take his eyes off her.

It was then as she led the horse from the stable that he decided he had allowed this nonsense to continue long enough. She was unaware as he approached that the horse jerked in panic and fearful that the girl would get hurt, his arm wrapped around her small waist to pull her out of harms way.

He had not expected her sudden attack as she burst into a fit of struggles. Dorian dodged her flailing arms as he jerked her back from the frightened horse and lost his footing, stumbling backwards. He released an impatient growl as he fought to control her wrestling limbs. He stepped sideways only to catch the rim of her skirts and send them both falling to the ground.

As he turned in midair to take the brunt of the fall, his arms tightened around her frame and they collided roughly in the dirt. As she attempted to right herself, he became increasingly aware of her little body pressed intimately against his own. His temper soared as his body ignited with desire.

His eyes clashed with those soft depths and he froze at the evident display of fear etched into her lovely face. Her hair framed her face in a tangled array of spun silk and he resisted the sudden disturbing notion to brush the silken tresses aside. His eyes settled on her lips, full and luscious, parted in her labored breathing. He had the swift urge to taste those lips and the sweet nectar of her kiss.

She scrambled off of him in a sudden panic and in her haste lost her balance and fell on her backside. Dorian's gaze shifted to something that caught his attention and his groin hardened at the expanse of creamy skin exposed to his hungry gaze. In their struggle, the gown had torn in several places. His heated gaze caressed the creamy shoulder and than fell to the rip at her thigh, revealing smooth, tantalizing skin that brought a moan to his throat.

A wave of anger seized him for how could a mere-slip-of-a-girl such as this cause such uncontrollable desire to stir within him? It was unnerving and painfully arousing and yet the vision of her with those wide, doe-like eyes and her disheveled hair and the creamy flesh exposed to him did something entirely foreign to him.

His demeanor hardened as he gained his footing and moved towards her. She flinched as he approached and this only agitated him further. His fingers seized her roughly by the arm and he quickly sought to ease his grip at her painful gasp.

She stiffened beneath the pressure of his fingers and appeared as though she would flee if given the opportunity, so for this reason alone his fingers remained firmly around her arm as he glared down at her. "I think you've stirred enough trouble for the evening." He growled in frustration.

The fear lingered in her pretty eyes but a sudden glint of anger rushed to the surface as she attempted to wrestle her arm free of his grip. "Release me."

He resisted a grin at her sudden boldness. He was well aware of her fear of him and yet she continued to stand her ground, a trait he found seemingly admirable. The frightened child he remembered from three years ago lay somewhere dormant in this defiant, little woman standing in front of him, demanding he release her.

She was by far the smallest woman he had ever met. Her head just reached his chest and he was keenly aware of the small, fragile bone he gripped in his hand and yet, she challenged him with her eyes. If provoked, he could easily break her in two but the thought of harming this delicate yet defiant woman shook him uncontrollably. His eyes briefly assessed the gown that barely revealed any curves of interest and he found it odd that she had aroused him when he had a preference for curvier women.

"Where will you go in the dead of the night?" she flinched at the rough baritone of his voice, clearly unaware that his anger wasn't the only reason for his sudden harshness.

"Why is it any of your concern?" she questioned, tugging on her arm encased in his iron grip.

His temper flared and he stepped towards her and she would have retreated if not for his fingers wrapped tight around her wrist, reeling her closer until they were a breath apart. "It is my concern because you are my responsibility."

"Simply because you are honor bound?" she seethed, glaring up at him and refusing to back down even though fear clouded her senses. "You care not for what happens to me but simply that you are obligated to care for a burden that which you did not want."

The muscle in his jaw flexed but he refrained from saying anything further which only convinced Ginelle of her statement.

She was painfully aware of how close they were. She could smell the dark spices of his skin, could see that his eyes were rimmed in a metal gray and could just make out the lines of laughter around his eyes. For a moment, she wondered if a man such as this was even capable of laughter. "Let's make something clear." He started; his voice dangerously low caused a shiver to race up her spine. "Did you not willingly agree to remain at Ashford?" he didn't wait for a response, "Was it not my sister that had cared for you? Did that not make her your guardian?"

Eloise had been her guardian but also her mentor, her sister. How could she explain that to him? "As rights of guardianship, everything that belonged to her is now mine. You are my responsibility by the rights of the arrangement that you and my sister had agreed upon the moment you consented to remain at Ashford."

Ginelle gasped, "That is absurd!"

"Is it?" he growled, his grip tightening a fraction around her arm. "Did you not agree to it?"

She opened her mouth to respond but nothing came forth and so he proceeded. "I'm sorry to disappoint you Little Fair but as you can see, the plantation belongs to me and all that which inhabits here." He paused and than said, "Which means, I am accountable for you."

Ginelle gritted her teeth for there was nothing else she could say that would prove otherwise. She had agreed to stay at Ashford only because Eloise had wished it and she wanted to escape Pierino, but it didn't mean that she would submit so easily and Dorian Ashford was keen to see the obvious challenge in her brown eyes.

She lifted her chin to glare defiantly up at him, refusing to cower beneath the intensity of his hard stare. "So will you take the whip to me as well?"

Dorian stiffened.

"I intended to steal your horse." Her voice shook as she said this and he could see the fear in her eyes that lay within but she stood her ground.

He was stunned that a woman so small would expect punishment when most men would cower at the notion. She must have overheard the servants gossiping about his laborers. He cared not for what she thought of him. Let her continue to make the wrong assumptions of him.

Reluctantly, he released her and stepped aside. Her expression shifted to one of uncertainty. "Return to your room."

For a moment, he thought she would defy him but she reconsidered and quickly left the stable. A grin formed at the corners of his mouth for she feared him and yet she challenged him defiantly. Half of the men he knew did not have the courage of one mere female. Mayhap having her here at his plantation would not be as troublesome as he half expected. He would be lying if he said he didn't find her lovely and at the same time the effect she had on him was most afflicting. His grin all but vanished as his mood darkened. She was indeed lovely but nothing more. He was a fool to even consider the possibility that he found her desirable.

Chapter 5

Ginelle made sure she was aware of her guardian's whereabouts so she could avoid Dorian Ashford as much as possible. She kept to her room most of the day, engrossing herself with books and needlework and yet it did nothing to appease the seldom boredom that came with being confined inside when the weather outside was pleasant and enticing. Since their heated encounter a few nights ago, she had not seen the dark lord nor had he demanded she be whipped for attempting to steal a horse. Had she been wrong about his cruel nature?

If he thought she would so willingly give in, he was quite mistaken. She would remain at Ashford only because her heart couldn't bear the thought of parting with Eloise. Her memory was painfully fresh and she wanted to linger a little longer to hold onto the sisterhood they had shared. Her thoughts strayed towards the disturbing image of Pierino. Surely the man had forgotten her, even if he were to see her today, would he recognize her? She trembled at the thought and quickly dismissed it. She would not dwell on that despicable man.

Thrusting her needlework aside, she got to her feet and moved to stand by the window. It was noon and the sun gleamed brightly in the cloudless blue sky, its beauty and warmth beckoning. The weather had increasingly grown warmer an indication that the seasons were changing. It had been some time since she had gone for a ride over the countryside. The last time she had allowed such a pleasantry was when Eloise had been alive and well. She was overcome with a sudden heaviness that she could only recognize has grief and she quickly sought to ease her heavy heart. She would not wither to nothing inside her room. She would not hide from Dorian Ashford. Eloise would not want her to waste such a beautiful day.

Smiling, she quickly rushed to her wardrobe to find a more suitable riding attire; her heart soaring at the thought of doing something she loved and escaping the dreadful enclosure of her bedroom.

The tobacco fields were steadily improving. They had a sufficient amount of barrels prepped and ready to be shipped. Dorian had spent hours in the past couple of days working his laborers to the point of exhaustion. The fields were producing an abundant of crops. He dedicated a portion of his day inspecting crops and the warehouse. He managed the workers, keenly aware that several that had been brought in a month ago were proving to be uncooperative. They refused to submit to the intensive labor or that of his commands. Some were rebellious but easily detained and put to rights and yet there was a selected few that remained resistant. He gave his men strict orders to keep a wary eye on the laborers that proved difficult for they would be the ones that could cost him.

As he did one last round through the fields and paused to give orders to one of the guards, he decided to retire to the house and freshen up. He smiled at the thought of Lucile scolding him like a disobedient lad for skipping a meal.

He pulled on the reins and turned Lafeu onto the path that would lead him back to the house. The black stallion was indeed a prized horse to be had and he had raised the horse since it was a colt. The stallion was a stubborn animal but its loyalty to him was impeccable.

Dorian jerked on the reins as a sudden movement caught his attention from his peripheral. He averted his gaze just to catch a flash of silver-blond hair before disappearing in the thick foliage. He felt an immediate wave of anger wash over him as he dug his heels into Lafeu's side and started after the object of his fury. The insolent chit would dare defy him!

Ginelle was aware of nothing but the heavenly caress of the wind in her unbound hair as it flowed freely behind her in waves of silver blond. How could she have possibly thought she could spend hours inside when beauty such as this was impossible to ignore? The mare beneath her moved at a steady and gentle canter and Ginelle hastened the horse's pace as they ventured further into the forest. At one point she had feared this desolate place with its towering trees and finger-like limbs, but in the daylight, the foliage was alluring. She didn't fear the dangers the forest presented for Eloise had explained that as long as she didn't wonder far from the plantation that she was perfectly safe.

With that thought in mind, she continued on towards the one place that offered comfort and serenity. As she fell onto the familiar path that would lead her to the river, she allowed herself a moment of happiness. She would not think of anything else but this moment. As the clearing came into view she immediately tugged on the reins and directed the mare to a spot were she could tie the reins around a hanging limb. She dismounted and brushed a hand over the horse's mane. She proceeded to wrap the reins around a tree limb and than turned towards the flow of the stream.

Though spring had just nearly blossomed, the sun beamed hotly upon her forehead and she brushed an arm across her face, suddenly aware of how hot the day had become. She moved to stand beneath the branches that entwined to shelter her from the sun except for a few several strays of sunlight that pooled through an occasional opening. She smiled to herself as she moved to the bank and knelt to gather water into her palms. She splashed her face and than rubbed the nape of her neck with her fingers. The sudden relief of coolness against her face brought a sigh to her lips and her fingers moved to the buttons of her fitted riding jacket. She didn't hesitate to abandon the itchy material to reveal the bodice beneath as she tossed the jacket aside. All thoughts of modesty fled as she slowly made her way into the water. Her black skirts pillowed around her as she sank waist-deep into the water, sighing blissfully as it rose to her breasts. She swept her arms outward, delighting in the ripples she created.

Dorian spotted the mare and felt an immediate anxiety as his eyes searched the region. He pulled Lafeu to a halt and dismounted, clearly perplexed as to where the little chit had vanished. It was than he heard the water and he slowly turned in that direction. The vegetation was thick and kept him concealed as he approached the river and it was there that he froze at the sight before him. He wanted nothing more than to wrap his hands around her little neck for defying him, but now his hands burned with the distinct urge to touch the flawless skin now exposed to his ravenous gaze.

She was unaware of his presence as she bathed. The sun captured the different shades of blond in her hair as it flowed freely around her shoulders. The sleeves of her bodice had fallen from her shoulders, leaving them bare. He felt the sudden tightening in his groin as his gaze dipped lower to find the treacherous material clinging to the soft mounds of her breasts. The material left little to the imagination, revealing small yet firm breasts that would mold perfectly into the palms of his hands. Her waist was impossibly small with a narrow ribcage and a flat stomach and he ached to feather his fingers over that ivory skin.

He groaned inwardly at the immense physical pain thrusting against the seams of his breeches. She affected him as though he hadn't had a woman in a long time and his immense arousal infuriated him. He shouldn't feel anything for this impertinent female.

At this thought he stepped into the clearing to make his presence known. She turned then as if to come out of the water and froze in sudden horror as her arms instinctively came up to cover her breasts.

"How dare-" her eyes widened as he started towards her. She found herself retreating further into the water as he waded in after her. She dropped her arms in a sudden panic as she turned to elude him.

His arm latched around her waist and he reeled her in against him. She turned to pummel his chest with her fists but he easily caught her wrists in one hand. She was intimately aware of his arm around her waist, holding her against the hard contours of his body. Her eyes dropped of their own accord to the black tunic clinging to the sleek muscles of his chest clearly outlined through the wet material. Her stomach did a strangle flip as she inhaled sharply at the venomous look in his glacial eyes.

He was angry. What had she done to provoke him so? Her body trembled as she was overcome with fear. Would he strike her? Inflict some sort of physical pain to ensure who had power between the two?

"You deliberately disobeyed me." His voice was rough as though he suffered from an internal pain.

She was suddenly aware of her breast thrusting against the edge of her bodice from her labored breathing. She could feel every inch of this powerful man against the smoothness of her body and it disarmed her in a way she couldn't comprehend. She felt the strength in those fingers wrapped securely around her wrists and wondered if he would retaliate for her disobedience but she was uncertain to what exactly she had done.

"I-I don't understand." She whispered and for a moment panic hastened through her as those eyes of steel fell on her mouth. A dawning realization caused her to stiffen in alarm as she was suddenly aware of something hard and large pressing against her abdomen.

"You were not to leave the estate." His words were released on a hushed growl.

She frowned, "You did not make that clear to me."

That smoky gaze darkened, "You were wrong to assume."

She wanted desperately to escape his iron grasp. He was doing strange things to her and the look in his eyes frightened her. She had never seen such a look and it terrified her to the very core of her being. "Let go of me." She whispered, refusing to show the pressing fear beneath the surface.

He didn't release her. His gaze had once again fallen to her parted lips. "Do you know what happens to a beautiful woman such as yourself, alone and unguarded in a region such as this?" his eyes never wavered from her mouth.

A new fear settled in the pit of her stomach. She jerked on her arm in an attempt to free herself but to no avail. Her eyes were wide pools of uncertainty and fear as she struggled to keep her wits about her. "I said let me go."

She wrenched free of his hand and pressed her fists against his chest in an effort to push him away. She released a sharp breath as his fingers tangled in the hair at the nape of her neck and stilled her frantic struggle. She felt a fleeting moment of panic before his mouth crashed down on hers. Her cries of protest were muffled against the sudden sweep of his tongue as his arm tightened, pulling her closer to deepen the kiss.

Ginelle struggled against him, terror causing her to panic at the sudden turn of events. Dorian was kissing her! This man whom she had been quite certain detested her, was kissing her! No one had ever kissed her before and it sent shocks of electricity throughout her body.

Just as quickly as the kiss had begun, it ended abruptly and he shoved her away. She quickly righted herself and pressed a shaky hand to her swollen lips as she stared at his livid back. "Get out and get dressed." She detected the imperative warning in that tone that if she defied him, there would be consequences.

Hesitantly, she made her way from the water as she cautiously watched his turned back. She quickly gathered her discarded jacket and donned it to cover the wet material that clung to her like a second skin. His kiss had not only frightened her but startled her. He had done it to make a point and his point was quite clear. She should not have ventured alone into the forest; though she was familiar with the stream, there were some uncharted regions that could have imposing dangers. She shivered at the thought and the warning in his kiss.

He turned then and she flinched as those cold, assessing eyes moved over her. He was right to make his point but it did not justify his actions, even now her bruised lips burned from the remembrance of his kiss.

Anger flooded through her for she had not deserved any of his cruel treatment. She closed the space between them and instinctively, delivered a slap to his roguish face. Strong fingers seized her wrist and tightened a fraction as the muscle at his jaw flexed where the imprint of her hand remained. She stiffened; horrified that she had slapped him as a minatory rage darkened his smoky eyes.

He jerked her forward until they were a mere breath apart, a glint of warning deepening the blue of his eyes as he said, "You tread on dangerous ground, milady."

As much as her body quivered with fear she wouldn't allow this man to control her. "Do not ever kiss me again." She wrenched her arm from his grasp and moved to untie her reins from the dangling limb. She felt his eyes boring into her back as she mounted the mare and turned the horse widely about. She took off at a frantic pace, not caring if he followed. Her heart thudded within her chest as she sought the sanctuary of her room. It wasn't until she reached her bedroom that she allowed the tears to come.

He swept an unsteady hand through his unkempt mane of black hair as he gripped the brandy glass nearly drained of its contents. Since he had returned to the estate he had refused to see anyone; his mood as black as the approaching night. His thoughts were plagued with images of large, unguarded brown eyes fringed in thick, black lashes. He brought the brandy glass to his lips as he remembered the taste of her kiss and how lovely she had felt against him.

He sneered as he slammed the glass down on the table and leapt from the chair. He paced the floor of his room, his temper rising for he could not rid himself of this sudden attraction that left him burning. Was it simply because he had not had a woman in so long? Or the fact that he could not have her?

This thought brought a grunt to his lips for he could have any woman he wanted, including a small, doe-eyed female that stirred him in ways unlike any other.

A sudden anger forced him from the study and into the narrow hall. He stalked the empty corridor until he found himself outside her bedroom. He lifted the latch and pushed open the door, all rational thought fled as he stepped into the quiet, dusk of the room. Instantly he found her sleeping form in the massive, canopied bed. He moved towards her, the candle on the side table flickering in protest as he stood over her, his eyes moving leisurely over the length of her body clad in a sheer, white chemise.

The warm glow proclaimed by a single candle cast a golden hue across her sleeping face, producing shadows to enhance the delicate cheekbones and defiant arch of her jaw. He reached out to touch a strand of white-blond hair dispersed across the pillows and marveled at its rich, softness. His heated gaze rested on the firmness of her mouth, slightly parted in her sleep. A sudden impulse to taste that honeyed mouth caused the muscles of his body to tense as he curled his fingers against the urge to touch her.

He was suddenly enraged. What was he doing? Why did he lust for this chit who had done nothing but stir foreign feelings and provoke him beyond recognition? This unwelcoming attraction was most disturbing and it was best he find a more willing and curvier woman to appease his lustful appetite.

Immediately he thought of Victoria but the image of the curvaceous redhead did nothing to the fire burning in his groin as his eyes studied the dark lashes caressing those delicate cheekbones. Victoria had been his mistress for years on end and always satisfied him but he suddenly found her exquisite beauty lacking in comparison to the angel sleeping before him. He allowed himself a moment to imagine what it would be like to have her; to claim her as his own.

Almost as abruptly as the thought occurred, he dismissed it for he was certain once he spent his lust in Victoria's arms that he would rid his body of this fire.

The best thing for him to do was marry the little chit off to the first suitor that came along. His hands curled at his sides at an unexpected emotion that bordered the line of jealousy seized him. He nearly laughed aloud at the ridiculous thought yet the feeling remained which only darkened his mood.

Ginelle had slept very little that night so when she had managed to sleep for a few hours, she was relieved when her eyes fluttered open only to feel immediate disappointment as her room still bore the remnants of darkness.

She felt her heart leap against her chest at the looming silhouette standing beside her bed. She was seized in an icy shroud of terror as a whimper escaped her lips and she bolted upright to put space between her and the man. Only then did she realize the shadow was immense and could not possibly be Pierino, but her recognition did nothing to appease her fear.

The man turned and his face was caught by the single candle still burning on her beside table. She released a startled gasp and her fear was overcome with anger. "What are you doing here?" she demanded.

"There is something you and I need to discuss."

That deep, authoritative voice made her tremble but she remained firm against his domineering front. "It couldn't wait till morning?" and then realizing she wasn't appropriately dressed, she quickly snatched up the coverlets and pulled them to her chin. "Or until I was properly clothed?" she seethed, as if he hadn't gotten his fill earlier that day.

Deep shadows played across the lines of his face and for a moment she fancied him handsome but she was quick to notice the deep scowl of disapproval and automatically dismissed the absurd compliment. "Pray tell what is of utmost importance that you had to come to my room in the middle of the night to tell me?"

"You are at a proper age for marriage." He stated solemnly.

She felt the blood rush from her face and she inhaled sharply. "What?"

"I have found a solution to our disagreement."

Ginelle gripped the blanket in a maddening grip as she stared at him, "Our disagreement? What are you saying?"

"I'm saying I will marry you off." His bold statement made her flinch. "You do not wish to reside at Ashford, nor do I. The solution is quite simple."

Ginelle narrowed her eyes at him, "I will not marry."

She stiffened as he leaned forward, forcing her back against the headboard as he planted both arms on either side of her. "You do not have a choice in the matter. You will marry because I demand it."

"You seem to forget that I am not of noble birth. Who would marry me, a lowly female with no title to her name?"

Dorian straightened, his face hardening as he replied, "My sister left you a sufficient dowry that would prove acceptable to a man pursuing a woman such as yourself."

His words stunned her. Eloise had left her a dowry? "I cannot accept that."

"The decision is not up to you." He said this coldly before turning and heading to the door. Ginelle inhaled sharply, outraged that he would dare make decisions for her.

She thrust the coverlets aside and jumped up from the bed. She came to an abrupt halt as he turned and she nearly collided against his chest. She refused to be intimidated by his hulking stature or the pressing fear that urged her back to bed. "How dare you!" she cried, "You could have just let me leave!"

"Where would you have gone?" he sneered, his temper flaring. "Would you have gone back to the streets?" she stiffened at this and he continued, "No, I did not think so."

Her eyes were smoldering and she wanted nothing more than to slap him as she had done earlier that day. "I will not marry."

His scowled deepened, "You will marry." With that said, he left, slamming the door in his angry departure.

Ginelle stood glaring at the door, her nails digging into the flesh of her palms as she bit down on a stream of words she had heard Pierino utter many times in a fit of rage. Her heart ached for Eloise and her father, the only two people who had ever loved her, yet both had abandoned her.

Dorian Ashford was absolutely infuriating. Eloise had given her a dowry, making her acceptable to all aspects of marriage but what if she found marriage unacceptable? How dare Dorian Ashford demand she marry!

She vowed that no man would make decisions for her. No man would possess her. No man would ever hurt her again.

It was quite evident that he couldn't wait to rid himself of his excess baggage. She was nothing but a difficulty to him.

She returned to bed as a thought came to her. She would play into his game. She would make him believe that she had willingly succumbed to his demands but she would not submit so easily. She would find a flaw in every suitor that came to court her. She would not be married off to the first money-grubber that came along, nor would she allow Dorian to have control of whom she married, if she married.

Chapter 6

In the duration of weeks to come, Ginelle found herself the topic of all gossip throughout the ton. During her time spent at Ashford, she had purposely avoided making contact with civilization outside the plantation. She was painfully aware of their hard stares and turned-up noses. They knew very little about her and she intended to keep it that way to remain hidden from Pierino. If the ton knew of her lowly status, they would not accept her as Eloise's ward. They would scorn her. They were nothing like Eloise. They all were mere puppets that dangled from the strings of society standards.

She grew wary of their loquacious chatter. Dorian had given word to several companions with loose tongues that his 'ward' had reached an agreeable age for marriage and there would be a banquet to launch her coming of age. This made her extremely fearful for what if all this immense gossip reached Pierino? If would not be difficult to track her whereabouts.

Pierino was quite familiar with social gatherings. He had attended many events simply to pick the pockets of those he secretly envied. He found it amusing to steal them blind while at the same time portraying a wealthy patron. She knew it all to be a farce façade. He enjoyed the hunt which made her believe he would not give up so easily on his pursuit in finding her.

The preparations for the banquet had been left to Lucile. She was keenly aware of Dorian's absence. He seemed to hoard everything off onto the housekeeper but she seemed not to care in the least for it was a great distraction from the grief she suffered at Eloise's loss.

Ginelle was entirely against the ordeal to come. It took every ounce of will power she possessed to continue with the arrangement. It could potentially ruin everything and jeopardize her wellbeing.

Ginelle was stunned one morning to find that she had several suitors waiting at the door; each eager to look at the woman that was the talk of gossip. All that Eloise had taught her about the proper ways of courtship forced her to endure their company. She pasted a smile on her face as each caller spoke of nonsense that was meant to impress her.

It was not all horrid as she had imagined. Some of the men were charming and respectable but her wariness of men kept her focused on her initial plan. As the time drew near for her banquet, the barriers she had built against the suitors that came to court her were steadily falling. As a child she had fancied marriage for is she was to marry why not marry for love? But those were the days when she could dream and nothing harmed her.

Though she was quite certain nothing could waver her from her decision, she was beginning to question her motives. Did she really want to live a lonely life? Eloise had been lonely and the grief she had suffered had nearly been her undoing. Yet, could she really succumb to love and risk her heart? Risk everything as she has done before only to be left alone with that heavy hole in her chest?

This stream of thoughts continued to run through her mind when a visitor came to see her. She was seated in the parlor with a book in her hand when Lucile appeared in the door to announce her visitor. Sighing to herself, Ginelle set the book aside and stood to greet another suitor whose presence she would have to endure for the next hour.

Ginelle was struck nonplussed as a man appeared with Lucile. Immediately, her eyes assessed his tall, slender frame equipped in an elaborate dark blue waistcoat. His long legs were dressed in fitting, black breeches and his feet adorned with riding boots fastened with silver buckles.

His hair was the color of wheat, short and cropped around his forehead. His complexion was neither pale nor dark but just the right medium tone to accentuate his hazel eyes. The bones of his face were sharp yet elegant and she found herself comparing this man to that of a dangerous laird whose eyes were cold like the artic sea and his skin dark from the sun. She shivered as Dorian's looming frame came to mind. The man standing before her was nothing like Dorian and for that single thought alone she presented the man with a smile.

His eyes were soft and warm as he smiled in return and she found him engaging. His smile was pleasant and inviting as he stepped forward to take her outstretched hand and gently pressed a kiss to her knuckles. She expected her body to react and shrink away in revulsion as she had done with the others but she was surprised when she did not.

She had been so absorbed in her assessment of this charming stranger standing in front of her that she had not heard Lucile's announcement.

Sensing her thoughts, the man smiled. "Tis a pleasure to make your acquaintance, milady. I am Nathaniel Sharp. I hope tis not too bold of my visit but I could not help but wonder if the rumors were true."

Ginelle blanched, "The rumors, Sir?" she felt the maddening pace of her heart and wondered exactly what the ton had been saying.

A dashing smile stretched across his lips as if to reassure her. "Many spoke of your exquisite beauty." The lilt of his voice was smooth and rich, a lot like chocolate.

She stiffened, expecting him to lavish her with compliments that did little but annoy her just as the others had done. The men who had come to call upon her had not been interested in her; they were merely interested in her supposed dowry. The suitors had varied from those with protruding bellies and gray hair to young lads whose eyes didn't stray far from her bosom.

Yet, the man standing before her appeared far different than her previous visitors. She sensed a kindness in him that settled her nerves. He had a gentle nature that was comforting and yet she sensed his self-confidence. He was indeed a handsome man.

Lucile suddenly appeared with a porcelain tray of tea and crumpets. Ginelle groaned inwardly for she was beginning to dislike the unsweetened bread that seemed to be a continuance with each caller. Ginelle motioned Mr. Sharp to the chair opposite of her own and accepted the tray from Lucile. She and the housekeeper exchanged glances but whatever Lucile intended to say was left unsaid as the older woman spared a glance at Mr. Sharp and than quietly left the room.

"I pray, Mr. Sharp that you do not waste your time with gossip." Ginelle said very adamantly as she set the tray between them and took her seat.

A corner of his mouth lifted in amusement at her remark, "You do not concern yourself with garrulous chatter, milady?"

"Nay, I do not." She said firmly.

"Are you saying you do not believe the rumors that are said about you?"

Ginelle stiffened, suddenly fearful. "I do not know what rumors are said about me, Mr. Sharp."

He leaned forward as he accepted a cup of tea, his eyes grinning conspicuously of sly amusement.

Ginelle straightened her spine and lifted her chin, "Do you mock me, Sir?"

His grin widened, "Not at all, milady."

Ginelle narrowed her eyes at him, "Would you care to explain what it is that you find so amusing?"

"You astound me." He said before taking a sip from his cup.

Ginelle frowned, her brow arching as she continued to stare at him.

"You state your opinion very blatantly and you do not concern yourself with social affairs." His eyes darkened before adding, "I admire that in a woman."

"You admire an assertive woman?"

"I do, milady." He replied coolly.

"Not many do."

"When I marry, the woman that I take as my wife will be beautiful and she will not waste time on vanity and social affairs."

"You have such high expectations, Mr. Sharp."

"Are you insinuating that they are unachievable?" he smirked and Ginelle couldn't help but grin in return.

She nearly laughed aloud for she found this man impossible yet likeable. He was handsome and intelligent but most importantly, he admired her willfulness. She scowled inwardly at the thought of Dorian for he fought to control her every whim. Nathaniel Sharp appeared to be a man who would not shun a woman's opinion.

"You like to read, Lady Pattinson?"

Jarred to awareness, Ginelle spared a glance at the book forgotten on the table. "Yes very much. Do you, Mr. Sharp?" she was suddenly excited that he had asked her a question that most gentlemen did not bother to ask.

He nodded, "I am quite the scholar."

She smiled but just as quickly as the smile appeared, it vanished abruptly at the dark presence looming in the door frame of the parlor. Immediately, Mr. Sharp gathered to his feet to address the man who assessed him with cold eyes.

Ginelle got to her feet as those icy depths met hers from across the room. What had she done now to bring on such a blackened mood? Dorian Ashford had all but disappeared in the past couple of days. Why now would he make his presence known when she was beginning to like one of the many suitors to call upon her?

Those vivid, blue eyes barely acknowledged the man standing in the parlor as he said to Ginelle. "I'd like a word with you."

Agitated by his authoritative manner, Ginelle excused herself from the parlor and followed Dorian into the hall. It wasn't until she reached his side that her senses were alert to the sheer size of him. Why did his presence unnerve her so much?

His fingers, warm and strong curled around her upper arm. She gasped as he pulled her close. Shocked by the sudden rush of her heart at the touch of his fingers on her skin and the closeness of their bodies, she wrenched her arm from his grip and stepped back to put space between them. "What have I done?" she demanded her breath short and quick as she struggled to keep her wits about her.

He towered over her, his broad chest donned in a black tunic opened at the throat to reveal smooth, bronze skin. She avoided that expanse of flesh and forced herself to meet his angry expression. "What is that man doing in my parlor?" the bone of his jaw flexed with obvious distaste.

Ginelle did not question why Dorian detested Nathaniel Sharp for what man or woman did not spark his temperament?

Instead she said, "Were you not the one who insisted I marry?"

He leaned forward and she inhaled sharply as he trapped her between his arms on either side of her and she realized than he had backed her against a wall. "You will not marry that man."

Her eyes narrowed with sheer anger. She would marry no man she fumed silently but she would not relate that to this brutish barbarian. In fact, she found it amusing that she actually had something to use against him for making demands of her and something to unravel his cold disposition.

She smiled coolly, "I will marry whichever man of my choosing."

She felt his big body stiffen and for a moment she thought she may have pushed him too far. Would he strike her? Why did it matter to him whom she married as long as she married? He said nothing as he straightened his eyes boring down at her before finally he turned and stalked away.

Within the next hour she and Mr. Sharp whom insisted she call Nathaniel talked vigorously of interests they both seemingly enjoyed. She found it odd that they shared many things in common and the more they talked the more she enjoyed his company. He appeared unaffected by Dorian's apparent rudeness. She was delighted when he insisted that she play from the piano.

Whichever reason Dorian detested Nathaniel Sharp she cared not. He was the first and only suitor that showed great interest in who she truly was. Though, she would not submit to marriage, she couldn't help her immediate attraction to him but a man like Nathaniel Sharp could never know of her past. The evening whisked on quickly and it wasn't long until they were standing at the door and he was bidding her a good night.

He smiled a charming smile and curtsied, "Twas a pleasure to spend the evening with you, Lady Ginelle. I pray that you and I will spend more time together. Mayhap at the banquet?" he did not wait for her reply but took her hand gently and graced it with a kiss and than left.

Ginelle closed the door and moved to the parlor, she stopped abruptly to stare at the large, muscled frame standing at the window with fists curled at his sides.

Instantly, she felt as though the room were too small despite it being a spacious parlor. She gathered her skirts with the intent of continuing on to her room but his displeased tone stopped her short.

"You are forbidden to see that man again." His eyes remained transfixed on the departing carriage outside the manor.

Ginelle's eyes narrowed heatedly as she said, "If I wish to see Mr. Sharp again that is my decision and mine alone."

He turned from the window then to glare at her and she immediately caught herself stepping back in panic at the black expression contorting his features. "Disobey me and I will be the one choosing you a husband as it are accustomed."

She inhaled sharply and her nostrils flared in sudden frustration. She stalked towards him until they were scarce apart. "Why do you insist on controlling everything I do?" she resisted the urge to jab her finger in the center of that hard chest as she lifted her chin defiantly up at him. "What is it that displeases you so about Nathaniel Sharp?"

Dorian enclosed the remainder of space hovering between them and she suddenly found it extremely difficult to breathe as the rich spices of his skin seeped into her senses. "That man is known for his wild streak of courting various women with considerably pleasing inheritance." He leaned forward and she felt his breath fan her forehead. She felt a blush creep up her neck and into her cheeks as her heart did a strange flip within her chest. "He is a fortune hunter."

His words jarred her past the sudden exhilaration of her heart and shortness of breath. He was doing something strange to her and she didn't like it one bit. For some anonymous reason unknown to her Dorian Don Ashford loathed Nathaniel Sharp but she would not be played a fool.

He was lying; Nathaniel was not a fortune hunter. He had given no indication that he knew of her supposed inheritance or that he was only interested in her dowry. In fact, he had stated quite clearly that he wanted an assertive woman as his wife. Is that not what she wanted, to be free to make her own decisions? If she really did want to marry, Nathaniel Sharp would be a definite choosing for a husband. Dorian Ashford was the sort of man that took pleasure in authority. He was evidently aware that she found Nathaniel a gentleman and his company enjoyable. He was anxious to be rid of her so why now this sudden objection?

He could conjure as many lies as he wanted and she would not believe a word of it. The stubborn oaf insisted on making decisions for her and if she were a meek and docile female, he would most likely continue with his governing up until the altar! She had endured too many hardships to allow a man such as Dorian Ashford to reign over her.

"Mr. Sharp is a very genuine man and I look forward to seeing him again at my banquet." She turned to leave but strong fingers circled her forearm and jerked her back around.

A breath rushed up from her throat and her eyes widened at the suddenness of his grip but the fingers around her arm were not bruising but they gripped her with warning. "You seem to forget milady that I arranged your banquet. Yourbanquet is being held at the grand hall of the Duke of Hadley in which the Duke happens to be an old companion of mine. Therefore milady, I have the power to arrange your banquet and I have the power to take it all away."

Ginelle stiffened as those icy depths fell to her lips and she was struck with the vivid image of his mouth crashing down on hers at the river. She felt a crimson blush stain her cheeks and she wrenched her arm from his grasp.

She stepped away from him and straightened her spine and said, "Do as you see fit, Master Dorian." She gathered her skirts and gripped them until her knuckles were white and stalked from the room, unaware of the grin curving the corners of his mouth as he watched her leave.

Dorian sat behind his mahogany desk, completely absorbed in the map in front of him as he studied the black print and intricate engravings. His gaze never wavered far from the brandy bottle and the map dispersed in front of him. With a growl of frustration he shoved the map aside and lunged to his feet, turning to the window behind him as he swept a hand through his tousled mane.

A streak of warm hues pierced the horizon just beyond the mountain peaks. He braced his weight against the window frame, staring beyond that point as if peering into the past. A dormant memory he thought buried surfaced within the walls of his troubled mind and as much as he struggled to shove it down, it refused to remain buried, rushing to the surface.

He stood in the darkened corridor, pressing his little frame flat against the wall, his arms coming out on both sides to balance his trembling body. His eyes fixated on the flickering light beneath the wooden door looming before him and he watched carefully as shadows stirred on the other side. He could hear their muffled words, one of anger and the other just a whisper. He waited, his heart pumping wildly in his chest. He could hear his voice, definite and frightening, a deep voice that cracked with uncontrollable rage.

The first slap came without warning and he stiffened as he heard his mother's distinct cry as the blow forced her to the floor. He pressed his fist against his mouth as he heard her silent plea while his father advanced and her unheeded cry did little to prevent the heavy fist coming at her face.

A sudden tapping jerked Dorian alert and he turned towards the door as he slowly unclenched his fists and relaxed the muscles in his face to greet Bogart. The steward was instantly aware of the sudden tension seeping from his Laird but said nothing as he cautiously entered.

"Lieutenant Cummings has arrived to see you, milord." The elderly man stepped aside to allow Cummings entry but the Lieutenant barely acknowledged the steward as his eyes settled on Dorian's rigid frame standing across the room.

Bogart took his leave as Cummings studied his Captain's dark face, void of any expression. "You look like death, Capitaine."

Dorian motioned Cummings to a chair opposite of his and settled into his own. He stretched out his aching limbs and leaned back into the leather chair to better observe his Lieutenant. "What news do you bring?"

Cummings poured himself a hearty glass of brandy and quickly downed it, bracing himself for Dorian's anger. "As you know most of the cargo was sold and remainders of the crates are unattainable. As for the crew many were rumored to have been sold into slavery. Some were killed during the siege. There whereabouts are uncertain but I've been tracking the Spanish bastard for weeks. He's gone off of his trail."

A heavy silence settled between them and Cummings leaned forward in the chair, the leather beneath him protesting against his shifting weight. "With London Officials and several Bounty Hunters on his tail, he's well aware of the reward in his capture. The bastard is fleeing."

"He has also made the mistake of changing his course. He has a concealed nest." Dorian added as he seized the map lying on his desk.

Cummings pressed a finger on the engraved map, "He was spotted off the coast of Portugal. This is where the bastard shifted routes. He started north-east continuing onward into the English Channel. In taking that risk, he has London Officials on his tail. Two sets of Bounty Hunters came from the Netherlands. The Spaniard has been plundering along our coast and the coast of France. They trailed him along the North Sea but he vanished. They can't seem to track his whereabouts."

"He's gone into hiding." Dorian puzzled over the engraved map. "It will be some time before he shows his cowardly face, at least until some of the heat dissipates. London Officials will be the first to give up their search for they have no authority elsewhere, as for Bounty Hunters, their paid to pursue and capture."

"What do you recommend, Capitaine?"

Dorian gathered to his feet and moved back to the window, "I have a sufficient amount of hogshead ready to be shipped." He turned from the window to stare at Cummings as he continued, "In several weeks time, I need you to ready a vessel."

"The Silver Wind?" Cummings asked, puzzled.

Dorian shook his head, "Nay, would be too conspicuous." He returned to his seat and grabbed the brandy bottle, he met Cummings stare from across the desk. "I need the biggest and most powerful vessel we have; a seemingly impressive prize to be had, one that the Spaniard King cannot pass up."

Cummings cocked a brow at his Captain. "What are you conducting?"

"I plan to lure the bastard from his hideaway, where I'm certain a majority of the crew and cargo is being detained. He has to have a retreat, a desolated refuge concealed from authorities."

"What happens after you manage to lure the Spaniard out?"

"We drop the element of surprise."

"Which is?" Cummings asked certain of the reply.

"We attack."

Cummings nodded, "You have only to send word and I will prepare the vessel with the readied hogshead, in the meantime I will set about purchasing fur, spices and fabrics. I'll ready the preparations when I am able. How long before we set sail?"

Dorian pondered this for a moment. If he knew the Spaniard well enough, the bastard would hide low until he felt his trail had gone cold. "I'll give the bastard a month."

"What will you do in the meantime?" Dorian frowned at this and averted his attention to his Lieutenant.

A swift image of silver-blond hair and soft, brown eyes rushed to mind and he realized than he had completely dismissed the banquet from his thoughts. "There are a few matters I have to tend too."

Cummings suddenly grinned a knowing grin as he studied Dorian's vexed expression. "This certain matter wouldn't happen to come in the form of a small woman with pretty, dark eyes?" Cummings hesitated before adding, "Do you have feelings for the girl, Capitaine?"

Dorian stiffened as he cast a dark and dangerous glare at Cummings. "Have you gone brash, Lieutenant?"

Cummings lazily shrugged his shoulders, "I am merely asking out of curiosity."

Dorian narrowed his eyes at his comrade, his mouth set in a grim line of irritation. "You best watch yourself Lieutenant for your curiosity could very well cost you your tongue."

Cummings straightened, suddenly intrigued as his mouth twisted into a grin. "Forgive me, Capitaine."

"The girl tries my patience." Dorian exclaimed. "She is intolerable."

"You hate her then?" Cummings urged.

"What exactly are you getting at, Cummings?" Dorian demanded, his eyes narrowing in speculation.

"Mere curiosity, Capitaine."

Dorian slammed his fist on the desk and jerked forward in his seat. "Damn you, Stefan! What is it exactly that you are implying?"

"Have you decided to marry the girl off?"

Dorian settled back into his chair, trying desperately to get a grip of his anger. Cummings was doing his best to unravel his temper and damn the bastard he had done so masterfully. "Aye, the sooner the better. Her small stature does little justice to her temper and defiant nature."

"Aye but with the short temper and defiance comes remarkable beauty, mayhap I should marry her myself? She is very lovely and would make a fine wife."

Dorian jerked upward and slammed his fists onto the smooth surface of the mahogany desk, his livid face revealing immediate anger. "I'll be damned if I stand by and let that happen!"

Cummings couldn't contain his humor any longer. He released a stream of laughter as he fell back into his seat. "Is that an impulse strictly of guardianship or that of jealousy?" Cummings insisted as he watched Dorian gather to his feet.

Dorian turned and scowled darkly at Cummings. "I grow weary of your jesting, Lieutenant." He cast a considerable glance at the brandy bottle and decided against it. He had much tedious planning and hard labor to face in the day to come; he needed a clear state of mind.

"I'll take my leave now, Capitaine. Shall I relieve you of the brandy?" Cummings eyes widened and he ducked just as the whiskey bottle whisked past his head to shatter against the far wall. Cummings straightened, turned to survey the mixture of spirits and glass before turning back with a wide grin plastered on his face. He curtsied and sauntered from the room, still grinning.

Chapter 7

Ginelle had awakened some time before the sun had arisen. She had slept very little throughout the night, her mind plagued with fond memories that brought terrible pain to her heart. She had dreamt of warm, blue eyes and a smile that always comforted her fears. Her memories revealed moments of laughter and excitement as she and Eloise endured the velocity of time discussing literature and indulging on sweetened pastries.

Ginelle gripped the edges of her robe as she stood before the window, her distant thoughts forcing unshed tears to her weary eyes.

The dream had given her a moment of happiness but her happiness was short lived and she was standing before a casket, peering down at a listless body so pale and cold, empty of warmth and compassion, only the body before her was that of her father. Her loving devoted father who had abandoned her to this dejected world.

Ginelle released a sharp breath followed by a heart-wrenching sob. She pressed a curled fist against her mouth to muffle her cry. Her chest ached with that familiar stab of pain and the erratic pace of her heart hastened with the profound grief that filled that deep hollowness in her chest.

Her fingers curled around the locket dangling from around her neck and she whispered a silent prayer to her mother to take care of her father whose pain had been so unbearable that he left his daughter to brace the world alone on a misguided path of sorrow.

How could he have been so selfish; to take his own life and abandon his child? Would she ever be able to forgive him?

Her thoughts shifted to Eloise. Eloise had spoken very little of her family. She claimed Dorian had been her only kin left to her. What had happened to their mother and father? Her heart suddenly ached for Dorian. He was as much alone as she was in the world. Was his grief as deep? How badly did his sister's death affect him?

She knew very little to nothing about Dorian Don Ashford except that he stirred feelings in her that were both of fear and exhilaration. What was it about her reluctant guardian that left her breathless whenever he was near?

He was indeed a menacing and challenging man who struck a fear in her that was quite unnerving but along with that fear were curiosity and a smidge of-what? Surely that feeling wasn't admiration?

Yes; admiration. She affirmed silently. She admired him because despite his short temperament and overbearing dominance, he had yet to lift a hand to her for her deliberate antagonism. In spite of her colored opinion of men she found she had the courage to stand her ground, even to a man like Dorian but what if she were wrong? What if Dorian were very much like the men she feared? He insisted on making decisions for her; could his ulterior motives be that of dominating her simply because she refused to submit to his demands?

She pressed her fingers unknowingly to her lips at the remembrance of his kiss. She remembered the shock of electricity that coursed through her body at the memory of his fingers at the nape of her neck and the way his mouth invaded her own. She had never been kissed by a man and the sheer exhilarated feeling left her breathless and shaken, even now as she remembered the abrupt intimacy.

She had expected fear and revulsion but in fact his kiss had flared a spark of inquisitiveness. If another man were to kiss her, would she feel the same jolt of heat and liveliness? She had never been so aware of a man except in that defining moment when he had kissed her.

Ginelle shook her head in alarming awareness. What was she thinking? She detested men, all men. Dorian Ashford was no exception just because he hadn't laid a hand on her, that didn't mean he wouldn't in time. She had to convince herself that all men were despicable beings that forced their will on women.

She felt a slight pang of guilt for all men were not so heinous. Her father had been nothing like Pierino Basilotta. Yet, had he not sealed her fate with his selfish impulse in taking his life?

"You are up early, pet." Ginelle stiffened and brushed the tears clumsily from her face as Lucile's voice came from behind. She turned and attempted a smile.

Lucile stopped suddenly, her eyes settling on Ginelle's distraught expression. Her brows knitted together with immediate concern as she crossed the room and seized Ginelle's upper arms. "What troubles you, child?"

Ginelle quickly sought an explanation that would appease Lucile's anxiety. "I had a restless night."

"Nightmares, eh?" Lucile's fingers squeezed her arms in reassurance. "They will go away in time, my dear."

Ginelle managed a weak smile before Lucile released her and crossed the room to her wardrobe. She opened the bureau and studied the row of gowns displayed on the bar. "I think it best you wear some pigment today. No more black, tis most unbecoming for your complexion." She sifted through the large collection of gowns, selecting a few as she sorted through them.

"Lucile-"

"I won't hear to your objections." Lucile said sternly. She approached the bed and placed several gowns for Ginelle to observe.

Ginelle had donned a gown of pink muslin with a neck-line that dipped low in the front trimmed in white lace. The dress was absolutely beautiful but the color did not fit her saddened state. If Lucile had not insisted on the lovely gown, she would have chosen another black dress. "I have to go into town today. Would you like to go along? Get some fresh air?" Lucile asked as she worked at putting the other gowns back into the bureau.

Ginelle turned abruptly to look at Lucile, her face pale against the morning sun. "What reason do you have to go to town?"

"Cook has asked if I would go to the market and purchase a few satchels of fruit and a portion of mutton for this evening's meal. I thought mayhap you would like to go along?"

Ginelle shifted her hands nervously in the skirts of her gown. She had only ventured in to town with Eloise at her side and even than the particular places they ventured had been safe but each trip she had been fearful.

If she traveled to the market she would be taking a big risk. The market hummed with life and plentiful pockets for crooks like Pierino lurking in the shadows to slip in and out of the crowd effortlessly stealing patrons. What if he spotted her?

But she desperately wanted to escape the manor. The weather was beautiful and inviting. It had been several years since Pierino had seen her; she has changed much over time. He could not possibly recognize her now?

She was no longer that frightened, broken child. If she was ever going to overcome her fears she would have to face them eventually.

After a long pause and little hesitation, she said, "Yes. I would like very much to go along."

Lucile nodded, "Good then. After you break your fast we will go."

Dorian studied the assortment of food laid out before him. Cook had gone out of her way this morning, preparing a seemingly sufficient course befitting a king and yet, Dorian's plate remained untouched while Lieutenant Cummings to his left helped himself to a large portion of buttered eggs with cream.

He leaned back in his chair to better observe his ravenous friend and felt a grin tug at the corners of his mouth. For a slender, tall man, Cummings could surely pack away an excessive amount of food.

Cummings suddenly paused in his chewing as his gaze averted from his plate to a spot behind Dorian. Dorian frowned and turned in his chair and felt a sharp breath leave his body.

She was radiant. The soft pink gown hugged her small frame, accentuating her tiny waist and the fullness of her breasts. Her silver-blond tresses had been piled high atop her head in a mass of curls and Dorian suddenly had the urge to wrap his fingers around a loose strand framing her face.

Cummings shot to his feet as was custom, to stand in the presence of a Lady, and Dorian slowly followed, his unwavering stare forcing a deep blush to her porcelain skin.

Ginelle found breathing to be extremely difficult as she entwined her hands to still the sudden trembling as she was keenly aware of those piercing blue eyes studying her intensely.

She avoided Dorian's face, fearful of the expression that darkened his features. She was certain his blackened countenance would reveal distaste.

Instead, she directed her attention to a slender man with inviting, clever russet eyes. Ginelle was suddenly struck with the memory of a man catching her as she fainted in the corridor the day Eloise passed. The man who had grabbed her before she hit the floor was smiling back at her now.

"You are a breath of fresh air, milady." The man said as he curtsied and than straightened to flash a dazzling smile.

Ginelle missed the deep scowl etched into Dorian's face as she stepped towards the man and smiled timidly. "Forgive me but I-" she hesitated, not wanting to offend him. She had met him once before when she first arrived at Ashford, but she couldn't place a name to his face.

His smile broadened, "Lieutenant Stefan Cummings, milady."

Her face brightened with recognition and Dorian's scowl deepened. "Lieutenant Cummings." She stated, "It is good to see you again and under better circumstances."

He laughed, "Indeed milady." He replied as he motioned her to the seat next to him. Cummings cast a mischievous glance at Dorian whose face revealed evident displeasure.

They settled into their chairs as a servant appeared to pour Ginelle a cup of apple with a pinch of sugar and honey. Ginelle took a sip of the pleasant concoction and her eyes met that icy stare from above the rim of her cup. She quickly averted her eyes to the plate set before her.

"Allow me." Cummings said as he began filling her plate with a variety of food.

Dorian's finger curled around his cup as he cast a dark glare at his Lieutenant vowing later to scold the fool for his forwardness.

He stiffened with a jolt as sweet laughter bubbled up from Ginelle's throat and she extended a hand to prevent Cummings from filling her plate with more food. "If I am mistaken, Lieutenant Cummings, I would think you are making a discreet indication that I am too thin?" she arched a brow as she observed him through humorous eyes.

Her laughter affected Dorian in a confounding way. He suddenly yearned to hear her laughter, to watch that distinct glint in those gentle eyes catch the light. He wanted to see that blush stain her cheeks in a delicate shade of pink. He had a swift and sudden yearning to kiss those lips and taste her sweetness.

He swallowed back the sudden groan that surfaced in his throat and jerked his attention to his plate.

He was a handsome man. He could have any woman he wanted. Women swooned at his feet. So why did he find it absolutely infuriating that she would smile at Cummings? That she would laugh at his thoughtless jesting? Why did he have this intense desire to touch her skin, to run his fingers through her hair?

Dorian had never heard her laugh or seen her smile but he had witnessed her anger. Her anger magnified the soft beauty of her eyes, brightening them in a way that revealed specks of green and gold. She was breathtaking in all her unrestrained anger but in the daylight with laughter illuminating her brown eyes and her sweet mouth titling in a delighted smile, her beauty magnified tenfold.

He could hear their distant conversing through the course of his thoughts and his grip tightened around the silver goblet in his hand.

"Will you be attending the banquet, Lieutenant Cummings?"

"Are you inviting me, Lady Ginelle?" Dorian stood abruptly from his chair, startling both Ginelle and Cummings. He threw his napkin down onto his place, turned and stalked from the room.

Cummings turned back to Ginelle and smiled sheepishly. "You will have to disregard his rudeness. He is in a foul mood this morning."

Ginelle caught Dorian's retreating back before he disappeared from the hall. "You do not have to apologize for his boorish behavior. He is a complex man."

"He has had a complex life, milady."

Ginelle shifted her attention to Lieutenant Cummings, suddenly intrigued. "What do you mean?"

Cummings cast a wary glance down the hall before cautiously continuing, "He is a man of many sorrows, painted black from his darkened past."

Ginelle leaned towards him at his lowered tone. “Darkened past?”

“His father, Clayton Ashford was a powerful and wealthy man. His wife, the beautiful Lady Charlotte, had brought him a satisfying dowry that conciliated his greedy appetite for wealth and lay to rest any objections to their arranged marriage.”

Ginelle listened intently, eager to know more about her dark, reticent guardian. “Did they love each other?”

Cummings mouth formed a grim line, “They were strangers bound to hate each other.”

Ginelle’s brows drew together in deep empathy. “What was Lady Charlotte like?” Cummings smiled a distant smile. “She was a beautiful woman; very quiet, soft spoken.” His smile filtered away and he added, “Dorian loved her as much as a child could love their mother.”

“What happened to her?”

He hesitated, a look of anguish altering the lines of his charming face. “She was murdered.”

Ginelle inhaled sharply at the declaration. “No!” she exclaimed, pressing a hand to her mouth. “Who would do such a thing?”

Cummings met her gaze, “Her husband.” He proclaimed despondently.

Her eye’s widened, “Dorian’s father?”

Cummings nodded.

“Why would he murder his own wife?” her voice was tiny and hollow, her heart aching for the small boy who lost his mother so young.

“Clayton Ashford was a greedy man. All the wealth and power he conducted was never enough. He wanted more therefore he took to gambling and with gambling came ale. He drank every night and came home to his wife in a fit of drunkenness and rage.”

Ginelle trembled at the dreadful image. She could not picture Clayton Ashford; instead she pictured a face with sharp, black eyes and a mouth that cracked with a sneer. A man she feared would haunt her infinitely. "Did he strike the children?" her voice trembled at the thought. Had Eloise and Dorian endured the same abuse she had suffered?

"Lady Charlotte sent her daughter to boarding school, fearing her daughter would become tainted if subjected to her father's abuse." He fell silent and Ginelle felt her heart beating harshly in her chest.

"Dorian?"

A distant look shadowed his face. "He remained at Ashford. He was the rightful heir to the Ashford manor. All of it would be his one day so he was to remain at the plantation and learn his keep."

"Was he a victim of his father's abuse?" Ginelle clenched her hands in her lap to still their trembling.

Lieutenant Cummings looked up at her, taking keen notice of the deep sadness in her brown eyes. "There was nothing that would drive him from Ashford, including the horrible beatings." He fell silent as a maid entered the room to clear the table of forgotten plates. After the maid departed, he continued. "He would not leave his mother, knowing the pain she suffered. He waited for the day that he would overshadow Clayton Ashford. He waited for reckoning."

Ginelle knew that day of reckoning did not come.

"His father returned one evening from a gamble, drunk and furious. They argued and eventually it progressed into a struggle."

"He killed her." She whispered despairingly.

He nodded. "He choked her." He cleared his throat, "He was beyond himself; too far gone in his rage that he killed his own wife. He had gambled away their fortune and he had been stripped his Earldom. Dorian found his mother dead and his father hanging from the banister."

Ginelle gasped, horrified.

"Dorian had to tell Lady Eloise of their horrifying deaths. He had to fight for the plantation for it was gambled to a man who cared less about a scrap of land." He fell quiet as he took a swig from his cup before continuing. "Sending Lady Eloise to boarding school saved her from her father's wrath. She had a heart of gold and Lady Charlotte knew Clayton Ashford would have done anything to break his daughter's spirit."

Ginelle studied Cummings face taking note of the sudden distant look of warmth and adoration in his russet eyes. "You loved her." It wasn't a question but an assertion based on the obvious affection in the Lieutenant's face.

He nodded as he dropped his head to brush the crumbs from his lap. "I loved her from afar."

"Did you ever proclaim your love to her?" Ginelle asked softly, her heart aching for this heartbroken man.

He lifted his head, "Her heart belonged to another." Ginelle reached out and placed her hand on his above the table. She could see he struggled to not reveal his pain but it was their behind the depths of his eyes. "I miss the sound of her laughter, sweet and subtle, and the euphony of the piano as it came to life beneath her finger-tips."

"I loved her as well." Ginelle related, lowering her head as she said, "She did more for me than anyone." She felt the sting of tears and quickly fought them at bay.

Cummings reached over and gently touched her shoulder, a genuine gesture as he asked, "You have suffered many hardships yourself?"

She stiffened and leaned away, suddenly overcome with apprehension. She wasn't ready to reveal her darkened past and she surely shouldn't have meddled in Dorian's. She cleared her throat and got to her feet, Cummings mirrored her movements, a puzzled look crossing his brow at her evident anxiety.

"Forgive me Lieutenant, I've seem to have loss track of time." She smiled apologetically as she smoothed her skirts of wrinkles. "I hope to see you again at the banquet." She added in hopes he would not be offended by her abruptness.

He smiled hesitantly, "Would be a pleasure, milady."

She left quickly, all the while feeling his russet eyes on her back. She felt terrible as she headed to her room to get her cloak. She should not have pried into Dorian's past, but she was suddenly seized with a profound eagerness to learn more about her troubled guardian. She was struck with an astonishing realization. They were alike in all their suffering.

She should not have been so quick to pass judgment. She had allowed her prejudice thoughts to form her opinion of Dorian without really seeking to understand him.

Lieutenant Cummings left the breakfast table in search of his Captain. He expected Dorian in a detrimental state for he had felt his sharp glares from across the table and he couldn't help but grin.

After having questioned a few of the servants, he headed out to the stables where he found Dorian saddling Lafeu.

Cummings paused in the doorframe and braced his weight against the wall, smirking as he crossed his arms against his chest.

Dorian cast him a venomous look, "Do you make sport of provoking me, Lieutenant?" he growled.

Cummings frowned with a hint of wry humor glinting in his russet gaze. "I know not what you speak of."

Dorian released a sigh of exasperation as he stepped from Lafeu to better observe the triumphant expression etched into Cummings face. He narrowed his eyes in irritation. "You deliberately antagonize me and I intend to know why, Lieutenant."

Cummings shrugged, "Simply for my amusement, Capitaine."

“Whatever ploy you’re conducting, I suggest you drop it for I’m in no mood for your games.”

Cummings gasped as he pressed a hand to his heart, feigning offense. “You would me, Capitaine.” He dropped his hand and grinned a toothy grin as Dorian turned back to Lafeu.

Cummings straightened and moved to the opposite of the horse, somewhat relieved that a beast stood between him and his Captain. “I know the look of intrigue when I see it.”

Dorian stiffened, “What the hell are you talking about?”

“You want her and whether you want to admit it or not, you like her.”

Dorian’s eyes narrowed dangerously to dark slits of ice. “I’ve warned you, Lieutenant about jesting.”

“Tis not just desire that have you intrigued.” Cummings continued.

Dorian growled impatiently, “What exactly are you implying?”

“What you feel for her is beyond physical attraction.”

“And you are such an expert on insight?” he demanded furiously.

Cummings rolled his shoulders, “I am merely stating what I see with my own eyes, Capitaine.” his mouth mischievously quirked at the corners.

“I’ve had enough of your inquiries, Lieutenant.” Dorian mounted the stallion and turned the horse towards the entrance, he paused to glare down at his Lieutenant. “I think it best you carry on with your duties. We have much of greater importance than those of mere observation to concern ourselves with.”

All traces of humor fled the surface of his face as he nodded, keenly aware of the reason he had first come to Ashford this morning but beneath the surface, he couldn’t contain his amusement. He wanted Dorian grip the leather reins and steer Lafeu from the barn. Cummings had witnessed rage and jealousy etched into Dorian’s features earlier at breakfast, whether Dorian wanted to acknowledge it or not.

Chapter 8

They had taken the carriage into town. The weather was exceptionally pleasant with a subtle breeze stirring the trees that dotted the land and white, fluffy clouds drifted languidly across the bright, blue sky. The sun emitted warm rays of light upon the township and its inhabitants crowding the cobblestone streets.

Ginelle stayed close to Lucile as they ushered their way through the crowd of bodies jostling through the market. There was a combined smell of freshly baked bread and the rancid odor of raw fish clinging to the air. Ginelle gasped just as a chicken released a high-pitch cry and hustled past her feet. A stray dog stood off in the corner street barking repeatedly at those who dare get too close.

Vendors stood aside, eagerly persuading bystanders to examine their merchandise. The crowd contained men in top-hats and fancy threads; women garbed in genteel attire clung to the arm of their gentleman and children of the street nudged their way through the crowd after a tiny ball dancing between the many sets of patent-leather boots and dainty slippers.

Lucile was unaware of the clamorous array, so absorbed in her task the older woman hastened through the crowd with swift strides towards her intended destination. Ginelle struggled to keep pace with the housekeeper as her eyes danced warily through the crowd.

She tried to convince herself that she was safe. Would he single her out in this vast crowd?

Her fear kept her on edge and aware of every motion. It was her keen observation that made her come to a sudden halt in the hub of bodies crushing her. She could just see Lucile's ample frame disappear in a flood of color as men and women swept by her.

Her gaze fixated on a small child, a tiny boy, slipping close to a cart consisting of sweets. She felt her heart constrict as the child peered around, his sad eyes sunken in his small face as he looked to see if anyone noticed his little body creeping toward it.

When he thought no one watched, he reached up with much strain to wrap his little fingers around a candy.

It came so suddenly, neither Ginelle nor the small boy expected it. The vendor stepped forward without warning and slapped the boy down. Ginelle inhaled sharply; horrified as she recalled the fear she felt that day she attempted to take an apple.

She knew the vendor would retaliate and she could see the utter terror etched into the child's face as she pushed her way through the crowd toward the boy.

The vendor's face flushed a vivid red as he reached within the cart and seconds later withdrew a folded object from within. Ginelle's eyes widened in profound horror as he unraveled the object and revealed a bullwhip. The long, leather lash spiraled to the ground and the vendor twisted his wrist to situate it between his hands before extending it above his head with the intention of bringing it violently down on the boy.

Ginelle couldn't bear the idea of the pain the boy would suffer and she wouldn't stand for it. Taking the risk of being struck dead on, she rushed forward and firmly placed herself between the vendor and the whimpering child. She knelt at the child's side, quickly assessing the boy for injuries.

The vendor blanched and lowered the ugly whip but his hand remained firm as he gripped the handle. He narrowed his eyes at her and hissed through clenched teeth, "Get out of my way, woman." He growled, "I will teach this boy a lesson."

Despite her fear and the curious audience growing around them, she remained firm, determined to protect the child. "I will not!"

His face pinched with immediate rage as his fingers tightened around the handle of the whip. "Then I will strike you!"

Her unyielding gaze never wavered, daring him to follow through on his threat. When he lifted his hand she felt a fleeting moment of panic as a number of gasps collected from the crowd.

The vendor jerked his hand back, unwinding the leather whip. He snapped his wrist in full circle and brought the lash fully around. Ginelle reacted in fear as she swung her arm upward to protect her face and braced her body for the pain.

There was a sudden flicker of black as a heavy shadow fell at her side and the unmistakable sound of leather wrapped itself around flesh and bone.

Ginelle pressed a hand to her mouth as she stared at the ghastly sight of leather tightly bound around bronze skin. She jerked her eyes to Dorian's enraged face, his eyes like blue fire as he jerked on the whip and the vendor stumbled into Dorian's iron grasp.

Strong fingers curled around the vendor's throat, lifting the man easily above the ground. Ginelle stood and stepped back as Dorian hurled the man backwards, his body snapping the cart in two as sweets littered the cobblestone.

Chaos erupted on the street, beggars rushed forward to seize the fallen pastries as women scolded the unconscious vendor and men glared, ushering their women from the horrendous display. Some spectators stood aside, whispering amongst each other, exchanging inquisitive glances.

Ginelle spun around, expecting to find the small boy, but there was no child. She lifted her head to spot the boy running through the crowd, he paused and turned back to look at her. He smiled tentatively, clutched in his arms braced against his chest was an accumulation of sweets. She smiled, relieved to see the boy unharmed.

She stiffened as her gaze connected with sharp, blue eyes. He had been watching her, all the while the ugly leather wrapped around his arm.

Ginelle drew in a sharp breath as she stepped towards him, her eyes transfixed on his arm. "Can you get it off?" she asked, fearful of what lay beneath.

Slowly, he began to unwind the leather. The lash had cut clear around his arm and fresh blood oozed from the lacerated flesh.

Ginelle reacted instinctively, reaching down she ripped a good portion of her skirt and moved to take his arm delicately between her fingers, and unaware that she caused him further pain that had nothing to do with his injury she began to wrap it tenderly around his wound.

"Thank you." She said in a soft, gentle voice as her fingers worked to bind his injury.

He stood motionless, marveling at the touch of her fingers moving tenderly over his arm and the tears glistening in her gentle eyes. Did she cry for him?

He had felt a maddening instinct, a momentum bordering the line of possessiveness surge through his body as an unspeakable rage drove him to her side. The very thought of the lash marring her skin enraged him beyond conveying.

His arm burned but he paid no heed to the injury for it was in no comparison to the fire burning in his veins. He watched as a breeze lifted a single strand of blond hair, releasing it to rest lightly on a delicate cheekbone. He resisted the urge to reach out and remove it and trace that very spot with his fingers.

The moment he entered the market and spotted her, he had envisioned Eloise doing the same for a pretty child but that child was now a woman and she had dared a man to strike her down for a small boy. Her bravado amazed him. The tears she shed now for his lacerated arm stunned him.

He focused on her blond head, bent over his arm, focused intently on the task at hand, unaware of his smoldering gaze moving over her.

Aye, he wanted her, desired her with a fire in his belly. She knew nothing of a man's touch. She knew not what transpired between a man and a woman and he had a compelling compulsion to teach her the thralls of passion.

He felt that swift tightening in his groin and immediately stiffened. The way she affected, by the merest touch, drove him mad.

Dorian jerked his arm from her touch, feeling as though she had seared him. She stepped back, her eyes wide with uncertainty to his sudden change in mood.

The muscle at his jaw tightened as her expression altered to puzzlement. The fire in his groin combined with the unnerving affect she had on him only worsened his temperament.

"Mayhap you should think twice in risking your life for a lowly peasant; tis feeble-minded." He hissed through clenched teeth. "The boy had what was coming."

She stiffened, suddenly furious. "Is that what you think?" she demanded, "That a mere child should suffer intolerably because he is hungry? That a lowly peasant deserves such harsh treatment?"

His expression hardened and he stepped towards her and she tensed beneath the harsh scrutiny of his stare.

"Ginelle!" Lucile's cry rang out from the crowd as she suddenly appeared, carrying her purchase in her hands as she rushed forward.

The housekeeper stopped abruptly as she spotted Dorian's bloodied arm. "Milord, what happened?" her face paled as she examined the torn flesh.

His eyes remained on Ginelle as he said, "Lucile, take Ginelle home-" he turned then to glare darkly at the older woman, his mouth set in a grim line as he continued, "-and the next time you take an outing, make sure she is not compelled to do anything foolish again."

Lucile merely nodded and stepped away as Dorian swept past her and disappeared in the thickened crowd. The older woman averted her worried stare to Ginelle who merely stood gripping a piece of her dress soaked with blood.

The carriage ride back to Ashford was silent. Lucile had flooded her with questions but Ginelle had been too angry to answer them and eventually the older maid had given up.

His harsh comment continued to replay in her mind.

Risking your life for a lowly peasant is feeble-minded. The boy had what was coming. Did he think so poorly of those less fortunate? Did he think so poorly of her? She had been a lowly peasant; did he believe she had deserved to starve, to be beaten?

She fought against tears but they came anyhow, rolling down her cheeks to fall in her lap. How could she have ever admired him? How could she have ever thought him different?

Yet, he had taken the brunt of the lash. Why would he do such a thing if he thought so little of her?

He couldn't rid his thoughts of her. She had somehow slipped beneath his skin, smelling sweet of heather. He could still smell that lovely scent. Her innocence and delicate beauty stirred him unlike any other. He wanted her as if he had never had a woman.

Dorian resisted a low growl as he trotted towards the fields, eager to place his mind elsewhere. Once he had returned from town, he bandaged his injury and proceeded on towards the croplands to relieve some of his men.

Instantly, he noticed many of the laborers stiffen at his approach. Dorian surveyed the slaves as they worked intensively, digging at the ground with grub hoes.

Most of the men tending his fields had been purchased from the slave market. A majority of them were thieves with a small handful of criminals added to the mix. These were the particular few he ordered whipped. They cast venomous looks occasionally his way in between digging.

He narrowed his eyes, accessing them from behind. He was not one to stand over his men with a lash and snap the whip any time they dared to glare his way. He was accustomed to their sharp stares and rigid spines. There were many that loathed him and wanted nothing more than to cut his throat in the night but others respected him for he was not as other masters, eager to flog their man at the slightest mishap. He neither starved them nor deprived them of shelter. They were given meals throughout the day and after working an extensive dawn till dusk, proceeded to their lodgings.

As their overseer, he maintained ordinance and respect. For those that dare step out line, attempting revolt, were immediately corrected. The whip was obtained only when he saw fit to use it and whenever something or someone stood in his way of the trade, the lash was significant.

The sudden roll of a carriage brought his laborers up short and Dorian stiffened. He turned in the saddle to see Lucile descend from the carriage. He unknowingly held his breath, anticipating the sudden blast of silver-blond hair to follow in wake of the housekeeper.

When she came into view, he released the sharp breath he had been holding. She held her skirts in one hand as she extended the other to the coachman. Even from the distance separating them, he could clearly make out the crimson blush staining her cheeks.

As if sensing his eyes on her, she looked up and their eyes clashed. His heart accelerated in his chest, his blood hastening through his veins with a burning desire to feel those lips beneath his own; to taste her as he had done at the river.

The moment his lips had touched hers, he had been ensnared. His intention had been to punish her, but the punishment was his own for he suffered intolerably.

Lucile muttered something and instantly the trance was broken. She tore her eyes away and continued on towards the manor.

He forced his attention back to the task at hand and felt an immediate rage seize him at the many eyes following the blond-beauty into the house.

"Get back to work!" he roared.

Immediately, the slaves jerked into motion and began digging, Dorian took notice that a few lingered, slowly moving back to their task.

He narrowed his eyes at them before stealing another glance towards the manor. He was relieved to find her out of sight but far from his mind.

"What were you thinking?" Lucile demanded as they stepped into the parlor. Ginelle turned her back to the housekeeper and stared at the piano, her heart sinking as an image of Eloise came to mind, her fingers gliding smoothly along the keys. "You could have severely been injured." The older woman continued.

Ginelle curled her hands at her sides and turned to Lucile with tears in her eyes. "What would you have me do? Watch helplessly as a poor child is beaten because he is hungry?"

Lucile stiffened, taken aback by Ginelle's broken expression. The housekeeper was stunned for it was as if Eloise were alive, her spirit planted firmly in Ginelle. How could she be angry with the girl for doing exactly what Eloise had done nearly four years ago?

She softened her visage, "I am sorry, my dear." The older woman's face revealed a sadness that Ginelle had only witnessed in brief moments. "Just promise me that you will not do anything like that again."

Ginelle nodded but she knew in her heart that she could not watch an innocent suffer. She was not so cruel and merciless like him.

Lucile straightened and all traces of emotion fled as her solemn disposition resurfaced. She gathered her purchase from earlier and proceeded on towards the kitchen in search of Cook.

Ginelle slowly turned back to the piano to run her fingers along the smooth, black surface. She would not regret what she had done. Though Dorian had been harsh in his words, he couldn't be so cruel as to wish harm upon a mere child?

Her thoughts were skeptical as she left the parlor and continued upstairs towards her room. As she turned the corner, she collided roughly with another body. She gasped as two hands shot out and shoved her roughly back. She stumbled into the wall, just narrowly missing the stair way. Her heart thrust against her chest in sudden alarm and she jerked her head up to the body standing over her.

Ingrid's eyes narrowed to bright, green slits of deep distaste. Her red hair was pulled back into a tight chignon at the top of her head, enhancing the cruel angles of her face. She planted her hands firmly on her hips as she glowered down at Ginelle, a nasty sneer curling the corners of her mouth as she said, "I apologize, milady. I did not see you." Her voice dripped with malice and she smirked as she sauntered away.

Shaken, Ginelle pulled herself upright and stared after Ingrid's retreating back. Her hands trembled at her sides but she refused to show her fear. Had Ingrid truly intended to push her down the stairs?

Gathering her skirts, she hastened towards her room, fearful that the maid would be lurking behind. When she came to her door, she paused as she reached for the latch. The door was parted, as if someone had already been inside.

She straightened to peer down the hall but Ingrid was gone. Turning back to the door, she waited a moment before pushing it open. She stared around to find nothing amiss and than she heard the distinct chirp of birds and the flood of sunlight pouring into the chamber from the open window, eased her fears.

Even as she closed the door and felt somewhat secure, she couldn't help but fathom a lingering thought in the back of her mind. Had Ingrid intended to hurt her? Had she imagined her Ingrid shoving her?

Chapter 9

Evening approached with rolling, gray clouds and a sinking chill. Ginelle moved to the window and watched as rain began to pelt the window. She shivered inwardly as she wrapped her arms around her body and stepped away. The rain forebodes a deep inkling of apprehension. She had never liked the rain, it only increased her anxiety.

Turning away from the window she quickly assessed her room for a distraction. She spotted a book lying on the table she had finished the previous day. Mayhap a new book would keep her occupied for some time.

She left the room, closing the door gently behind her, and started towards the study where the books were kept. There were two separate studies. The one she was headed towards which was at the end of the hall and the other, Dorian's study. He spent a majority of his time there. She wondered for a moment why he spent so much time in his study. What kept him so occupied? What was he always thinking? Was he always managing business or did he think on his troubled past, the loss of Eloise?

She took her time sorting through the many books lining the shelves along the walls. After debating between several, she decided on two. Pulling them from the shelf, she tucked them under her arm and started back towards her room.

As she headed towards the end of the hall to her chamber, she stopped half-way. Gripping her skirts in one hand with her books tucked under the other, she stared down at the crease of light emitting through the parted door.

Her heart began to pulse with unease. She had shut the door when she left, of that she was certain. Had Ingrid come back?

Hesitantly, she moved towards the door and pushed it open. Ginelle inhaled sharply at the overturned mattress and coverlets dispersed beneath it. Her eyes widened as she studied the room in utter disarray. Objects lay scattered through out the room, along the floor in a disordered fashion.

Stunned, she could only stare in bewilderment at her destroyed room. A sudden noise to her right jerked her attention around, expecting to find Ingrid, instead she found a looming frame garbed in black.

Her mouth fell open in outrage as she took several angry steps towards him. "What do you think-"

Dorian turned and the fire in his eyes brought her up short. She blanched at the evident signs of anger and for a moment, she thought him capable of violence. The muscle in his jaw clenched painfully and she could just see the pulse beneath his skin, throbbing from the fury within. She had never seen him so enraged. She didn't recognize this menacing stature of a man with eyes like blue fire. She had witnessed Dorian's anger, but this was in no comparison.

She swallowed back a sudden lump lodged in her throat as she stepped back, a flood of fear and confusion swallowing her whole as he started towards her. It was then she noticed his fist clenched between them, clutched between his fingers was a long golden chain.

Frozen and startled by his black expression, she could only stare dumbfounded at his hand. "Where did you get this?" his voice had dropped dangerously low and fear settled heavily in her stomach.

Ginelle opened her mouth to say something but words failed to come out. Her apprehension choked her of any response and she could only stare wide-eyed as he closed the space between them to tower over her. She could only hear the frantic beat of her heart, pounding in her ears as images came flooding back. For a startling moment, she thought she saw the face of Pierino standing over her.

"Answer me!" he demanded.

She winced and would have stepped back but his fingers snaked around her upper arm and an alarming fear scuttled through her as his grip tightened, jerking her forward. The books from under her arm flopped to the floor and she nearly tripped over them as he dragged her towards the bureau.

She hadn't noticed that it was open or that her gowns had been tossed aside. She could only focus on the unforgiving fingers wrapped painfully around her arm. Ginelle gasped as the blood rushed from her face as she stared, horrified, down at the pile of jewels lying at the bottom of her bureau.

She paled as a nauseated feeling came over her. Her eyes widened and before she could utter a word, Dorian pulled her away. "How did you get these?" he dangled the necklace in front of her, his face shifting viciously with his anger.

Ginelle opened her mouth to respond but again her fear left her breathless. "These were my mother's." his ice, blue eyes regarded her accusingly.

She stood helplessly beneath his cold, intense stare as a tremor seized her. "I didn't-" she fumbled with words but his harsh accusations left her hollow. Why did his distrust of her hurt so badly?

"You had me fooled." He said bitterly, his voice flat and hard. "You had us all fooled."

Her stomach churned with dread and she felt the sting of tears as he released her and turned his back to her, his body shaking with uncontrollable rage.

"So you thought you could steal us blind? What was your plan? What did you think you were going to do with my mother's jewelry?" he whirled and stalked towards her, she retreated, frightened.

"Tell me!" he demanded as he gripped the golden necklace with maddening force. His blue eyes suddenly brightened with comprehension. "Ah, I see." He retorted as if she had spoke aloud. "I should have known you would have done something, anything to escape the marriage forced upon you." He sneered, taking another angry step towards her. "Is that what you were planning?"

"No!" she cried, "You accuse me unjustly!"

"Enough!" he roared, silencing her. "I don't want to hear your lies." His eyes suddenly wavered to the locket around her neck and narrowed suspiciously. "Did you steal that as well?"

Ginelle felt a wet streak on her face but refused to wipe the tears away. Her heart felt as though it had shattered. His cruel accusations hurt her beyond meaning, and she couldn't fathom why. Isn't this what she expected of him? There was nothing she could say that would convince him otherwise. He thought the worst of her and always has. She was nothing but a lowly peasant to him, whether she was garbed in fancy gowns or not, she would always be nothing more than worthless.

Her prolonged silence seemed to convince him further of his accusations. "If marriage is what you were escaping, than my lady, you've accomplished that." Still clutching the necklace between his fingers, he said in a low, harsh tone. "I want you gone this very evening."

He stalked from the room and slammed the door with deafening force. Ginelle stood staring helplessly at the door. The tears came uncontrollably as she stared at the disrupted chamber.

She was a fool to think she could live here. Her heart lay heavy in her chest as she turned to survey the room. Eloise had been kind to take her in, but no matter how well educated or finely dressed she was there was no changing who she really is.

She searched the remnants of the room for her cloak and found it where she left it. She slipped it on and cast a look out the window where the rain continued to fall mercifully. She would remember Eloise and there time shared together. She would hold onto that memory.

Dorian stared down at the golden necklace that once belonged to his mother, the Lady Charlotte, devoted wife of Lord Clayton Ashford. His fingers curled painfully around the chain, his eyes closing at the memory of his mother. The memory was far too painful to dwell upon; instead he focused on his anger.

She had lied to him, betrayed his trust. Yet, despite the fury at finding his mother's precious heirlooms in her room, he couldn't shake his disbelief or his gut instinct that he was wrong.

His anger had only intensified of her fear of him. She flinched beneath his anger as though he had struck her, and that unnerved him the most. Aye, he had been enraged and he should not have handled her as roughly as he did, but he had not lifted a hand to her, so why than this fear of him? Was it because she was guilty, or did she really think he would hurt her?

He felt the muscle at his jaw throbbing as he continued to stare at the necklace. One of the servants had informed him of the open chest containing all of his mother's valuables. The chest had been empty.

Dorian stood abruptly from his chair and moved to the window. The rain continued to fall heavily from thick, dark clouds. He imagined her, alone and crying. Her tears had affected him deeply. Even with anger, he found her irresistibly beautiful. Had he been fooled, blinded by her beauty? Was it all farce?

She had objected to the idea of marriage. Had she planned to barter his mother's jewelry to leave Ashford, to escape his plans for her?

He wondered for a moment where she had gotten the locket around her neck. He never saw her lovely neck bare without it. Where did she get it? Did it belong to her or had she stolen it?

There was an abrupt knock on the door and he turned just as it opened. Lucile entered, her hands gripping the latch as she observed him with wide, disheartened eyes. "Milord, what have you done?"

He narrowed his eyes at the older woman, clearly in no mood for her objections.

The housekeeper closed the door firmly behind her before turning back to him. She lifted her face to better meet his hard stare. Dorian noticed the intense anxiety in the older woman's face and her struggle to keep it at bay. "What have you done?" she demanded, her voice on edge.

Dorian had never witnessed Lucile frantic. Even when Eloise had passed the older woman had managed to contain her composure. "The servants say you have banished Ginelle?" her voice rose with panic.

His face was grim as he said, "I am in no mood to discuss this now." He turned away from her as if to dismiss her but the older woman moved around the desk to gain his attention.

"Milord, you will listen to me." Lucile said firmly, "With the good Lord as my witness, if you do not bring her back, as much as it pains me to do so, I will relieve myself of my position and leave Ashford this very moment."

Dorian arched a brow as he turned to fully study the housekeeper. "You would give up your position for her?" he asked curiously.

She nodded. "I would, milord."

"Why?" he asked.

"I know in my heart that Ginelle would never steal from us. She is not capable of such wrongdoings."

"You seem certain."

"I am quite certain, milord."

Dorian wanted to believe the older woman for his instincts were telling him the housekeeper was right but the evidence was there. How did Ginelle come by his mother's valuables? Why hadn't she claimed her innocence?

Another knock sounded curtly at the door and it opened before Dorian bid them entry. Mirabelle stepped timidly into the room, an edge of nervousness about her as she immediately dropped her head, her fingers entwining in her apron.

"What is it, Belle?" Lucile demanded.

The maid peeked up from under her lashes to spare a glance at Dorian. "I must speak with Master Dorian, tis urgent."

"What is it?" Dorian growled.

Belle straightened her spine as she slowly met that cold, blue gaze. "Mistress Ginelle is guilty of naught, milord." Her voice was hushed, fearful.

Dorian felt a strange flutter in his stomach. Had he been wrong? "How do you know this?" he demanded.

Belle spared a glance at Lucile and the older woman nodded, encouraging her to continue. "I saw-" she paused, biting down on her lip with anxiousness. "-I saw Ingrid-"

His eyes narrowed harshly with recognition. The red-haired servant that had informed him of his mother's empty chest claimed she had suspicions of Ginelle.

Belle swallowed, "I saw Ingrid take Lady Charlotte's things. S-she took them from the chest and planted them in Mistress Ginelle's room."

"You are certain, Belle?" Lucile prodded.

She nodded, "I followed her-" she jerked aside as Dorian swept past. The door fell back hard against the wall as he turned down the hall, his mind plagued with images of Ginelle alone and frightened.

Ginelle felt a wave of trepidation seize her as she paused beneath the rain to study the narrow paths leading her further into the forest.

She felt a rising panic and quickly sought to calm her fears. She couldn't allow her anxiety to overwhelm her, not now. Her eyes burned with unshed tears and mixed with the rain her vision became clouded.

Gripping the leather reins tightly until her knuckles turned white, she focused on steering her horse onto another path.

The rain soaked her clothing to the bone. Despite the warm evening, she shivered in her cloak. She had lost track of time and somehow managed to get lost. The unfamiliar path only heightened her apprehension.

She had packed nothing knowing none of it belonged to her, even the horse but she would not risk traveling on foot.

Her heart felt like stone in her chest. He had blatantly accused her of a crime she did not commit. Why did it hurt so much?

Someone had deliberately plotted the jewelry in her bureau to be rid of her. She should of left Ashford long ago. She had been a fool to stay, to allow herself to get close to Eloise and Lucile.

Her only other option was a convent.

Why hadn't she thought of it before? She would be safe in a convent. She did not want to marry and she wanted to be free of Pierino. In a convent she would never be subjected to marriage or come in contact with men like Pierino and Dorian again.

She felt a flutter of relief as the rain slowly began to let up. The sun drifted low in the sky, making a lazily descent with the approaching night. Ginelle tugged on the reins to pull her mare to a slow trot.

She had a sudden foolish urge to peer over her shoulder but she would not think of Ashford as her home. It had never been her home. She brushed tears from her face for she would miss Lucile and Belle, even Cook. She would not think of Dorian. He had wanted her gone from the very beginning.

How could she have ever thought him capable of compassion? He had cast her out so cruelly without the slightest remorse, had accused her so quickly without giving her a chance to declare her innocence.

Ginelle cared not for she was free, free to do as she pleased. She should have gone to a convent long ago to avoid the pain she continuously endured when allowing others into her heart.

It was then she heard the thunderous approach of hooves. Every muscle in her body stiffened with warning. Her fingers tightened around the reins as she pulled the mare to a halt. Her eyes strained against the forest as her heart erupted against her chest.

She suddenly remembered Eloise's warning that the uncharted forest could conceal brigands and dangerous outlaws.

Her fingers tightened around the reins and she nudged her mare with her heels. Instantly her horse took off at a frightening pace. She felt dangling limbs stab at her cloak as she caught speed, ducking to dodge a hanging branch. In her sudden flight, her hair flowed freely down her back and she struggled to keep the wayward strands from her face.

Her heart accelerated against her chest as she heard the stranger's vast approach and than an immense shadow fell in at her side.

Ginelle felt a scream in her throat as long, lean fingers reached out and seized her reins. She caught a glimpse of the massive black beast riding alongside her horse just as she came to a jerky halt. The sudden momentum wrenched her sideways and she felt herself falling.

A band of muscle wrapped tightly around her waist and Ginelle gasped as she was easily plucked from the air and placed right onto a large, masculine thigh.

Her eyes widened as they collided with a glacial stare.

"Are you hurt?" Dorian's gruff tone brought her alert as that intense, blue gaze moved over her face looking for injuries, and she was instinctively aware of his arm wrapped around her waist, holding her in his lap.

She realized then that her hands lay firm and flat against the hard wall of his chest and she jerked them away as if he burned to the touch.

"Put me down." She squirmed in his lap in efforts to get down but his arm only tightened, pulling her closer against the heat of his body.

"I said are you hurt?" his voice was deeper, tinged with a huskiness that startled her. The rain had soaked his clothing. His black tunic clung to the muscles of his chest, emphasizing the breadth of broad shoulders. The open v at his chest revealed smooth bronze skin with ripples of rain dotting the muscle beneath it.

She peeled her eyes away from his chest and gasped for the heat in his eyes made her heart flutter. His jet-black hair lay wild and untamed, framing the sharp angles of his face. His vivid, blue eyes moved boldly over her face to rest firmly on her mouth.

She stilled as he reached up and pushed wet strands of hair from her face. The tender gesture ignited a searing heat in her belly. His fingers lingered along the arch of her cheek and she held her breath as he fanned her skin with his knuckles. His hand turned and she felt his fingers brush her lips and her mouth fell open on its own accord.

She felt his breath, heavy on her forehead as if he struggled with an internal confliction. His fingers traced her lower lip, trailing lower to the arch of her jaw to dip under her cloak.

Ginelle gasped as she felt his fingers peel her cloak off her shoulders. She felt a strange heat at the tips of his fingers as he caressed the hollow at her throat.

Instincts warned her to stop him but she sat paralyzed, unable to resist the strange temptations urging his touch. No man had ever touched her so tenderly and this wasn't just any man, this was Dorian.

His fingers spanned her throat, forcing her head back. She inhaled sharply as his dark head lowered and he pressed his lips against the pulse at her throat as the arm at her back tightened, forcing her back into an arch, and pressing her breasts firmly against his chest.

She clenched her eyes shut as he trailed kisses along the smooth expanse of her throat, his mouth leaving a trail of heat over her flesh as it tingled with sensation beneath his lips.

Stop this now. Her instincts warned. He's dangerous. She suddenly recalled his fury and how quickly he had accused her of thievery. He had cast her out into the rain without a chance to claim her innocence and now she was letting him kiss her?

Her thoughts demanded he release her, but her body protested as it eagerly sought his touch. Her breath quickened at the gentleness of his lips, moving tenderly along her flesh. She felt the evening air, moist from rain, against her skin, followed by the gentle brush of his fingers.

She molded perfectly against him, aware of every sinewy muscle. His hair tickled the side of her face and she shivered, a feeling of exhilaration sweeping through her as he rose higher to claim the spot below her earlobe, his mouth a mere caress, doing strange, invigorating things to her.

She felt the strength in his touch, in the arm binding her to him. Shouldn't she be angry with him? Shouldn't she be frightened?

She couldn't seem to focus clearly past the manipulations of his lips. He lifted his head and their eyes connected, and Ginelle was struck with the raw desire burning in the depths of his icy stare. How could eyes so vivid, so arctic blue, burn with such a deep fire?

His raven tresses framed the sharp angels of his face, accentuating his straight jaw and full lips. The chiseled features indicated a rough, dominating exterior, but there was a softness that could be detected. She could see faint lines of laughter around his eyes and mouth and wondered for a moment when last he had laughed?

He was by far the most handsome man she had ever encountered, and the most dangerous. He stirred things in her that she had never felt, never imagined feeling. They were both frightening and stimulating.

His eyes burned so blue they almost appeared silver beneath the approaching twilight. They moved over her face as if studying every arch and curve, mesmerized by her features. His gaze fell on her lips and her heart leapt.

Dorian knew he should resist her, resist the fierce demands of his body, urging him to taste her, to take her. He had never yearned for a woman as he did for her. She was like forbidden fruit, one taste and he was doomed.

She felt lovely against him, her little body cradled in his lap as her hair tumbled over his forearm. Her skin was flawless, smooth and perfect like fine porcelain. A rosy blush tainted her cheeks and her eyes were large and round, a soft, gentle brown that kindled his body in flames.

Her gown molded to the curves of her luscious frame as her breasts fell and rose with her labored breaths.

His eyes rested firmly on her lips, parted with her breathing and he was seized with a fierce longing.

He reached up and gripped her chin delicately between his fingers and she inhaled sharply, her lovely breasts rose against the seams of her dress and a hot stab of arousal gripped him mercifully.

He leaned forward, unable to resist her sweetness, yearning to claim her lips with his own. Her eyes grew wide and he felt her tremble against him.

He knew the moment he had kissed her at the river that one taste would not quench his insatiable hunger.

His mouth captured hers, and she gasped, opening to him and allowing his tongue to sweet passionately inside. She arched against him and he felt a thrilling sensation as she accepted his kiss with an inquisitive shyness.

He kissed her tenderly, aware that she was credulous to what transpired between a man and a woman. He imagined taking her maidenhead, teaching her the depths of passion and the wonders of lovemaking.

He deepened the kiss and felt his groin harden with anticipation as a soft moan escaped her throat. He savored the way her lips moved beneath his own, cautious but curious as he claimed her mouth with an intensity that surprised as well as excited him. His manhood throbbed with an insufferable urge and every fiber in his being demanded he take her, take her here on the forest floor.

His free hand spanned her little waist, marveling at her petite body and how perfect she would fit against him. His fingers skimmed over her ribs to rest below the swells of her breasts.

He reached up and seized the material at her shoulder. He caught her gasp with his lips as he jerked the material down, exposing one, milky breast.

She stiffened against him, suddenly aware of her nakedness as the cool, evening air caressed her flesh. He cupped her breast into his palm; his body jerked with fiery desire as he rubbed his finger over her nipple and traced the curve of her breast with his thumb.

Unable to resist the fire burning low in his belly, he released her mouth and bent her back over his arm and captured her nipple in between his teeth, tugging lightly. She gasped aloud, her sharp intake of breath doing strange and hot things to him.

He traced her nipple with his tongue as his hand slid around her ribcage, gliding smoothly along the expanse of her back. She jerked against him as he tugged and sucked, pulling gently until she released a pained cry of desire.

He felt a grin tug at the corners of his lips as he reached over and jerked the material further down, exposing her other breast. Exposed entirely, Ginelle straightened as if to cover herself, but he seized her wrists in one hand and pinned them behind her back.

His mouth captured her neglected breast and began the same ministrations, tugging and pulling until she squirmed in his lap, igniting an inferno until he feared he would bust at the seams.

"I want you, ma petite." He whispered the plea against her breast and Ginelle arched into his mouth, her body burning with a fever that nearly consumed her.

Dorian reached down and pulled at the skirts pillowing over his lap. He jerked them up and exposed her long, slender legs.

When she felt the cold air against her legs followed by the intimate trail of his fingers, it was as if a cold bucket of water had been splashed over her. She stiffened against him and jerked against his hands.

Immediately, she felt his big body tense and their eyes connected. She saw the raw hunger burning there, the fire to claim her and though shamelessly, she had wanted his touch, his desire frightened her.

For a moment, she thought he would continue; she could see the struggle on the inside. The fire in his eyes slowly diminished and an implacable resolve settled across his dark, handsome face.

The moment he released her, her body became chilled, as if needing his warmth. She quickly righted her dress and pushed her skirts down over her legs.

She attempted to get down off his lap on her own but the height of the stallion proved difficult, instead his arm circled her waist and easily lowered her to the ground.

Ginelle spun around to glare murderously at him, suddenly ashamed at how wanton she had acted. How could she have let him touch her so intimately after what he had done?

"Don't ever touch me again!" she hissed.

Her eyes widened as he swung one powerful leg over the saddle and easily jumped down. She backed away as he approached her, towering at a massive six-foot-two. His blue eyes moved leisurely over her frame and she felt a deep blush paint her cheeks at his boldness.

It wasn't until she felt a tree at her back that she realized she was cornered. He loomed above her and leaned forward, pressing an arm against the bark above her head as he peered down at her. "I was merely checking for injuries." He stated nonchalantly.

Ginelle gasped at the abrupt indifference in his manner. He had been so gentle, so tender when he had kissed her and now this coldness? She wanted to slap his dark, handsome face but refrained.

She narrowed her eyes at him, "Never touch me again."

The muscle at his jaw tightened as he pondered her retort. He leaned closer until his breath fanned her forehead. "You think your Nathaniel will bring you to such heights?"

She slapped him, hard. Her hand burned from the impact but not as hot as the anger in his eyes. Ginelle recoiled, fearful that he would strike her, but he merely grit his teeth and wrapped his fingers around her arm and pulled her from the tree towards his horse.

"What are you doing?" she demanded, tugging at his arm.

"We are going home." He growled, as he reached for her waist to lift her up onto the horse.

"No!" she turned in his arms and pushed against his chest, "I'm not going back to Ashford with you."

"Do you have somewhere else to be?" he grounded between clenched teeth.

Ginelle lifted her chin to meet his hard stare. "I'm not returning to Ashford. I'll join a convent. I should have done it long ago."

Dorian felt a grin tug at the corners of his mouth as he imagined this lovely, desirable creature in a convent. He couldn't, wouldn't allow it. "I think not, milady. Your home is at Ashford."

A somber look crossed her lovely face, "Ashford was never my home." He frowned as she said this and than jerked away from his touch. "Why would you harbor a thief?" she demanded, her eyes narrowing with anger. "Is that not why you banished me?"

"Your name has been cleared of any wrongdoing."

She shook her head at him, "That does not change what you really think. The next time something is stolen, will you be so quick to blame me?"

He stepped towards her and she resisted the urge to step back. His intense, blue eyes bore into her face, a mask of emotions that she could not fathom. "Milady." He said in a deep, hushed tone. "You have stolen something, but that remains a mystery."

Her brows knitted together in puzzlement but before she could comprehend his statement, he lifted her off the ground and planted her firmly in the saddle. He mounted behind her and whipped the horse back towards the direction of Ashford.

Chapter 10

The banquet was being held in the grand hall by the Duke of Hadley. Ginelle knew very little of the man except that he and his wife, the Duchess of Hadley were members of English nobility and highly admired among the ton. During the following weeks before the banquet, she had learned that Edmund Wilkinson was a prominent diplomat and before his title as a duke, an armed mercenary.

Ellison Wilkinson, the Duchess of Hadley was rumored to be quite striking in beauty and profoundly refined in etiquette. According to Lucile, the Duchess was the epitome of perfection when it came to nobility standards.

Ginelle found herself in a chaos of frantic maids and an assortment of accessories and extravagant gowns. She was keen to notice that Ingrid was absent from the circle of maids crowding her. She had not given much thought to the girl since that day she returned to Ashford and received the news that Ingrid had been the one to plant the jewelry in her bureau. She later learned the maid no longer resided at Ashford, but at a neighboring plantation.

Despite the continuous somersaulting of her stomach and jittery nerves, she couldn't but laugh as Lucile hastened about the room in a distressed manner. She had never witnessed the maid so frenzied.

"You must look your very best this evening." Lucile stated as she gathered a few gowns from the bureau.

Ginelle managed a peak from beneath the mass of curls atop her head as Belle poked and prodded with pins to sort the tedious tresses.

After nearly an hour of Lucile's indecisive study of gowns, they decided on a gorgeous dress of satin maize with elbow-length sleeves adorned with falling ruffles. The neckline and hem was trimmed in a white lace with an embroidered bodice. The tiered skirt had been intricately stitched with moderate care with full, flowing skirts to accentuate the fitted gown.

Once fully dressed, Ginelle took a moment to admire the reflection staring back at her in the mirror. For a moment, she almost fooled herself into believing that she belonged in such a magnificent gown and the woman staring back at her was Lady Ginelle Pattinson and not Ginelle Hayes, impoverished orphan.

How did she get here? How could she have allowed this nonsense to continue? And now she was to attend a banquet for her coming out, hosted by the Duke and Duchess of Hadley?

She turned from the mirror, suddenly dispirited. Lucile approached and handed her a pair of lovely white slippers. Ginelle slipped them on her feet and waited as Lucile accessed her appearance.

"You are going to have every man swooning at your feet!" exclaimed Belle.

"Belle!"

Belle straightened and flattened her palms on her apron. "Well, you will." She stated with a sheepish grin.

"I do not wish to speak of men swooning at my feet."

Lucile clasped her hands together to gain their attention. "We've prolonged the evening long enough." She turned to look at Fannie, another maid who had assisted in getting Ginelle ready for the evening. "Fannie, please go and fetch Ginelle's cloak and inform Master Dorian that we shall be down shortly."

At the mention of Dorian, Ginelle's heart pitched whether from excitement or dread, she knew not. She could not say that she had forgotten that Dorian would be escorting her for the evening for he had rarely left her thoughts since that night in the forest. She felt a blush stain her cheeks as she recalled vividly how he had touched her, claimed her with his lips.

How could she have acted so brazenly knowing Dorian wanted to be rid of her? If he wanted her gone, than why would he kiss her, touch her?

She had rarely seen him since that night. She knew not how her body would react once she did. Her mere thoughts had her brain rattled with questions and uncertainty to the reaction of her body whenever he came to mind.

She would have rather endured the company of the tons most notorious gossipmonger than have that unbearable brute as her chaperone!

Dorian braced his weight against the window sill, his left arm extended above his head and in his right hand, a glass of brandy. Ah, how he enjoyed these moments of distilled liquor and disturbing thoughts, he mused silently, anything to chase away the burning desire in his body.

He downed the last remnants of the glass and set it aside as he stared down at the arriving carriage. He was going to need a lot more brandy to get him through this night. Though Edmund Wilkinson was a dear and old companion, who willingly obliged his request to host Ginelle's coming out banquet at his grand home, he loathed the night's event and all its inhabitants attending. He had to continue to remind himself that this was a good happening.

Some poor sap was going to come along and offer a proposal that would finally rid him of his burden and he would gladly oblige the unfortunate bastard. His hands curled into fists at the thought of another man touching her.

He heard a knock at the door and ignored it. A second knock followed and he grounded his teeth until finally the door squeaked open. "Milord?"

Dorian turned to cast a dark glare at Bogart, but the older serf was not deferred by his Master's black expression. "The carriage has arrived milord; and one of the maid's have informed me that Mistress Ginelle is ready."

He said nothing but turned back to the window. He waited until Bogart left the room until he left the window to retrieve his waist-coat draped across the back of the chair. He eyed the brandy bottle with much contemplation and decided against it. He needed a clear head for this evening.

He left the confines of his study and descended the winding stairs where he found Bogart waiting with the coachman. He paused at the last step to retrieve a cigar from within the pocket of his coat but his fingers froze half way; his eyes captivated to the top of the stairs.

Ginelle made her way down, carefully gripping the banister as her legs melted like butter beneath that riveting, blue stare. Immediately she was taken aback by how striking Dorian appeared in his black waist-coat fitted to the contours of his big frame. Beneath it he wore a white linen shirt, opened at the front to reveal rippling, bronze muscle. His long, lean legs were encased in black breeches with patent leather boots to adorn his feet. His jet-black hair had been tamed for the evening, pulled back by a leather thong to accentuate the severity of his handsome face.

She felt a hot sensation stir in her belly as she remembered the way his arms felt around her, the way his mouth claimed hers so diligently and she blushed deeply. How could anyone look so wickedly handsome?

The way he looked at her, those glacial eyes moving slowly over the length of her in bold appraisal, intensified the searing flame threatening to consume her.

She felt that familiar shock of electricity and wondered if any man could affect her the way Dorian did? Those blue eyes seared her to the last step and she nearly lost her balance for that smoldering look had such an intense lure on her senses. His disposition reeked black with a grim expression etched into his granite face and she wondered where is that man who had kissed her so tenderly, so passionately in the forest?

Fannie must have given Dorian her cloak for he had the garment draped over his arm. He helped her into it and she gasped as she felt the brush of his fingers along the nape of her neck. She turned and he offered her his arm and she tentatively accepted.

As they made their way outside, she unknowingly shrank closer to his side as the blackened sky released a deep rumble of thunder. The humid air struck her face in a clammy caress. As Dorian assisted her into the carriage she felt her stomach churn at the thought of the approaching storm.

She settled into the leather seat and stared out the window, her eyes widening at the tree limbs struggling against the unexpected gust of wind.

"The storm frightens you?"

Ginelle jerked to awareness at Dorian's deep, gruff voice, unaware that he had been watching her from across the space of the carriage, taking keen notice to the display of emotions crossing her face.

"Yes." She said lightly.

He said nothing but flexed his jaw as he continued to stare at her. Ginelle was suddenly annoyed despite her fear of the storm. In some way or another, she provoked his temper without meaning to do so. "Do you find my fear childish?" she demanded, lifting her chin.

He tilted his head to better survey the sudden spark that lightened her eyes to soft amber. "When fear is absolute it is never childish."

She narrowed her eyes at him, "Then why do you look at me so as if I have upset you? Have I done something to displease you?"

Dorian's expression darkened as he crossed his arms against his chest. What could he say to her? That he was angry? Aye, he was angry.

He was angry because he demanded that she marry. He was angry that she even suggested going to a convent when her home was at Ashford. He was even angrier that he was confined to this blasted carriage with its small compartment to entice his senses with the sweet smell of heather.

She was a vision in that yellow dress that enhanced her ethereal beauty. He loved the way her silver-blond hair settled on her head, a mass of curls piled high with several strands caressing the distinct line of her jaw. How he ached to replace those wayward strands with his fingers as he recalled the softness of her skin.

He loved her petite frame and small breasts pressed firmly in the bodice that accentuated her tiny waist. His groin hardened with a stab of lust as he remembered the feel of her breasts in his hands and her immediate response to his affections. He admired her delicate hands and small, pert nose lifted now in defiance. He had never been more captivated. Even now his body burned with that fire, that quick and swift demand to take her, now in this carriage. He wanted her, damn it, and he envied the bastard who would have her.

His hands curled against his chest and he averted his eyes away from her. He couldn't stare at her without wanting to taste her honeyed mouth and if he had to endure her presence any longer, he might very well act on selfish impulse and take what his body demanded.

Ginelle gritted her teeth and forced herself to look out the window. He was absolutely infuriating. He avoided her questions or just wouldn't give her straight answers. He was intolerable!

The remainder of the ride, a heavy silence settled between them and both were keenly aware of the other. It wasn't until they arrived to their destination that Ginelle released a sigh of relief.

The carriage rolled to a stop and the coachman opened the door and stepped aside as Dorian stepped down. He turned and extended a hand to

Ginelle and she accepted only because she feared her legs would give out beneath her. When her feet touched the ground, she started to pull away from Dorian but his fingers, strong and assertive, seized her wrist in a firm grip.

"I am to escort you, milady." He said as he pulled her closer to his side. She would have gladly jerked her arm free if not suddenly aware of the boisterous noise of an immense crowd waiting inside.

Ginelle could hear the quadrille band as they made their way inside. As they passed the front staircase lined with bodies, she caught a group of women standing close together, leaning in to whisper amongst each other. They spotted her and eyed her with deep curiosity. Ginelle quickly averted her eyes dreading the night to come for she was to be the topic for the evening.

The room was marvelous with high ceilings adorned with crystal chandeliers. The polished floor stretched out before her, dotted with powdered faces and fancy waist-coats. The windows were draped with gold tapestries including a set of double doors at the opposite end of the room leading to what seem to be a garden.

Ginelle felt herself shrinking against Dorian, seeking the comfort of his familiarity as numerous amounts of eyes turned to survey them. She noticed instantly how many turned to whisper in the ear next to them, others stared curiously, eager to know more about the woman on Dorian Don Ashford's arm.

She knew the contrast of the two of them was indubitably striking. He was tall, dark and irrevocably handsome where as she was small and fair. As more turned to study them in apparent interest she felt a crimson red stain her cheeks. She would have liked nothing more than to simply disappear.

Long, trestle tables lined each side of the grand hall, each decorated with an assortment of diverse dishes from an array of sweetmeats to a selection of roast quail, glazed ham and chicken. Refreshments consisted of tea, coffee and a variety of wine and brandy for the gentlemen.

The orchestra struck a merry tune and Ginelle stopped to admire a display of theatrics. She had heard that some banquets hosted spectacles meant to amaze the guests but surely all this wasn't for her coming out?

"I was beginning to wonder if you and the young miss were going to make your debut." Ginelle turned as a voice rang out from the crowd.

A man approached them, equipped in a cutaway coat of black velvet embroidered with gold ornamentation and black breeches that hugged his lean frame. He was tall and lean; his hair a deep auburn with eyes the color of cocoa.

The man smiled a beguiling grin as he extended a hand to Dorian who immediately accepted. They shook hands and than roughly embraced and slapped each other delightedly on the back.

Ginelle stepped aside, amazed as humor brightened Dorian's eyes, transforming his face completely; he was absolutely beautiful when he smiled.

"You forget your manners, darling." A woman separated from the crowd and fell in at the man's side, placing a small hand in the crook of his arm.

A smile touched Ginelle's mouth as the woman looked at her in genuine interest; her green eyes were warm and inviting, resembling that of an emerald meadow beneath the summer sun.

The man smiled as he wrapped a secure arm around the woman's waist. "Dorian, this is my wife, Lady Ellison Wilkinson, the Duchess of Hadley. Ellison, this is Lord Dorian Ashford, an old colleague and dear friend of mine."

Dorian grinned as he took Ellison's extended hand and pressed a kiss to her knuckles, "A pleasure, milady." He straightened, released her hand and added, "My thanks your grace for hosting the banquet at your hall."

The Duke laughed, "Dorian has very little patience for social gatherings."

Lady Ellison smiled softly, her green eyes twinkling with merriment. "I have heard much about you, Lord Dorian. I am honored that I could accommodate you."

"My wife has out done herself with the festivities." The Duke said amusingly, purposely avoiding Dorian's dark glare.

Ginelle was amazed. This man and woman were the Duke and Duchess of Hadley? The Duke was charming and enlightening, not at all what she expected, and a friend of Dorian's? The Duchess was indeed a vision of perfected beauty with flawless skin and jet-black hair pinned high atop her head. She had chosen a gown of sparkle tulle with an embellished bodice done in gold rhinestones to match that of her husband's ensemble. They were the ideal couple of nobility, she mused quietly, admiring them in discreet observation.

Dark, brown eyes shifted to her and instantly she felt her face blush a deep red. "You must be the lovely Lady Ginelle?"

She nodded as she offered a shy smile and extended her hand to the Duke. "Edmund Wilkinson, at your beck and call, milady." He smiled a dazzling grin and Ginelle's smile broadened.

"I pray that the festivity is to your liking?" the Duke asked, his dark eyes glinting back at her.

Ginelle nodded, "Yes, very much, thank you your grace." She turned to address the Duchess, "I am very grateful for all your efforts."

The Duchess smiled, her green eyes brightening with contentment. "I look forward to such events so that I may make new acquaintances."

"Well, we will not keep you." The Duke said, taking his wife's offered arm. He turned to Ginelle, "I hope milady that you will enjoy the evening and mayhap grant this old fool a dance?"

Ginelle smiled, unaware that Dorian watched her. "It would be a pleasure, your grace."

He laughed, "That is where you are wrong, my dear. The honor is mine."

One curtsied and the other bowed, as was custom and Ginelle watched as Edmund led Ellison away, his arm wrapped gently around her waist, ushering her through the crowded room. Her heart soared at the thought of befriending such a genuinely, friendly couple.

Dorian took her arm and led her to a table. She imagined what Eloise would have thought of the festivity and how she would have loved the occasion. Her laughter would have mesmerized the room.

Ginelle settled into her seat and watched as Dorian stalked away without so much as an explanation. Immediately she felt his somber mood and she felt her temper flare as she glared at his disappearing back.

She kept her posture straight, remembering that proper etiquette and posture were vital. Lucile continued to remind her that improper behavior was unacceptable and could very well taint her image. Her eyes searched the room, instinctively aware of the many eyes staring back at her.

Her heart somersaulted in her chest and she cursed Dorian beneath her breath for leaving her alone, subjected to the many probing eyes watching her.

Lucile had claimed it was imperative to impress the ton. Ginelle cringed on the inside at the thought.

Dorian returned with a glass of wine in one hand and a glass of brandy in the other. He settled into the seat across from her and handed her the glass of wine. She accepted it gingerly and gently swirled its contents. She had never tasted the fermented juice but she was eager to experience new things for the evening itself was an experience all its own.

Those blue eyes studied her over the brim of his glass and she quickly shifted her gaze else where, sudden vivid images of their moment together in the forest came rushing back and she felt heat creep up her neck.

Ginelle quickly sought an escape, anything to not think of their intimacy shared. "Do you plan on being foxed for the evening?" she narrowed her eyes at the glass in his hand.

Dorian lowered his brandy and arched a dark brow at her as his mouth quirked into a grin, "Would my drunkenness concern you?"

She quickly concealed her scowl, aware that many watched her. "I am merely concerned that you will make a spectacle of yourself." She averted her eyes to survey the band across the room.

Dorian released a low laugh as he set his glass down and Ginelle turned to peer back at him. "What do you find so amusing?" she demanded.

"I would think you are concerned that I might scandalize your image?"

Ginelle clenched her mouth shut against the sudden words that rushed to mind. She knew he favored the intoxicant but would he really dampen his reputation and ruin her image? She couldn't fathom Dorian going to such an extreme all because he disapproved of her? Remembering the way he had kissed her in the forest, she wasn't all too sure on how Dorian felt about her.

She knew he wouldn't do anything irrational. Eloise had relished in social occasions such as this and she was certain he wouldn't do anything to taint his sister's shadow.

His blue eyes gleamed back at her and she wondered for a moment if he really would make a spectacle.

A shadow fell over their table and both paused in their silent anger to peer up at Lieutenant Cummings. Dorian narrowed his eyes at his Lieutenant and his expression darkened as Ginelle's face brightened, her lips tilting into a tantalizing smile as Cummings greeted her with a dashing grin.

Dorian scowled deeply. He was all too aware of Cummings winsome antics in seducing youthful beauties.

He glared venomously at the Lieutenant over the rim of his glass as he brought it to his lips for an eager sip, anything to chase away the sudden jolt of jealousy surging through his veins.

"You are exquisite, milady." His russet eyes glinted mischievously and Dorian could barely refrain from slamming his glass down.

Ginelle extended a hand to Cummings and he proceeded to kiss her offered hand. "May I inquire for that dance, Lady Pattinson?"

Ginelle nodded eagerly, anxious to escape Dorian's company and the feelings he stirred in her. Cummings helped her to her feet but as she straightened, strong fingers seized her arm and pulled her back against a hard body. Her face flushed a deep red as her heart jerked against her chest in a frantic flutter.

"As is accustomed, the lady is to dance first with the partner in which she arrived with." His voice, deep and dangerously low, sent a shiver through her and she could all but drag air into her lungs for his mere presence robbed her of breath.

Cummings grinned and than bowed, easily submitting, "Of course."

Ginelle watched him leave. She gasped as Dorian's fingers tightened around her arm. Heat spread beneath his fingers, along her skin, warming her senses in a frightening but exhilarating way. Why did the merest touch unravel her so?

She was whisked out onto the floor in blinding haste as the orchestra pit created an unlikely tune with the fierce stroke of several violins blending in union to create a mystical waltz.

Ginelle inhaled sharply as Dorian's arms pulled her close, pressing her intimately against the hard contours of his muscled frame. She peered up and felt her legs turn to liquid as he stared down at her in pools of smoldering, blue heat. She trembled as he whirled her out, her skirts billowing as he spun her, and than jerked her back against him.

She attempted to pull away but his fingers only tightened as he twirled her away and reeled her back again. His arm slipped around her waist and she felt heat spread at the base of his fingers. That glacial blue stare remained frozen, fixated on her as he fell into step with other couples joining in on the waltz.

Ginelle was intimately aware of every inch of his solid, masculine frame. The firm set of his jaw and the sharp glint in his icy eyes set her heart at a pulsating pace. She felt that tingling sensation, spreading wide, a distinct, fierce urge for him to claim her lips, to kiss her as he had done in the forest. She felt the rise and fall of her breasts and remembered distinctively the way his fingers had done tantalizing things to her.

How could he have such an effect on her? He was dangerous. Everything she warned herself against. How could her body react in such a way, by a mere touch, a scorching look?

His face was a dark mask, concealing any expression with a hardened layer of resolve, but the heat in his eyes spoke of his hunger, his burning desire.

The violins blended into perfect captivation as if a gypsy played a tune for her enchanted beholder. The cadence of the melody lessened to a provocative rhythm, creating a hazy moment that stirred Ginelle in an indescribable way.

She released a tiny, sharp breath as heat spiraled low in her belly at the touch of his hand, caressing the underside of her breast. She struggled to focus on the steps of the waltz as her body turned to liquid beneath his smoldering gaze. She moved along the dance floor on unsteady legs, as her heart beat wildly in her chest, his eyes blazed with a fervid heat, a burning that unraveled her completely.

Suddenly, his eyes lifted to a spot above her head and Ginelle frowned as his mouth stretched into an exasperated grin.

They stopped in the middle of the floor and through the haze of crowded bodies, she found Nathaniel, watching from afar, his body seething with contempt before he turned and slipped into the shadows, disappearing from Ginelle's line of sight.

She whirled, her jaw dropping with outrage and mortification as Dorian stared down at her with cold reprisal glinting sharply in the depths of his icy glare.

Angry and humiliated by her body's treacherous reactions to his touch, she opened her mouth for a cutting retort to his antagonizing manner but he stepped towards her, his face darkening as he leaned close enough to say for her ears alone, "Curb your tongue milady, for your every gesture and motion is being observed."

Ginelle bristled silently. She was such a fool. He had purposely touched her to provoke Nathaniel!

She narrowed her eyes at him as she stepped away from him. She would have liked nothing more than to give him a tongue-lashing but she was instinctively aware of her every move being scrutinized. She refrained from speaking the lingering thoughts on her tongue, instead she turned and slowly walked from the room, her spine rigid and her chin held high.

Dorian watched her retreating back with a minatory rage. He returned to his seat and glared murderously across the dance floor where Sharp had been moments ago. He had succeeded in flaring the bastard's temper, which was very clear from the discernable hatred in the man's eyes.

He would not feel remorse for humiliating her. The very thought of Sharp touching her had his temper in an uproar. He was well aware of Sharp's reputation and Ginelle would not fall prey to his covetous appetite for wealth. He would be damned if Nathaniel Sharp were to lay a hand on her.

"You seemed to have improved in the techniques of ball room dancing, mon amour."

Dorian groaned inwardly as he averted his gaze from the vacant entrance of the grand hall to look up at the flame-haired beauty with eyes of smoldering blue. She had donned a gown of shimmering red wine with a flattering neckline that dipped low in the front to flaunt her bountiful breasts. Her red hair rested high atop her head, clearly in the latest style, adorned with a crimson ribbon. She chose the gown specifically for the way it molded to her luscious curves, leaving little to the imagination.

Dorian arched a black brow, "I don't recall you getting an invitation, Victoria."

Victoria Petroff shrugged carelessly as she settled across from Dorian. "You know that I cannot resist such an occasion, especially when their might be a vigorous gentleman eager to pay for my services." She grinned a lustful grin but Dorian was unaffected.

She studied him for a moment, contemplating another tactic. "I had hoped that you would be that gentleman." She leaned forward with a mischievous glint in her eyes. "Then again, you were never a gentleman."

Dorian straightened as Ginelle reappeared in the hall. He took notice to the faint blush in her pale face and the way her eyes searched the room. His eyes narrowed angrily. Was she looking for Sharp?

Clearly annoyed, Victoria scowled darkly and followed the direction of Dorian's intent gaze. When she noticed the little blond he had been dancing with standing in the entrance of the hall she was aghast.

"I see." She huffed; she turned in her seat to glare more directly at him. "Have you replaced me with that little whore?"

She stiffened as those cold eyes fixated on her and she froze. He had never looked at her in such a way and it terrified her. He had only looked at her with raw desire in his eyes but the sheer impact of his icy glare frightened her to the core. She knew Dorian was dangerous but she had never witnessed his anger.

"There's where your mistaken, Victoria." His eyes rested on her flushed face, "You are the whore." He said, undaunted.

Her mouth fell open in downright shock and her eyes widened at his harsh statement.

Dorian leaned back in his seat and crossed his arms against his chest, "Don't look so horrified, Victoria. Your reputation is quite notorious."

Victoria clamped her mouth shut and straightened her spine as she reached up to pat the side of her hair. "You need not state it so blatantly."

He grinned, "Ah, but whoring comes so naturally to you."

Victoria was deeply wounded. She cast a dark glare at the blond nymph across the room. "So who is she?" she demanded.

Dorian's eyes fell on Ginelle. She was clearly making it a point to avoid him. He nearly growled aloud when a man approached her.

Victoria tensed, frowning as a black expression contorted his handsome face. She had never seen Dorian react in such a way and she was absolutely, intolerably outraged that it wasn't her he responding so irrationally for.

Dorian recognized the young man as Byron Macaulay, barely a man and quite naïve in his youth. If Dorian was not mistaken, the boy might actually think himself in love with Ginelle by the way he was looking at her.

He felt a deep growl surface in his throat as he watched them from across the room, his eyes intense and waiting for the boy to make a move that could prove fatal to his wellbeing.

When the waltz ended and Macaulay curtsied to Ginelle, Dorian had every intention of intervening but as he moved towards her, a small hand landed on his arm, halting him.

He peered over at the Duchess as she smiled gently up at him, her attentive green eyes glinting prettily beneath the dim chandelier light. "Would you dance with me, Lord Ashford?"

Dorian resisted the urge to grit his teeth and produced a smile that didn't quite match the blood boiling in his veins.

He extended his arm to her, "Would be an honor, your grace."

As he led Lady Ellison to the floor, he spotted Ginelle and was slightly relieved to see her conversing with Edmund. "Are you enjoying yourself, milord?"

Dorian jerked his attention to Lady Ellison and smiled, "Yes, your grace, and yourself?"

"Please, call me Ellison." She insisted, "And yes, the evening has been quite joyous."

As they danced, Dorian's eyes wavered occasionally across the room, following a trail of maize skirts. He was unaware that Lady Ellison watched in silent humor, very aware of the grim expression contorting his rugged face.

"She is lovely, is she not?"

Dorian stiffened, his eyes shifting to the Duchess, "Your grace?"

"Your ward." She indicated with a nod to Ginelle, "She is quite lovely."

Dorian gritted his teeth, his eyes straying to the object of his thoughts. Lovely was not the word he would have used to describe her in that moment.

She was absolute perfection in all her innocence and pale beauty. No woman had ever driven him to jealousy but something about another man touching her drove him to the point of insanity. The thought of her marrying another seemed ridiculous. She belonged with a man who would protect her and love her above all things.

"Edmund and I did not see eye to eye when we married." He turned to Lady Ellison as she spoke, "I was quite against our betrothal." She admitted, "I was very certain I detested my husband." She smiled than, her green eyes brightening with adoration, "Love finds you when you least expect it, Dorian."

The waltz ended and Lady Ellison stepped back to dip in a curtsy. "It was a pleasure, milord."

"There you are!" Edmund appeared from the crowd, his brown eyes alight with affection for his wife as he took her arm gently in his hand. "You owe me a dance, lady wife." He nodded to Dorian as he led her away.

He leaned down and whispered in her ear, "What mischief are you at, clever one?" The Duchess smiled a beguiling grin up at her husband, and felt her heart swell with love and affection.

"Wait and see, mon amour."

Chapter 11

Dorian returned to his seat as Edmund led Ellison away. His eyes moved over the dance floor and found Ginelle. Her laughter vibrated across the room, stirring him deeply. He was pleased to see that she was enjoying herself but he greatly disapproved of the number of men pining for her attention.

"You know, jealousy furrows your face in the most unbecoming way. It dampens the appeal." Cummings fell into the seat across from Dorian, his mouth quirked into a teasing grin.

Dorian ignored Cummings and surveyed the floor. She was dancing with Douglas Campbell. He was a pragmatic youth with charismatic charm.

The two of them would be a beneficial pair. He was charming and handsome, exceedingly wealthy for one so young. He would make her a good husband, treat her kindly.

His face darkened considerably as Campbell leaned forward and said something and Ginelle laughed gently. He felt a swift tightening in his groin at her sweet laughter. She would laugh for Sharp and even the Campbell boy, but she had only anger for him?

"Lust on the other hand, alters your face completely."

Dorian jerked his gaze to Cummings, "What nonsense are you muttering?"

Cummings smirked, "Why do you fight it?"

Dorian's gaze wavered to Ginelle as Campbell twirled her about the floor, her eyes revealing sheer delight for the waltz. "She would resist me."

"You have charisma; why not woo the bonny chit?" He grinned knowing how absurd the suggestion sounded as it rolled off his tongue.

Dorian grinned, "You and I both know that my reputation is anything but flattering, least of all charismatic like our Campbell boy."

He caught a glimpse of red approaching their table and scowled deeply as Victoria sauntered forward. She acknowledged Cummings with a grin before addressing Dorian, "You need not look so vexed, mon amour." Victoria purred, her eyes smoldering as she studied the length of him.

"What do you want, Victoria?"

"The evening is quite boring but I was hoping you and I could have a dance before I leave?" she pouted prettily, "Can you not at least grant me that before you discard me so carelessly?"

Dorian gritted his teeth and would have refused until he caught sight of Ginelle crossing the room to their table.

"Just one dance, mon amour?" Victoria's voice penetrated his thoughts and he turned to extend his hand to her.

The room flowed with numerous bodies and yet, Ginelle was very aware of Dorian's presence. Even as many suitors approached and asked to dance, she was instinctively aware of his eyes following her.

He knew she would defy him at one point and she cared not. He had deliberately humiliated her and her intention for the rest of the evening was to avoid him as much as possible. He was naught but a brute!

Her eyes scanned the room for Nathaniel and once again she was disappointed to find him absent. Had he left because of Dorian's boldness? Was he no longer interested in her? Shouldn't she be thanking Dorian? She did not want to marry, therefore any proposal from Nathaniel would have been rejected but she couldn't help the likeness she felt whenever Nathaniel was near. She would have enjoyed his company for the evening.

Her scattered thoughts kept her distracted and she tried focusing on the boy in front of her. Douglas Campbell was very tall and thin, but his gaunt stature held little to no muscle. His hands gripping hers were a bit clammy and by the beads of perspiration dotting his forehead, he was racked with nerves. His eyes were a deep cobalt blue and she considered him passably handsome but couldn't help comparing his soft eyes to a pair of intense, sharp depths that resembled the artic regions.

Once the dance ended, she quickly concealed her relief and after a brief exchange of words with Douglas Campbell, she sought her table.

As she started towards it, she paused half way as she caught a flash of deep red. A beautiful woman in a tantalizing gown of red wine that was in striking resemblance to the flowing curls down her back stood next to Dorian. He was talking to her with a grin and that devilish glint in his sharp, blue eyes. Did he know the woman, a lover perhaps?

Ginelle felt a tightening in her chest that confounded her.

Jealousy? Surely not!

She shook her head of the absurd thought. What did she care if Dorian had numerous lovers? But that tightening in her chest intensified as Dorian led the pretty red-head to the dance floor.

She was being ridiculous. Realizing she watched their retreating backs, she jerked her eyes away and continued on towards their table where Lieutenant Cummings waited.

His russet eyes warmed at her approach and he motioned to the seat across from him. "How are you, mademoiselle?" he asked with great mirth.

Ginelle smiled despite the intense urge to look for a distinct towering figure in black moving fluidly along the dance floor. Instead she focused on Lieutenant Cummings. "I am well, Lieutenant, and yourself?"

His smile broadened as he turned to survey the room. "Enduring the festivities, milady."

She laughed, "I assume social events are not your preference, Lieutenant?"

He leaned casually back into the chair and smiled, "Nay, not my first choice. I prefer the brisk ocean air and rolling waves of the deep, blue sea."

Ginelle leaned forward, suddenly intrigued. "Have you spent much time at sea?"

He turned to grin at her, "Aye, since I was a young boy."

Her eyes wavered to the dance floor, "How did you come to know Dorian?"

He paused for a moment before saying, "I was but sixteen, aboard a vessel that had been attacked by brigands." The warmth faded from his russet eyes as he relayed his past and Ginelle caught a glimpse of the sad youth he had once been. "The crew and I were left for dead. It wasn't long before another vessel passed by. The Captain found me dispersed across a plank, clinging to life."

"Dorian is your Captain?"

Cummings smiled over at her, "Aye, milady. He is the commander of many a merchant vessels."

Ginelle turned to study Dorian. That swift tightening returned in her chest as he smiled down at the woman in his arms. He was strikingly handsome when he smiled. The woman must be of some significance to Dorian to get such an unlikely response. They appeared the ideal couple. She was exotic and curvaceous, her beauty fit to appeal too many, including Dorian.

"Mademoiselle Pattinson?"

Ginelle averted her eyes from Dorian and the pretty red-haired woman to a man standing above her. He was tall with broad shoulders, emphasized by a deep, gray tailcoat. Glorious locks of pale blond hair peeked out from beneath a woolen, gray top hat.

The man smiled gently at her as he curtsied, his dark eyes glinting curiously at her from beneath full, thick lashes.

Hesitantly, she extended her hand to him and he took her palm lightly between his fingers. He pressed a kiss to her knuckles and than straightened to his full height.

Something about the man's demeanor aroused deep inquiry. His elegance and fine attire indicated his wealth and authority.

"You are Lady Ginelle Pattinson?" his voice was soft, yet firm, inquisitive as he studied her expression.

Ginelle stiffened as a warning sounded in her head. His analytical stare warned her to be wary despite the warmth in is dark eyes. She was comforted by the fact that Lieutenant Cummings sat across from her, studying the stranger in discreet regard.

"I am." She said cautiously, tilting her chin slightly to peer more firmly into the stranger's inquiring gaze. "And you are, Sir?"

His smile broadened as a light appeared in his dark eyes, "I am Lord Edric, milady. I have just recently arrived to London and heard of your debut."

She smiled tentatively, "I am flattered, monsieur. What brings you to London?"

His face brightened as he said, "I am here visiting family."

Ginelle lifted a brow, "Are they here as well?" her eyes scanned the room curiously, suddenly intrigued to know more about this mysterious stranger despite a lingering notion of cautiousness.

"Just one, milady but they are at the moment, occupied." Something about his expression startled her but not so much in a frightening way. The way his eyes studied her, Lord Edric seemed very eager to know her, to learn more about her and she wasn't quite ready to reveal more than necessary to a complete stranger.

"May I interrupt?" Nathaniel suddenly appeared in front of her and she inhaled sharply, stunned to see him. She had worried all evening that he had left but realized he was waiting for an opportune moment to speak with her.

Lord Edric turned to Nathaniel and offered a smile that didn't quite match the gleam in his eyes. He turned back to Ginelle and took her hand in between his. "It was a pleasure speaking with you, mademoiselle."

Ginelle smiled and nodded as his hand lingered around hers until slowly he released her and walked away. She watched him disappear through the crowd before turning to Nathaniel.

Nathaniel did little to conceal his sour expression. "Who is that man?"

Ginelle than realized the man had not revealed his last name. Her heart suddenly dropped in her chest. She didn't know a thing about him aside from his first name.

Her eyes moved warily along the room but it wasn't until they settled on Dorian that she felt the tension slightly ease from her body. Dorian would not let any harm come to her, even if they were at odds with each other.

Nathaniel smiled down at her, all traces of the stranger forgotten as he extended a hand to her. "May I have that dance now, Lady Pattinson?"

She needed a distraction, anything to keep her thoughts from straying towards Dorian and lingering feelings.

She smiled at Lieutenant Cummings before allowing Nathaniel to assist her away. For some reason, she felt as though Lieutenant Cummings had been on the verge to say something but refrained. Did he too, disapprove of Nathaniel?

She dislodged the thought. Of course Lieutenant Cummings would disapprove; he was Dorian's first in command. Dorian could conjure as many absurd allegations of Nathaniel all he wanted. After his humiliating display to ward Nathaniel off, she cared not what Dorian thought, nor would she muse on the startling effect he had on her sensibilities.

"Many are striving to catch your attention." Nathaniel said, pulling her from her thoughts. Even with Nathaniel, she could think of none other than Dorian. "I hope that I have not paled in comparison to any of the young chaps that you might fancy."

Ginelle laughed, "I do not fancy any of them." Instantly her thoughts turned to Dorian and she was greatly relieved when Nathaniel spoke next.

"Ah, so I am still in your favor?" his mouth tilted in a grin. She stared at his mouth, wondering if his kiss would differ from Dorian's. Would she feel that shock of electricity, that tingling throughout her limbs? Would he affect her as intensely as Dorian?

He held her gently as they twirled across the room. His hands didn't move over her as Dorian's had done. He was tender and sweet when Dorian had been rough and abrupt. Yet, something about the way Dorian had touched her had her emotions in such an uproar of chaotic combustion. It was as if she had no control over her body's reactions. Shouldn't she be shocked by her body's wanton response to Dorian's caresses? She was ashamed to admit that there was a longing, buried beneath denial, eager to learn more, to explore the deep recesses of these foreign feelings. No man had ever touched her in such a way. As a child she had feared such a touch and yet, the mere intimate brush of Dorian's fingers along her skin left her breathless.

"Ginelle?"

She jerked to awareness as crimson stained her cheeks, suddenly embarrassed as she realized the direction of her thoughts. "I'm sorry-did you say something?"

He frowned at her, "I said the room is a bit stifling, would you care to get some fresh air?"

Ginelle hesitated, Lucile had stated quite adamantly that leaving the hall was improper, especially with a man who was not her chaperone but she couldn't bare the crowded room a moment longer. She needed some air, anything to clear her head of these unwanted thoughts.

"Yes, that would be nice." She gathered her skirts in one hand and felt Nathaniel grip her elbow as they slipped effortlessly from the room.

The humid air had dropped to a frightening chill and a sudden fiery gust pulled at her hem, bringing her still as a sense of foreboding snaked up her spine.

Ginelle shivered, regretting not having grabbed her cloak as she surveyed the black sky with faint visible lines of thick, rolling clouds.

"I think we should return inside. There is a storm approaching."

Nathaniel stepped in beside her and for a moment she was comforted by his warmth and strength. "There is a terrace just right around the corner. It will shelter us from the rain." Ginelle hesitated, her eyes widening at the bended limbs straining against the menacing wind. Her instincts warned her to return to the hall but she was not ready to return to that crowded room or that piercing hot stare of those vivid blue eyes.

Fingers circled her wrist and she swallowed back a protest as Nathaniel ushered her around the garden to the terrace on the other side before the rain began to fall and a deep rumble of thunder shook the terrain.

She trembled as she stepped further back beneath the canopy, a sudden flare of lightning forcing the air from her lungs. "Can we return to the hall, please?"

"You are safe here." Nathaniel said to ease her fears but somehow she had a deep inkling that she wasn't. A strong innate feeling warned her that something was amiss.

"I want to go back." Her heart began a frantic rhythm and her voice cracked with her fear. She felt small and frightened, just like the child she had been years ago.

"Just a few moments." He said, "Tis difficult to steal you away when Ashford keeps you within his reach. If I weren't mistaken, I think he wants you for himself."

At this, Ginelle turned to stare more directly at Nathaniel, her brows knitting together at his absurd allegation. "Surely you don't think that?"

"I am speaking only from having observed his manner, the man is completely, and hopelessly infatuated with you."

Ginelle blanched as her heart did a strange, somersault in her chest. "Nathaniel you speak nonsense!"

He stepped towards her and she stiffened, "I cannot blame him, any man would be a fool to not want you."

Dorian's distinct warning about Nathaniel's reputation rushed to mind. Was he truly a fortune hunter? She didn't want to believe it. She couldn't fathom the very thought that she had been so naïve to trust another man and yet, the feelings she had hoped to feel for Nathaniel were not there.

She wondered for a moment if Nathaniel's kiss would be as electrifying as Dorian's? Could he stir her senses in a heated frenzy like Dorian?

Nathaniel reached out and cupped her face. Her reaction surprised her. She was not affected by his touch; in fact, his touch had no real strong pull on her senses.

He closed his eyes and leaned towards her. She knew he was going to kiss her and sudden curiosity kept her still as his mouth plastered against hers. Instantly, she felt revulsion stir in her belly as his mouth moved sloppily over her own. His kisses were wet and did little but disgust her.

Ginelle pulled away but his arm around her waist stopped her. Fear scuttled through her but she remained firm as she said, "I think it best we return to the hall." Her eyes sparked with defiance as she struggled to conceal the rising anxiety to the swift and unexpected change in Nathaniel's disposition.

"I studied you, Ginelle. I watched you discard suitor after suitor. Their excessive wealth could not appease you." His finger traced her chin and she shivered inwardly with revulsion. "I know I can be that man to make you happy."

Ginelle wanted nothing more than to shove Nathaniel away. How could she have ever thought him charming, or handsome? He thought she turned suitors away simply because their wealth did not satisfy her? That alone sickened her deeply.

"I am sorry Nathaniel, but I will not marry you." She exclaimed.

He frowned, suddenly perplexed. "I do not understand."

She pressed her hands against his chest to push, an indication for him to release her. "I have no desire to marry." She said, "I am sorry but I will only disappoint you."

A sudden crack of thunder startled them both but Nathaniel's arms did not fall away. Rain began to descend in dark torrents, soaking the terrain around the terrace. "Mayhap I can change your mind?"

His mouth suddenly crashed down on hers. She opened her lips to object but her protests were smothered by his roughened kisses and the rain pelting the ground. She squeaked in alarm as his lips bruised her own as thunder rumbled deeply in the clouds. She felt a fleeting moment of panic as she felt the strength in his arms as they tightened around her, pressing her closer against him. Her fingers curled in his shirt in an effort to shove him away but his tightened embrace proved futile to escape his clutches.

Suddenly, a large and solid frame separated from the shadows. A looming and frightening silhouette that advanced on Nathanial, wrenching him away.

Ginelle quickly stumbled back as a massive body placed itself between her and Nathaniel. She stared at Dorian's rigid back shaking with fury. Her eyes widened as he drew back his fist and delivered a thunderous blow to Nathaniel's face, the fierce momentum sending him sprawling backwards off the terrace.

Ginelle leapt forward as Dorian followed Nathaniel's sprawling body. As he reared back to deliver another hard crack to Nathaniel's bloodied face, she reached out and grabbed his upraised arm. "Dorian, no!"

Her distinct plea jarred him from the haze of red clouding his vision. He peered down at Sharp, nursing his bloodied nose and snorted in disgust.

"Let's make something clear." The words were released on a deep growl, "Touch her again, Sharp and I'll kill you."

Nathaniel's eyes narrowed but he refrained from saying anything that could potentially break another bone in his face. He staggered to his feet, careful to cradle his broken nose in his palm as he left on hastened strides.

Dorian slowly turned to Ginelle. She was drenched and trembling. The rain had ruined her curls, plastering her hair to her face and shoulders. His eyes narrowed on her swollen lips from Sharp's kisses and he felt a maddening rage seize him and her large eyes widened with fear. Did she fear for her lover?

"Did you enjoy playing the harlot?" his voice revealed his anger and Ginelle winced beneath the hardness of his cold stare. "You let him touch you? Kiss you?" he stalked towards her, forcing her to retreat back under the terrace.

Ginelle was breathless, stunned by his livid manner. He stood over her, dangerous and unpredictable in all his untamed fury.

"I gave you fair warning." His gazed seared her, his eyes like shards of ice as panic seized her.

She narrowed her eyes at him, enraged that he would make such a blatant remark of her. How dare he say such things when he had acted irrationally, with the full intent of humiliating her and even have the audacity to order her about!

"I do not find fault in kissing the man I intend on marrying." She would never admit that he had been right all along about Nathaniel, nor was she going to acknowledge the fact that she had been utterly naïve to Nathaniel's pretenses.

A blue flame gathered in his eyes as he stepped towards her, and immediately Ginelle realized her mistake in taunting him. She felt cold stone at her back and stiffened as his arms stretched out on either side of her.

Her mouth parted on a gasp at the proximity of his body and that strange and explicit heat spiraled low in her belly, tingling throughout her limbs until her knees threatened to buckle. She stared up at him through large eyes and had an uncontrollable urge to reach up and tuck loose strands of black hair from his face.

His blue eyes moved over her, peeling away her defenses until her body trembled from the burning desire in his icy depths.

Her heart jumped against her chest and her stomach fluttered as his eyes averted to her mouth, and the fire in his eyes intensified, burning with a heated promise.

Dorian reached up and traced the delicate curve of her cheek and brushed a tendril of hair away with his thumb. He was furious with her, so angry that he could tear Sharp from limb to limb for touching her as he so painfully longed to do.

She deliberately taunted him and yet, she stood before him, trembling and frightened of his temper. It angered him that she would think him capable of hurting her. He couldn't fathom the disquieting notion; it sickened him.

He could see the fear in her eyes, just below her thin resolve and it unsettled him deeply. A disturbing thought came to him as he studied her face. What had his mother thought in the brunt of his father's anger?

He felt the muscle at his jaw flex. He was nothing like his father. He would never hurt a female, especially the beautiful creature standing before him but did she think him certain of violence?

Another step brought him closer until he felt her breasts pushing against his chest, she tensed, her eyes widened to large pools of soft brown as she peered up at him. "Why do you fear me?"

Her unguarded gaze revealed surprise and his eyes fell to her mouth as she spoke, "I do not fear you." He searched her face knowing beneath her defiance was a frightened woman with secrets of her own.

Dorian had every intention of unraveling her defenses. He wanted to know the woman past the barriers. "You are a pretty liar, Ginelle." He leaned towards her and felt his body harden as she responded, her chest rising sharply with her shortness of breath.

Her heart quickened in her chest as her blood rushed through her veins with anticipation. He thought she feared him and she did, but for reasons other than his temper. She feared this man because she had never met another like him. His body spoke of intimacies that stirred her in ways that she thought incapable of experiencing and that frightened her the most.

She knew as she stared up into his dark face that she wanted his kisses, wanted the touch of his fingers on her skin and ached for those intoxicating feelings that left her yearning for more, but she feared her body's reaction, she feared she would give her heart to this man who would never return her love.

He had stated quite adamantly that he wanted her, desired her as a man would for a woman but was that all? Did he simply want her because his body demanded it? Did his heart bespoke of affection?

Her heart somersaulted in her chest as his mouth descended and captured hers and he crushed her against his chest. She gasped, opening her mouth to him as his arm tightened around her waist and he reached up to cup her face in his other hand. She felt his heart beating against her own as if the two of them were meant for each other.

She grew breathless with the intensity of his kisses and the possessiveness of his claim as his tongue delved inside and her legs buckled, forcing her to rely on his strength. She felt her fears slowly dissipate with the moment as everything around them spiraled out of place as that tiny flame flickered to life, growing with each sweep of his tongue. His mouth skimmed lightly across her own, a gentle butterfly caress; making her heart flutter chaotically against her breast.

His kiss was tender and rough; passionate in its claim on her but as badly as her body yearned for this moment, logic began to take place. She had been so naïve of Nathaniel, she had actually considered him passably acceptable to marriage only to be played a fool for his advances spoke of his true nature.

How could she allow Dorian to touch her when he wanted only to claim her? He wanted to control her, just like every man. She did not love Dorian, but what did it mean when her body responded so wantonly to his touch when Nathaniel sparked revulsion?

His hand reached up to cup her breast and an intense burning erupted at the base of his fingers, flowing through her body like a hot stream to douse her coherent thoughts. She struggled to gain her composure but the tantalizing effect left her trembling and her womanhood tingling for something she knew not.

Dorian hated her, she said as if to convince herself. She had to stop this before he hurt her, before he left her hollow and broken.

"No, stop." She stiffened as she shoved her hands against his chest, feeling the rippling muscle shift beneath her fingers; she jerked her hands back as if to ward that hardened flesh for it burned with his raw desire.

Dorian pulled back, his eyes narrowing to dark slits of ice, studying her intently with sudden pique. "You submit wantonly to Sharp's advances but deny me your affects?"

Ginelle gasped in outrage, startled by how abruptly his mood had shifted from tender and passionate to a sudden cruelness that altered him completely. Stunned by how hurtful his words had wounded her, she acted on impulse and brought her hand around to smack soundly against his face.

His arms fell away at the impact of her hand and he watched her flee from beneath hooded eyes. Ginelle wiped blindly at the tears streaking her face and the rain combined made it impossible to see where she was running.

The wind struck her full blown in the face and she cringed as a bolt of lightning cut across the blackened sky. She gathered her sodden skirts and rushed from the garden, not caring if Dorian followed. How dare him! How could he stir such startling feelings that left her yearning for more and yet, make her hate him so!

She swept past the double glass doors, unaware to the figure garbed in red as she slipped along the wet grass and rounded the corner, colliding roughly with another body. She and the stranger tumbled to the ground and rolled twice before she was able to steady herself. Her heavy skirts made it difficult for her to gain her footing and when she finally did, the stranger had already risen to stare at her through gleaming black eyes of shock and malice.

The dark face leering back at her instilled absolute fear and she froze with horror, her feet riveted to the ground as she stared wide-eyed at the man sneering back at her. Ginelle gasped in profound dismay as she took a step back, her mouth parting to utter the name of the man who implanted terror in her bones.

"Pierino."

Chapter 12

His face had aged much over the past couple of years, a significant amount of alcohol partaking in the unmistakable withered face staring back at Ginelle. His eyes were still as sharp and obsidian. His hair was brushed back from his face, revealing those familiar distinct angles of cruelty.

Pierino's granite eyes moved over the length of her, taking in her soaked gown and slipper-adorned feet. His mouth twisted into a sinister sneer as he reached down to retrieve his hat and righted it atop his head. "Ye startled me, kitten."

"Don't call me that." Her voice cracked as she watched him cautiously, carefully stepping left as he advanced right.

A glint of surprise surfaced in his black eyes as he studied the defiant little woman glaring back at him. If not for the large, unguarded brown eyes, he would have overlooked this impertinent female but there was no mistaking the eyes or pale hair.

A deep chuckle rose from his throat as he swept out his arms, "Who would have thought out of sheer luck ye would fall practically into my hands while I am out plundering, eh?" he began circling her, his eyes assessing her appearance. "Ye have managed far better than I expected. Tell me-" his eyes narrowed as he nudged his head towards the golden hall, "-who are ye to these braggarts?"

Ginelle struggled to keep her fears at bay. She cast a glance towards the hall where the murmur of the crowd and band were barely intangible over the loud crack of thunder. No one would hear her scream if she attempted.

"What are you doing here?" she asked hoping to distract him as she searched for a means of escape.

Her chest swelled with fear as he took a step towards her, "One has to make a living." He said in a toneless voice, his eyes narrowed dangerously. "I am not entirely satisfied with how ye have compensated for me generous act. Yer debt is not paid."

"Who are you to extract this debt?" she demanded, "I owe you nothing."

His face twisted with anger that darkened his ebony eyes. "It seems time apart, garbed in fancy garments has made ye brave, but yer bravery has made ye foolish." He extended a hand to her, "Ye will come with me now lest I drag yer body myself."

Terror threatened to render her numb and she struggled with her wavering defiance. "I will never return to you."

He dropped his hand, "Vera' well."

Pierino lunged for her and a cry of anguish tore from her throat as she turned to flee. Trepidation paralyzed her limbs and she stumbled while those fears and horrors that lay dormant, came flooding back in horrifying recognition. The memory of her father's death and those torturous years spent with Pierino came rushing back in vivid detail, shattering her sheltered solace.

A scream lodged in her throat as his hand seized painfully around her arm. She pivoted her body and raked her nails across his face, drawing thin streaks of blood across his cheek. Pierino yelped as his face shifted with malice and his fingers tightened around her arm, drawing a cry past her lips as he drew back his fist.

Pain exploded across her jaw as the impact sent her reeling. Her body collided roughly with the ground and her surroundings spiraled into vertigo. She clenched her eyes against the hazy red cloud as she struggled to pull her body up.

She felt herself being lifted and panic erupted in her chest as she raised her elbow, bringing it up with enough force to connect with Pierino's ribs. He released her abruptly and clutched his wounded side. Ginelle gathered her heavy skirts in one hand as she scrambled to her feet and began to run.

She cleared the garden and spotted a row of carriages lined side by side. Her eyes searched warily for a means of escape and she spotted a lone horse just beneath a tree.

The storm erupted violently and a streak of lightning lit the sky, revealing towering trees looming in the distance. Tears streaked her grimy face and the pain registering left her jaw throbbing. She felt bile rising in her throat as her fears threatened to consume her as she started towards the single horse.

A voice called to her from beyond the thunder and she felt her heart skip in her chest as she fought to bring air into her lungs.

Her hands shook violently as she seized the reins and jerked them from the tree. In her frantic efforts, her feet slid along the wet grass and she fell. Her abrupt approach sent the horse reeling upward, panicking as thunder rumbled, shaking the ground beneath her.

That voice again called to her, demanding.

Terrified, Ginelle gained her footing and fumbled for the reins of the panicked horse. The frightened animal whinnied and reared, her eyes widened in horror as its hooves raised high above her and she faltered back, paralyzed in a shell of shock.

An iron band wrapped around her waist as an alarming fear gripped her and as she turned to fight her attacker, everything went black.

Dorian lifted Ginelle as her body went limp in his arms, cradling her against his chest. Perplexed by her reaction, he reached up and gently brushed wet strands of hair from her face. As his hand skimmed lightly along her cheek, his fingers paused and his expression darkened fiercely at the tender, swollen jaw beneath his touch.

His eyes moved over her unconscious frame, taking note of the dark streaks of mud staining her skirts and pieces of her dress torn in several places, indicating a struggle. Gritting his teeth, he knelt to lay her gently on the ground; quickly removing his cloak to wrap her trembling body within its folds.

He reached beneath her and lifted her easily against him. Her head lolled back over his arm and as he moved towards their carriage, he vowed silently to kill the man that would dare harm his woman.

Victoria watched from the shadows, a curvaceous silhouette fuming silently, observing Dorian and the unconscious girl in his arms as he made his way to a carriage.

She narrowed her eyes venomously for she was keen to notice the way her former lover cradled his new obsession so tenderly. She felt bile in her throat at the affectionate display.

Who was this Dorian that harbored such warmth and ardor for a small sprite of a girl? What did the little wench have that she did not? The girl was nothing more than a mere child with no curves to appease a man's arousal.

Did she not possess the body for Dorian's lustful appetite?

She felt a grin tug at the corners of her mouth for she was well aware that Ginelle Pattinson was not whom she claimed to be. Having witnessed her violent encounter with the dark-eyed stranger, she had an immediate means to ridding herself of this unwanted distraction.

Who was Ginelle Pattinson, she wondered? Whoever the girl happens to be, she knew of someone in particular that wanted the girl and she would see to it that the man get what he wanted so as long as she gets what she wants.

She stood in the darkness, alone and frightened. No, she wasn't alone; Ginelle could hear a deep, heavy breath as if it bore down upon the nape of her neck. She reached up to grip her mother's locket only to touch skin bare of the silver chain. She gasped, horrified as her fingers skimmed her throat and neck, frantically searching. Her locket was gone!

She whirled violently, her eyes moving warily around her surroundings but she could see nothing in the dark, could feel nothing but a dull pain surfacing from her jaw and a fear combined. There was nothing in the extent of the black void, that is, until a lithe shadow slipped effortlessly into her line of sight.

She froze.

The shadow inched forward, taking shape and form into a horrifying image, a face with sharp, glinting eyes like pointed daggers stared back at her, menacing and violent. Large hands snaked out from the darkness and seized her roughly around her throat, that bare flesh vacant of her precious necklace now bore the marks of a monster.

She screamed.

"Be still, ma petite, you are safe." A voice, deep and masculine, spoke to her through the darkness; whispering and drawing her away from the creature vowing to destroy her. She held strongly to that voice for it was reassuring, a hushed promise to keep her safe from her demon.

She felt herself surfacing and was instantly aware of arms holding her, cradling her gently as fingers brushed strands of hair from her face.

For a moment, she thought her father had finally come for her, to take her with him to heaven but as she opened her mouth to utter his name, pain resonated sharply through her jaw. She struggled to open her eyes but they remained heavy and firmly shut.

She was so cold. Why did her body feel so cold? Didn't that mean she was dead? Where was her father? She felt panic swelling in her chest and sought the blissful darkness. She listened for his voice and felt a rising alarm. Her savior was fading; his voice and the comforting strength of his arms, all fading, whoever he may be.

Her body was afire, her limbs scorching as she thrashed against layers of cloth holding her down. She felt hands, all over, prodding along her legs, fingers digging, searching. A bolt of alarm shot through her as she tried opening her eyes. They were so heavy, a black heady cloud kept her motionless, unable to respond.

She drifted in and out of oblivion, struggling against the hands moving over her heated flesh. Her mouth felt raw and dry, as if sand had been poured down her throat but the scream came easily to her.

Her body arched on its own accord, thrashing against the hands to hold her firmly in place. Confusion and fear collided within her mind as her eyes flailed in a feeble attempt to ward off her many attackers. Had her demon found her?

"Lay still, little one. I am here." That voice, so dark yet beautiful like black velvet came to her, calming her fears. She felt that familiar strength wrap around her, pulling her close against something solid and warm.

She wanted to fight, fearful that her demon would come for her, its obsidian eyes and wicked sneer revealing its malicious intent. She would never be safe.

I am here. The voice had said. Her fear lessened with the reassuring notion that her savior had returned, that no harm would come to her so as long he was near.

Blackness.

Flames gathered and cracked within the hearth, exhibiting a subtle glow to sketch the small form lying in the center of the bed in soft shades of gold.

Dorian moved to the side of the bed, his eyes moving over her sleeping face to rest firmly upon the large, ugly bruise marring her dewy complexion.

She groaned in her sleep, relaying a name that had been a reoccurrence since he put her to bed.

A budding fury swelled within his chest for this Pierino had left his mark of violence on this small, delicate woman for a reason he knew not and he vowed to find and kill the bastard.

He moved and settled on the mattress beside her and reached out to brush a silver strand from her face. As if sensing his touch, she turned her cheek into his palm.

She had been bedridden for two days, her body fighting a fever that would not submit. Her mouth parted on a gasp and Dorian stiffened as her head jerked against the pillow. Beads of perspiration gathered along her forehead, bathing her throat and chest. Cursing under his breath, Dorian swept to his feet and moved towards the door, jerking it open he bellowed for Lucile.

Lucile appeared within moments with a frantic Belle trailing at her heels. Dorian stood aside, his fists clenched as the older woman moved to press the back of her hand to Ginelle's forehead. "I have summoned the doctor, Monsieur."

Dorian felt a sickening, increasing fear rise in his chest, churning his stomach as he watched her thrash, her ashen complexion indicating the depth of her fever.

"Milord!" cried Belle as the maid stumbled away from the bed as Lucile struggled to keep Ginelle down against the mattress.

He moved forward and gently seized her flailing arms, pressing them down at her sides to cease any further movement. Her skin burned beneath his fingers as she arched against the pillows, her mouth parting with incoherent words slurred in her delirium.

A servant appeared at the door and Lucile moved forward to speak with him.

"Where the hell is the doctor?" Dorian roared.

"The doctor is unobtainable, Monsieur." Her face paled with apprehension, fearing she would lose her young mistress.

"Take her, Lucile." The older woman moved forward as Dorian reluctantly released Ginelle. He rushed to his feet and swept an unsteady hand through his tousled hair. Belle stood helplessly aside, wringing her hands nervously in her apron as she watched Dorian pace back and forth.

He halted his face darkening as he addressed the maid, "Have my men bring a tub immediately to my room. Fill it with cold water." Belle nodded and rushed to his demand.

Dorian stood over the bed as her body twisted in the coverlets, her chemise soaked to the skin. He reached out and stroked her hair as he whispered to her, his voice coaxing her to relax, unaware that the housekeeper watched.

Eloise was gone. He was not ready to lose Ginelle.

His men arrived moments later, bracing a tub in their hands as they placed it before the hearth followed by others trailing behind lugging pitchers of water. He continued to stroke her hair, watching her face as they proceeded to fill the tub.

Lucile fell in at his side and gently laid a hand on his shoulder, "Monsieur, allow me."

He moved to his feet and bellowed, "Leave."

The men hastened from the room but Lucile lingered, "Milord, let me-"

He reached down and gathered Ginelle in his arms, nestling her close against his chest as he turned and carried her to the tub with Lucile at his heels. The older woman remained silent as he lowered her to the tub and the cold water swept over her feverish body.

He proceeded to palm water into his hand, gently caressing her face and chest and slowly her wrestling limbs settled in the water.

"Give me a cloth."

Lucile handed him a cloth and he dipped it in the water and continued to dab at her face, the expanse of her throat and chest.

"Her fever is breaking." Lucile said from over his shoulder.

He felt the tension steadily slipping from her limbs as she fell blissfully asleep. "I need more blankets." He ordered.

Lucile nodded, "I will have Cook prepare some tea and toast." She said as she quietly left the room.

Dorian continued to dab her face with the wet cloth, relieved to see a bit of color return to her cheeks. He knew in that moment that losing Ginelle was simply intolerable. He cursed the day his sister had brought her to the plantation, for he had forever lost his heart to her.

Chapter 13

Her eyes fluttered open to stare blankly up at the wide, extended ceiling above her. Ginelle closed her eyes and opened them again to clear her vision as she searched the walls of her mind for a means to how she ended up like this.

Her eyes widened as she stared around the room, the surroundings unfamiliar to her. Panic escalated through her chest. Where was she?

She lay unmoving, her mind plagued with questions. The room was dark, lit with a dim glow provided by the dying fire across the room. She could just make out the outlines of furniture, masculine furniture. The room was done in dark, warm hues which indicated the presence of a man.

Her panic increased with each parched breath as she studied the contents of the empty room. What manner of man occupied the room?

Suddenly, vague images scuttled through her mind. Ginelle froze, her eyes relaying the events that led her to this moment.

The banquet. She squeezed her eyes shut, specifically recalling the storm that had soaked her gown. Her heart became an erratic drum within her chest.

Nathaniel. Her eyes jerked open, remembering their moment beneath the terrace. She groaned as she turned her head on the pillow, eagerly pushing pass the foggy haze. Why was she clouded? Why couldn't she think straight?

Dorian. She had been angry with Dorian.

Pierino!

"No!" she gasped. She bolted upright in bed as her eyes moved warily around the remnants of the darkened room, suddenly aware of every shifting shadow. Had he found her?

Everything was so terribly clear. Pierino had found her!

Ginelle pressed her lips firmly together against the bile rising in her throat as her stomach churned with dread. Her hair fell over her shoulder as she jerked on the layers of coverlets.

She reached out to grip the post of the canopy, surprised that her legs were unsteady as she gathered to her height.

She whimpered as a tear streaked her face. No, she could not register the thought. Pierino knew where she was, he had found her, nearly four years later and he had found her.

Her knees threatened to buckle and she grasped the post to steady her balance as she clenched her eyes shut against the wave of vertigo.

She had to run; he would find her. He would always find her or was it too late? Ginelle jerked her head up to peer around the room, her face paling against the dusk glow emitting from the hearth.

Was this Pierino's room? It couldn't be, she thought, shaking her head as if to convince herself. She remembered the horse as she rushed to get away but after that moment everything went dark.

She acted on fear and alarm as she pushed away from the bed-post and moved towards the door, her instincts warning her to flee. A sudden, intense wave of dizziness seized her and she felt herself fumbling to catch her balance as she stumbled over the carpet. She hit the floor with such an impact, it rendered her breathless.

Stunned and suddenly furious by how weak and helpless she was, she scrambled to pull herself up just as the door to the room jerked open.

The tears came flooding in a rush of panic for she couldn't fight Pierino in this weakened condition. She was defenseless.

Ginelle braced herself for the attack and stiffened with shock as something warm and solid slipped beneath her back and legs lifting her effortlessly. She stiffened in the solid arms wrapped securely around her and twisted against the masculine chest, frantic and afraid.

"Easy, little one." That voice. She knew that voice and the relief that flooded through her was so immaculate that she began to cry, not from fear but from the realization that she was safe, safe and with Dorian.

Dorian settled Ginelle on the bed, clearly taken aback by the fear in her eyes and the tears that streaked her pale face. She trembled beneath his hand as he reached up to push her hair from her face and she turned her head away to shield her eyes, to hide the tears that kept coming.

His jaw tightened.

Pierino. The name came to him along with the tide of fury. She had uttered the name many times. He realized just how little he knew about her and he had every intention of finding out just who this man, Pierino, was to her.

He continued to stroke her hair, loving the way the silken tresses easily slid through his fingers. His eyes drifted over her and realized in her fall the chemise had drifted lower, revealing a smooth creamy shoulder and the soft mounds of her breasts. He felt a groan in his throat and he shifted his eyes from the beautiful skin that had tempted him every night this past sennight.

"What frightens you, ma petite?" his voice coaxed her to look at him. When she turned her head, he was struck by how lovely she was in that moment. Her large eyes rimmed in thick, feather-black lashes wet with her tears, and he resisted the urge to lean down and kiss the tears from her eyes.

She said nothing but just looked at him. He reached out to trace her lower lip and she jerked from his hand.

Dorian shook his head, "I would not hurt you, Ginelle."

She wanted to believe him, so desperately she did. She had been so naïve to let her guard down. She had allowed herself a moment to trust a man and it had nearly cost her, her life. Pierino had come close to finding her. If she had not trusted Nathaniel as she had done, she would not have been in the garden and she would not have fallen into Pierino's hands.

"Who is Pierino?"

Her heart lurched in her breast as she jerked her eyes around to Dorian. How did he know about Pierino? She averted her gaze to the door, frightened to speak of the man whom she thought never to think on again.

Strong fingers circled her chin and pulled her head back around to peer into those intense, blue eyes. "You will answer me."

"Why?" she demanded, her voice dry as she spoke, "So that you can deliver me back to that monster?" she was breathless, her voice rimmed with pain.

Dorian frowned, "What makes you think I would do that?"

"It is clear to the both of us that you have not wanted me here from the beginning. Why must we prolong this any longer?" despite her unshed tears and the weakness in her voice, she lifted her chin with defiance, "You may send me anywhere but back to that man."

His eyes narrowed to dark slits of blue ice as he said, "Who is he to you?"

"Why does it matter to you?" she hissed.

Ginelle stiffened as he leaned down; pressing a fist into the lushness of the pillow surrounding her head as his face hovered above her own. "You will tell me, Ginelle because I ask it of you." She sensed the danger in the undertone of his voice and shivered.

"He is- was my guardian."

He made no indication of moving and Ginelle found it extremely difficult to breath for the air was filled with a masculine musk, tingling her senses as his blue eyes searched her face.

Her tongue darted out to lick her parted lips and his eyes followed the innocent gesture. "How did this man become your guardian?" the tone of his voice dropped to a deeper pitch and a spark of hunger flared in his icy depths, startling Ginelle.

"I-I was orphaned at nine. Pierino found me on the streets. He took me in."

Dorian's eyes moved over her face, knowing she was leaving out crucial details but he didn't press her, not yet.

"You can trust me, Ginelle."

He took notice that her lower lip trembled as she said. "I trust no man."

"You gave me such a fright." Lucile said, crossing the room to push open the heavy drapes.

Ginelle lifted a hand to block the sudden flare of sunlight as it flickered throughout the room, which consisted of an armoire of deep mahogany done in rich, intricate carvings. The bed in which she sat was massive, fit for a king or yet, a man of intense size. A small dining table took up one corner of the room adorned with candles and a spread of what looked to be a map of some sort. A love seat of walnut base sat before a grand hearth made of elaborate marble and she wondered how many nights Dorian sat before the fire, his massive size filling every inch of the love seat.

"I want to thank you, Lucile."

Lucile paused in gathering the discarded clothing about the room. "For what, pet?"

"For tending to me while I was ill."

Lucile shook her head, "I did not tend to you, my dear."

Ginelle frowned, "You did not?"

The older woman shook her head, "You may say I was not permitted."

"What do you mean?"

Lucile bent down to retrieve a towel from the floor and rolled it up in her hands as she moved to stand at Ginelle's side. "Monsieur Dorian would not permit anyone to see to you, including myself."

Ginelle gasped, "What?"

The housekeeper nodded, "He is the one that saw to you." As the older woman turned away to finish straightening the room, Ginelle could specifically recall strong arms holding her, reassuring her during those feverish moments.

"I shall have water sent up for your bath." Lucile said as she started towards the door and at this Ginelle turned crimson. Surely Dorian had not bathed her as well?

It wasn't long before the men arrived; lugging pitchers of steaming water and Ginelle shielded her body from the men as they proceeded to fill it to the rim. She noticed that neither of them looked her way and she turned even redder at what they might be thinking with her lying half naked in Dorian's bed.

Lucile returned moments later and helped Ginelle from bed, despite her protests that she was perfectly fine, the older woman insisted on assisting her. She removed her chemise and slipped blissfully into the water.

Lucile stoked the fire once more and than started for the door. Ginelle sat up abruptly and water splashed over the edges of the tub onto the floor. "Where are you going?"

The older woman paused with her hand on the latch, "I'm going to get some fresh linen for the bed and a clean towel. I had Cook prepare a tray of porridge for you. I will only be but a moment."

Ginelle sank deeper into the tub as Lucile left the room. She closed her eyes and focused on the water and how it soothed her tired bones. She detested being confined to the bed, having others to wait on her so it was nice that she could have this moment to herself.

Suddenly, images of Pierino flooded her thoughts, startling her. She jerked her eyes open as she focused on steady, even breaths as she quickly sought her mind for a distraction, something to keep her from straying towards the terrifying realization that Pierino could find her again.

He is the one that saw to you. Lucile's words startled her. Dorian had tended to her while she was with fever? Dorian had held her, whispered to her as she treaded on the edge of darkness with her demon, Pierino, trailing at her heels?

Why would he do such a thing if he cared nothing for her?

A noise indicated that Lucile had returned with the towel. She closed her eyes, comforted by the fact that the older woman was there as the water molded to her body, keeping the slight chill of the room at bay.

She felt a butterfly caress along her shoulder. Her eyes wrenched open as she jerked around to peer up at Dorian, standing over the tub. She gasped as her arms instinctively rushed to cover her nakedness. "What are you doing?" she gasped, outraged. "Get out!"

He grinned as he dropped the towel and it landed on the floor at his feet. He knelt beside the tub, his eyes like ice in the morning sunlight. "This is my room." He said as he reached over the rim of the tub and his fingers dabbed at the water, his hand not far from her naked thigh.

She watched him cautiously, breathless as her eyes fixated on his handsome face. "Then allow me to return to the privacy of my own room."

His grin broadened as his eyes moved leisurely over her body, making her keenly aware of her nakedness. "I think not." He said, "I like the thought of you in my bed. "

Ginelle stiffened. What game was he playing? She was not a possession. She fumed silently. He had seen to her illness, had taken good care of her, but that did not give him the right to invade her privacy.

"I think you should leave." She turned her head, unable to stare into that heated gaze.

His hand left the water and she hadn't realized she had been holding her breath until she released it. He stood to his full height, towering over her in all his masculine glory and she felt a shiver of excitement race up her spine.

She had not seen him since she had been well and obviously, he had been working in the fields. The sleeves of his tunic were rolled to his elbows, the collar open at the chest to reveal hard, bronze muscle. His black hair lay loose and untamed on his broad shoulders, swept back from his face as if he had run his fingers through it continuously.

He bent down and picked up the towel and held it out to her. She stared at him as if he had lost his wits. "I can see to myself, thank you."

He smirked, his blue eyes glinting like shards of ice. "You seem to forget that I've seen every inch of your loveliness."

Ginelle gasped as heat crept up her neck.

His face hardened, "Now get out of the tub."

"I would rather wait for Lucile."

"She's occupied at the moment."

Her eyes narrowed on his handsome, rugged face as she said, "I care not that you've seen me naked but I refuse to get out until you leave. It is improper."

The corners of his mouth quirked into a devilish grin as he said, "I am not a man of comeliness, Ginelle. I see fit to do as I please."

"Why are you doing this?" she demanded, "Why can't you just send for Lucile?"

Dorian leaned down and braced his hands on the tub, his eyes burning into her as they settled on her mouth. "I want you." His eyes moved over her face as if searching for a reason to why he burned so badly for this small female, "I want you and I will make sure no man will have you."

Ginelle was stunned into silence. What did he mean?

As if reading her thoughts, he continued. "You will not marry Nathaniel Sharp, or any of the men that appeal to you."

She released a rush of air in outrage. "You think you can just change your mind when it pleases you to do so? I am not some possession to be placed on a shelf and then taken down!"

A black brow arched, "You are not pleased?"

Ginelle quickly clamped down on the words that rushed up from her throat. Of course she was pleased, she was absolutely ecstatic that she was not being forced to marry, but she was furious that he would make demands of her so easily without her consent.

She narrowed her eyes at him as a thought occurred to her, "If you do not wish for me to marry, then what is it that you want?"

Her eyes widened as he reached down into the tub and lifted her out of the water. She gasped, furious and humiliated as her naked body fell against his chest. She scrambled in his arms as he crossed the room in three easy strides and deposited her on the bed.

He settled beside her as she scrambled to hide her nakedness from him but he reached out and began to dry her arms with the towel. She jerked away from him, her eyes like daggers. "Stop that!"

Dorian dropped the towel, smirking as his blue eyes burned a trail over her lithe body. Ginelle fumbled for the coverlets and wrenched them over her body, burning to the tip of her toes as she resisted the urge to pummel him with her fists.

"You will answer me." She demanded, lifting her chin to glare venomously at him.

He leaned forward, forcing her back against the pillows. His mouth hovered inches above her own and she was struck by the hunger burning blatantly in those icy depths. "That is a matter that should be discussed at a more convenient time when you are-" he paused, his eyes dropping to her parted lips, "-properly dressed."

Ginelle clenched the blanket tighter to her chest as he released her and stalked from the room, the message in his eyes leaving her shaking, with fear or excitement, she knew not.

Ginelle was relieved to return to the familiar confines of her room. She deliberately avoided Dorian. His words had stirred something deep and unknown within her. He frightened her. Yet, something about the way he looked at her, despite her fear of him, warmed her blood. She had never known a man like Dorian Don Ashford. His sheer size alone intimidated her but his frankness alarmed her.

I want you.

Each night she went to bed with those words replaying in her thoughts. She avoided him because she couldn't fathom the feelings he made her feel. She couldn't control the way her body trembled when he was near, aching for his touch. She was always painfully aware of his presence. She had thought he hated her but he had tended to her so gently.

He spent most of his time in the fields, working along side his men. She would watch from afar, fascinated by the rippling muscles of his hardened physique, the way they strained as he moved about, his back flexing with each movement. She would catch herself and immediately withdraw from these thoughts, ashamed that she would think such things.

She dressed that morning in a gown of soft, green muslin. She had lost a little weight so the gown was not as tight around her midriff. Her flaxen hair lay straight on her shoulders, falling down her back in a silken stream. She basked in the morning light as a northern breeze caressed her face, stirring the silver-blond strands into disarray.

She paused on her way outside, her eyes settling on the barn. It was a pleasant day to go riding. She could hear the horses on the inside, whinnying and pacing within their stalls, beckoning to her.

Ginelle stiffened as she heard the distinct fall of hooves. Her heart somersaulted as she turned to assess the black stallion coming her way.

Dorian stared down at her from the saddle, his ice-blue eyes moving over her frame in a smoldering caress. The acute angles of his face were sharp and more direct beneath the sunlight, his white tunic bright in contrast to his golden, dark skin.

"You are causing a commotion among my laborers." His voice was laced with anger and disapproval.

Ginelle frowned as she peeked around him, aghast to see that all eyes were on her. "I am but walking." She said, turning back to him.

Dorian dismounted and stepped towards her. Ginelle stepped back. He stood a good several inches over six feet where she barely reached his chest. "Any man would be a fool to look upon you and at the moment my field is full of them."

She blinked up at him. If she were not mistaken, she sensed jealousy on the edge of his voice. "There is no injustice in taking a walk."

The muscle at his jaw ticked as he said, "I would prefer if you stayed well out of sight of my men."

Ginelle shivered at the thought of falling into the hands of one of his laborers. She knew not what the men had been convicted of, nor did she have any intention of finding out.

She nodded, "Very well." She glanced at the stable, saddened at the thought that she would not be able to ride.

She turned to leave but his voice stopped her. "Ride with me."

Ginelle looked up at him, "Pardon?"

He stepped towards her and the deep spices of his skin stirred her senses. "Take a ride with me."

Her heart accelerated at the thought but when she stared at the black, snorting beast behind him, she took a step back.

He extended a hand to her, "You'll be safe with me, Ginelle."

She stared at that hand and than at the dark, handsome face peering back at her. He would keep her safe from the horse but what would protect her from him?

Hesitantly, she placed her hand in his.

Chapter 14

This ride was unlike any other. She could feel the stallion's powerful muscles shift beneath her as the beast took flight, its massive hooves pounding into the dirt. Exhilaration rushed through her veins as she closed her eyes and let the wind tease her hair but it was the solid male at her back that made her heart pulse erratically in her chest.

Ginelle was keenly aware of the muscled arm wrapped around her waist, holding her firmly against his chest and encased between his large thighs. The scent of him, musky and strictly male, wrapped around her senses.

So absorbed in the ride and the man at her back, she wasn't aware of their destination until they reined in before the stream she bathed in the day he found her.

Dorian said nothing as he dismounted and lifted his hands to help her down. She immediately stepped back from him for the heat from his body scorched her. She watched as he turned and approached the water than knelt to splash water onto his face.

"Why are we here?" she asked.

He continued to rub water along his forehead and along the nape of his neck. She stared at his back and watched the muscles beneath his cotton tunic shift marveling at the strength in which those arms possessed.

He straightened to his height and turned to look at her. He stared at her as if he wanted to say something but refrained. She watched as he reached within the pocket of his breeches and withdrew an object.

Ginelle felt her heart leap against her chest. Surely he hadn't brought her here to accuse her of thievery again?

She frowned as he extended the object to her and slowly unraveled his fist. Her mouth parted on a gasp as she stared down at the familiar length of chain, and dangling from that chain was her locket.

Intuitively, her hand fluttered to the bare spot at her neck. She reached out and took it from his hand. "Thank you." She whispered, tears forming in her eyes. She thought she had lost her mother's necklace forever. "Where did you find it?" she looked up to peer at him.

He moved forward and gently took the necklace from her, motioning for her to turn around. Reluctantly she turned and lifted her hair as he placed the locket around her neck. His fingers lingered along her nape, eager to touch her silver-blond tresses.

Dorian dropped his hands and stepped away as the locket settled around her throat. "The woman-" he nodded towards the picture concealed within, "Who is she?"

Ginelle reached up and unclasped the locket, revealing the beautiful woman inside. "My mother." She whispered, lightly tapping a finger against the tiny portrait.

"She is beautiful-." He said and she looked up, a small smile curving her mouth. "-like you." He added.

Her smile faded and she turned her back to him. She couldn't let him see the affect he had on her. How could she tell him that when he was sweet and gentle, he made her heart beat for a reason entirely foreign to her, a reason that she couldn't fathom possible, especially with a man like Dorian.

"Why are you afraid of me?" his voice hardened and she turned to him, stunned by how quickly his demeanor changed.

She shook her head, "I told you-"

"I don't believe you." He stepped towards her and she retreated. His blue eyes narrowed, "What has colored your opinion of me?"

Ginelle swallowed back a heavy lump lodged in her throat. She wasn't ready to reveal anything, especially to him.

He reached out to brush her face and she turned away from his touch. His hand curled into a fist and he dropped it to his side. His features darkened as he demanded, "Who is Pierino?"

Her eyes widened and her face paled beneath his questioning glare. She gritted her teeth and turned abruptly around, "I think it best we return home." She made a move towards the horse but strong, lean fingers seized her arm, steering her back around.

"Answer me dammit!" his fingers gripped her upper arms as he searched her face. "Did he hurt you?"

Tears filled the rim of her eyes and she struggled against the rising storm of emotions. "Yes!" she wrenched from his grasp and stepped away, quickly wiping the tears from her face.

Dorian stared at her rigid back, her shoulders shaking with her fear. "Was he there?" he asked gently, "At the banquet?"

She nodded.

"What does he want with you?"

Ginelle whirled, her eyes flashing like daggers as she cried, "I don't know!" she gasped for a breath, "He is an evil man who will stop at nothing to see that I suffer and that's just it, I don't know why. I cannot tell you his intentions but he seems to want me for a reason that I cannot explain."

She stalked away from him, unable to look at him for revealing too much of her painful past. He grasped her arm, pulling her back towards him. "Let go of me!"

"Ginelle." His arms tightened around her waist as he reached up to cup her chin, forcing her to peer into his eyes. He traced a finger along the curve of her cheek as he said, "This man will never hurt you again, and so as long as I am alive, no harm will come to you."

She shook her head, "Do not make promises that you cannot keep."

His face hardened, "My word is my vow."

For a moment they stared at each other, locked in their embrace, their hearts beating as one and Ginelle was startled by a swift and sudden notion, that here, in Dorian's arms is where she belonged. She wanted to believe him, believe that she was safe and Dorian would protect her, for a moment she would allow herself that comforting thought, but it would not last long.

He released her and she immediately put space between them. She felt his eyes on her back as she moved towards the horse. She reached up and gently patted the thick, black mane and the beast nudged its head against her shoulder.

"You have seemed to tame the beast." Dorian said as he stepped towards her. "He does not take well to others, but he seems to like you."

Ginelle smiled as she continued to run her fingers through the stallion's mane. "What is his name?"

"He is Lafeu." Ginelle's smile broadened and Dorian felt his heart leap against his solid chest. "I have had him since I was a young boy."

"He is quite a magnificent animal." She said as she stroked his neck.

"Have you ever had a horse for your own?"

She shook her head, her blond strands stirring with the gesture. "No, my father was a poor man, he did not have much."

"Your mother?"

She froze and dropped her head, her lashes lowering over her eyes to conceal her sudden sadness. "I did not know my mother."

"Did you have any siblings?" he couldn't help but pry, this fierce intrigue nagged at him and he yearned to know more about her.

"I have no siblings to speak of, 'twas only my father and myself." he had moved closer and now stood a mere space apart. She lifted her head and their eyes clashed. There in her unguarded gaze, he saw her pain, her deep sorrow and loneliness.

"What happened to your father?"

Her lovely face twisted with raw pain and she quickly averted her eyes from his face. "I wish to no longer speak of this." Her voice broke with unshed tears and he resisted the urge to pull her in his arms. He knew that if he touched her, she would not allow it in her fragile state.

He said nothing and moved to the other side of Lafeu and extended a hand to her. This time, she did not hesitate to accept his hand but paused as he moved to lift her into the saddle.

"Thank you, Dorian." She said softly as she reached up to touch the locket around her neck. "You do not know how much this means to me."

The sunlight played gently across her delicate face, enhancing each little hollow and arch of bone. In that moment, with her lips parted and her eyes alight with her happiness, he yearned for nothing more than to kiss her dewy lips, to claim this woman as his own.

Instead, he refrained and assisted her into the saddle. He mounted behind her and turned Lafeu back towards the direction of the manor.

The next morning, Ginelle was awakened by a subtle tapping on her door. She stirred and rolled over, taking note that her room was still dark, and that dawn had barely broken the horizon. Wary as the tapping continued, she arose and quickly slipped into her robe. She pulled the edges together as she moved towards the door.

She nudged the door open and was startled to find Dorian standing on the other side. "Monsieur, is something wrong?"

"There is something I need to show you. Can you get dressed?" he asked.

She frowned, "Is something amiss?"

"Just get dressed. I'll wait below." With that he turned and disappeared down the hall. Closing the door, Ginelle moved towards her bureau. She donned a simple day dress and pinned her hair to the nape of her neck.

As she slipped from her room into the darkened hall, she noticed that even the servants had yet to awaken. Concerned that something terrible had happened, she proceeded on down the stairs. Dorian stood at the bottom waiting for her. He did not wait for her to reach his side; instead he continued on out the front door, leaving it ajar for her to follow.

When she stepped outside, the sun barely peaked over the mountains. Streaks of orange and yellow with a hint of pink painted the morning sky but it was not the approach of dawn that startled her with surprise, it was the beautiful white mare grazing in the grass.

Her mouth fell open and she froze at Dorian's side, unaware that he watched her reaction, eager for her smile. "Do you like her?" he asked.

Ginelle nodded, "Where did you get her?"

He left her side and moved towards the mare as she continued to gnaw at the strays of grass. He reached up and trailed a hand along her thick mane. "I purchased her from a plantation not far from here."

"What is her name?" Ginelle smiled as the horse lifted her head and nudged her nose against Ginelle's shoulder. She laughed and reached up to scratch the mare's ear.

"She is whatever you wish to call her."

Startled, she averted her eyes from the horse to the man at her side. "She is for me?" she asked, her voice a whisper.

He nodded, a small smile curving his mouth. "She is yours."

Ginelle dropped her head as she cradled the mare's nose in her palm. "I do not know what to say." Her heart thundered against her breast as she lifted her eyes to stare at the man who continued to surprise her.

"You need not say anything." He said, "If you are going to remain at Ashford you are going to need a horse for your own personal use."

At that moment, Ginelle was too ecstatic to think on his statement. Instead she focused on the beautiful white thoroughbred and felt her heart swell within her chest. She reached up and trailed a hand along the mare's smooth, white neck. "I shall call her Millie."

"Would you care to take her for a ride?" he asked.

Ginelle paused, "Now?"

He nodded. "Now is a good time as any."

She smiled, "Yes that would be nice."

It didn't take long for them to saddle the horses. As Dorian led Lafeu from the barn, she stared at his broad back, curious to know more of this gentle side of him.

They mounted their horses and took off at a steady canter. Lafeu was much greater in size and strength, but the animal took its time, riding alongside Millie.

"I have never owned a horse before." She said, gripping the reins in her hand. She lifted her head and her eyes connected with Dorian's. "Thank you."

He nodded.

Her heart did a strange jump in her chest as she continued to stare at him. The sun had arisen and the morning light played beautifully across his chiseled face. His black hair lay unbound against his shoulders and she had a strange urge to touch those raven strands.

She wondered than, if she were not to marry, what plans did he have for her? He said that she was to remain at Ashford but there had to be more?

At that moment she cared to not think on it. She was happy and strangely enough, she was enjoying Dorian's company. She did not acknowledge the automatic flutter in her belly whenever he was near, nor did she assess any of the intense urges for his touch, or his lips to claim her own. She couldn't think such things with him so near.

They rode up until noon. The sun was high in the sky but a gentle breeze cooled their faces. They traveled the familiar path that led them to the river where they paused to let the horses rest and drink some water.

Dorian moved to a boulder and sat down. His eyes fixated on Ginelle as she moved to the edge of the river to pat her face with cool water.

When she straightened and turned, she paused, her heart accelerating as his heated gaze remained firm upon her face.

As if spellbound, he gathered to his full height. Ginelle stood motionless, frozen as he closed the space between them. He did not touch her as his eyes roamed her face. She felt the heat from his body as she craved his touch. She knew she should turn away, end this before it starts but her body couldn't register her thoughts.

He reached up and her mouth parted as his arm brushed her cheek. He tugged at the ribbon binding her hair until the silver-blond strands spiraled freely down her back. His fingers threaded through her hair and her head fell back, her mouth arching upward, eager for his kiss.

His left arm fell to her side and she released a sharp breath as his arm curved around her waist, pulling her against his chest. His right hand swept through her hair, brushing strands of blond from her face.

He leaned forward and pressed his cheek against her own and inhaled her scent as his desire flared, burning hotly in his belly.

She reached up and pressed a hand against his chest, "Dorian-"

He captured her mouth in a heated frenzy. Any words of objection died within her throat as his tongue delved inside, sweeping passionately in its claim on her.

Unable to control the feelings and her own curiosity, she opened her mouth to him and pressed her breasts against his chest.

A deep moan surfaced from his throat as he swung her up into his arms. He pressed tiny kisses against the corners of her mouth as he moved to a shallow patch of grass beneath a large oak tree. He lowered her to the soft terrain and followed her down.

Dorian stared at her, taking in every inch of her loveliness. Her pale hair lay dispersed beneath her, her lips parted and wet with his kisses. He smiled inwardly; he had fantasized many nights of her like this, beneath him, waiting for him to claim her as his own.

Her soft, brown eyes stared up at him, innocent and uncertain. His eyes trailed slowly over her petite frame. Her breasts, small yet supple swelled against the confines of her dress with each labored breath.

A fire burned deep in his groin as his manhood thrust against the seams of his breeches. He wanted her to the point of recklessness but he couldn't be rough, this wasn't simply a tumble and roll in the hay. This was Ginelle, sweet and beautiful Ginelle.

He reached down and spanned her waist with his hand marveling at how little and perfect she would fit against him.

His hand moved to her waist and curled into her dress, inching her skirts upward. Her breathing increased and he captured her gasp into his mouth as he bared her legs and reached down to caress a milky calve.

Ginelle felt her heart spiraling out of control within her chest. She knew she should stop him but found her body immobile.

He kissed her tenderly, as if she were the most precious thing he held dear. She accepted his kisses with a shyness that slowly faded as her desire intensified with his tender strokes.

His fingers glided higher and she felt her body twisting against his touch as his hand smoothed along her inner thigh.

Her eyes widened as he brushed that intimate spot between her thighs. A flutter of surprise rippled through her body as he probed her folds, seeking the delicate nub within. She arched against him as his finger dipped deeper, circling and stirring a deep longing that started a trembling in her limbs.

Her eyes fell closed as he pressed his hand against her, shocked that her body responded so erotically.

She nearly groaned aloud when he withdrew his finger. He reached up and tugged at the material at her shoulders. Her breasts fell free to his hungry gaze and he veered up to capture a pink nipple between his lips.

His hand slipped beneath her pulling her flush against him as he lightly pulled and teased, his tongue dipping out to trace the delicate curve of her breast.

He released her only to move and repeat the same to her other breast. Her fingers curled in his shirt as he pressed his hips against her, his manhood pulsating within his breeches. She opened to him as his hand fell between her thighs and he thrust a finger into her dewy folds.

She felt her desire brewing, a longing burning where his fingers stroked her tenderly as his tongue lavished her pink puckered bud. Passion swept through her and a swift tingling started at the base of his fingers. She knew not exactly what she craved, what her body yearned but she knew only Dorian could sedate her sudden burning, her fierce and swift desire.

He released her taut nipple and shifted his body against her, pressing his hardness against her inner core. Her eyes widened and a sudden fear gripped her. She had never seen a man naked and she knew not what lay beneath his clothes but it frightened her.

Logic took place and she suddenly questioned her feelings. She had been repulsed by Nathaniel's touch but somehow yearned for Dorian's but he did not love her. He wanted her to remain at Ashford but that could not be. If she allowed this to continue, she would lose her maidenhood, and not under matrimony.

As much as her body yearned for this moment, eager for Dorian to teach her the ways of passion and lovemaking, she couldn't. She would be ruined, spoiled as some women of the ton referred it. She would not be worthy of marriage or a convent and most of all, she could not give up her maidenhead to a man that did not love her.

She pressed her hand against his chest and felt his body stiffen. "Dorian."

The moment his body left hers, she felt a sudden draft sweep over her. She sat up and quickly righted her gown.

He paced before her and swept a hand through his hair. She gathered to her feet and brushed the dirt from her skirts. She knew she should say something but what could she say? What would become of her once he sedated his lust?

"It's best we return to the manor." His voice was stiff and she sensed his anger.

She said nothing as she moved to Millie and he helped her mount. The ride back to Ashford was quiet and tense. When they arrived, she was angry with him for having been so gentle and than suddenly cold towards her.

When she dismounted, he took Millie's reins and led both the mare and stallion towards the barn. He left her standing without as much as a word and his detachment wounded her. Struggling to keep her tears at bay, she spun on her heels and went inside.

Chapter 15

After seeing to the fields and his laborers, Dorian returned inside, eager to wash the grime from his back. As he reached the top of the stairs, he paused to stare down at the end of the hall.

Every fiber in his being urged him to go to her room and take what his body demanded. Curling his hands into fists at his side, he turned and stalked to his room. His eyes settled on the massive bed against the center wall and he felt a fierce groan of frustration surface to his throat. Vivid images of her lying in his bed rushed to taunt him, tease the struggling urges just beneath the surface of his feeble control.

Mumbling a stream of curses beneath his breath, he tore off his tunic and cast it aside. He moved to his bed and flopped down onto the mattress and sank into a restless slumber.

When he next awoke, there was a light tapping at his door. He stirred against the heavy grogginess and sat up; throwing his legs to the floor he cast an angry glare at the door.

His heart jumped against his chest as the tapping continued. He thought for a moment Ginelle had come to him and he found himself at the door, opening it with an urgency that startled the woman on the other side.

Immediate disappointment crossed his darkened face for the feminine body standing on the other side revealed voluptuous curves and striking red hair.

"What are you doing here?" he growled as he stalked away from the door.

Victoria's blue eyes narrowed as she sauntered into the room, her wounded pride clear on her regal face. "Expecting someone else, mon amour?"

She moved to discard her cloak and placed it across the sofa. She had specifically donned a gown of sparkling blue with a flattering neckline that accentuated her curves but she was keen to notice that Dorian did not appreciate or notice her efforts.

Struggling to contain her fury, she moved to pour herself a glass of brandy. She held the glass between her fingers and studied Dorian's muscular frame with a rapidly growing lust.

"You have not called upon me for some time." Her voice purred as she took another long drag of brandy. "This wouldn't be because of that blond nymph, would it?"

Dorian leaned against the bed post, crossing his arms against his chest; he turned his head to study Victoria. At one point, he would have gladly accepted her charms but her voluptuous curves seemed to have no strong pull on his arousal. He wanted a female but it wasn't the one standing across from him.

He arched a black brow as he said with a little amusement in his tone, "Afraid of a little competition, Victoria?"

He had considered her beautiful at one point but her jealousy and rage altered her face completely. "You think I find a spit of a girl challenging?" she slammed her glass down and moved towards him, swaying her hips with a clear indication that she wanted him.

She splayed her hands across his bare chest, trailing her fingers over the hard contours of his muscles as she pressed her heaving bosom flat against him. "I have never disappointed you before, mon amant." Her hand dipped low to grasp his shaft and he hardened in her palm. Her triumphant smile confirmed that he still desired her.

"She is nothing but a girl." Victoria spat, squeezing him in her hand and tugging lightly as she added, "Let a woman appease your desires."

Releasing a deep growl, he reached up and seized her arms. He spun her around and pushed her back against the bed. She fell upon the mattress with a delighted laugh and opened her arms to him as he fell over her.

She squirmed beneath him as she laid her hands flat against his chest, marveling at the bulging muscles in his arms and torso as his hand roamed over her ample breasts.

A fire licked at his insides and his shaft bulged against his breeches. Seized with an insatiable desire, he captured her mouth and tugged lightly at her lower lip but the mouth beneath his own responded not with shyness, but with a boldness that startled him out of his heated haze.

Dorian jolted backwards and released Victoria all at once. He leapt to his feet and crossed the room to grab the brandy bottle. He had wanted to rid himself of the drunkenness but tonight he needed something strong to douse the fire burning in his groin.

Victoria sat up, her eyes darting daggers at his broad back as she reached up and righted her dress. "Are you daft?" she spat harshly, moving to stand to meet his icy glare. "I am no fool, Dorian Ashford; I know this girl has your cock in an uproar. What is it about her that you find so appealing?"

Chugging his glass of brandy, he set the glass down and crossed the room to snatch up Victoria's cloak. He tossed it at her and she caught it with a gasp. "Get out." He growled.

Appalled, she froze as she bundled her cloak against her chest. "You want me gone?"

"Your charms are no longer needed, Victoria."

Her eyes narrowed viciously as she crossed the room to glare at him. Her eyes widened with a revelation and her mouth parted on a gasp. "You're in love with her."

When he didn't answer, this only confirmed her suspicion. "What do you know about this little bitch, Dorian? Do you know that she owes a man?"

Dorian stiffened. "How do you know this?"

Victoria straightened her shoulders, a small smile curving her lips. "I know many things, Dorian and I also know that a girl like that is not worthy of your love." Placing her cloak back around her shoulders she stalked towards the door and paused, "When the girl continues to deny you, you may seek me out." With that said, she closed the door quietly behind her, leaving Dorian quaking with fury.

Ginelle had just stripped away her gown when her door burst open, yielding a large formidable frame. She yelped as she clutched the dress to her chest, shielding her body from the icy eyes glaring angrily back at her.

"Are you indebted to him?" his harsh tone made her flinch as she stepped back from Dorian, confused as to his meaning. "Pierino." He growled, "Are you indebted to him?"

Her eyes widened and her face paled considerably with fear. Why would he ask such a question unless he had spoken with Pierino himself?

He reached out and gripped her arms, "Answer me, Ginelle." He said more calmly. "Did you give yourself to that man?"

She gasped; appalled that he would ask such a horrific question. She struggled against tears as she wrenched away from him.

Dorian turned to study her back, realizing she stood only in her chemise. Instantly, his body responded with hot desire. "Do you refuse me, because another man has had you?"

Ginelle spun around, suddenly furious. "What?" she stiffened as he crossed the room and stood over her. "I have been with no man."

He gritted his teeth and said, "Do not lie to me."

Ginelle was livid. How dare he barge into her room and make such blatant accusations and than accuse her of lying. “Get out of my room!”

It happened so abruptly she couldn’t respond automatically. She found herself dangling over his shoulder and half-way down the hall towards his room before she could react. She pummeled his back with her fists and struggled but his arm around the back of her knees prevented any damage.

He slammed his door shut and locked the latch before settling her on her feet. “Now, you will tell me the truth.” He demanded.

Breathless, she backed away from him and lifted her chin. “I have told you the truth, imbecile!”

He leapt towards her and she squealed as his hand snaked around her wrist and jerked her towards him. She stumbled forward but he easily caught her, swinging her high against his chest.

He released her and she flopped onto the bed. She moved to escape him but his arm lashed out and grasped her around the waist.

The moment her hands contacted bare flesh, she felt her heart accelerate tenfold and the passion brewing in his eyes was her undoing. She wanted to be angry with him for accusing her so harshly but the moment his mouth crashed upon hers, she was lost in a haze of heated bliss.

A low moan arose deep from his throat as he kissed her deeply, plunging his fingers through her hair to loosen the silken strands. His arm settled at her back, crushing her against him. She cried out as he reached up and ripped the chemise from her shoulders, baring her lovely skin to his ravenous gaze.

Her head fell back as his mouth left a hot trail of kisses along her skin, along the delicate bone of her collarbone to the hollowness between her breasts.

He carried them both down to lay flat on the mattress as he jerked the sheer material further down to her waist, baring her lovely breasts and flat stomach. For a moment, he spanned his hand over the smooth flesh of her abdomen, and pictured her belly growing with his child.

His hand skimmed over her narrow ribcage and he reached to cup a milky breast in his palm. She arched against him, her head tilting back onto the pillows as a nipple hardened beneath his thumb as he lightly brushed the delicate nub.

Ginelle felt herself blossoming beneath his caresses. She had never experienced such pleasures of the body or the wild fire soaring throughout her limbs. She welcomed his kisses with an eagerness that startled her.

She arched into his hands, her body yearning for his touch and than gasped as his mouth replaced his hand as he lightly teased and suckled her breast. She felt her face turn crimson red as she squirmed against him as an intense wave of desire washed over her. His hands grasped her waist, pulling her down against him so that he could do the same to her other breast.

She reached up and threaded her hands through his hair, teasing the raven strands as they settled on his broad shoulders. Her hands trailed softly over his flesh, amazed at the hard lines of muscles that protruded beneath the bronze skin.

A shudder trembled through her body as his tongue traced her budding nipple and she gasped as his hand reached beneath her chemise, seeking that intimate place between her thighs. She opened to him as a pool of heat spiraled low in her belly, tingling through her thighs and that delicate spot where his fingers entered.

He splayed her legs apart and fitted his body above her. Immediately she was aware of something large pressing against her thigh and a slight fear scuttled through her.

Sensing her anxiety, Dorian kissed the corners of her mouth. "I would never hurt you, ma petite."

The tension slightly eased from her limbs but her heart erupted in her breast as he reached down and released his swollen shaft.

Her eyes widened for she couldn't imagine how something so big could not do harm to someone her size.

Her thoughts fled when his lips feathered across her own. He captured her face with his hand and kissed her with an intensity that made her heart soar within her chest.

He entered her gently and she gasped.

The pain came unexpectedly as he thrust through her maidenhead, startling them both as he captured her cry with a kiss. Her nails dug into the flesh at his shoulders as he allowed a moment for her body to adjust to his size.

He kissed the tears from her face and gently began to rock his hips. Slowly the pain began to fade and her pleasure amounted to an exhilarating peak. Moans of pleasure escaped her throat as she arched her hips to meet his every thrust; the more he moved within her, the more her body became alive, the more she aware of his body adjoined with her own.

Dorian kissed her passionately, cradling her head between his hands as his tongue caressed her lip and his hands explored the small curves of her body, marveling at how fire spread beneath his fingertips along her sensitive skin.

His thrusts grew more intense and with the intensity, a fire that threatened to consume them both. Until she thought they both would be devoured by their passions, they fell back onto the bed, breathless and spent.

His arm curved around her waist and he pulled her flush against him, realizing he had rid himself of his breeches and now lay completely naked.

She almost reached for the blanket to hide her nakedness but paused for Dorian had already seen every inch of her. Fleeting thoughts of shame and what would come of her now that she was no longer an innocent brushed her mind. She quickly blocked them out, not wanting to ruin this moment of happiness shared in Dorian's arms.

She felt his fingers in her hair and slowly drifted to sleep, a small smile curving the corners of her mouth.

Chapter 16

He woke early and was immediately aware of the small, feminine body pressed against him. Dorian tightened his arms around Ginelle as she slept peacefully, his body responding automatically to her nearness.

He reached out and plucked a strand of silver-blond hair from the pillow, teasing the silken tresses between his thumb and forefinger.

He had taken her maidenhead. He relished in that notion for no man had, had her and no man would. She belonged to him; he would make sure of it.

He arose from the bed and proceeded to get dressed, all the while, his eyes straying towards the bed. He wanted nothing more than to crawl back beneath the coverlets and take her over and over as his body so badly yearned to do.

Instead, he finished dressing and reluctantly left the room. He would spend most of the day in the fields but his thoughts would continuously stray towards Ginelle and how he burned to claim her over and again.

It was nearly noon when her eyes fluttered open and she was immediately aware of a sudden soreness between her legs. Ginelle sat upright in bed and was overcome with disappointment at finding Dorian gone.

An abrupt knock on the door startled her and she stiffened as she bid them entry. Almost immediately crimson stained her cheeks as Lucile entered, yielding a tray.

Ginelle half expected the older woman to vent her shock at finding Ginelle in Dorian's bed, or at least cast a look that would indicate her horror, but the older woman said nothing, her pinched face remained expressionless as she crossed the room and set the tray down on the table.

When Lucile turned to face her, she tensed, bracing herself for the housekeeper's rebuke. "Monsieur Dorian has asked that a bath be prepared for you, will you need my assistance?" she arched a brow and Ginelle blushed even redder.

"Vera' well." The older woman said, taking her prolonged silence as an answer.

Ginelle frowned after Lucile had left. Dorian must have said something and the thought made her blush darken. Surely every habitant within the manor was now well aware that she had been in Dorian's bed.

Hesitantly, she peeled away the coverlets and gasped for dry blood coated her inner thighs, a clear indication that symbolized her loss of innocence.

She slipped from the bed, dragging the coverlets with her to shield her naked body. Her heart thundered in her chest as she turned and stared at the rumpled bed. Dorian's absence was like a splash of cold water.

What had she done? She had given herself to a man whom she barely understood; Who had proclaimed no affections for her? What did she expect?

She had spoken quite adamantly that marriage was not an option, but she had given herself to him, had experienced the desires that a man and woman shared.

What did it mean when her heart beat for him and no other? He had been so gentle, so tender in their lovemaking that even now her heart swelled at the remembrance of his caresses.

Ginelle gasped and her eyes widened as she was struck with a startling epiphany. She loved him. How could she have been so blind? His presence unraveled her completely, melting her limbs in a pool of heat as his searing gaze sought her out.

Though his dominance frightened her, she knew in her heart that there was no other that could make her feel this way.

She was struck with a sudden thought for though she loved Dorian, Dorian did not love her in return. He was a man of solitude, a man destined to live a life of loneliness, never to marry.

She was a fool to even think he would take her as his wife, and yet, she would allow him to take her to his bed?

A sudden anger filled her veins for she refused to become his mistress! Mayhap he was finished with her, and though the lingering thought pained her that he would use and discard her so cruelly, she would rather end this now than risk losing her heart further to a man who did not love her.

At that, she quickly washed and dressed, all the while, her mind plagued with their lovemaking. He made her feel alive, aware of her body in ways she thought never to imagine.

Quickly dismissing the heated thoughts from her mind, she fled his room, eagerly seeking a distraction. Her face burned red as she swept by servants, very much aware of their knowing gazes as they spoke secretly amongst each other.

She needed an escape and could think of only one place. Deliberately avoiding crossing paths with Lucile, she slipped through the kitchen, pass a suddenly perplexed Cook, and in to the midday sun.

Dorian paused beneath the blistering sun to wipe the sweat from his brow but a brief flash of movement from his peripheral forced him to stiffen.

His eyes narrowed as Ginelle disappeared within the barn and returned moments later with Millie saddled.

At the sight of her, his body responded instantly, hardening to the point where he nearly groaned aloud. He bit down on his sudden arousal as he watched her flee on horseback. Where the devil did she think she was going?

Once she disappeared into the thick foliage, he turned and noticed two of his laborers following her with their eyes, one in particular. He narrowed his gaze as a rage brought him to the man. "Find something of interest, slave?"

The man stiffened but his anger remained firm in the deep set of his dark eyes. A small grin tugged at the corners of his mouth as he said, "I am merely enjoying the view."

Dorian clenched his hands into tight fists as he stepped closer to the man, his temper magnifying to a dangerous peak at the thought of this man touching Ginelle.

Bent on rage, he had not heard the approach of one of his overseers. "Milord?" spoke Yves from above.

Slowly, Dorian turned to peer up at Yves sitting upon his horse. "I'll take over, milord." By the expression on Yves' face, he was quite aware of the storm approaching, having braced the brunt of Dorian's fury many times afore, he knew when to intervene.

The muscle at his jaw ticked as he turned back to the slave. His nostrils flared with the intense urge to pummel the bastard but instead, he spun on his heels and stalked from the fields.

The sun was scorching and she couldn't wait to rid herself of her restricting garments. As she disrobed, Ginelle eyed the water with a growing eagerness. Millie grazed in a patch of grass beneath a large oak and swung her white tail repeatedly to swat at the pestering flies.

Ginelle smiled as she set her dress on a nearby boulder and moved to the edge of the water. She lightly tapped the calm surface with her foot and delighted in the ripples created with the swift motion.

She needed this time apart. She needed to collect her thoughts and she could think of no other place to do just that.

She waded into the water and sighed as she sank waist deep. She had pulled her hair high above her head to keep from getting the tresses wet but at this moment with the sun searing her delicate face; she wanted nothing more than to sink below the surface.

Seconds later, she could withstand the heat no longer and dipped beneath the water. When she resurfaced, laughter slipped from her throat as she lifted her hands to push wet strands of hair from her face, unaware of the searing gaze watching afar.

His cock bulged against the seam of his breeches as his eyes moved hotly over her scantily clad body, drenched in nothing but a meager, tantalizing shift.

Dorian moved closer, drawn by her sweet laughter as she playfully spun around. Her small breasts protruding through the sheer garment forced another painful groan past his lips.

For a time, he watched her from the shadows as she moved through the water, relishing in the sun as the water cooled her delicate skin.

He was nearly aflame when she surfaced, like a water nymph, her blond hair piled high atop her head, several wet strands framed the nape of her neck as her chemise molded to every small curve of her body, enticing his inner demons.

When he stepped into the clearing, she froze, fear jolting her on the spot followed by a sudden flare of surprise to find him standing there.

His eyes dropped to her breasts, visible through the shift as her chest rose and fell with each labored breath.

"W-what are you doing here?" her voice small and surprised, pulled at him, drawing him closer.

His eyes roamed over her body in a hot caress until settling on her face. "I've come to collect what's mine." He said gruffly, stepping towards her.

Ginelle stiffened, struggling to conceal her desires for though she yearned for his touch, she fought to keep her heart guarded.

She tilted her chin, "I am not yours to collect."

A flash of anger glinted sharply in his blue eyes as he stepped towards her and seized her arm. He spun her around and she fell against his naked chest. Seized with an uncontrollable urge to run her hands over the hardened muscle beneath her fingertips, she fought to escape his grip.

"Release me." She demanded, shoving against his massive shoulders.

She gasped for in one swift motion, she was on the ground, beneath him. He seized her wrists and pressed them above her head as his free hand skimmed lightly over her breasts. She shuddered beneath him as she tugged to pull her wrists free but with little effort.

He reached down and feathered an erect nipple with his thumb, alighting a fire beneath his touch as his hand traced the soft curve of her breast beneath the sheer chemise; sparks of desire shot throughout her limbs, to tingle deep in her loins.

She moaned her displeasure when he suddenly released her but gasped as he ripped the front of her chemise, clear to her navel, baring her breasts to his heated gaze.

Ginelle clenched her eyes shut as she arched into his palm, eagerly seeking his touch as he leaned down and captured a breast with his mouth. A moan escaped her throat as he lapped a hardened nipple with his tongue that left her quivering.

She hadn't realized that he had released her wrists until her hands settled on his broad shoulders. His fingers trailed along her sides, rising higher to rest beneath the undersides of her breasts as he shifted his weight to seize her lips in a sensual kiss.

All sense of control fled and she was immobile with her desires as his kiss deepened, becoming rough and suddenly possessive. She clung to him as he devoured her with an intensity that frightened yet exhilarated her.

Her nails dug into the flesh at his back as he pushed the thin layer of chemise away that prevented their heated bodies from touching.

Her stomach somersaulted with a sudden flare of heat as he nudged her legs apart. She trembled not with fear but anticipation as he released his swollen shaft and settled within the cradle of her thighs.

The moment he entered her, she cried out with pleasure, clutching his shoulders as he thrust into her. Each abrupt movement sent needles of rapture tingling through her limbs as he drove against her, his muscles flexing beneath her fingers.

He grasped her breast and teased the swollen bud as he captured the other with his mouth, licking and rolling his tongue over her breast as he rolled his hips, pushing deeper into her soft, moist folds.

Ginelle couldn't think clearly through the rolling waves of bliss as Dorian possessed her body and soul. She knew she should have struggled but the moment his lips descended upon hers, she was loss forever in his embrace.

He veered upward and she moaned as he reached between them and brushed her intimate folds. She gasped and her body convulsed against his palm.

He leaned down and pressed his lips against the pulse at her throat. "You are mine." He whispered hotly, thrusting harder between her thighs.

Her heart thundered against her chest at his declaration but her heart sank for he had not confessed love but possession.

The thought evaporated as he plunged deeper and he shuddered with ecstasy, she felt his release as his seed spilled hotly into her. He fell upon her but kept his weight from crushing her. His arms circled her naked body, holding her close as their hearts beat as one.

Still joined, she relished in this moment when he was passionate and tender but her anger came all too swiftly for she had allowed him to sedate his lust once more, leaving her heart aching for his love.

When he finally released her and moved away, she quickly righted her torn chemise, very aware of his hot stare as she gathered to her feet.

As she gathered her dress against her chest she turned to glare at him. "Do not think you can have me whenever you see fit." Her chin jutted outward as his ice eyes narrowed on her, "I am not here to satisfy your needs."

Ginelle stiffened as he stalked towards her, closing the space that separated them. She gasped as solid rock brought her up short and his arms closed in around her, trapping her between the boulder and his massive frame.

His cold eyes moved over her face, searching as he said, "What prompted this response?"

Her eyes sparked with defiance as she said icily, "I will not become your mistress."

She watched the muscle at his jaw jump as he gritted his teeth. "It's a bit late for that."

Ginelle stiffened at his response and than ducked out from underneath his arms to escape the heat of his body. She didn't get far for his fingers latched around her arm, jerking her back around. His brawny arm swung around her naked back as she continued to clutch the dress to her chest. Her heart leapt against her breast as she was forced to peer up into his fiery gaze.

"Know this-" his voice dropped dangerously low as a feral gleam sparked in his glacial stare. "I will not abide another man touching you. So as long as I see it, you are mine."

Fear shuddered through her body for she knew not what kindled this sudden reaction and she dare not test it.

"May I go now?"

Slowly, he released her and remained silent as she quickly dressed. As she started towards Millie his voice stopped her.

"You will move your things into my room."

Furious, she spun around and jolted at his nearness for he had moved closer. "I will do no such thing!" she exclaimed.

He leaned towards her and she tensed. "You will or I will do it myself and none so gently, either."

Fuming, she curled her fists at her sides with the urge of venting her anger out on his hardened, stubborn chest. She had no intention of moving her things into his room for that meant she would share his bed and become his mistress.

She most certainly would not!

Chapter 17

Ginelle waited nearly till the afternoon before returning to the manor. Her heart was still aflutter within her chest and she knew she could not bare Dorian's presence without succumbing to his dark charm.

The desires he awakened within her tilted her entire world and she experienced wondrous feelings unlike anything she had ever felt.

If she declared her love would he shun her affections? Did he merely lust after her body?

She wanted nothing more than to dislodge her feelings, to shut out the emotions bombarding her very thoughts, her actions and motives, for fear of rejection and loneliness but she couldn't simply place her heart in a box for safekeeping. Her feelings for Dorian were raw; growing each and every day, every minute spent with him was a growing happiness and love that could not be suppressed. There was no denying her feelings for Dorian.

Yet could she really reside at Ashford as his mistress? Was she willing to face that sort of complication?

Her thoughts drifted astray as she reigned in before the stables and dismounted. The stable boy arrived to assist her with Millie. Once she was finished she proceeded towards the house but half-way she stopped as a rider approached from down the road.

Her eyes strained against the faint day light as the lone rider grew closer and it wasn't until the man was nearly upon her that she recognized him as Lord Edric from the banquet.

She frowned for what reason would Lord Edric come to Ashford? She stepped back as he came to a steady halt before her. He wore no hat, instead his glorious blond hair curled atop his shoulders and he was equipped in a simple white tunic beneath a brown fitted vest.

Ginelle struggled to remain calm for obviously this man continued to seek her out for a reason anonymous to her.

She presented Lord Edric with a small smile, "Good evening, Sir Edric. What brings you to Ashford?"

He smiled in return and dismounted, causing Ginelle to retreat another step. He curtsied before saying, "Forgive my abrupt presence, mademoiselle. I pray that I may have a word with you? I had little chance of speaking with you at the banquet."

Ginelle felt a shiver of warning for his expression had altered slightly to anxiousness. If he were anything of a threat to her, she needed to lightly dismiss him and flee for she knew nothing about this man but his name.

She quickly searched her mind for a ploy. "I am sorry Lord Edric but I must retire for the evening, if it is my hand that you seek, I have decided not to marry. If you'll excuse me." She turned quickly and started towards the house.

"I came not to speak of marriage but on another matter of importance." He exclaimed, his tone intense as she turned to study the taunt lines of his face pulled tight with tension.

Her heart jumped against her chest as she paused in step, her face paling as warning bells sounded in her head. "Than pray tell sir, what reason do you have to be here?"

He stepped towards her and she stiffened, her stomach twisting with the urge to run. “Do not fear me but the danger I speak of.”

Ginelle gasped as his hand circled her arm. “You must come with me.”

She inhaled sharply as a scream jammed tight in her throat.

“Please-“ he said gently, “I am not here to harm you. You must come with me for your life is in danger.”

Her eyes widened with alarm. “Of what do you speak of?” her voice cracked with apprehension. “Who are you?”

“I –“

“I will only ask once for you to remove your hand.” Dorian’s voice rang like hot steel, dripping with fury as Ginelle met that cold, calculating gleam.

His manner bespoke of aggressive intent as his massive shadow fell in at her side and he grasped her other arm, pulling her swiftly out of Lord Edric’s grasp as he moved to plant his body firmly in front of her.

Immediately, alarm hastened across Lord Edric’s face as he stepped away taken aback by the fierce expression painted black on Dorian’s face. “I have no quarrel with you, milord.”

“A quarrel is all you shall receive.” The muscle at his jaw flexed dangerously and Ginelle feared not for Dorian but for Lord Edric.

“Dorian-“ Ginelle said gently, reaching out to touch his arm. He barely budged or even noticed her silent plea. “He has not harmed me.”

“You have no business here.” Dorian growled, ignoring Ginelle. “I want you off my land.”

Edric nodded but before he mounted he directed his attention to Dorian. “I had no intention of harming her. I came only to deliver a warning.”

Dorian narrowed his eyes, “What warning?”

Edric averted his gaze to Ginelle, “He knows where she resides. She is no longer safe for he will come for her.”

Dorian heard Ginelle's sharp intake of breath and felt her small body quiver against him. Something barbaric and vengeful sharpened the fury within him for in that moment he felt Ginelle's vulnerability and fear. "She has nothing to fear for no harm will come to her. I will ensure it."

Edric nodded and than mounted his horse. As he gathered the reins, he turned to peer at Ginelle. "I apologize if I frightened you, mademoiselle." He hesitated as if to say more but refrained as he caught Dorian's scolding look.

As Dorian watched the man ride away, he waited until he was clear of sight before turning to Ginelle only to find her gone. He peered up and caught the edge of her skirts disappearing through the front doors.

Dorian followed inside and made his way upstairs. He knew he would find her barricaded within her room and was not so pleased to find the lock against him. He paused at the door but heard nothing from the other side.

"Open the door, Ginelle."

No response.

This only angered him and he beat his fist on the door. "You will open the door or I will break it open."

His body jolted as a stifled sob came from the other side. Her cry rushed through him, affecting him deeply and he found himself inside with the door hanging limply on the hinges.

Ginelle stood next to the window with her hand pressed against her chest, her mouth forming an O at finding her door completely torn apart. "Was that necessary?" she demanded.

He did not notice her anger but the tears that streaked her face and widened her eyes to pools of lightened brown. He crossed the room to stand over her and reached out to cup her face gently with the palm of his hand. "Why do you cry?"

Emotions flickered in her subtle gaze and he watched her struggle internally with her fears as she pushed away from him and motioned towards the door. "How am I to have some privacy with no door?" her voice trembled as she kept her back to him.

"You will not need a door for you will not be sleeping here." He replied.

She spun around, suddenly furious, and he saw fresh tears spill to the rim of her eyes. "This is my room!"

He shook his head as he stepped towards her. "It is no longer." Her shoulders trembled as he grew closer and grasped her shoulders gently. "Why do you weep, my sweet one?" his thumb caressed her lower lip as it quivered beneath his touch.

He peered into her large, unguarded eyes and saw the fear that left her feeling fragile and unprotected. He lifted his hand and lightly traced the curve of her cheek. "I would not let anything happen to you."

"But how does he know?" she gasped, "How does Pierino know where I live? How does Lord Edric know of him? What reason does he want me for?" she wrenched away from him and pressed her hands to her face to muffle her cry.

Dorian stood motionless, watching her tremble with sobs. She dropped her arms and spun around to face him. "I am weary of being frightened. I seek answers but gain nothing." Her expression shifted to one of defeat as she dropped her head. "Mayhap I should seek him out myself and demand his reasons?"

Dorian reached her in two long strides and seized her shoulders. "No!" he hissed, "You will go no where near this man! What ever the reason may be, I will be the one finding answers." He loosened his grip and reached up to push her hair from her face. "Do not fear for I will keep you safe."

Ginelle shook her head, "This does not make sense to me, Dorian. Pierino is merely a thief and I an orphan with nothing to benefit. His motives to me are unclear."

"He is not merely a thief; he is a skillfully equipped criminal. What do you know of this man?" Dorian asked.

Ginelle sought her mind and realized she knew absolutely nothing about Pierino aside from his pick-pocketing and abuse.

"You know nothing of him because you were just a child. He will not reveal his true motives to you, a small girl."

"But what of Lord Edric?" she asked, more perplexed that a complete stranger knew of Pierino and herself, and that he would warn her.

"I have every intention of unraveling that mystery as well. I have never heard nor seen this man."

"He claimed that he had family here but I know not where he resides." Ginelle said.

"How do you know this man?"

"He was at the banquet." She replied.

Dorian fell silent for a moment but than noticed the paleness of her face and the evident fear in her eyes. He cupped her chin as he said, "Think on it no longer. Gather your things for you're moving to my room."

"I most certainly am not!"

He had turned his back to her and at her protest a smile curved the corners of his mouth. Even with her fears she would dare to challenge him with defiance.

He turned to look at her and arched a dark brow. "Must I carry you?"

She narrowed her brown eyes at him. "Must I smack you?"

Dorian resisted a grin, "You wouldn't?"

She lifted her little chin and glared sharply at him. "I most certainly would and I would enjoy it since you insist on ordering me about."

This time he did grin, flashing his straight, white teeth as he stalked towards her. Immediately she backed up, throwing her hand out between them as if to ward him off. "Dorian I mean it!"

He stalked her as a predator would its prey and when she had no where to run, he made his move. He swept forward and seized her around the legs, shifting her completely up off the floor onto his shoulder. She began kicking and pummeling his back as he strolled from the room.

Ginelle felt red stain her cheeks as she caught a glimpse of Belle and Fannie standing huddled in the hall, clear out of Dorian's path as he walked by them. Their smirks only heightened her embarrassment before they disappeared around the corner.

"Put me down!" she cried as he pushed open the door and set her on her feet.

She brought her hand around to collide with his cheek but he easily caught her wrist in a firm, yet gentle grip. He shook his head at her as his grin broadened. "I expected that."

Her eyes narrowed angrily before wrenching her hand free and placing them on her hips. "Why must you insist on getting your way?" she demanded, "Does it pain you greatly to show a smidge of compromise?"

Dorian crossed his arms against his chest as he observed her amusingly. "Mayhap I am not accustomed to compromising."

"Well I am not accustomed to defeat." She started around him towards the door but he swiftly caught her up against him and immediately her body erupted in flames, suddenly eager for his lips upon hers.

He leaned forward and his breath fanned her forehead. "Why do you resist me?" his voice had dropped; laced with desire as a swirling heat sharpened his ice blue eyes.

She quivered against the hard muscle pressing against her breasts and the feel of his hands at her back. "Why do you insist on controlling me?" her voice was hushed as she fought against a sudden wave of heat spiraling deep in her loins at the feel of his hardened shaft pressing against her belly.

His arm tightened as his eyes fell to her lips. “I do not wish to control you, Ginelle.” He said as he reached up and traced the curve of her jaw. “I wish to make passionate love to you.”

Chapter 18

They made love all through the night. Every lingering bad thought seem to disappear in Dorian's arms. She thought of nothing but their time spent together and the tenderness of his lovemaking. How could she have been so blind to her heart's desire? Her heart seemed to expand within her chest for he displayed such gentleness in these precious moments.

She yearned for his love and the urge to declare her own. She had feared of becoming his mistress but that no longer mattered for she craved these moments where she was open to express her waking desires in his embrace.

Yet, the fear of his rejection, of being cast aside once she proclaimed her love was a dreaded worry. She had loss many dear to her heart and somehow, losing Dorian seemed the ultimate tragedy.

No man had ever treated her so wonderfully, so kindly despite his own demons. The only man to love her unconditionally had been her beloved father, never once did she think to look upon a man and fall hopelessly in love.

She imagined her belly growing with his child, a child with hair as black as the night and eyes like blue ice.

Her mouth curved into a smile at the joy of having Dorian's children and her hand fell flat to her belly. Could she now have a babe growing within her womb?

She turned her head on the pillow to study Dorian's sleeping face. In slumber, his face took on a boyish expression. She reached out and gently pushed aside a tendril of black hair. His face was smooth of any lines; those distinct lines that usually furrowed his brow whenever provoked. His face was soft and irrevocably handsome and she pictured the youth he had once been and her heart ached for the pain he must have endured in those fragile years.

He vowed to protect her and keep her safe, but what of his torment? What of the suffering from his darkened childhood and the loss of his sister? Would he let down his barriers for her?

She struggled with tears for she couldn't imagine the magnitude of his heartache and grief that he kept so tightly concealed.

Dorian awoke sometime later to find his bed empty. He shifted his body until he lay facing the side where the lovely smell of lavender drifted sweetly into his senses. Immediately he ached for her nearness and wondered after her absence. He would have seemingly enjoyed waking to find her curled against him; the thought brought an immediate grin to his face for he would have liked exploring her delectable curves while she slept.

Never had his mind or body lingered on one particular woman for such a prolonged time. He had imagined after having her that he would have been satisfied and move on, as he had done previous times afore with countless women.

But Ginelle was different. It seemed the more he took her, the more he wanted her and the thought of life without her was entirely intolerable. He no longer wanted to dwell among the shadows, drinking away his sorrows. After Eloise had died, he feared of living a nonexistent life; he feared loving again but what is life without love?

He knew the moment he laid eyes on Ginelle that there would be no other capable of ensnaring his heart. He wanted her at his side, as his wife, bearing his children. He vowed in that moment to make her his, forever so that no other could claim the woman of his heart.

Suddenly he thought of the stranger that had sought Ginelle out the previous day. Who was Lord Edric? What reason did he have for wanting to speak with her? He would see to it that he discover every little detail circling this mystery.

With that notion, he arose and quickly dressed. He left the room with the intention of finding Ginelle only to stumble into Lucile at the end of the hall.

"It is midday and now you think to arise?" she inquired, placing her hands on her hips in that accustomed manner of scolding. "It is well past breakfast, monsieur so you will just have to make do on your own."

Dorian resisted a grin as he addressed his housekeeper with wry humor. "Where might I find Ginelle?"

The older woman narrowed her acute gaze before saying, "She is in the garden."

He nodded his thanks.

"Before you go-" Lucile said, catching him half-way, he turned as she reached in her pocket and withdrew a letter. "This just arrived for you this morning."

Dorian accepted the letter and ripped open the seal. His eyes skimmed along the lines of ink informing him that Lieutenant Cummings had made port and had information on trade and most importantly, the Spaniard King.

He folded the letter and nodded once more to Lucile before continuing on down the hall.

The moment Dorian spotted her, sitting along the stone bench by a bushel of roses, his heart swelled within his chest; an immediate urge to go to her and possess her lips nearly drove a moan from his tightened throat.

Instead, he straightened and studied her from the shadows. A cooled gentle breeze, an indication that summer was nearly at an end, trickled through the garden, rustling the flowers that dangled in the midday sun. He crossed his arms against his chest and felt a smile tug at the corners of his mouth.

Seemingly unaware of his presence and occupied by a book that rested within her lap, with her head slightly bent, she proceeded to read.

She had donned a simple day dress that hugged her small frame and for a moment, he watched her, amazed at how little a female could make such an impact on his darkened heart.

"You let me sleep well pass dawn." He said, his voice stirring her aware as she lifted her head, surprised to see him.

She smiled and it nearly inflamed him. She smiled for him alone and that pleased him greatly.

"I did not wish to wake you." She said gently, setting the book aside as she rose to her feet.

Dorian grinned, "If you had awakened me at daybreak I would have likely dislodged the tongue lashing I just received from that cynical woman."

Ginelle laughed softly as Dorian crossed the space separating them and reached for her hands. He watched an emotion much like surprise flicker in her soft eyes as he lifted her palm and lightly pressed a kiss to her knuckles.

"I have to go into town today and would like for you to accompany me."

All traces of humor fled as she stiffened, hesitating before asking, "What reason do you have to go into town?"

"Lieutenant Cummings has made port and requested I meet him in town to speak on business."

Quickly she sought a reason to decline. "I would simply get in the way, Dorian."

He grinned as he reached up and cupped her face in his hand. "I can think of nothing more but having you at my side for the day."

Ginelle bit down on her lower lip, unable to resist the dark lilt of his voice. How could she refuse when she herself wanted nothing more than to spend every moment with him?

Something about his demeanor had changed; he was gentle and humorous as if the dark shroud that seemed to hover over his disposition had all but lifted. Could she be the reason for his sudden change in manner and happiness? Was it possible that he felt strongly about her as she him? Did he love her?

She feared going to town certain that Pierino or Lord Edric would be lurking, ready to snatch her from Dorian. Yet, with Dorian at her side, she felt certain he would protect her at all costs.

She peered up into his handsome face, marveling at the glint of life that brightened his eyes to a clear, crystal blue. His face revealed no harsh lines of anger or coldness; in fact, she could detect nothing but softness, a gentleness that amazed her.

If she proclaimed her love now in this moment, would he tell her that he loved her? Her heart jumped against her breast with a sudden rush of adrenaline as she opened her mouth but the words never came as a sudden anxiety warned her she was wrong.

Instead, she gripped his hand and nodded. "Yes, I'll go with you." She replied with a small smile.

Dorian assisted Ginelle from the carriage and she felt her heart skip in her chest as he placed her hand in the crook of his arm. Almost instantly she felt some of her anxiety ease at the comfort of his large body standing at her side.

They had traveled to the other part of town where poverty littered the cobblestone streets. This particular part of town was overcrowded with squalid conditions. Merchants bellowed from each side of the street as carriages rolled along and children garbed in rags chased through the thickening crowd.

Ginelle leaned closer to Dorian, somewhat wary as her eyes moved over Londoners. She half expected Pierino to suddenly appear, demanding his debt to be paid. These were the exact streets she had channeled her way through as a child, picking unsuspecting pockets to make a living.

She remembered that exact day she had ran, fleeing to the safer side of London to escape Pierino. If she had not escaped when she did, she would have never met Eloise on that fateful day. She would have never known this life or the man at her side that she would grow to love.

Her other life was now a vague memory, a memory that she wish to forget, aside from the fond remembrance of her doting father.

Her fear eased as Dorian wrapped an arm securely around her waist, as if sensing her discomfort. He led her easily through the crowd, his mood darkening with each step as they made their way to the docks.

Ginelle gasped when she spotted the many vessels varying in all sizes lining the docks. Large crowds gathered to unload the huge quantities of cargo, passing them along from the boats to waiting barrows. Ginelle gasped, stunned to see that some of the cargo consisted of slaves as she watched a row of men connected with chains make their way onto the dock.

Various crews rustled about, shouting, some singing merrily as they unloaded crates along with hammering while loosened ropes were released to splash loudly in the water. Barrels were rolled along, each laden with valuable merchandise.

When they reached the Eastern Dock, Ginelle inhaled sharply as they made their way towards a large vessel made up of several masts. She knew little to nothing about vessels or the business of trade and was quite in awe to see such a magnificent ship and suddenly intrigued to learn more.

"That is yours?" she asked Dorian, her voice light and curious.

Dorian nodded, "Yes, one of several."

"What type of ship is it?'

"It is called a schooner, rigged with three masts. It is specifically used for trade because of its agility in speed therefore it is a favorable vessel among traders."

Just than they spotted Lieutenant Cummings and he waved them over. Ginelle was somewhat curious to know why Dorian had asked her to come along and even noticed that Lieutenant Cummings was a bit surprised to see her as well.

Cummings aura usually bordered lively and humorous but today Ginelle sensed a change in his character, a severity that she had not witnessed before. "Should we speak in privacy, Captain?"

"We can speak in the Captain's quarters." Dorian said as he ushered Ginelle onward towards the ship.

Dorian took immediate notice to the crew's sudden perk of interest as Ginelle stepped on deck. He scowled darkly and cast angry looks over the men who thought to chance a look at his woman.

Once inside the confines of his cabin, he released Ginelle, not realizing his grip had been bruising until he noticed her fingers rubbing the skin where his hand had been moments ago, but she said nothing as she moved about the room, studying its confines.

"What news do you have, Lieutenant?" he asked, jerking his eyes from Ginelle.

Ginelle paused in her surveying to turn and peer at Cummings who seemed almost pallid in the dusked cabin. "The remainder of the crew is rumored to be dead."

Dorian stiffened and Ginelle immediately felt the fury seeping from his body. "You are certain?"

Cummings shrugged, "It is but a rumor, the truth of it is unknown."

"What of the Spaniard?" Dorian asked, his voice dripping with malice.

"There are rumors that he was spotted in the Shetland Islands."

Dorian arched a black brow, "Shetland Islands? It doesn't add up, why Shetland?"

"Shetland could possibly be a nest location; mayhap in Lerwick where vessels are serviced." Cummings suggested.

"Last we spoke you said the bastard was seen along the coast of Portugal and than the English Channel. That is the opposite direction? How did he manage to shift his course so suddenly?"

"We believe he has a replica of the vessel he steers, one that is a diversion to keep officials off his trail."

Dorian's scowl deepened, "I have merely an assumption to run on but one worthy of considering. The Spaniard is clever, forming a diversion when all along he may be shacked on Shetland." He was ready to make a move, ready to exact punishment on the blackguard that killed nearly an entire crew and stole an entire vessel of cargo costing him a pretty penny. He was not one to wallow in his loss, instead he sought retribution.

"We set sail in a few days. Have the vessel and crew prepped for departure."

Cummings nodded. "I'll send word when she is ready, Captain." With that he nudged his head in agreement and proceeded out of the cabin.

Dorian turned and stiffened, suddenly aware of the intense storm brewing in the soft brown eyes glaring angrily back at him.

Chapter 19

Why had he brought her here? Ginelle wondered as she stared angrily at Dorian from across the cabin. She was hurt and hiding her emotions proved to be difficult in that moment. She had listened keenly into their conversation and Dorian had immediately made plans to leave for sea once again, without a single thought to her.

"You plan to leave so soon?" she asked through clenched teeth.

"I have business to tend too."

Ginelle narrowed her eyes suddenly vexed at his nonchalant manner for he didn't realize how desperately she yearned for him to remain home, for fear that something terrible would happen to the man she loved.

"Who is this man that you seek?"

He straightened his back and crossed the room to stand over a desk piled with maps. "He's a wanted man." He said as he sifted through the papers, "He took the lives of many of my men and for that I seek justice."

Ginelle moved to stand behind him, "You do not have that sort of authority. Why not allow London officials bring this man down?"

Dorian spun about and Ginelle took a startled step back, surprised to find his face drawn with anger. "London officials have done little to nothing to see that this man is brought to justice. Therefore I will take matters into my own hands. I have been tracking him for some time now and am well aware of his methods. He will be brought down by my hand."

She curled her hands into fists at her sides, wanting to vent out her frustration and the words that jammed tight into her throat. How could she tell him that she feared she would lose him? She felt the words surfacing in her throat but stalled as she attempted to declare her love.

He was angry and bent on vengeance. She doubted he would proclaim what she so painfully yearned to hear.

She lifted her chin and hardened her stare, "What reason did you have for bringing me down here, to this part of town?"

His body bespoke his simmering rage and she sought for a smidge of the gentle, tender man who had made passionate love to her just the previous night but was disappointed to see that his coldness had returned.

His sharp blue eyes settled on her face as he said, "I brought you along because I enjoy your company." His voice was cold and did little to sedate her anger.

She would not ask him to stay. She knew his business was important to him and it would be selfish of her to make such a demand, yet at the same time, she was furious that he would risk his life all for a vendetta. She was terrified that she would lose the one stable thing in her life, the man whom she'd given her heart too.

Victoria stood aside from the lively crowd, her eyes grazing the many suitors passing her by, some blatantly admiring her with open interest. She felt a grin tug at the corners of her mouth as she lifted her chin, boldly meeting each intrigued stare.

She detested this part of town but knew better than to venture into the affluent parts of London. She would be frowned upon, shunned by many who knew of Victoria Petroff. She cared not of their opinions, she cared not that they called her harlot. She was a prideful woman who took no shame in flaunting her beauty for compensation.

She had many eager suitors along the side, some exceedingly generous but they were no longer of interest. She wanted a challenge.

As she searched the streets, she paused to study a few that would prove conflicting but continued to survey her options. She grinned, excited by the mere thought of taming another man who thought himself immune to a woman's power.

She turned and jolted, an immediate gasp escaping her throat as she caught sight of a familiar masculine frame moving along the dock.

Her eyes widened than narrowed with simmering rage as the sun glinted off the blond head beneath Dorian's shoulder. Almost instantly, a violent urge to rip the girl from Dorian's arms surfaced.

She hissed beneath her breath as she studied them from afar. She felt Dorian's rejection like a knife in her chest. Dorian had been the one incapable of taming. She thought assuredly he would come crawling back to her once the girl denied him, how wrong she had been.

Her hands curled into fists at her sides as she followed the two with a burning stare. Something violent and vengeful stirred from her soul, demanding she take back what once belonged to her.

Dorian loved this girl. Her Dorian! Not once in their lovemaking did he declare affection or endearments to flatter her. Did she not satisfy him? Had she not met his needs, his pleasures?

Dorian was her challenge. She would not obligingly sit aside and allow this impertinent female take her man.

One reason alone would bring Dorian to this particular part of town. He was here on business which meant a possible venture out to sea. If that is the case, her opportune moment would arise to seize control.

Victoria Petroff would not be discarded because of some pale haired, child-like wench. She would make certain of it.

When they returned to Ashford, Ginelle immediately distanced herself, unable to remain in Dorian's presence, fearful that her emotions would rise to the surface. She was angry that Dorian planned to leave and for how long she knew not. She was frightened that he would never return and with that, she would be alone, forsaken with a broken heart.

Once inside, she settled in the parlor, struggling to succumb to the pain that she would surely suffer from his departure. Did he not see her pain? Did he not feel her undying love?

She struggled with tears and turned to see the piano. Immediately, her heart swelled against her chest as the memory of Eloise, beautiful compassionate Eloise teaching her the basics of playing memorable pieces was as vivid as if they were yesterday.

She crossed the room and settled on the bench. She lifted her arms and her hands hovered along the black and white keys. She breathed in deeply as she closed her eyes, remembering that day that changed her life forever, the day Eloise brought her to Ashford.

With her eyes closed, she began a subtle, alluring tune. Her fingers moved gracefully along the keys, creating a methodic harmony that played throughout the room. She felt the tears slip uncontrollably from beneath her lowered lashes. Her chest shuddered with a sob and yet she continued to play, finding comfort in the familiar ballad.

The moment Dorian entered the manor; he stopped abruptly, taken aback by the beautiful stream of notes drifting from the parlor. The sweet euphony brought on a rush of tangled emotions, drawing him across the hall to stand in the door.

He watched in bewilderment as Ginelle's small, graceful hands danced along the piano's keys. He watched her silently as he was overcome with a state of solace, knowing in this defining moment that he would never love another. She had affected him in a monumental way, altering the man he once was into the man he is now, capable and worthy of love.

He had never known purity and light until Ginelle. She had shown him a different path aside from the narrow one he had walked his whole life.

His entire family was loss to him; his gentle mother and willful Eloise, even his tormented father.

There was that lingering fear that he could potentially harm those he loved, just as Clayton Ashford had done, ripping them apart with his anger and overwhelming darkness. He refused to believe that he would become his father.

He was certain she avoided her feelings, her emotions towards him, burying them beneath her defiant layers. She was frightened of her affections and he vowed that he would make her his, even if that meant marrying her without her consent. He knew not if she loved him, but he would spend the rest of his life loving her.

Later that evening, they dined in silence. Her stomached rumbled but her plate remained untouched for there was no desire to eat.

Ginelle studied Dorian from beneath her lashes. He had not said a word since their return from town. She wondered desperately for his thoughts but knew better to ask. It mattered not if she asked him to stay at Ashford; he would leave with or without her approval.

Her opinion seemed to not matter for he was determined to leave whether she liked it or not and that hurt the most. Had they not shared intimacies that meant she had some say in this? She was angry and yet, she could not help but love the way his black hair swept across his broad shoulders, or how his brow furrowed whenever deep in thought. Her heart fluttered for no other and the actuality of his departure was frightening as well as painful.

If she opened her heart completely, she would be vulnerable and she wasn't willing to take that risk. What if he never returned? What if he didn't love her?

She lifted her eyes and watched him from across the table, her heart beating profoundly against her chest for she longed to hear the words that would wipe out every last doubt.

As much as she disapproved of his determination to avenge his fallen crew, she knew it was inevitable to fight it. She just wanted that assurance, those distinct words that meant something of worth or was it naught but lust?

Her utensil dropped abruptly to clatter against her plate. Dorian peered over at her from across the table, his piercing eyes narrowing in the dim glow of the room as he studied the sudden affliction on her face.

"Are you ill?" he asked, his voice deep with concern stirred her distressingly, forcing tears to her eyes.

She nodded grimly and pushed away from the table. She cleared her throat and said, "I am not hungry and wish to go to bed."

"Ginelle."

She stopped short of the hall and clenched her eyes shut, wanting nothing more than to flee. She turned to meet his perceptive stare, "I make for port in the morning."

She hadn't the courage to utter the words jammed in her throat so she merely lifted her head, gathered her skirts and left the room.

When he entered his room, his eyes immediately swept across the bed, expecting to find her small frame asleep but found the bed unstirred. For a moment, he thought she had returned to her own room, knowing something of distress had come over her, but the moment he turned his head and spotted her asleep in the cushioned sofa before the hearth, he was immediately drawn to her side.

He knelt by the chair and gently pulled the open book from her lap. She stirred and lifted her head and the firelight flickered across her face, catching the dampness that trailed her cheek. He stiffened, affected deeply to see that she had been crying.

As he gathered to his height, he lifted her gingerly from the chair and cradled her against his chest as he moved towards the bed. As he lowered her to the coverlets, her eyes fluttered open, wide and glossy with unshed tears.

Her fingers grasped his forearm, curling into the sleeves of his tunic. "Don't leave." She rasped her fear in the edge of her voice.

He reached out and cupped her face, "What do you fear, my sweet one?"

He watched intense emotions flicker in the subtle brown of her eyes and yet, she refrained from revealing her distress. "Pierino will not come for you here. You are safe, ma petite."

She closed her eyes and turned her face away.

Dorian reached out and gripped her chin gently, pulling her eyes back to meet his own. "What troubles you, Ginelle?"

She remained silent, struggling internally with a confliction he knew not. "You leave tomorrow." She whispered.

He nodded.

Her fingers unfurled from his arms to flatten against his chest. "Would you love me?" her voice trembled and her lips quivered, "Would you love me tonight?"

"Ginelle-"

She reached up and pressed a hand to his lips, shaking her head lightly. "Kiss me." she cried fervently.

She pushed up from the pillows as his arms swept around her, pulling her flush against him as he captured her sweet mouth. He kissed her deeply, his tongue sweeping along her lush honeyed lips, as his hands caressed every delectable curve to plant in his memory, to remember the feel of her soft little body in his arms for the lonely nights to come.

She came to her knees and arched against him, her breasts pushing against his chest. A deep growl of desire rose from the depths of his throat as he reluctantly released her to rip the shirt from his heated flesh.

His lips found the pulse at her throat, kissing a trail along the delicate curve of her jaw as his fingers jerked on her nightdress. She met his kisses with an eagerness that heightened his rapture to near insatiable.

The fire in his groin spread throughout his limbs, demanding he taste every inch of her loveliness. He would never have enough of her, he would never be sedated. He would want her always; love her always.

He swept a hand through her silken tresses, his memory taking note of its softness and pale, moonlight hue. He reached up and cupped a milky breast, his fingers teasing and tracing, her voice gasping his name as he reached down and released his pulsing member.

He tried being tender in his lovemaking but the way she arched against him, pressed her body to the heated contours of his own, he was mindless with longing, unable to withstand a moment longer.

Her body quivered in his hands as he nudged her legs apart and thrust inside her, catching her lips as she cried out with fervor.

Their passions rose, his kiss deepening as she met each vigorous thrust. Dorian was intoxicated with the sweet scent of her, the feel of her skin and her dewy eyes brimmed with passion. He took her ardently that drove his name from her lips and her nails into his back. They collapsed together in each other's arms and he pulled her close to mold perfectly against him.

She closed her eyes and he kissed a butterfly caress along her feather-like lashes, and the small brim of her nose and the corners of her lips, wanting to implant every inch of her in his mind. It wasn't long before she drifted asleep and he remained awake for some time, watching her sleep, and brushing the wayward tears from her face.

Chapter 20

He was gone. Ginelle knew the moment her eyes opened that he was gone, and with his absence, an immediate pang of emptiness. Her eyes fluttered wide, brimmed with tears as she stared blankly up at the wide, ivory ceiling, her heart sinking heavily as a deep void of hollowness spread within her chest.

She sat upright and pulled the coverlets to her chest, inhaling deeply of his masculine scent. She shifted and than spotted the white lily resting against his pillow.

Her heart accelerated as she studied the beautiful flower, the tender gesture flaring hopes anew. As she reached for the lily, she couldn't help but feel a bit foolish for acting very much the lamented widow but somehow she feared the day of his return would never come.

She cradled the delicate flower, her thumbs gently caressing its milk-white petals. Her tears slipped uncontrollably as the night before embraced in his arms surfaced to mind.

A sudden, unexpected knock came to the door and Ginelle quickly brushed her tears away as Lucile entered, lugging a silver tray fraught with an assorted breakfast. The aromas struck her senses with a ferocity that suddenly churned her stomach. She felt her face grow pale and immediately pressed a hand to her suddenly unsettling belly.

"You have slept well unto midday, mademoiselle." Lucile's voice was stern and her dark eyes inquisitive and for a moment, Ginelle feared the older woman would question her afflicted disposition.

She was relieved when the housekeeper said naught, and preceded about the room. She jerked the drapes wide and immediate sunlight poured into the darkened room, emitting effulgent light amongst the masculine furniture.

Ginelle's fingers curled around the white lily as Lucile crossed back to the tray and removed the silver platters. "Cook has prepared a hearty breakfast I expect a good portion of it to be eaten."

The older woman turned and her severity wavered but she refrained from saying anything but her dark eyes beheld a deep empathy.

Clearing her throat she motioned towards the tray, "Once you've finished your morning meal, you are to get dressed for you are expecting a visitor today."

Ginelle stilled to awareness, her eyes averting from the flower to Lucile's face. "A visitor?"

Lucile nodded, "A missive arrived early this morning from the Duchess of Hadley. She asked if you would join her for tea later this evening but considering the circumstances, we informed her that you were feeling a bit under the weather, so we asked if she would come to Ashford instead and she gladly obliged."

She frowned, "Circumstances?"

"Monsieur Dorian gave adamant orders that you were not to venture far from Ashford while he is away."

Pierino. Of course. She thought suddenly, her heart budding with affection for though Dorian was at sea and at greater risk than she, he still thought of her wellbeing and that notion brought comfort.

After Lucile left the room, Ginelle arose from bed, her hand still cradling the beautiful small flower symbolizing Dorian's absence, and for a time she kept that flower in her palm as she stared out the window.

Belle appeared a short time later and assisted Ginelle with her bath. She donned a beautiful gown of peach, the dress emphasizing the tininess of her waist and the fullness of her breasts with a white sash along her midriff and adorning lace sleeves.

Belle situated her blond tresses at the nape of her neck, binding the silver mane with a matching peach ribbon.

She peered at her reflection and found that the lovely image did not reflect the saddened heart within. She could only hope that Lady Ellison could somewhat appease her melancholy.

It was a short time later when a servant informed Ginelle that the Duchess had arrived. As she ascended the stairs, she was taken aback by the sudden nauseated ache within her stomach and the thought of food seemed to deepen her nausea.

Inhaling deeply to abide her queasy belly, she made her way outside to greet Lady Ellison. For a moment she felt slightly nervous at seeing the Duchess again but remembering how much she had seemingly enjoyed her company at the banquet, a bit of her discomfort eased.

The coachman assisted Lady Ellison from the carriage and immediately the sun encompassed her flowing, black hair. She had chosen a vibrant gown of green, very much in striking resemblance to her startling green eyes as they glinted with mirth as they settled on Ginelle.

The two women grasped each other's extended hands and pressed a kiss on each adorning cheek. "I heard you were not feeling well?" The Duchess asked softly, her green eyes moving genuinely over Ginelle's pale face.

She nodded with a soft smile, "It is nothing, I promise. I pray that it is not much of an inconvenience, your grace?"

The Duchess laughed sweetly, “Nonsense!” her green eyes glinted with a smile, “And please, call me Ellison. We are friends are we not?”

Despite her unhappiness, she smiled wholeheartedly. She had not many friends so having a companion in Lady Ellison was greatly appreciative. “Would you care for some tea in the garden?”

Ellison nodded eagerly, “That would be lovely.”

The midday sun accentuated the exceptional day, shimmering beautifully along the flourishing garden of kaleidoscopic colors. A brisk autumn breeze caressed the hair at her nape and despite the high sun; she shivered at the sudden cool air skimming lightly along her skin.

Fannie appeared moments later, bracing a tray heavy with tea and crumpets. Ginelle groaned inwardly, her stomach rolling with distaste for the unsweetened bread. She imagined she truly was ill for the nauseated feeling lingered.

“How is the Duke?” she asked, focusing her attention on Ellison. “He is well I hope?”

Ellison chuckled softly, “He is thriving and as vigorous as ever, my beguiling husband.”

Ginelle smiled with amusement at the admiring affection in Ellison’s bright, green eyes. She took a tentative sip from her tea, hoping the aromatic beverage would settle her stomach.

“I heard of your illness recently after the banquet?” Ellison expressed, her face suddenly sympathetic, “I pray there were no lasting effects?” she inquired.

Ginelle set her tea aside and smiled reassuringly, “Not at all. I’m a bit under the weather today but nothing to be concerned over.”

“Tell me-“ Ellison began, “-did any of the suitors at the banquet appeal to you?”

Ginelle stiffened, remembering that night as vividly as if it were yesterday. She felt her face turn crimson with embarrassment at the recollection of Nathaniel Sharp and than the terrifying memory of Pierino.

Sensing her sudden detachment, Ellison felt regret. "Forgive me that was very untoward of me. I have no right to pry."

Ginelle smiled, quickly composing her thoughts. "No need to apologize." She said, "Many are curious to know for not much has been said on the matter. I'm afraid none of the men were of interest to me." she paused and than quickly added, "Do you think me vain?"

Ellison laughed, "Gracious no! I believe every woman has a preference when it comes to choosing a husband."

"What do you mean?" she asked, suddenly intrigued.

Ellison smiled unto herself, "Well, the Duke and I didn't quite see eye to eye when we married; in fact, I was quite against our betrothal."

Ginelle gasped, utterly surprised.

Ellison chuckled with laughter, "It is hard to believe now but at that time it was quite evident that my husband-to-be was anything but appealing to me."

"But you love him?"

Her green eyes lightened with heartfelt compassion. "Most ardently."

Her eyes met Ginelle's from across the table with a knowing expression. "Love is blind, Ginelle. Sometimes it is just beneath the surface."

Ginelle's thoughts turned inward, instinctively towards the man who had stolen her heart, against all her objections and distrust of him, she had fallen hopelessly in love with him.

"He loves you, you know."

Ginelle's head jerked up, startled by Ellison's declaration. "Pardon?"

"Dorian." She said, "He loves you, with a fire that may be grander than your own."

Ginelle wanted to laugh at how ridiculous the notion was, but found she could not find any humor in it. “I don’t know what you mean.”

“I know that your heart cries.” Ellison said softly, “I see it in your eyes and you wonder if he loves you too.” She fell silent, smiling as she added. “I have never seen Dorian so enamored by a woman. The way he looks at you and follows you with his eyes, the very way his demeanor alters completely whenever you are near. The evident signs of enrapture are there, Ginelle.”

Could enrapture be mistaken for lust? She wondered.

“I am being untoward again.” Ellison said and yet, Ginelle did not detect sincere remorse. As she studied Ellison’s expression, there was a keen sense of awareness glinting beautifully in her green eyes, a longing to ease another’s discomfort.

Was Ellison right? Did Dorian truly love her?

They continued the afternoon with a livelier, flowing conversation of theatrical events and latest fashions. She believed Ellison knew of her distress and wished not to upset her, so they avoided the discussion of Dorian.

When the time came for Ellison to leave, Ginelle immediately felt that heaviness in her chest, realizing Ellison had been a wonderful distraction, slightly easing some of her doubts.

“I had a wonderful time.” Ellison said, grasping Ginelle’s hand in her own. “Mayhap we could do this again, soon?” she inquired.

Ginelle smiled and squeezed her hands lightly, “Yes I would like that very much.”

Ellison’s smile widened, “Do not hesitate to call upon me if you need me. I have not many friends that I trust and you will find a worthy ally in me.”

Ginelle felt a great deal of comfort in knowing that she had a worthy companion in Ellison. “Thank you.” She said gently.

With that said between them, Ginelle watched as the coachman assisted Ellison into the carriage and as it strolled down the winding path leading away from Ashford, Ellison waved out the window her goodbye.

A sennight had passed and some of her relief she had felt with Ellison's reassurance seemed to diminish with each passing day. She had not received word from Dorian on his whereabouts and she could detect nothing from town that usually teemed with gossip.

She immersed herself with books and music and domesticated labor but found that even the tedious house work could do little to cease her thoughts, or the rising fears.

She called upon Ellison frequently, comforted by her presence and warm manner. She visited often, sipping tea and dining of late. They soon became inseparable and Ginelle found it easier to cope with Dorian's absence so as long Ellison was there to keep her troubled thoughts at bay.

"I am so glad you could join me for supper." Ginelle said cheerfully as servants bustled around the room, supplying heaps of cookery.

"As am I." Ellison replied happily, eyeing the food hungrily. "I'm so sorry that Edmund could not join us, he has been quite occupied lately."

Ginelle smiled but as soon as her gaze settled on the immense display of food spread before them, her stomach turned.

Startled by this reoccurrence since Dorian's departure, she tried pondering an explanation for her sudden illness. She couldn't fathom the sudden nausea that plagued her continuously each morning.

Cook had done an excellent job preparing a hearty meal but found that she could not stomach the boiled beef or the fresh, savory vegetables and buttered bread. Though her stomach groaned with hunger, she knew she would not be able to stomach much of anything so chose a latter option of hot tea and chicken broth.

It wasn't until both women were alone that Ellison asked, "You are not Dorian's ward are you?"

Ginelle stiffened, startled by the unexpected question. She peered at Ellison from across the table, noting the sharp glint in her evergreen eyes.

She frowned as she cleared her throat, "What do you ask?"

Ellison lowered her knowing gaze, "London ton is quite loquacious. Your banquet stirred quite a significant amount of curiosity."

With Ginelle's prolonged silence, Ellison immediately exclaimed, "I am sorry, Ginelle. I find myself prying without limitation."

Ginelle smiled, "I understand your curiosity. I am quite a mystery to others but you are my beloved friend, I have no fear in confiding in you."

Ellison hesitantly continued, knowing something of graveness hid beneath the surface. "How did you come to know Dorian?" she took immediate note to the sudden anguish contorting her beloved friend's face.

It was a stretch of estranged silence before Ginelle answered. Her eyes focused on her lap where her fingers entwined to still the sudden rush of grief that she had for so long blocked from her mind. "I was orphaned at a very young age." Her voice trembled as she spoke, "It wasn't until I met a woman that would change my life forever."

"Eloise."

Ginelle met Ellison's attentive, green eyes and smiled gently, her eyes brimming with unshed tears. "She had bestowed such kindness on me when others had turned away for they saw only beggary." Her eyes jumped to Ellison's for now the Duchess truly knew her heritage was nothing but meager but she detected nothing but sincere comprehension.

"She took me in when I had no where else to go. If it were not for her, I would have surely died."

Ginelle was stunned to see that Ellison's green eyes glinted with tears in the dusk glow of the room. "I could imagine her death was devastating for you?" she asked softly, her voice laced with immense heartache.

Ginelle dropped her head, her shoulders shuddering at the painful memory of Eloise lying lifeless in bed, her brilliant blue eyes growing dim. "She had been everything to me that I had never known; a mother, mentor, a sister and most graciously, a beloved friend. Her death was the most painful thing that until this day, I suffer."

Tears streamed Ellison's cheek and she found herself immobile to brush them away. "I'm terribly sorry for you loss. Lady Eloise was the most compassionate woman I had ever met."

Ginelle met Ellison's gaze, "Did you know her well?"

She shook her head, her black curls bouncing atop her shoulders. "We had met occasionally during social gatherings but sadly she had spent a majority of her time as an adolescent at a boarding school." She paused, her eyes relaying a glazed look, "She was the light of the Ashford lineage." she said, "And Dorian was the dark."

Ginelle shuddered, knowing just how engrossing Dorian's pain truly was.

"Eloise was the light in Dorian and with her death; I truly thought it would be his undoing." She paused and than added, "That is until you."

Ginelle felt her heart swell against her breast as she met her friend's glowing stare. "I could never compare to her."

Ellison smiled gently, "It is not about comparison, my dear friend. Love is a profound, inexplicable phenomenon. You, my dearest companion, have bestowed in Dorian what many other women had failed to do. That light that brightens his tormented soul has returned in the budding form of love, all because of you."

Ellison smiled than, "This is all from observation of course."

Ginelle laughed gently, "Simply from observation? Are you certain you are not a scholar on the physics of love?"

Ellison grinned, "Perhaps."

The mood had changed instantly from cloudy to cheerful with Ellison's enlightening perspective but as farfetched as her explanation sounded, Ginelle couldn't help but wonder if she was right? Had she truly sparked such a love in Dorian?

Her doubts immediately settled in the back of her mind to dwell upon later so she continued with the evening meal, conversing happily and Ginelle was greatly relieved to see that Ellison seemed unaffected by her poor, troublesome past.

She smiled inwardly for there was a slight sense of acceptance of herself despite her hardships and heritage; a feeling of belonging.

Chapter 21

The season grew colder with lingering nights and pale, gray skies. Leaves fell from their tangled limbs littering the roughened terrain in autumn hues of yellow, red and orange.

Ginelle shivered as she rubbed her arms, sinking deeper into her cloak. She had been looking forward to taking Milly for a ride and now decided against it with the sudden cold draft sweeping from over the hills. She had not been feeling well as of late, plagued with backs pain and fatigue, so she thought better of it and returned to the manor.

Mayhap a nap would ease her troubled mind and tired body. She paused half-way down the hall, her heart sinking in her chest as she pressed a hand flat against the mahogany door leading into Dorian's study.

She sparred a glance sideways before entering the room and closing the door quietly behind her. She pressed her back flat against the door and felt a shudder quiver through her body. She closed her eyes as she inhaled his scent, drinking in his memory as troubling, subliminal thoughts rushed to mind.

Her mind seemed to conjure every frightening threat likely to endanger Dorian's life but she couldn't seem to shake the notion that something dreadfully unimaginable had happened to him and the idea of another heart ache was all too catastrophic.

Lerwick, Shetland Islands: November, 1816.

Time transpired without recollection and though he could not prevent the duration of time, he held strongly onto the vitality of his thoughts; they were all that kept him sane.

He tasted the copper tang of blood along his tongue, felt every inch of the rusted shackles encased around the bone and flesh of his wrists. He could feel the sticky substance of his own blood seeping profusely from the inflicted wounds along his limbs, soaking his tattered clothing but none of that mattered for the remainder of his crew were alive and well on their way home.

His temples throbbed, forcing his head forward, the pain doubling with every little movement of his beaten frame. He fought against waves of churning disorientation and the pain, growing spreading throughout his weakened body to burry deep into the recesses of his mind rendered him debilitated but through it all, he kept her in mind.

Through his blackened haze, Dorian sought the only image of beauty that brought immediate comfort, the only lingering thread of sanity he could hold onto.

She was like lemons and sunlight. The purity and beauty of Ginelle swept away all the sorrows of his predicament, allowing him to maintain some semblance of his sanity while buried in this blackened hell.

Dorian clenched his eyes and imagined the sweet scent of heather, the softness of her doe-like eyes and the ivory complexion of her skin. He knew the moment she came to Ashford that she would be his. He had made a grave mistake in ignoring his feelings for her. He should have made Ginelle his long ago and vowed that if he ever escaped this blasted hole, he would see to making Ginelle his forever.

A sudden noise jarred him aware and the sudden sweep of his head brought on a fierce stabbing at his temples. He moaned despite himself as the latch rattled, indicating his captor's arrival.

Nearly a month in this darkened cell and he had yet to set eyes on the man known as the Spaniard King. Reyes crewman had dragged him down to this rancid box and since than, he had not met the infamous blackguard plundering his vessels.

He knew that time was now as he braced his weight against the wall at his back and watched through dark, hooded eyes as the door swung inward, and the shape of a man filled its frame.

Dorian narrowed his eyes against the strain of darkness and jerked as a flare of light struck his wearied gaze. He listened intently as his captor crossed the space, his slick leather boots stepping methodically along the damp floor.

His eyes slowly adjusted to the sudden flow of light and he peered up to meet the face of the Spaniard King.

Black, wild eyes glinted sharply in the light. Donned in a rich velvet waistcoat; equipped with knives, a distinct gold hoop dangled from his left earlobe, he sported a thick, black beard and a gold chain hung from around his neck, silk, black breeches and a brimmed hat with a black feather protruding from the top all preceded the Spaniard King's reputation of appearance.

""¿Señor Ashford, no?" His mouth twisted as his black eyes glinted curiously back at Dorian. "I hope your stay has been-" he smirked, ""-cómodo?"

The Spaniard King paused, his black brow arching with wry humor. "I find your English language essential, Capitán, so I will speak in your tongue. You have been expecting me, sí?" when Dorian remained silent, the Spaniard King continued, "You are a clever hombre; you've been tracking me, quite successfully." He grinned a toothy grin, "You have sought me for a reason, no?"

Dorian listened intently.

"Your crew, they are alive-"

"A handful of men don't compensate for the lives of many." Dorian accosted, his voice dripping with untamed fury.

The Spaniard King paused, considering this before continuing. "I do not keep count of men that I kill, Señor Ashford. However, I deliberately sought your vengeance to lure you to me, so the lives of your men were vital."

Struggling to understand his words through a haze of heated red, Dorian remained silent.

"Allow me to explain so that we may have an understanding. You have something I want, Señor Ashford, something that plays a key point leading up to the capture of your vessel, the lives of your crew, and your stolen cargo." He paused, allowing his words to sink in, "I am not accountable for the remainder of your men, as you can see, I am exceptionally merciful when it comes to self-gain." He grinned and than his face darkened. "I have taken you in exchange for the remainder of your crew but in exchange for your freedom Capitán, you have something I want."

Dorian resisted the unsettling fury and tried pondering reasons that would strike an attack on his vessels and cost him the lives of half his crew.

"My brother, Romano de Reyes, was captured by European slave traders during a raid. He was taken a slave and rumored to have been sold to a plantation owner, that plantation owner being you, Señor Ashford. So you see, my intentions are clear, no?"

Dorian gritted his teeth, knowing full well of the man he spoke of, one of the few slaves who had done nothing but give him problems since the moment he was brought to Ashford years ago. "The man you speak of is a convicted criminal."

Reyes' black eyes glinted acutely, "As am I, Capitán, but you do not see me laboring your fields as a slave. I deliberately attacked your vessel and misled you for some time. I am a very busy man Señor so much has kept me occupied."

"That would explain your delay." Dorian grinned but his eyes flashed murderously.

Reyes grinned, "I imagine the bounty on my head is considerable. I have plundered quite a many buques. I've managed to mislead every authority hunting me, including you."

"You take pride in your accomplishments, Spaniard coward." Dorian spat, "You altered ships whenever the fire got too hot. It won't be long before London Officials catch you, I'll happily deliver you into their hands myself."

"Ah, but you will be dead when that day comes, no?"

Dorian grinned, "I don't fear death, Spaniard."

Reyes leaned back on his hunches to better observe his prisoner. "You amaze me, Señor. I thought you a simple hombre, but you have more courage than a thousand men I have known."

Dorian's face darkened, his blue eyes flashing daggers of impending rage. "Don't presume to think you know me, Spaniard. I am the Captain of many vessels; I'm quite adapted to the likes of you. Don't let my plantation upbringing fool you into believing you know a thing about me."

Reyes smirked, "Yet you are imprisoned in my cell as my prisoner therefore I have the advantage?"

Dorian leaned back against the wall unable to support his heavy body any longer. "Do what you will Spaniard, your brother shall remain a slave for decree has deemed him a criminal, I find comfort in that."

Silence fell between them and Dorian watched the Spaniard King struggle with his repressed anger. A brief flash of maddening fury darkened his obsidian eyes but he refrained from saying more. He gathered to his height and crossed the room to the opening of the cell; he paused to turn back to

Dorian. "You may rot in here, Señor Ashford, you may rot until you have set my brother free, if that means you must wither and die in this rotted place in order for me to gain his freedom, than so be it."

As the door slammed closed with deafening force, Dorian settled back against the wall and closed his eyes, quickly seeking the lovely image of the woman he loved.

Ginelle woke with a start, startled to see that her room remained dark, traces of the morning light barely admitting through the window. She pressed a shaky hand to her forehead and closed her eyes, drawing in a few breaths to chase away the remnants of her nightmare.

Settling back into the pillows, she focused on the fire across the room and for a time stared into the gathering flames her mind plagued with lasting images.

As morning light filtered into the room, Ginelle pushed aside the coverlets and arose from bed. The moment her feet touched the floor she was seized with a sudden vertigo as a violent wave of nausea gripped her stomach, sending her sprawling for the chamber pot.

Suddenly, Lucile was there, holding her hair aside and gently rubbing her back until the morning sickness passed.

Ginelle settled back onto her heels and Lucile handed her a glass of water to wash out her mouth. "Thank you." She mumbled, reaching up to brush strands of blond from her pale face.

Lucile set the glass aside and pulled out a cloth to gently dab at Ginelle's forehead. "When was your last monthly flow, my dear?"

Taken slightly aback, Ginelle turned to look at Lucile, her face furrowing into a frown. "It was-" she fell silent and than her eyes widened with a startling realization. "You don't think?"

Lucile nodded, "You get sick quite often before the sun?"

Ginelle fell silent contemplating the signs that had been there for some time. Her morning sickness, the constant fatigue and back pains, she had even noticed a little weight gain but hadn't given it much thought. "Are you certain?" she asked, her voice shaky.

The older woman nodded, "If you'd like, we could have a mid-wife examine you, just to be certain?"

Despite her newfound fear and shock, her heart accelerated at the thought of Dorian's child growing within her womb. Slowly, she pressed a palm flat to her belly and noticed the roundness of her stomach and smiled a tiny smile. All the sadness she had suffered since Dorian's departure vanished in that defining moment. As scary as it was to realize she was carrying a child, her heart blossomed with the idea of being a mother.

She carried Dorian's child.

"No." she said softly, her eyes aglow, "I don't need a mid-wife."

The weather grew colder and with each passing day that did not bring Dorian home to Ashford, or a missive to inform of his whereabouts, her heart darkened with despair, dashing any hopes of his return. Instead, Ginelle found comfort in the small bundle of life growing within her belly, easing some of the pain that left her feeling hollow and empty.

She busied herself with daily chores and complex events to keep her occupied and far from the depths of her mind. Along with Lucile, she helped to maintain Ashford, working and completing numerous tasks. She buried herself in cooking and cleaning, especially reading where the endings were always joyous.

Ellison was ecstatic when she learned of the pregnancy. They spent a majority of time speaking on the joys of motherhood and doing all the necessary means in preparing for the child and as exciting as it all was, Ginelle found it difficult, fearing Dorian would never return to learn of his unborn child.

A few days later, Ginelle was awakened by a noise outside her window. Her breath rushed from her lungs as her heart leapt against her breast at the sound of a carriage rolling to a halt.

She shoved the blankets aside and rushed to the window. She pushed the drapes aside and gasped as Lieutenant Cummings stepped from out of the carriage. Her heart seemed to stop for a scarce second, her eyes widening as she reached out to grip something steady.

Dorian! Had he returned?

Overwhelmed with a bombardment of emotions she cried out in glee, unable to contain her overpowering excitement and the flood of relief she whirled from the window and gathered her robe in one hand as she rushed for the door. She cared not that her appearance was disheveled or that she was not properly dressed; she cared for nothing in that moment except that Dorian had finally returned to her!

She fled down the hall, her hair pillowing freely around her flushed face as she gathered the edges of her robe together, her heart pulsating against her chest as she eagerly sought Dorian's embrace.

Bogart was there at the bottom of the stairs to greet Lieutenant Cummings. Lucile joined Ginelle at the bottom and the older woman's look of disapproval on Ginelle's current appearance was overshadowed by her anxiousness to see her Lord finally come home.

Ginelle stiffened as Bogart stepped aside and only Lieutenant Cummings followed inside. Her heart suddenly dropped in her chest like a heavy stone and her hand lashed out to grip the banister for support, her face paling beneath the soft, russet stare of the Lieutenant's eyes.

"Lieutenant Cummings?" Lucile spoke and Ginelle was keen to notice the edge of fear in the older woman's somber tone and knew that something terrible had happened.

Stefan reached up to remove his hat and stepped aside as Bogart closed the door against the cold draft. The Lieutenant cleared his throat and fumbled with his hat, unable to meet the fearful stares around him. "I had to come and tell you myself."

Ginelle struggled to bring air into her lugs for she detected the sorrow in Stefan's voice, there was no shred of his usual charismatic manner and that alone confirmed her fears that a foreboding happening had occurred. "What has happened, Stefan?" her voice was small and hollow.

He lifted his head and met Ginelle's alarming stare. "I had to tell you myself. I could not send a missive."

"What is it, Lieutenant? Has something happened to Monsieur Dorian?" Lucile stepped forward her face pinching with apprehension.

There was a heavy, prolonged silence along with a strange buzzing in Ginelle's ears as she struggled to keep her body from swaying. A sudden trembling crept up her legs until her entire frame shook with tremors.

"He is dead." Stefan proclaimed, his voice sinking with his devastating words. "He was captured by the Spaniard King in exchange for the lives of his men. I have brought them safely home but-"

"Ginelle!"

Stefan rushed forward and seized her before she crumpled to the floor. He swept her gently against him, startled to find her unconscious and frighteningly pale.

Chapter 22

After settling Ginelle in bed, Lieutenant Cummings stepped aside as two maids moved forward to see to their young mistress.

Stefan turned to the housekeeper who stood in the corner, silent and pale. Gathering her composure, the older woman motioned him into the hall.

"I thank you Lieutenant, for coming all this way to inform us of this unfortunate news." Stefan had rarely seen moments of weakness in this tenacious woman but he could see the tears brimming in her dark eyes while her hands trembled in gripping the front of her apron.

He dropped his head and cleared his throat, "Your heartache is as grave as mine, mademoiselle. You do not know how difficult it was for me to come here but if it is any consolation, Ashford is my second home, Dorian was many things to me."

Lucile reached out and smiled despite her suffering and squeezed the young Lieutenant's arm in a comforting gesture. "Ashford shall always be a home to you, Lieutenant."

Her hand dropped to her side and she cast a longing stare at the closed door.

"Will she be alright?" Stefan asked, following the older woman's stare.

He noticed a distinct shudder pass through the housekeeper's shoulders. "I do not know." She whispered tightly, "She carries his child."

Stefan blanched, "You are certain?"

Lucile nodded, "Yes, I fear for her health as well as the unborn child. Dorian's death may very well destroy her."

"She loves him?" Stefan already knew the answer but somehow had to hear it from another.

The older woman turned to peer up at him. "Her love for him is what will destroy her. There has been much sorrow at Ashford, first Lady Eloise and now Master Dorian. Ginelle is all that we have left."

"He would have married her." Stefan said more to himself, realizing than that Ginelle's reputation was ruined. She was unmarried and with child and somehow he could not bare any more travesties for Lady Ginelle. He knew Dorian had loved her and would have wanted the very best for her. Dorian had not only been his Captain, but many things, a father, brother, a mentor, everything he had lacked in is life.

He was painfully familiar with the depth of Ginelle's pain, having lost the woman he loved and never confessing his affections. "I shall marry her."

Lucile gasped her mouth parting in a distinct O. "Pardon, Lieutenant?"

"She is unmarried, mademoiselle and carrying a man's child. She will be the object of many taunts along with her suffering; I cannot bear to see it."

"You are an honorable man, Lieutenant, but I fear Lady Ginelle may not accept your offer." Lucile fell silent, knowing full well that he was right. She could not bear to see her young mistress whom she had grown to love as her own suffer another hardship. "Would you give her time?"

He nodded, "Of course. She is in a critical state right now." He squeezed her shoulder before descending down the hall.

She should be accustomed to pain by now but somehow every tragedy, every blow directed towards her heart seemed to intensify, leaving her broken and utterly drained of emotion. Her eyes fluttered open and immediately the numbness was there, sinking deep into her soul. She willed the tears to come but found she hadn't the strength to weep.

She could hear rustling throughout the room but focused her attention on the window, staring blankly at the empty, blue sky. She heard voices, speaking softly to her but nothing registered past the insensitive barriers. It felt better to not feel anything so she held strongly onto that obstruction.

Hours seem to drift obscurely as vague shadows moved in a cloudy haze around her. There was nothing but a deep oblivion, dragging her further into its depths and she welcomed it for deep beneath those layers of emptiness, there were no sensations, no particular feelings of warmth and pain, just a consciousness of nothing.

Finally when her eyes drifted closed; Ginelle was thrust into the whirlwind of pain as her mind became flooded with every imaginable emotion leaving her pillows ruffled and her nights restless.

Days turned into weeks and the Ashford household fell into a central of lifeless inhabitants. Lucile did all she could in managing the estate but her servants were dismal and saddened by the heavy loss of their master and the listless state of their mistress.

Fear for her young mistress and her unborn child grew increasingly with each passing day. Ginelle refused to respond, let alone eat a thing until Lucile was forced to call upon the mid-wife. The woman did all she could in convincing Ginelle to eat but she remained passive and showed little signs of cooperating.

She feared that Ginelle would waste away in her bed, refusing food and potentially harming the unborn child and eventually resorted to drastic measures. She called upon the mid-wife and from there they forcefully fed her. Her efforts in struggle lasted only a minute until finally she resisted no longer and finished her meal but as soon as the tray was taken away, she retreated to her usual state of remoteness.

This continued for days until Lucile sought the only woman who in hopes could possibly reach her young mistress and pull her from the depths of depression.

It didn't take long for Lady Ellison to arrive at Ashford and Lucile greeted the Duchess immediately, filling in minor details for Ellison was well informed of the travesty that had befallen Ashford.

"Has she spoken since?" the Duchess asked, her lovely face etched with utmost concern.

Lucile shook her head, "No your grace, she has not uttered a word and I fear for her health and the state of her child."

Ellison gathered her skirts and followed the housekeeper upstairs and down the hall. When she opened the door, Ellison was immediately struck by the gloom of the room and a lingering sadness and gasped despite her collectedness.

Her green eyes immediately settled on the crumpled frame lying motionless in the bed and her heart sank to a degree of horror. "Have this room brightened immediately." She ordered her harmonic tone taking on a serious note of measure.

Lucile wasted no time, crossing the room she shoved open the heavy drapes and the evening light chased away loitering shadows.

"Have your cook prepare some broth and a hearty loaf of bread, and some ginger tea."

"Right away, your grace." Lucile hastened from the room and Ellison moved about, straightening things and rousing the diminishing fire beneath the hearth.

She turned towards the bed and her heart sank deeply. She crossed the room and settled beside Ginelle, and gently stirred her awake.

The moment her eyes fluttered wide, Ellison saw the weight of her pain. "You must get up, Ginelle." She said earnestly, "This has gone on long enough. You need to get up."

She remained unmoving, her eyes staring vacantly at the wall.

"I refuse to sit idly by and allow this nonsense to continue. Think of your child, Ginelle."

A small light flickered in her brown eyes and Ellison knew she had sparked a flare of life. "You're stronger than this." She said determinedly.

Slowly, those brown eyes met Ellison's green stare and the weight of all her pain came crashing down and her dear friend released a heart-wrenching cry.

Ginelle wept for hours cradled in Ellison's lap and her friend held her as a mother would a weeping child until she could cry no longer. Ellison dabbed the remaining tears from her face and settled next to her friend in the bed.

"It is okay to cry, Ginelle." Ellison said softly.

Ginelle shook her head, sniffling as she stared across the room into the embers burning low and dim. "I've cried nearly a lifetime of tears." She mumbled, "I'm tired of feeling."

Ellison straightened, "You don't mean that."

Ginelle peered over at her, "Yes-" she whispered, "It is all too much."

Suddenly, Ellison reached over and took Ginelle's hand, pressing it flat against her rounded belly. "Do you feel that?" she said thoughtfully, "That is life growing in you, a blessing from God. How could you not want to feel that?"

Ginelle stared down at their hands and felt a tiny motion beneath her hand. She gasped, her eyes teeming with a sudden flow of tears.

"You can't ignore your feelings." Ellison said, releasing her hand, but Ginelle's remained, her heart jumping against her breast as the little bundle in her belly filled her with an overwhelming light. "You need to feel every thing that life can offer you, the good and the bad, for the sake of your child, you need to live."

Silence settled heavily between them and Ellison allowed Ginelle to register her thoughts. One of the servants appeared, carrying a tray with a recap of ginger tea. Ellison nodded towards the table across the room, it wasn't until the servant had left that Ginelle finally spoke.

"He didn't know I was with child." Her voice trembled with turmoil. "Now he'll never know."

Ellison reached out and lightly gripped Ginelle's shoulder. "Your pain will go away. Once you hold your baby, all that you're feeling will slowly diminish and though it is bittersweet, you have him in your heart. The memory of him will live through you and your baby."

Ginelle peered over at Ellison and for the first time in several weeks felt a small smile curve her lips. She wrapped her arms around her beloved friend and knew she had to live, for the sake of Dorian; she had to live for their child.

Chapter 23

As the tiny bundle within her womb grew, her pain lessened moderately through the approaching weeks but Dorian's loss remained branded on her heart. She knew she would never love another and slowly came to means with her new life of loneliness, and yet, her life was not as lonely as she imagined it to be. She had her child and Lucile, even the servants who adoringly waited on her, and her beloved friend Ellison. She was not entirely alone and somehow that brought a bit of reassurance.

The approach of winter brought heavy snowfalls and vast white skies. Ginelle spent a majority of her time with Lucile, preparing for the holiday season. Cook was especially excited for this was the season that induced hearty meals and delightful desserts. The servants bustled into preparing Ashford for the Christmas holiday, creating hand-made ornaments and decorations made of glass beads, tinsel and an assortment of lace and ribbon. Days were spent devoted to preparations for the approaching festivities and it gave Ginelle much distraction from a monumental absence.

She noticed particularly that Lieutenant Cummings visited often, his warm demeanor brought on a sense of security but at the same time, his company reminded her painfully of the man she loved.

That evening, Ginelle settled into the parlor, finding comfort next to the fireplace. It was one of her favorite rooms in the entire house. Every inch of the room displayed an assortment of gilt porcelain and hand-crafted pottery. The ceiling bestowed a beautifully silver chandelier that in the full-bloom of spring, the crystals glinted light stars on a crisp night. Oil paintings adorned the pale walls and floral carpets extended along the smooth surface of the parlor floor. Sheer lace curtains ran the length of tall windows where the light of day could shimmer across the sleek black surface of the piano.

She had settled into one of the velvet seats before the hearth and occupied a book to pass the time. She could hear the servants hustling about, engaged in their daily tasks, and could smell sweet aromas drifting from the kitchen where Cook prepared the evening meal.

She closed the book in her lap and stared blankly into the fire.

"I thought I would find you here."

Ginelle jerked to the present, her attention averting to the front of the parlor where Lieutenant Cummings stood, smiling gently, his arms folded modestly behind his back.

"May I join you?" he inquired.

She straightened and offered a tentative smile, "Of course." She said lightly, motioning towards the seat across from her.

He settled across from her and she was discreetly grateful for the sudden distraction. "Will you be staying for supper?" she asked gently, noticing his gaze strayed away from hers.

"Thank you but no, madame." He replied.

Ginelle frowned; did she detect a slight edge to his voice? She folded her hands in her lap and studied him with due consideration until finally she asked, "Is something troubling you, Lieutenant?"

His eyes fixated on her and she noticed a slight unease in his warm, russet stare. "I've been meaning to ask you something, Ginelle. I have just been waiting for the opportune moment."

Her heart fluttered lightly in her chest as she leaned forward, "That moment being now?" she asked gently.

He nodded and turned fully in his chair towards her. She was taken aback when he reached across and gently took her hand in his. He cleared his throat before asking, "I would be honored, if you'd accept my hand in marriage."

Her eyes widened and she released a startled gasp at his unexpected question. Her mouth parted but she found herself at a loss for words.

"I would treat you kindly." He said quickly, "I would give you everything you need, for you and the babe."

Her heart accelerated tenfold and she found herself on her feet, pulling her hand from his. "Lieutenant-"

"I know this seems all so sudden-" he said, gathering to his height.

"I am truly flattered but you do not want to marry me, Lieutenant."

"Because you carry another man's child?" he asked gently.

Ginelle fell silent, her heart taking on a sudden pain. Not just any man, she thought brokenly to herself.

"I assure you, my intentions are honorable."

She smiled a small smile but her eyes remained saddened. "Why do you wish to marry me, Lieutenant?"

He gathered her hand in his and stared down at her in honesty. "I admit, I do not love you as of now, but in time, we could grow to love each other. We are friends, are we not?"

Slowly, she nodded.

"I do not wish to see you succumb to the vicious taunts of society. They are unaware that you carry Dorian's child. I would marry you and cease any mockery before it begins."

Ginelle smiled as she reached up and admiringly brushed Stefan's face. "You were always a dear friend to Dorian; you do this for his child?"

He nodded, "And you."

Her eyes fluttered down and she stared at there entwined hands. "I need time." She whispered softly.

"Of course, please, take all the time you need." He lifted her hand and gently brushed a kiss across her knuckles. After he had left the parlor, she settled back into the chair by the fire, completely lost as of what to do.

"He did what?" exclaimed Ellison.

Ginelle nodded, staring out the window of her bedroom window, pressing fingers to the cold glass. "He asked me to marry him."

Ellison's green eyes brightened with a sudden flare of elation. "I always did like him." She said with great mirth.

Ginelle turned from the window to study her friend, a small smile curving her lips. "You agree than, with the proposal?"

"Of course I do." She said diligently, "Lieutenant Cummings is a charming, young man."

Ginelle withdrew into her thoughts, knowing how right Ellison was.

"The child would be assured and well taken care of, my dear." Both women lifted their heads as Lucile entered the room.

Ginelle straightened, surprised to find the older woman at the door. "You are already aware of his proposal?"

The housekeeper nodded, "He told me of his intentions the day he arrived; it seems he has given it much thought."

Ginelle bit down on her lower lip, struggling internally with her own conflictions. She knew Ellison and Lucile wanted the best for her but she couldn't cope with the idea of marrying Stefan. Indeed, he was exceptionally charming and handsome, and very clever, but she did not love him.

"He has said that he's ready to settle down." Lucile explained, "He's finished with the mercenary life."

Of course, Ginelle thought sadly, struggling with tears, his Captain was dead. Her hand fell to her belly and she felt the evident bump that concealed her little blessing.

She lifted her chin and met their waiting stares. “You’re right.” She said meekly. “I must do what I can for my child.” She turned away from them, unable to hold her tears any longer.

The following week leading up unto Christmas, there was a great happening of festivities. To announce their engagement, Ginelle and Stefan attended many, including the great hall of Hadley.

The night of the occasion, she had chosen an evening gown of azure blue with flowing skirts that concealed her evident bump. She wanted to keep as much speculation to a minimum for she feared if asked, she would burst into a flood of tears.

Stefan had selected a fitted pair of gray trousers with an adorning vest beneath a flowing frockcoat. He completed his ensemble with a matching tall hat.

Ginelle smiled inwardly. Stefan was very much the appeal of every admiring female but she found it difficult to enjoy the evening, especially since the last time she had been to the Hadley estate, Dorian had been alive.

She proceeded into the evening in mute silence. The weather was exceptionally cold reminding her all too well of frightened nights wondering the streets of London as an orphan. She abruptly pushed those memories away, not wanting to dwell on her second life that seemed all a bad dream.

Stefan escorted her from the carriage once they arrived to the Hadley estate and Ginelle trembled within her wintry cloak as she cast a meaningful stare around her, wondering if Pierino lurked in the shadows. Her heart began an erratic beat as she imagined their last encounter.

“Are you alright?” Stefan asked his youthful face etched with evident concern.

She turned to face him and quickly nodded a reassuring nod and slowly placed her hand in the crook of his arm and they started up the snow-laden path into the Hadley manor.

Ellison had outdone herself once again, creating a room specifically assembled for entertaining her lively guests. The room exhibited exuberance and excitement, glittering colors of holiday décor and the combined smells of pine and cranberry, etched perfectly for the holiday celebration.

"Ginelle!" Ellison appeared from out of the crowd, her green eyes shining beneath the bright chandelier light, donned in a full-skirted gown of deep crimson, her raven curls bouncing atop her slender shoulders as she moved forward for an embrace.

"Everything looks so lovely." Ginelle said appreciatively.

Ellison's smile widened, "As do you, my dear friend. Lieutenant?" she turned to Stefan, "You wouldn't mind so much if I steal your betrothed, do you?"

Stefan grinned, "Of course not."

Ellison wrapped an arm around Ginelle and motioned across the room. "My husband is somewhere in this room-" she paused, scanning the room with her emerald stare. "Ah!-there he is! Come!"

Ginelle released a delighted laugh, knowing Ellison was doing her best to ease some of her anxiousness at being in a crowded room with many curious stares. They strolled across the room until they reached Edmund's side and immediately the Duke turned to plant a kiss gently against Ellison's temple.

Ginelle quickly turned away, feeling a pang of grief at the tender display. "It is good to see you, Lady Ginelle. How are you faring?" she turned back to greet Edmund, his eyes warm and genuine as he studied her quietly.

"I am very well." Ginelle said as convincingly as she could. "Ellison has been very adoring of late, treating me exceptionally well."

"She is a darling." Edmund cast an admiring look onto his wife. "My lovely wife has told me that you are engaged?"

Ginelle found herself nodding.

Sensing Ginelle's detachment, Ellison quickly added, "I'm sure you're famished; let's get you something to eat."

As the two women crossed the room, they were distinctly unaware of the large silhouette blended obscurely in the shadows of the room, a piercing pair of ice-blue eyes watching in curbed contempt.

Chapter 24

Several hours later, Ginelle was tucked comfortably in the cushioned seat of the horse-drawn carriage. Despite the frigid air of the wintry night, her velvet cloak kept her considerably warm. She peered across the space to peek at Stefan from beneath lowered lashes. He had been kind to her all evening, escorting her about the room, introducing her as his betrothed but her affections for him had not changed. He was merely a friend.

She closed her eyes and breathed in gently. She had to continue to remind herself that this was all for her unborn child. She wanted her child to have a better life than she did when she was younger.

"Did you enjoy yourself?" Stefan asked gently, drawing her from her thoughts.

Ginelle sifted in her seat and smiled. "Yes, very much, thank you." She fell silent, feeling the sudden effects of sleep creeping forward.

It wasn't until she drifted asleep that the carriage rolled to a stop and they were suddenly at Ashford. Ginelle stirred awake and blinked repeatedly to clear her head.

The coachman opened the carriage door and the frosty draft struck her face, sending a spasm of tremors through her body as she stepped down into the snow encased ground.

Stefan was there to take her arm and lead her towards the manor. Once inside, Lucile greeted them at the door and Ginelle bid Stefan a good night.

"These terrible cold conditions are just wrecking havoc." Lucile muttered with disdain, trembling as she hurried to close the door. "You must be tired, go on to bed my dear and I'll have Belle bring you some tea."

Ginelle smiled as she shrugged out of her cloak. "Thank you Lucile but I think I will just retire for the evening."

She made her way upstairs, her limbs dragging as she moved on down the darkened hall, eagerly seeking the comforts of her bed.

Warmth wafted from the fireplace as she stepped into the room, exuding a subtle glow, enhancing shadows to creep along darkened corners. She closed the door gently behind her and tossed her cloak carelessly aside, wanting nothing more than to collapse into her bed.

With slow, tired fingers, she worked at disrobing until she stood in nothing but her chemise. As she moved to gently lay the gown aside, it was than her peripheral caught the large, looming frame lounged precariously in the corner.

She released a startled gasp, her eyes widening with alarm as she fell back, her body colliding against the bed-post as the shadow lazily unfurled it's long, lean legs to stand to its towering height. Ginelle felt her heart hastened until it threatened to burst from her chest; it wasn't until the figure stepped forward, that her eyes widened in stunned awareness.

"Oh my-" her eyes welled with tears as bewilderment combined with disbelief propelled her forward, only to halt as those haunting, blue eyes hardened cruelly to slits of ice.

"Dorian?" her throat convulsed as she uttered his name in a small, pained whisper, fearful that she imagined him and he would vanish abruptly.

"Disappointed?" he snarled his voice low and menacing.

Ginelle frowned, struggling to control the sudden rush of air escaping her lungs. She felt an onslaught of incredulity and sheer delirium. Dorian was alive!

She felt tears of profound happiness slip abundantly down her face and she wanted to rush into his arms and feel him, flesh and blood, to assure herself that he was very much alive.

She stepped forward, her eyes wide pools of anguish. "What happened to you?"

"You seem baffled to see me alive?" Ginelle frowned, detecting hard accusation in the timbre of his voice.

"Dorian-"

He stepped forward and she jolted with a sudden rush of apprehension. Her mouth fell open on a horrified gasp as her eyes traveled frighteningly over his tall, thin frame. His hair now slightly longer, fell in loose, untamed waves around the sharp, cruel angles of his face revealing sunken cheeks and dark circles beneath cold, blue eyes.

Words escaped her as she assessed his gaunt stature, horrified for she did not recognize the man staring viciously at her, an air of violence surrounding his detached manner.

"What happened?" her words trembled as they escaped her throat and she stiffened as he stepped towards her, his strides deliberate and foreboding.

A shudder trembled through her limbs as his cold, blue eyes traveled insolently down the length of her, lingering on the swell of her breasts. "Do you know how many nights I dreamt of you, like this?" his voice sent a tremor down her spine as she retreated until her back came up against the bed-post.

His mouth curled into a sneer as he stared callously, his eyes taking on a feral gleam of simmering rage. Her mind scrambled for an explanation but she couldn't seem to think clearly with his body towering over her.

"Dorian-" her brows knitted together in utter confusion as she reached out and lightly touched his chest.

His hands lashed out and seized her roughly by the forearms, jerking her forward and forcing a cry past her lips. "I rot in a black hole and all this time, you're spreading your thighs for another man!" he hissed.

Ginelle gasped as his fingers painfully tightened, forcing a whimper from her throat as tears rushed to cloud her vision. "You're hurting me!"

"You know nothing of suffering." He growled, reaching up to grip her chin roughly, forcing her to peer into his penetrating stare. "I thought of you, my sweet woman, little did I know you planned to wed another when you diligently refused me!" he jerked her away from the bed-post and she gasped as he shoved her onto the bed. Ginelle scrambled in haste, frightened but eager to explain. She barely released a breath before he seized the front of her chemise and ripped the material in half.

She cried out as he shoved her down onto the mattress and pinned her there with his body. She shoved against his chest, pummeling him with balled fists as tears of hurt and betrayal rushed forth.

"Dorian, stop!" she cried desperately. "You're wrong-" he captured her lips and gripped her chin cruelly between his fingers, his mouth crushing and bruising, punishing as his hands ravaged her frame, jerking on her torn chemise.

Ginelle struggled in vain, her emotions torn as his mouth devoured her sensitive skin, and his fingers tugging until he grasped her breast, forcing a moan past her lips. She fought against rational thoughts and the sudden flare of heat uncoiling through her limbs. Unable to resist, she opened her lips to his kisses and they softened, his hands no longer tugging but caressing as they moved hurriedly over the curves of her body.

"Ginelle, my sweet one." he rasped, his voice strained and heated. His lips trailed hot kisses over her throat and the swell of her breasts and she felt the length of him pressed against her outer thigh.

He reached up and seized the pins holding her hair in place and tugged her tresses free curling his fingers in the silken wealth of her hair.

A deep ache spiraled in her loins and she arched in his arms, pressing her body flush against the heated contours of his male frame.

He pushed her legs apart and thrust inside her, their cries of passion joining in union as he sank deeper into the cradle of her thighs, his hips rolling in slow, deliberate thrusts as he captured her lips, his kiss possessive and branding.

Suddenly, he left her side like a flame of a candle abruptly diminished. A sudden gust of cold air swept over her heated flesh and she scrambled into a sitting position, jerking the blankets against her chest. A cold splash of realization struck her hard as she stared at his rigid back and averted her tearful eyes to the torn chemise lying heedlessly across the bed.

Rational thoughts took place along with immense betrayal and hurt of his treatment towards her. She peered up from beneath lowered lashes and was surprised to find him staring at her. "Feeling guilty?" he asked maliciously, his eyes leveling coldly on her.

"Dorian, what have I done?" she cried brokenly.

He stalked towards her and she stiffened as he loomed above her. "Every unimaginable wrong doing." He growled low, his eyes narrowing with cold rebuke, "Do you carry his bastard?"

Ginelle gasped, "Dorian-"

He gripped her arm, his fingers curling painfully around her flesh. "Answer me, damn it! Do you carry Stefan's child?"

Her body trembled in his hands and her brown eyes brimmed with tears. She hadn't the words to tell him that the child she carried was his, the pain of his accusations opened old wounds, and the afflictions left her feeling as empty and hollow like never before. She loved this man and yet, he continued to think the worst of her. Did he not see? Did he not feel how her heart ached for him?

Her waited silence confirmed his suspicions and he shoved her away in disgust. "Dorian!-wait!" she cried but he jerked away from her and stalked from the room, slamming the door with frightening force.

Chapter 25

He spent the night wallowing in despair, finding little solace at the bottom of a whisky bottle.

He stumbled away from the window, his long limbs heavy with lethargy as he sank onto the floor of his study. The room was dark, as dark as his black heart, he thought bitterly.

Brief fragments of the previous night rushed forward to plague his befuddled mind. He pressed a hand to his forehead, disgusted by the tremors that wracked his body, how the room spun uncontrollably even while sitting.

He clenched his eyes shut, struggling to think past the throbbing of his temples and the heavy lump lodged in his throat.

He had hurt her, he thought despairingly, and here he was, the epitome of Lord Clayton Ashford. He had not struck her, but the pain in her lovely eyes had been as though he had laid a hand to her delicate face.

A violent growl surfaced deep from within his throat. His sudden remorse overshadowed by a fierce and menacing rage. She had betrayed him! She had given herself to Stefan, his own mercenary and the bastard had taken his woman for his own.

The moment of his arrival he was stunned to hear of their betrothal, enraged by the rumors of a child and vague signs of grief of his supposed death and all the while, he wasted away in a blackened hell, thinking of naught but the beauty of the woman who had stolen his heart.

He knew the moment the manor came alive with servants, the scuffling of footsteps outside the halls brought him aware but his thoughts remained cloudy as the pain of his inflicted wounds intensified intolerably, forcing his conscious mind deep into the depths of oblivion, just as his eyes grew heavy with lassitude, the door of the study swung open and wavering voices bellowed, “In here, milord is here!”

Lucile paced back and forth, casting looks of disbelief and anxiety towards the master bed where her liege laid, unconscious and pale. She thought her eyes betrayed her for all this time, she had believed him dead, but he was alive and very much at death’s door.

Her eyes strayed from her master to the small shadow sitting alongside the bed. Ginelle’s brown eyes gleamed with tears, a lingering thread of hope glistening in the subtle glint of her eyes as she sat rigidly in her chair, clutching tightly into the material of her skirt.

Lucile knew something had transpired between her liege and young mistress but Ginelle had refused to say.

A tall shadow fell in at her side and Lucile peered over at Lieutenant Cummings, his handsome face etched with evident signs of concern. “The doctor will be here shortly.”

The older woman reached up and gently grasped his shoulder until his russet gaze settled on her. “Take your leave, Lieutenant. I will see to master Dorian.”

He nodded grimly and started for the door, he paused halfway, his eyes settling on Ginelle. He was at her side, gently touching her elbow to lure her gaze to him. “Come mademoiselle, the doctor will arrive shortly, you mustn’t be here.”

She shook her head, averting her eyes back to Dorian. “I do not wish to leave him.”

His eyes left her momentarily and strayed towards the bed, he was startled to see cold, blue eyes observing him harshly.

His hand fell to his side as he turned fully around, "Captain?"

Lucile moved forward just as Belle opened the door, ushering the doctor inside. "The doctor is here, madam." She exclaimed.

"Don't touch her." The words were released on a deadly hiss and everyone in the room paused and there was a distinct, sharp gasp as his icy stare settled on Ginelle. "Leave me." He growled his voice pitiless and stinging.

Lucile stepped forward and gently took Ginelle's arm. "Come, my pet." And she wrapped an arm around Ginelle's waist as the doctor stepped forward to examine his patient.

Once in the hall, Ginelle stepped away from Lucile and pressed a shaky hand to the wall, her eyes on the floor to hide her unveiled tears.

"Monsieur is in pain, is all." Lucile said softly to console her young mistress.

The older woman watched a shudder pass through her mistress' shoulders. "He cannot stand the sight of me." She wailed softly, turning to peer at Lucile, her brown eyes filled with sadness.

Lucile froze, shaking her head as she reached out to grip Ginelle's shoulder. "You mustn't think that-"

"He thinks I carry Stefan's child!" she cried brokenly.

Lucile blanched, "Surely he knows?"

Ginelle shook her head as she pressed a hand to her rounded belly beneath the heap of skirts. "He will not listen to reason. He thinks I have betrayed him." With that said, she swept down the hall, eager to flee.

The holiday went unnoticed for a state of melancholy fell upon Ashford. Ginelle was torn, pained by Dorian's refusal to see her. The doctor visited often, tending his wounds that were horrible beyond imaging.

Every night she cried herself to sleep, damaged by his hatred for her and the cruelty he showed her the night of his return and despite it all, her heart still yearned for his love.

She wanted desperately to confess her love, reveal her undying heart and the passions he awakened in her, but she feared he would never think on her again, and never see her in the light as before. He had accused her unjustly of wrongdoings before, but these accusations hurt more than his unrequited love.

The passing weeks she remained barricaded within her room, her heart growing heavy every night he did not call for her.

She yearned for his embrace, his gentleness and sweet, tender kisses. She ached for his warmth and adoring affections.

She pressed a hand to her growing belly. She smiled a tiny smile regardless of her pain, her heart blossoming for she had a piece of Dorian in the small form of her little blessing.

Ginelle decided a nap might ease her saddened thoughts, but as she turned away from the window, a carriage came strolling down the widening path leading up to the front of the manor. She paused as she peered through the cold glass, a frown creasing her brow as her eyes rested on the unfamiliar carriage.

A sharp gasp uncoiled from her throat as a woman materialized from out of the carriage, her striking red curls piled high atop her head as she extended a gloved hand to her coachman. Ginelle was suddenly breathless, the room tilting beneath her feet as the woman from the banquet who had danced with Dorian stepped down into the snow, her crimson skirts in striking contrast to the blanket of snow carpeting the plantation grounds.

Ginelle stumbled away from the window, her eyes glazed with tears as she pressed a hand to her heart, her breaths coming quick and short.

Dorian's mistress.

She crossed the room and settled languidly onto her bed as her heart sank heavily in her chest. Her heart twisted with misery. He didn't love her. How could he love her and call upon his mistress?

"What the hell are you doing here?" Dorian growled, his eyes flashing daggers of pain; gritting his teeth as sharp spasms darted throughout his limbs while he straightened his frame to sit upright in bed.

"Are you not happy to see me?" Victoria asked, her brow arching as a small smirk curved her rosy lips, "Did you not ask your servant to see me in?"

"You did not answer me question, woman. What are you doing here?" he growled as his eyes swept dispassionately over her curvaceous frame.

"Surely you know the heartache I suffered?" she said halfheartedly, her eyes glinting like deep sapphires. "But alas, you are alive, mon amant."

"And that pleases you?" he snarled, his eyes narrowing coldly.

She stepped towards the bed, her dark eyes moving leisurely along his lean frame. Her red lips curled into a grin, "Considerably."

"What is it that you want, Victoria?"

She settled onto the bed beside him, her gloved hand reaching across to trail slowly down the length of his muscled arm. "Haven't I made that clear?" she purred softly.

Dorian wrenched from her touch, "I've stated before, you're affects are no longer of interest."

Her sapphire eyes darkened and her spine stiffened. "You are still smitten with her?" she hissed.

He said nothing but turned away from her penetrating stare. "How could you love her, a peasant?" she asked, her voice dripping with disdain. "When you could love me?"

He turned and met her sharp gaze. "You do not have room for love in your blackened heart, Victoria. You seek only to climb the social ladder to satisfy your excessive taste because you know that spreading your thighs will gain you nothing but merely fancy dresses."

Her nostrils flared as she struggled to suppress her anger. "How very perceptive of you, mon amant." She gathered to her feet and lifted her chin, "I have ruthless, social ambition, but it has gotten me all my heart desires, all but one." She turned back around to face him, "I do not have you, monsieur."

"And you will never have me, Victoria." He replied coldly.

He was surprised to see a small flicker of pain in the deep set of her sapphire eyes, but as quickly as the emotion flickered aware, it vanished abruptly, her eyes converting to smoldering blue. "Leave my estate, Victoria. You are no longer welcome here." He dismissed her with the simple wave of his hand and his rejection burned tenfold.

She lifted her chin defiantly, her eyes sparkling like blue diamonds; her kindled anger propelled her towards the door. She paused, her hand lingering on the latch as she turned back to say, "You will regret it, monsieur, I assure you." She said icily and than she was gone.

Chapter 26

Sleep eluded him but his thoughts remained relentless. Dorian struggled from his bed, pressing a hand to his thigh where the cutlass had severed his flesh. The wounds inflicted along his body were steadily healing, but the wound in his heart was another matter entirely.

His hands curled into fists as he braced his weight against the wall, clenching his eyes shut as he imagined her alabaster skin, hair like moonlight, and eyes the color of golden brown.

The length of his frame erupted in flames, his desire demanding he claim his woman. Mindless of his actions, he left the confines of his room and stalked the dark corridor leading to her room.

The room was dim but warm, a gentle fire burning low in the hearth as he closed her bedroom door. His ice-eyes immediately sought her sleeping form, small and curled in the large four-poster bed.

He moved toward her, his undeniable hunger intensifying with each step that brought him closer to her side.

In her restlessness, she had kicked the covers away, her nightgown rising high on her thighs. He felt a moan rise deep from within his throat as his hands resisted the temptation of running the length of her silky skin with the tips of his fingers.

His eyes moved higher and fell firm on the evident roundness of her belly. A minatory rage gripped him fiercely, and he jerked away, tearing his eyes from this lovely creature that he'd given his heart too.

How could she have given herself so carelessly to Cummings? Had he been so enraptured with her, so oblivious to their discreet love that he had not noticed any wayward glances, lingering touches? But the flattery, he thought bitterly, the flattery had been there, clear as the morning light.

Infuriated, he spun back around, cringing as the abrupt movement caused him pain. He settled beside her, the mattress sinking beneath his weight as his eyes roamed the extent of her small frame.

Her chemise was thin and flimsy, like a whisper of silk concealing the object of his insatiable hunger. Her breasts swelled, rising with each sleeping breath and he had the fierce urge to rip the material apart and lavish her lovely flesh with his mouth.

Heedless with desire, he reached out and lightly caressed a creamy shoulder, trailing his fingers smoothly down her arm. Her shudder passed through him and he gasped, his manhood jerking with anticipation, thrusting against the seams of his breeches.

His hand dipped lower, brushing lightly over the soft mounds of her breasts and her mouth parted in her slumber. She stirred but did not wake, her body shifting towards his touch, and her legs slightly parted.

A rush of heat spiraled low in his belly as he reached down and gently caressed the inside of her thighs. It would be so easy, he thought, his hand straying provocatively close to her moist center.

Her head turned on the pillow and it was there he noticed the wet streak that trailed her cheek. His hand froze and his brow furrowed as he reached up and cupped her face.

She had been crying for whom he wondered?

He forced himself from her bed and for a moment, stood staring down at her. Had he been wrong in accusing her? How could he think otherwise when she had been betrothed and she had not denied carrying another man's child?

The morning light was heavy and grim, as her eyes fluttered wide; Ginelle slowly sat up and stared around the room.

Had she imagined it? Surely she had thought Dorian had come to her in the night? She shook her head for he repelled the sight of her, what reason would he have to come to her?

The notion brought sudden tears to her eyes as her hands fell lightly on her budding belly. She wouldn't give up hope, she vowed determinedly. She would convince him of her love and prove to him that she carried his child.

She had suffered many hardships and refused to cower from this. Surely if his hatred burned so deep, there must have been some sort of affection before it all? He must have felt something for her to shun her so painfully? He had not banished her from Ashford, certainly that meant something?

Her chest expanding with a small ball of hope, she arose from bed and began to dress. She took her time, contemplating ways of expressing her everlasting love. She would make him see; she thought with a hopeful smile, she would make him see how wrong he had been in his allegations.

As she started for the door, she stopped suddenly, remembering the beautiful red-haired woman from yesterday. She shook her head of the image, not wanting anything to deter her from her purpose. She would make him see.

"Where is Master Dorian?" Lucile peered up from beneath the cupboard to stare curiously up at Ginelle looming above her.

The housekeeper straightened to address her young mistress, "I believe he's gone into town, my dear."

Ginelle frowned, "But his wounds have not completely healed?" she said, her words laced with concern.

The older woman shrugged helplessly, "He refused to reason. He said he had important business to see too, concerning Sir Stefan."

Ginelle's heart dropped in her chest. Surely Dorian wouldn't hurt his own Lieutenant, he had to know that Stefan's intentions had been honorable?

"Thank you, Lucile." She said before walking away, knowing the older woman sensed her unease.

She couldn't allow Stefan to suffer Dorian's wrath on her expense. She had to find him and explain before something harrowing happened for she sensed a terrible, foreboding dread.

She dressed in her warmest cloak and gathered it close, chancing a glance towards the rear of the manor in fear Lucile would be standing nearby and when she saw no one, not even a servant, she opened the door and rushed out into the frosty, morning air.

The coachman assisted her into a carriage and she gave specific orders to start for town as she clutched anxiously at the locket dangling from around her neck, her heart beating erratically in her chest as she stared blankly out her window as they bypassed snow-encased hills.

She loved him; she had to convince him of that.

Aboard The Silver Wind, docked along the Eastern harbor, Stefan opened the cabin door and stepped into the dimly lit room. He shrugged out of his waistcoat, oblivious to the man lounging in the corner.

"Did you bed her, Stefan?" his words cut through the quiet like a jagged blade, startling Stefan as he turned to peer at Dorian's hulking frame.

"Captain? What are you doing here? Your wounds-"

Dorian stood slowly from his chair and stepped closer, his eyes like shards of ice as they settled on Stefan. "Answer me, Lieutenant." He demanded coldly.

Stefan shook his head, "No." he said indubitably.

Doubt flickered in his icy stare as he stepped around Stefan, his stride unbalanced, his wounds causing him great discomfort. "I find that hard to believe, especially since at my arrival, I find you escorting her around as your betrothed." He hissed suspiciously.

"Dorian, you have it all wrong." Stefan conveyed, shaking his head. "We all thought you dead. There were rumors that the Royal Navy attacked the Spaniard's vessel and sank every merchant ship on sight?"

Dorian grunted with pain as he shifted his weight to better ease the shooting spasms spiraling through his leg. "You heard right, Lieutenant. The Spaniard is dead, but as you can see, I am very much alive." He said breathlessly, "And I returned to claim my woman only to see that she is betrothed to you, my own mercenary, and confidant. She carries your bastard!" he exclaimed furiously.

"You are wrong in your allegations, Captain." Stefan replied calmly. "She loves you, always has."

"Yet, you intended on marrying her? Why is that, Lieutenant?"

"Because she carries your child!" Stefan proclaimed, "'Tis your babe that she carries and I could not abide her reputation to be tainted, so I did the honorable thing and asked her to marry me, to see her unharmed by society's cruelty because you and I both know she has suffered enough in this life."

Dorian felt the blood rush from his face. "You speak the truth?"

Stefan nodded, "I have never misled you, Captain."

"Your feelings for her are strictly amiable?" he asked, his eyes narrowing with intensity.

"She is merely a friend." He confirmed, "My affections have not changed."

"Does she love you?" Dorian asked, surprised by the sudden somersault of his heart as he anxiously awaited Stefan's response.

Stefan smirked, "Every woman cannot resist my undeniable charm-" he paused, his russet eyes glinting with that familiar wry humor. "-aside from one." He added.

Dorian fell silent as a pang of guilt seized him abruptly. He had treated her cruelly the night of his return and all along, she had not betrayed his heart, and she carried his child.

"She was a shadow of herself." Stefan spoke, drawing Dorian's attention. "When she thought you dead, she withdrew from the world. She loves you undeniably."

"I have made a grave mistake in doubting you, old friend." Dorian collapsed into a chair and swept an unsteady hand through his tousled hair. "I have made a grave error of this whole misunderstanding."

Stefan settled across from him, "You shouldn't waste time with lingering regrets. You love her, so claim your woman and child." Dorian peered over at his friend as Stefan added, "Marry her."

The carriage carried her further into town and Ginelle shivered uncontrollably as a slight fear shuddered down her spine. She had never ventured to town alone but she had to find Dorian, she had to resolve everything.

She peered through the window as children swept along the street, dodging patches of ice as snow flurries began to descend from the milky sky.

Ginelle tried to keep her anxiety at bay but the familiarity of these roughened streets, the dangers lurking in every corner despite the midday light, left her shaking with dismay.

The carriage suddenly rolled to a precarious stop, wrenching her forward. She cried out as she quickly caught herself and straightened against the leather seat.

The door suddenly opened, revealing the coachman. "I am sorry, mademoiselle, but the streets are too crowded for me to continue."

Inhaling a deep breath, Ginelle gathered her cloak tightly together. "No need, Henry. I shall continue on foot."

"Milady?" he frowned with disapproval. "These streets are not safe for a woman like you." he objected.

"I know, Henry. I will only travel a short distance if you'll just wait here?" she asked gently as he assisted her from the carriage.

"Aye milady, but please do hurry."

The moment her slippered feet touched the frozen cobblestone, a feeling of trepidation settled heavy in her belly. Grateful that the cloak concealed her small frame, she reached up and pulled the hood over her head and started into the thickening crowd.

Her brown eyes scanned frantically for the docks but through the crowd she had poor sense of direction. Bodies jostled her about and she felt panic rising in her throat as grimy faces leered back at her. Struggling to not get alarmed, she pushed her way through the crowd and managed to step onto the sidewalk and there she spotted the docks with a gasp of aspiration.

"Looking for someone in particular?" spoke a velvety voice laced with distaste.

Ginelle stiffened and slowly turned to peer into a pair of dark, sapphire eyes. Her eyes widened for a fraction to find her affronted by Dorian's mistress.

The woman radiated beauty but the animosity that glinted cruelly in her deep blue eyes, resembling a stormy sea sent an inclination of intended harm. "He is not there." She said coolly, her blue eyes peering past Ginelle's shoulder.

Ginelle lifted her chin, determined not to be swayed by this woman's indifference. "I'm sorry but I do not know who you are talking about."

The woman's blue eyes met hers once more, narrowing with contempt. "Don't play coy with me girl, I know you seek Dorian."

Her heart jumped against her breast, "How are you so certain of that, madam?"

Her mouth twisted into a smile that didn't quite reach the blue of her eyes. "He sent me for you, of course."

Ginelle stiffened; startled that Dorian would send his mistress to fetch her! She lifted her chin more defiantly, compelling herself to remain firm. "If he sent you for me, than where is he?" she demanded.

The woman grinned, her head turning slightly as she motioned Ginelle to follow her. "He is this way, please, come with me." Her voice had softened, drawing Ginelle forward as a sudden inkling warned her to be cautious.

She followed the red-haired woman and realized she was leading her away from the crowd and into an alley. Her heart hastened within her chest and she hesitated as she darted a fearful glance back towards the crowded streets.

"This way." The woman beckoned and proceeded on down the darkened alley. When she saw her disappear around the corner, Ginelle quickened her steps, eager to escape the damp, deserted passage.

She appeared on the other side of the building, the street less crowded but crammed with carriages lining the cobblestone.

Just as Ginelle managed to catch her breath, the hairs at the nape of her neck tingled in warning as a shadow fell over her. A startled gasp escaped her throat as a large hand seized her arm, jerking her roughly about and her gaze connected with a familiar pair of hazel eyes.

"Nathaniel!" she rasped, her eyes widening a fraction as his grip tightened mercifully around her arm. "What are you doing?" she cried in desperation, struggling to wrench free of his grip.

His expression was made of stone but his eyes were almost remorseful as he said, "I am sorry Ginelle but you left me little choice in the matter."

She frowned, fear clogging her throat as she struggled against him. "What are you talking about? Release me, Nathaniel!"

His face hardened and he jerked her closer until his breath fanned her forehead. "I did not take Dorian's warning lightly when last we met." He growled, "I am touching you, yet he is no where to be found?" he growled ominously.

She blanched, the color draining from her face as she caught a flash of red from her peripheral. "Why are you doing this?" she cast a fearful glance at Dorian's mistress, her red lips curving wickedly.

"I find myself in financial straits." Nathaniel said, drawing her attention. "Miss Petroff has obligingly liberated me from my current predicament with one minor exception."

Ginelle paled, her stomach churning with dread as she stiffened in his grasp. "I have to keep my end of the bargain." He said and than he started forward, dragging her along as he started towards one of the carriages.

"No!" she cried, "Nathaniel, please!" her plea lodged tight in her throat as she struggled in vain to escape his clutches.

He reached out and jerked the carriage door open and shoved her abruptly inside, slamming it closed before attracting unwanted attention.

Frightened, Ginelle stared dumbfounded at the door, her heart pounding forcefully against her chest as she struggled to catch her breath.

Suddenly, her skin prickled in alarm for although the carriage was dark with the curtains drawn closed, she felt the presence of another concealed in the small compartment.

"I tired of these cat and mouse games, kitten." The voice that spoke from the darkness sent an alarming rush of terror down her spine as the curtains were wrenched apart, revealing the recipient of all her fears.

Chapter 27

Ginelle felt a scream wedge tight in her throat as she scrambled to escape the carriage. Just as she reached for the door, rough fingers seized her arm, jarring her backward as the carriage propelled forward, accelerating her terror tenfold.

Gasping to bring air into her lungs, she hastened to put space between her and the sum of all her fears regarded her through cold, black eyes.

"Pierino..." his name escaped her throat on a horrified gasp, her limbs tensing for the unexpected as his thin mouth twisted cruelly into a grin.

Her eyes slanted fearfully towards the door, her body stiffening with anticipation.

"I don't think it wise to provoke me, kitten." Pierino's guttural voice growled, his eyes glinting sharply in the small compartment of the carriage.

Her heart leapt against her breast, her mouth suddenly dry as her mind hastened to think logically past her fear. "I have not forgotten our last encounter." He said harshly, "Ye seem to forget that I am yer guardian."

Despite her fear, Ginelle felt an immediate rush of anger. "I forget nothing." She exclaimed, "You took advantage of a helpless child, you are scum!"

Pierino's eyes glinted suddenly with surprise, "I do not approve of yer newfound bravery, girl, and I tire of it already. What has prompted such a change in ye, eh?"

Her stomach rolled with revulsion as his black eyes assessed her from head to toe. "Ye no longer fear me?" a black brow arched curiously, his eyes twinkling maliciously in the dim light of the carriage. "Mayhap I should test yer bravado, if I remember; ye fought me like a wildcat the last time."

She paled beneath his black gaze, her blood rushing with a sudden, gripping fear for her unborn child. She lifted her chin, her eyes flashing defiantly. "I will fight you tooth and nail if you touch me."

He laughed the sound rolling precariously from his throat like venom. "Methinks ye speak with a pretense tongue, girl."

Her hands trembled in her lap and she prayed he did not see her fear lingering just beneath the surface as she straightened her spine and met his onward stare. "I'm not a child anymore. I am no longer afraid of you."

There was a moment of stillness, just the slight rocking of the carriage and Ginelle tensed, expecting the blow. It came so suddenly, rocking her backward with enough force to wrench a cry from her throat.

Instinctively one hand rushed to her inflamed cheek, her eyes clouding with tears as her other hand moved to her swollen belly, terrified that another blow would be struck to her midriff.

He chuckled, forcing her attention as he leaned back against the leather seat. "Precisely what I had assumed." His eyes hardened as he said, "No need to worry yer little head, ye are no good to be dead."

Her heart shuddered in warning when his gaze fell to her hand pressed protectively against her belly, hoping he wouldn't notice the evident bump beneath her layers of clothing. She quickly rushed to interrupt the process of his thoughts.

"How do you know Victoria?" her voice trembled as she asked the question and slowly lowered her hand to her lap.

His eyes met hers, his lips peeling back from uneven teeth as he said, “Ah, the avaricious red-head? She finds ye a great obstruction. She called upon me. She wanted ye gone, I merely obliged her, twas as simple as that.”

The banquet. Ginelle thought suddenly. She must have seen us. “And Lord Sharp?”

Pierino grimaced and waved his hand in the air as if to dismiss the man. “He was derived from the woman he was not apart of my agreement with the red-head.”

Ginelle’s eyes averted to the window, her heart sinking heavily in her chest for they were no longer in town and now traveled a desolate road.

“Ye have led many to believe ye are this – Miss Pattinson?”

Turning away from the window, she peered at him coldly. “To rid myself of you.”

He smirked, “Ah, but ye failed miserably in doing so.”

Her jaw hardened as her hands squeezed the material of her cloak. “It would appear so.”

“Are ye not curious to know where I am taking ye?”

She tilted her chin, “I cannot make sense of your reasons for wanting me, and I am tired of running.”

A knowing glint sharpened the edge of his black eyes and she shivered despite her wavering bravery. “Mayhap ye would be more interested in the happenings of yer father’s death?”

Ginelle jolted as if the carriage had come to an abrupt halt. Her heart leapt against her chest as though it would burst through flesh and bone, unaware that her fingers grasped the leather seat beneath her. “What did you say?” her voice quivered in a whisper.

“Yer father?” he said tauntingly, “Was yer father not Ross Hayes, the blacksmith?”

Ginelle pulled away from the leather at her back, the profound beating of her heart pulsating in her ears as she struggled to contemplate his jeering words. "H-how do you know my father?"

"I know great deal more, kitten." He said his voice laced with satisfaction at having drawn her back into his control.

"W-what do you know of my father?" her chest rose and fell with trepidation as a numbness filled her limbs, she felt her throat closing tightly as a terrifying notion set heavily in her mind. "Did you kill my father?"

His thin lips peeled away into that sinister grin, his eyes favoring a savage gleam. "I take my profession very seriously and any distraction that may get in the way must be removed effectively."

The tears came painfully in a flood of emotions as Ginelle struggled to absorb his words and the horrifying realization that her sweet, doting father had been murdered by this heinous man. "Why?" she demanded, her fists curling in her lap as she glared at him through tearful eyes. "He harmed no one!" she resisted the urge to leap across the space separating them, for fear of her child, she remained seated, her limbs trembling with suppressed fury. "He was a sweet man and you killed him, you bastard!" she hissed uncontrollably.

He startled her by jumping forward and seizing her around the neck. She gasped, her eyes widening with fear as his fingers tightened warningly. "Cease yer tongue, girl. Ye will learn to submit and know yer place for I can snap yer little neck like a twig." He shoved her away and she gasped for air, her fingers along her reddened throat.

"Why?" she rasped, a single tear slipping along her face, "Why did you kill him?"

"As I said-" he started, "-I take my profession very seriously. I was informed well enough to know what was asked of me. Kill yer father and bring ye to the baron."

Ginelle frowned, "I-I don't understand? Who is the baron?"

Pierino smirked, "My employer."

Her frown deepened, "You were paid by this man to kill my father and take me to him? Why?" she demanded.

Black eyes glistened knowingly. "What do ye know of yer mother, girl?"

Ginelle stiffened, taken aback by the sudden alarm of fear that coursed through her body. "My m-mother?" her stomach churned with dread, her mind turning to the locket close to her heart. "Did you kill her as well?" she spoke the question so softly, fearful of his reply.

"Hah!" he laughed coldly, "I am afraid I cannot take credit for that one."

Ginelle frowned, "Than why do you ask? What do you know of my mother?"

"Yer mother was a baroness, kitten, did she not tell ye?"

Ginelle blanched, "You speak falsely." She shook her head, her thoughts spinning uncontrollably.

A black brow arched, "Ye are so certain that I speak an untruth, yet ye do not know anything of yer own mother, but her name?"

Her chest tightened painfully, "My father would have mentioned it."

"Nay, Ross Hayes conjured a life of lies to keep ye protected, to keep ye from yer real father, the Baron of Cambridge."

She shook her head, "You are lying!"

Pierino jerked forward, his expression twisting with annoyance. "Yer 'father' was an English lord, companion to Lord Alfred Sterling betrothed to the Lady Anne Montgomery, yer mother, no?" he paused than continued, "The marriage proceeded as intended but yer mother had other plans. Infatuated with another man she fled the baron and intended for a peaceful life with her English lord." He sneered mockingly, "They thought to conceal themselves as peasants, live a life of poverty all for the foolishness of love." He said the words with disgust as he sank back into the seat. "The baron learned of my talents and called upon me to bring ye to him."

"How do you know for certain that I am this man's daughter?" she demanded, her heart heavy.

"I know naught of fact on that part. Yer whore of a mother was not so discreet in her endeavors. The servants informed their lord of secret meetings with the English man. She fled like a coward and it wasn't long before a servant informed Sterling that she carried either an heir or a bastard." He laughed, "It matters naught to me what ye are, ye are simply a means to an end on my part."

"Was it the baron's plan to keep me a prisoner of your cruelty as well?"

Pierino laughed harshly, his grin contorting his face all the more heinous. "I claimed I am a man of many talents, I seek only to please myself and myself alone. I could not resist in taking full advantage of the opportunity that presented itself. A baron was asking for my assistance, how could I not take control in my favor?"

Ginelle's eyes narrowed in disgust, "I was just a child."

He smirked, "All the easier to mold ye as my puppet. It was all very simple; I had ye in my grasp and squeezed the baron dry."

"You ransomed me." She said assertively, disgusted by this evil man sitting across from her.

"Bribery goes a long way, girl, and I thought why not make a profit off ye, no? I was yer benefactor, I deserved a bit of compensation for my generosity."

"You are pathetic, weaseling your way through pockets."

His face hardened, "I make a living how I choose, wench. Ye have done just the same, swindling the wealthy; tell me, has the Ashford bastard tasted ye?"

Ginelle paled beneath the black scrutiny of his stare. "I am nothing like you." She stated adamantly. "Will the Baron not be angry that you trifled with his money, misled him all this time?"

Pierino smirked, "I expect naught else but his fury. He is not expecting us so that may buy me some time to get what I came for. I have ye to dangle before the baron, any threats made on my person will be put upon yer head."

Ginelle shivered as she sank deeper into her cloak and peered out the window, her heart persistent in its hammering against her chest. Her thoughts shifted to Dorian and immediately her heart sank with grief. He would never know what happened, he would never find her because who would suspect she was the supposed daughter of the Baron of Cambridge?

Would she be a prisoner or a guest? Was this man truly the man who sired her? She cared not for Ross Hayes was and always will be her father, he raised her, adored her as his own, whether her blood bespoke of a different heritage, she knew in her heart that he was her father and he had loved her, he had not taken his own life as she had suspected, he had been brutally murdered, no matter what the Lord of Cambridge intended to say, she would not be deterred by the love and adoration she had as the daughter for Ross Hayes.

Dorian left The Silver Wind, his heart feeling light and elevated, a feeling he had rarely known his entire life. How could he ever make amends for his accusations? Stefan claimed that she loved him, than why had she not told him? Why had she not said anything of the child cradled in her womb belonging to him?

He had to make things right, he desperately needed to know if she loved him as Stefan had maintained, he needed to know for his very own heart beat with an everlasting love that could no longer be denied. He would claim Ginelle as his wife; love her for all the days to come. He couldn't imagine life without her sweetness, the fire in her eyes that asserted her defiance, her big heart nestled in her little frame. He would be a hollow, desolate soul without this woman.

He found his horse and mounted, his body aching from the lingering results of his wounds. He had not given much thought to his condition when he left the manor, his thoughts had clearly been elsewhere, but with the combination of the bitter cold, it all but worsened his state.

He had been fortunate to escape that blackened hole. With the capture of the Spaniard King, the Royal Navy had discovered several of the Spaniard's retreats, including the imprisonment where he had been kept. Once he informed the Captain of his station, he was released without further questioning.

He had wanted nothing more than to personally deliver Reyes to the ground but he would have to settle for the outcome that had occurred. He had wanted to avenge the lives of his crew lost, and though Reyes had not died by his hand, his death would compensate for his departed men.

Once he reached Ashford he could not withstand the anticipation any longer. He dismounted and the stable boy rushed forward to take Lafeu as he started for the manor. His wounds caused him great discomfort but he gritted back the pain and started up the stairs towards Ginelle's room.

He was startled to find her room empty and cold. Frowning, he turned and proceeded down the hall, checking rooms as he passed them by. A feeling of unease started heavy in his belly as he searched the manor, his unease growing towards an unsettling fear.

"Milord!" Lucile rushed from the parlor as he reached the bottom stairs, the older woman's face pinched with distress as she approached frantically.

"Where is Ginelle?" he demanded.

The housekeeper shook her head, "She left without any notice, monsieur. I found her gone several hours past. I believe she went in search of you."

Dorian felt a coldness envelop his limbs. "What did you tell her?"

"I told her you had to speak with Lieutenant Stefan, monsieur. I did not think she would go alone to find you." The woman's voice trembled with evident worry.

Dorian felt a terrible and unimaginable fear seize him in a black shroud. She knew he had gone to the other side of town, to the Eastern harbor.

Immediately he thought of all the perilous dangers that awaited a woman on the streets of that part of town. His thoughts quickly shifted to Pierino and his heart lurched against his chest, a sickening feeling twisting his gut.

The two of them jolted as the sound of wheels rolled to a stop before the manor. Whirling on his heels with Lucile close behind, they rushed outside to find Henry, the coachman, leaping to intercept them.

"Henry-" Lucile gasped as Dorian swept past the older man and housekeeper to jerk open the carriage door only to find the small compartment empty and dark.

"Milord-" Henry started fearfully.

He pivoted his face red and his expression torn as he seized the smaller man by his collar. "Where is she?" he demanded, his fingers tightening around the man's shirt.

"I-I warned h-her, milord." Henry stammered his eyes wide and alarmed. "She w-would n-not listen." The muscle at his jaw flexed dangerously as he struggled to control his rising temper and the terrible feeling that something inconceivable had happened to her. Pierino must have taken her. She had gone looking for him and must have been abducted by the bastard. "I'll kill him." He vowed murderously, shoving Henry from his grasp as he spun around and started for the stables.

"Monsieur-" Lucile rushed at his heels, "Monsieur- what do you think you are doing? You need to rest, you are not healed, please allow me to call upon-"

"No!" he growled, turning to catch the housekeeper by the shoulders, her expression shifting to astonishment at the apparent signs of fear clouding his blue eyes. "Have Ives seek out Stefan, do you understand? I do not have time to find him myself."

Lucile nodded, her dark eyes widening with tension. "What has happened?"

"I fear Ginelle's past has caught up with her." He said more to himself than to Lucile. "Find Stefan and have him meet me in town once more, understood?"

She nodded and he released her as he turned and headed into the stables. Lucile felt a tremor shiver down her spine. Had something happened to Ginelle? Would she lose her young mistress? The alarming thought brought on a rush of tears, and for the first time in nearly four years, the older woman cried.

Chapter 28

The small confines of the carriage darkened as the day transpired, with that, Ginelle struggled to remain passive despite everything Pierino had revealed. Could she truly believe his accusations against her mother? Could she believe this man, Alfred Sterling, was her supposed father? Was it possible that the man who raised her had not sired her at all?

Her head began to throb with her whirlwind thoughts and she moaned inwardly as she leaned back against the seat, her eyes darting nervously to the brooding man across from her. Her thoughts immediately turned to Dorian. Surely they would know by now that something terrible had happened to her? Henry would have told them.

Her heart ached within her chest, fearing the unknown of the situation soon to unravel. What was to become of her and her unborn child? What were the baron's intentions? She shivered, imaging brutality and cruelness.

Had her mother truly loved Ross that she would escape her privileged life, all for the sake of love? Had she fled for a reason entirely unbeknownst to anyone? Had the baron treated her mother so cruelly that she fled, fearing her life? She pondered all the scattered thoughts wracking her troubled mind, each making her heart pace all the more fearful.

The sun descended, evoking a gloomy stretch of blackness to extend wide over the flat, green land. The carriage rocked without difficulty, making it all the more complicated for Ginelle to remain awake. She had eaten very little that day and felt a slight weakness creeping into her limbs.

She was nearly asleep when the carriage suddenly jolted to a stop, jarring her alert. She stiffened as her head snapped upright, her eyes moving warily about, taking in her surroundings. She barely had time to access her situation before Pierino hurried forward, grabbing her wrist and dragging her along after him.

She nearly lost her footing as they stumbled from the carriage. Her heart pounding, her eyes strained against the looming darkness, searching for a means to escape but Pierino kept a firm grip on her wrist ensuring her that an easy escape was not possible.

Ginelle knew that if she struggled she would be endangering her child so she obediently followed at his heels. Her heart somersaulted in her chest as her eyes averted to the extravagant manor dominating the blackened sky.

"Pull yer hood up over yer head." Pierino demanded and when she did not comply, he grumbled nervously and turned to fumble with her hood until it rest firmly atop her head.

She stood frozen, mindless as of what to expect as a young servant answered Pierino's abrupt knock. The girl appeared startled by Pierino's suddenness as she studied them curiously, her brows pulling together in slight puzzlement.

"I wish to speak with the baron, tis urgent." Pierino commanded, his grip tightening around Ginelle's wrist in warning.

The girl hesitated, shaking her dark head. "I am sorry, Sir. Monsieur is not accepting visitors at this hour, mayhap if you return on the morrow-"

Pierino shoved the girl aside and dragged Ginelle over the threshold. "Ye may tell yer lord that I will see him now." Pierino exclaimed.

Frightened by his brusque manner, the girl merely nodded and fled the hall. Pierino turned and seized Ginelle roughly by the arms. "Ye will remain silent, understood?"

Ginelle lifted her head, her brown eyes glinting challengingly beneath the rim of her hood. "If I don't?"

His fingers tightened and she resisted a whimper as he leaned in close, his black eyes penetrating her calm reserve. "If ye do not abide, I will see yer child dead before it sees the light, understood?"

She paled beneath his accosting stare, her body jolting in alarm at his jarring words.

He sneered, "Aye, I know ye carry a bastard in yer belly, so take note and remember my warning."

He shoved her away and her hand lashed out to steady her sudden quaking frame. He stood a pace apart but she felt his nearness like a black cloud intending to suffocate the very life from her body and that of her babe. She kept her distance and remained silent, fearing if she angered him, he may retaliate. She had little choice but to submit.

Lord Alfred Sterling, baron of Cambridge, paced the lavished carpeted floor, his arms entwined at his back as he waited anxiously for the unexpected visitor to appear in his study. He was livid to have a visitor calling at this hour, more so that the man had demanded his presence.

A knock sounded at his door and he turned as the maid tentatively opened the door, their eyes connected and he nodded curtly, allowing her to bid the man entry.

When the man stepped into the light of the study, Alfred froze, his limbs stiffening with a maddening fury. "Basilotta." He hissed the name with underlying malice.

Pierino smirked as he strolled casually into the room, the maid closing the door firmly behind him as he crossed the floor to the brandy sitting atop a glass table. "Ye are not pleased to see me?"

Alfred's hands curled into fists at his sides until his knuckles turned white with pain. "You are a fool to come here, Basilotta." The baron hissed,

"You have misled me for the last time, diminishing my finances with your deceit. If you think I'm going to allow you to walk unscathed from my estate, you are mistaken."

Pierino slowly turned, his fingers curling around the glass in his hand to still the concealed tremors declaring his unease. "If ye think to kill me, Sir, ye would be wise to reconsider yer threats."

Alfred paused despite his frosted anger, "You best have a good reason for your presence, Basilotta, if I have to endure another one of your lies, I will end you here and now. I've wasted precious time and money relying on your incompetent methods."

Pierino lifted the glass and downed the brandy, his hands trembling as he set the glass aside. "I would have yer word, baron." He demanded nervously, a slight edge to his tone as he met Alfred's hard stare. "I would have yer word that ye intend to see out our bargain, with my head attached?"

Alfred felt a small flutter in his chest, a sudden anxiousness sweeping throughout his limbs. "You found her?" the words were barely spoken, "If my child has been found, than I will ensure that our bargain is met." He said firmly and than narrowed his eyes suspiciously, "But if you intend to beguile me, it will be for the last time."

Pierino nodded grimly.

Alfred watched, waiting anxiously as Pierino crossed the room and jerked open the door, he stepped for a moment into the hall and than entered the room, his fingers wrapped around a small wrist, pulling an unwilling concealed body into the study.

Pierino stepped back as Alfred observed the small cloaked figure standing several feet from him. His heart beat like a persistent drum, his hope flaring to a colossal magnitude that he nearly rushed forward to reveal the concealed figure. How would he know for certain Pierino had not failed him?

“Take down yer hood.” Pierino commanded.

His heart jumped as there was a moment of hesitation, he sensed her fear, her reluctance before small hands reached up, trembling in their ascent, to push the hood away, revealing the mystery beneath.

Alfred felt as though the very room itself shifted beneath his weight, conjuring the image of a woman he had loved from the moment they were betrothed. It was as if he were staring at Anne Montgomery all over again, her dewy-brown eyes wide and fully-lashed, her skin pale like ivory and hair the color of moonbeams, only this small woman standing in front of him, had a firm yet small jaw, set in determination, her subtle eyes sharpening with a boldness that surprised him.

He stepped toward her and she tensed, her eyes darting warily like a frightened doe, but he sensed her eagerness to fight if she must and he wondered for a moment what kept her restrained. “You have no reason to fear me, my child.”

“I am not your child.” She stated adamantly, her chin thrusting upward to indicate her sudden anger.

He resisted a grin, stunned by her courageousness. “If you are not my child, than pray tell, who sired you?” he asked curiously.

Her chin remained firm, “Ross Hayes is my father.”

He winced inwardly, knowing the name painfully well. “You are so certain he is your father?” he inquired.

“You are so certain that I am your daughter?” she challenged.

He smiled, “You are a striking semblance of Anne. There is not a slightest bit of uncertainty that you are her daughter, and mine.” He took another step towards her and she retreated. “I did not search years for you my child to have you fear me.”

He noticed her eyes glance nervously at Pierino and this angered him immensely. “You have nothing to fear here, no harm will come to you.”

He turned to address Pierino, “Your work is done here, Basilotta. I am no longer in need of your assistance. You may seek Reeves; he will see that you are greatly rewarded.”

Pierino’s dark eyes rested firmly on Ginelle and she met his stare boldly, determined not to cower beneath his obsidian stare, remembering all too well the cruelty and pain she had endured at his hands, the fears he had placed in her little heart as a child.

Once Pierino left the room, Ginelle averted her eyes to the man standing across from her. He was tall and lean with an abundance of hair the color of mahogany, swept back from his face to reveal streaks of gray forming at his temples. His nose was sharp and his features aristocratic and angled in preciseness. He stood with an air of exactness and proclaimed a keen intellect.

Ginelle remained wary of this man, knowing very little of his manner and reputation. His cobalt eyes studied her silently, his thoughts working tediously behind his masked expression.

“You fear him?” he asked than, taking her by surprise.

She shifted uneasily beneath his acute, blue eyes.

“I believe I am at fault for the pain you have suffered.” He said suddenly, his tone taking on a sadness that startled her. “I was informed that he was exceptionally skilled in tracking a missing person’s whereabouts. Unfortunately, I was not informed of his deceitful and cruel tactics. How can I make amends for all that you have suffered?”

“There is nothing you can say that will make amends for what you have done. He murdered my father. If you had left well enough alone, none of that would have occurred.”

“Your ‘father’ betrayed my trust.” He said indignantly. “When I learned your mother carried a child, I had to know for certain if the babe was mine.

When I learned of your mother's death, I was devastated." He fell silent and Ginelle sensed a deep sadness in him.

"You loved my mother?" she asked, surprised.

His blue eyes softened, "I loved your mother the moment I laid eyes on her. She was against our betrothal and unbeknownst to me, she loved another."

"Did you treat her cruelly?" Ginelle knew the question to be absurd, but she had to know.

Alfred stiffened, "I never laid a hand to her. I pined for her affections, not once did violence occur. I could not abide the thought of harming your mother. She was a gentle soul. You are like her in many ways."

Ginelle smiled despite the circumstances. "I never knew my mother. I was told she died giving birth to me."

He nodded, "I was told the same but your name was never given."

Ginelle hesitated, she knew he wanted to know her given name but could she truly trust this man who claimed to be her father? She had studied him for a time, searching his face for similar features but she could detect nothing that would confirm this man as the one who sired her. He had not been cruel to her mother. He had not intended harm on her part in any way. She sensed a kindness along with a lingering sadness that matched her own that elicited a response from her lips. "I am Ginelle."

He smiled a light forming in his cobalt eyes. "I have a proposition for you, Ginelle."

She frowned, sensing a slight unease. "A proposition?"

He nodded, "I would like for you to remain here, with me, at Cambridge."

Her heart jolted, "I cannot, I am sorry but I wish to return to London."

He frowned, taken aback as if expecting a different response entirely. "London?" and than as if suddenly taking note of her clean appearance and fine garments, he asked, "Do you not live in hardship?"

She shook her head, "Whether I live in poverty or not, milord, I wish to return home."

He took a step toward her, his expression curious. "Where exactly is home?"

Ginelle bit down on her lower lip, "Home is where I wish to be."

"You refuse to tell me?" he appeared almost agitated.

"I do, milord."

He pondered this for a moment but did not press the matter. "My proposition stands." He said assertively.

She shook her head, "I must decline."

He was quiet and she noticed the muscle tensing along his jaw. He was angry and she grew wary. "I had hoped you would agree to live here willingly." With that said, he started around her towards the door.

Her heart plummeting, Ginelle whirled to catch him. "You mean to keep me here against my will?"

He stopped before the door with his back to her and she caught the rigidness in his spine. He turned than to look at her, "I do." He wrenched open the door and slammed it closed as she rushed forward, her hands circling the latch as the lock fell into place.

Chapter 29

Mindless of his wounds, Dorian spent every waking hour rummaging the darkened streets of London searching frantically for any evident signs or bystanders they may have some information to Ginelle's disappearance. He vowed silently that he would not rest until she was safely in his arms. He entrusted in Stefan's aid and the two of them ransacked every crevice, every corner and building, hoping to stumble upon any evidence that could lead them to her.

Hours elapsed without any knowledge but Dorian was quite certain the man responsible for her abduction was Pierino.

Reluctantly, he returned to Ashford with the fixed intention of finding the bastard and seeing that he would never again harm the woman he loved.

His stomach knotted with tension, his thoughts shifting to Ginelle's wellbeing and his unborn child. He prayed silently for their safety, cursing himself for his ill-advised treatment and cruel accusations. He had been such a misguided fool, hindered by his own judgment and the uncertainty of his feelings, he should have claimed her long ago and now it may be too late.

The very thought of someone harming her sent his senses reeling, his mind spinning with unimaginable happenings that he stumbled through the manor doors. He collapsed on the floor; his hands shaking as he fumbled to get to his feet.

"Monsieur!" he heard Lucile's frantic cry as the older woman rushed forward, followed by Stefan as he moved forward to grab Dorian's arm and help him to his feet.

"He is not well." Lucile said to Stefan as the two of them balanced his massive weight between them. "His wounds are festering. We must get him to bed." Her panicked voice jarred Dorian alert, suddenly aware of the pain shooting through his exhausted limbs.

He mumbled a disgruntled groan as the two of them assisted him up the flight of stairs, each struggling to maintain a firm grip on his muscled frame as he attempted to pull away from them. "Must f-find her." He groaned, his head spinning uncontrollably.

"You are no good to her like this." Stefan said sternly, his grip tightening as they started down the hall, "You've caused your wounds much distress, and you need to rest. I will continue to search for her, rest easy, Captain."

Ginelle woke the next morning, exhausted from a restless night and fearful of what would become of her. She stared blankly around the room, the elaborate furnishings and costly paintings lost its appeal, her mind and heart heavy with uncertainty and fear that she may never return to Ashford.

She rested a hand against her belly, her fingers probing for the life that lay within. Her little bundle was the only means to her sanity, the only thread keeping her sane while her scrambled thoughts conjured an escape. Dorian must love her; she thought convincingly, his manner towards her bespoke of a passion that surely matched her own.

Yet, even as she thought this, she wondered for a moment if it all had been merely for possession, for control over her wellbeing. The thought made her heart sink deeply in her chest and she quickly thrust the horrid thought aside.

She had accomplished many fears, vanquished a lot of doubts and she refused to believe that Dorian thought so little of her. He had to have some feelings, some affection towards her?

She felt tears at the back of her eyes and struggled to keep them at bay. Whether Dorian loved her or not, she refused to submit to these circumstances. He would come for her and she would unveil everything, convince him that she carried his child and that her love was undeniable.

There was a gentle knock at her door and Ginelle stiffened as it cracked open and a young girl stepped into the room. She was slightly tall but slender, with a timid smile and shy but equally curious dark eyes as they scanned momentarily over Ginelle. "Good morning, mademoiselle." She said softly, crossing the room to place the silver tray down, "I am Thora, monsieur has asked that I see to your needs."

Ginelle jerked her chin upward, her eyes flashing as she said, "I have no need for your assistance. There is nothing I want from you or your lord. I wish for nothing more than to leave this horrid place."

The girl's slender shoulders stiffened offensively, her young face contorting with remorse as her dark eyes shifted uncomfortably from Ginelle. "Surely mademoiselle this place is not so bad?"

Suddenly feeling a slight flare of hope, Ginelle came up on her knees in the bed, her hand gripping the bedpost. "Thora, you could help me?" she asked gently, "You could help me escape? I have no reason to be here. Your lord keeps me here against my will."

Thora jolted, her face paling as she shook her head, "Nay mademoiselle, I cannot. Monsieur would be very angry with me." The girl started for the door and Ginelle felt her hope depleting.

She hastened from the bed and quickly implored, "I am with child, Thora."

The girl stiffened and turned slowly to peer at her, her dark eyes averting to the small bump beneath Ginelle's layers of clothing. "No harm will come to you and your child, milady." She said reassuringly.

Ginelle shook her head, her tears forming at the rim of her eyes. "I am in great distress here, Thora. Do you not think that will have some effect on my unborn child?"

The girl hesitated as if considering this but her uncertainty shown bright in her dark eyes, and her confliction as of what to do. Without another word, she fled the room, feeling cornered and unsettled.

Ginelle sank slowly back onto the bed, her head hanging as her shoulders shuddered with a sob. She would never escape unless Dorian came for her. She clung onto that hopeful thought as she settled into the bed and clenched her eyes shut.

A sennight passed and doubt began to take place in her frantic thoughts. The baron did as much to please her, to make her comfortable but Ginelle remained aloof, her replies brief and curt. She held onto the solid notion that Ross Hayes was her father, not Alfred Sterling. She found little to no resemblance but uncertainty began to take place. How would she ever know for certain?

She gripped her mother's locket, dangling loosely from around her neck, finding slight comfort in the precious trinket. She opened it to reveal her mother's tiny portrait and for a time stared at the beautiful woman within. She pressed her hand flat to her belly, her heart suddenly aching with an urgency to know everything about the woman who had given her life. She brushed tears from her eyes and moved to stand by the window.

Thora appeared moments later to announce the evening meal but Ginelle simply ignored the girl, feeling a small pang of guilt for the girl tried immensely to gain her friendship. She would have liked Thora very much under different circumstances but she couldn't befriend the maid, she had to think on escaping. The longer she remained at Cambridge, her heart cracked a little more each day, deepening her distraught that she would never be found.

Her shoulders stiffened at the approach of footsteps outside her door followed but a subtle knock before the door swung inward, producing the baron.

"Thora says you are not hungry?" he inquired. When she remained silent, he continued, "You should eat, considering your condition." He added knowingly.

Ginelle closed her eyes and groaned inwardly. Blast Thora. "It is not the food I find so displeasing." She said grudgingly, she turned and watched the muscle tighten at his jaw.

"It does not please me to see you unhappy." He said, "You are not a prisoner here, you are welcome to explore the manor, the servants are at your every whim, you have only to ask, but you understand that you cannot leave the estate?"

She lifted her chin, "Do you keep me here simply because I resemble my mother?" she watched his expression carefully, taking immediately notice to the slight alteration in his features, the glint of pain in his cobalt eyes before abruptly hardening his countenance.

"What do you think?" he asked gently.

"The resemblance to my mother is undeniable, we are alike in many ways but I am not Anne Montgomery." She fell silent, watching him intensely, "I cannot replace her memory."

For a moment, she thought she saw a flicker of tears but he was quick to conceal his pain. "You are very observant." He said, "Her disloyalty of our vows pained me gravely. When Anne fled with Ross, their betrayal was devastating. I have never truly recovered. So you see, letting you go is not a possibility." He turned towards the door and felt her immediate fury.

"You cannot do this! Do you hear me?" she stalked towards him, her fists clenched and her face red with anger. "You keep me prisoner based on selfishness!"

He turned back around, "No, I keep you here because you are mine by birthright." He stated adamantly.

Her nostrils flared with composed anger. "You are not certain of that."

"Nor you." He replied and than left the room, jerking it shut and twisting the lock.

The moment his eyes opened wide, he felt the immediate emptiness filling is chest like a black mass, smothering out every lingering remnant of light she had replenished to his shattered soul. The pain from his past seem to rush tenfold to the forefront of his mind, evoking streams of heartache of the raw remembrance of his mother's murder, his father's abuse, and the illness that drained the life from his beloved sister. The very thought of losing Ginelle sent him over the brink of madness. He couldn't withstand a day without her innocence and beauty. He would walk a perilous path to see her safely home. He would give his life to renew the lives of his beloved and child.

He forced himself to sit upright in bed, gritting his teeth against the shooting pains that seared his body. His chest was bare for all but a bandage that wrapped entirely around his midriff, the minor wounds had been tended too, and a small portion of salve lay on the table by his bed. He was grateful for what his servants had done for him but his major priority at that moment was finding Ginelle.

"How do you feel?" he was startled to see Stefan standing across the room, leaning casually against the hearth.

"Have you found her?" he demanded, his voice laced with concern.

Stefan dropped his arm and moved away from the mantel. "No, Captain. We have had little to no leads to her disappearance."

"What of Pierino?"

The Lieutenant shook his head, "I have beseeched Edmund's assistance, Ellison is very distressed and both are eager to see Ginelle safely home. They are out questioning the ton as we speak."

"How long have I been out?"

"Nearly a week." Stefan replied.

Dorian groaned disapprovingly as he shoved the blankets aside and struggled to arise. Stefan moved forward to assist him and Dorian waved him off, refusing to be coddled.

"Captain, you are not-"

"I am well enough." Dorian growled, his eyes piercing as he staggered around Stefan and snatched up his tunic and fumbled to get dressed. Once he was fully clothed, he poured himself a hearty glass of brandy and downed the liquid in one swallow, his weakened body savoring the harshness of the drink as it burned down his throat. He slammed the glass down and contemplated another drink but the memory of his father lingered in his mind and he turned away from the bottle. "I will not rest until she is brought to me." He said more to himself than to Stefan.

"We have searched every remnants of the town. I know not where else to look." Stefan said deploringly.

"Find Henry, he will go with us to town and there we will trace their steps." Pushing himself forward, he snatched up his cloak and followed Stefan from the room. He would search well unto the night and onward until she is found.

Chapter 30

Dorian grew apprehensive, a deep gut-wrenching feeling of trepidation settling heavily in his stomach. The hour was late, his room permeating a substantial darkness that corresponded to the lightless soul dwelling within his body.

He sat before the hearth, his limbs tense and his eyes glazed with the subliminal thoughts engrossing his mind. An empty brandy bottle sat depleted on the table at his side as he stared pensively into the kindled fire.

They had searched to the perimeter of London without the slightest indication to Ginelle or Pierino's whereabouts. He was beginning to doubt that Pierino was accountable in Ginelle's abduction; his mind began to conjure other possibilities.

Had Ginelle decided to flee because of his treatment towards her? Had Stefan spoke falsely of her affections for him? Had she fled to a nunnery? He remembered the day Lord Edric had attempted to steal her away, had he some involvement in her disappearance?

All these thoughts and more flowed through his mind and he was jarred suddenly to the present as a gentle rattling sounded at his door. Frowning, he forced himself to his feet and crossed the space to the door and jerked it open.

Instinctively, he felt a wave of revolt creep up his throat as he jerked around from his unwanted visitor. "I will have to advise my servants that your presence here is no longer welcome." He sneered, turning his back to the fixed, sapphire gaze eying him creditably.

"I had hoped you would be pleased to see me, mon amour." Victoria said, sauntering slowly into the room, her eyes dancing wickedly along the masculine furniture to rest firmly upon the bed.

"Did I not make it clear the last time, Victoria that you and I are no longer?" Dorian growled, turning to glare at her.

Victoria tossed her red curls over her shoulder as her red lips peeled away with a grin. "Nonsense." She said convincingly, "There are no men that cannot resist me, and no woman that can compare." She crossed the room to the bed and trailed a gloved hand along the blanketed surface. "I have missed you, Dorian." She turned to peer at him, "And I know you have missed me."

He stood before the hearth, his arm resting lightly against the stone above his head as he stared deeply into the crackling flames. "The hour is late, Victoria. I wish for you to leave."

Victoria stiffened, having not expected his coldness. She approached him and admired him with a long favorable look. She slipped her arms around his torso, her fingers exploring the rigid lines of muscle beneath his tunic. "Have I disappointed you before, mon amant?" she said silkily, her hands dipping lower over the hard contours of his body to wrap around his manhood.

Muttering a curse, Dorian seized her hands, his fingers tightening to an almost painful degree as he turn around and glared dangerously down at Victoria. "Enough!" he snarled, "We are done, Victoria. What do you not understand about that?" he shoved her away and she stumbled back, her face turning red with humiliation and anger.

"How dare you, you detestable wretch!" she hissed with chagrin. "A woman scorned is a dreaded thing, Dorian, you should make note of that and remember it well. I had thought with the little bitch gone you would see just how much of a besotted fool you were-"

"What did you say?" he hissed ominously.

Victoria jerked her chin sharply, her eyes flashing like daggers as she said, "That little nymph had you acting like an infatuated youth. I do not like being replaced, especially with some little chit with no curves to please a man!"

She stiffened as he unexpectedly moved forward, closing the space between them in three angry strides as he grasped her wrist in a bruising manner. "You better pray, Victoria, that you had no part in Ginelle's disappearance." He growled with such menace that a shiver of fear raced down her spine. "If you have harmed her in any way, I will personally see your reputation in shambles."

Her sapphire eyes narrowed in sudden distaste. "If not for her, you would not treat me so cruelly. You would not make threats on my person so harshly."

"She is not at fault for any of this."

"What makes her so different?" Victoria snapped.

He was silent for a moment and than he said, "I love her." Her blue eyes widened with horrified astonishment, "So I suggest you take what pride you have left remaining and leave my manor for good. If she is harmed in any way possible, I am holding you entirely responsible."

Victoria gasped, outraged. "I cannot believe you are choosing her over me!"

His grip tightened and she winced as he jerked her closer, his blue eyes jutting like blades of ice. "I have no confliction in ending you now." He snarled maliciously. "I know you did not accomplish this feat on your own, who aided you?"

She clamped her mouth shut, her sapphire eyes glinting challengingly as he glared violently down at her.

He shook her roughly, "Tell me!"

"Nathaniel Sharp." She disclosed, attempting to pull free of his grasp.

Dorian stiffened, "Sharp?"

She grinned, "The man was easily persuaded, having a great deal of dislike for you, and harboring a bit of revenge for having been rejected by your precious Ginelle, he was easily lured into my plans, especially since the man is in a financial crisis. Flash a bit of coin and he was hooked like the imbecile he is."

His fingers tightened and her glint of triumphant wavered, "Who else?" he demanded, "What did you to do her?"

She lifted her chin, suddenly breathless as she struggled lightly against his grip. "I did nothing!" she exclaimed, "I merely devised the scheme and it worked like a charm."

"Sharp?" he questioned.

Victoria smirked, "He handled the girl roughly, shoved her into a carriage."

Dorian felt the sudden impulse to smack the savage grin from her face but he restrained, all his anger curling into a nut shell as he struggled with his rising fury. "Was Pierino involved?" he shook her again, enraged by her victorious sneer, "Answer me dammit!"

"He was the one in the carriage." She snapped, "How else do you think I got rid of her? I simply handed her back to the man she belonged too! Let go of me, you're hurting me!" he shoved her away and stalked across the room, his hands destroying every inanimate object that fell into his path.

His chest rose and fell with untamed fury as his fists curled at his sides. His nostrils flared as he came to a stand-still, his body trembling with concealed rage. "Where did he take her?" he demanded sternly.

Startled by his reaction, Victoria struggled to maintain her composure, her eyes glancing nervously towards the door. "No questions were asked. I simply wanted her gone; he was the man for the task."

Dorian pivoted to glare at her, "If that man hurts her in any way, I will personally rip out your vindictive heart." He growled the threat through clenched teeth, his voice hardening with inevitable confirmation. "Get the hell out of my house."

It was nearly dawn and Dorian continuously paced the floor of his room, his steps taking him from the hearth to the window, from the window to the chair as he sorted through the information he had received. He was racked with uncertainty and concern, his mind struggling to make sense of Pierino's intentions. Ginelle had revealed very little of the man aside from his abusive and violent manner. The thought nearly unraveled him, his gut twisting mercifully.

Just as the first streaks of sunlight painted the break of day, a sudden recognition came to him. Who exactly was Lord Edric? Since all that had occurred, he had not given much thought to the man or attempted to unveil the mystery surrounding him.

Had they been searching London for the wrong man all this time? Pierino left no trail, no evidence that could lead him to Ginelle but what of the other man? He had warned them once of Pierino. Was he somehow connected in all this? Did he have vital information that could lead him to Ginelle? With that last thought in mind, he gathered his cloak and left the room. He needed to find Lord Edric and fast.

Tracking the whereabouts of a Lord Edric with no last name to speak of proved more difficult than he expected. Today, the cobblestone streets were less crowded, the icy weather a great discomfort to the London inhabitants.

Dorian questioned every individual he crossed but gained nothing on a Lord Edric. Ginelle had told him once that Lord Edric possibly had family that resided in London, but without a surname, it would be impossible to track him. He had attended the banquet so was it possible Edmund would have records of that night, of all the guests who attended?

He mounted Lafeu and started in the direction of the Wilkinson estate. On his arrival, Lady Ellison was making her way outside, a maid trailing at her skirts as she started towards a waiting carriage. Once she spotted him, her emerald eyes widened with apprehension.

"Lord Ashford?" a gloved hand fluttered to her chest, "Pray tell you have found her unharmed?"

Dorian shook his head as he dismounted and approached the Duchess. "No mademoiselle. I have come to speak with Edmund. Tis urgent."

She waved him forward, "Of course, please." She led him inside, her beautiful face creased with concern.

He followed her closely as she led him through the hall and towards the grand parlor where Edmund sojourned.

Edmund lifted his head, startled to see Dorian as he followed Ellison into the room. "Is something amiss?" he asked, rising to his feet to greet his friend.

"Do you have a list of all the guests who attended the banquet?" he asked urgently.

Edmund paused a moment as he considered this, "I believe I have yet to discard the list, why?"

"I am seeking a Lord Edric. The banquet was highly secured which means no one could attend without an invitation, and those who had an invitation were put on the list. I need to see that list."

Edmund shook his head, "Even if that were so, there were several guests deemed uninvited who gained admission, it is highly likely that the man you seek is one of them."

"I am aware of that, but I am not taking any chances. I need to be certain. This man was of aristocracy. I am positive he would have done things just, instead of barging into an event uninvited."

Edmund nodded, "Very well. Give me a moment." He left the room quietly.

"Have you learned anything?" Dorian was surprised to see Ellison in the room; her pale face conflicted with grief.

He hesitated, not wanting to worry the woman further more but he knew that if he told her what he had gained, it might bring a bit of reassurance. "She was abducted." He said, watching her face carefully, taking note of the shudder that passed through her slender shoulders. "I do not know where this man takes her, but I intend to find out."

Tears surfaced to the rim of her emerald, green eyes and she nodded as she turned away, relying heavily on his oath that he find her dear friend.

Edmund returned moments later, carrying a rolled article of paper. They moved to a table where he unraveled the bundle to its length and there the three of them scanned the list of names.

Dorian was startled when his eyes caught sight of the name he sought and he mumbled the given name aloud.

"Lord Edric Collins, Marquis of Northampton."

Chapter 31

Dorian traveled the 67 miles north-west of London to Northampton by carriage, along with the company of his Lieutenant. He knew very little of Northampton aside from the great fire that had occurred many ages ago and destroyed many lives. The town eventually rebuilt becoming extensive and very prosperous with the aid of marketing.

As beautiful as the land was, much of the earth was littered with small pebbles and the sloped hills topped with soft stone. The hollow lowlands were heavily wooded, assembled with tall trees and a blanket of snow to coat the softened terrain buried beneath.

Once they reached town, Dorian was surprised to find the noticeably small town teeming with commerce. From what he had gathered, much gossip had been said that the town was allegedly the finest in all of England with its structured buildings and widened streets.

His essential motives drew him immediately into the lively crowds. With Stefan's help, the two of them began their search for Lord Edric Collins. Most inhabitants knew of the Marquis, claiming the man was a highly admired advocate of the town with an exceptional background and education that proclaimed his aristocracy but most knew very little of the man's whereabouts at that time.

What information they had gained led them to a grand h-shaped manor with a spacious cobblestone courtyard. As their carriage rolled to a stop before the extravagant house, a servant appeared from within and waited.

They announced their names along with their purpose and the hesitant servant led them into the great hall where they remained to be seen.

As the two of them waited, Dorian caught a woman's voice coming from another room speaking to the servant who had showed them in. He heard someone approaching and he turned as a woman followed by Lord Edric entered the hall and what he saw made his body go still with complete shock.

Ginelle had spent a majority of her day roaming the halls that were now her prison. Despite the circumstances, she was finding it more difficult to be cold to the friendly servants, especially Thora. Her demeanor remained the same with Lord Sterling. She refused to submit to this sudden life thrusted upon her and to the troubling thoughts that Dorian may very well be happy to be rid of her. Doubts were beginning to set heavily in her mind and weigh deeply on her heart.

She was moving quietly through the hall when a hushed voice came from the other side of the door. She paused, suddenly intrigued as the voice carried on, revealing the man to be Lord Sterling.

"You have done what I asked?"

"I have, milord." Spoke an unfamiliar tone.

"You are certain that the man is dead?" Ginelle felt her heart jump against her chest as she leaned in closer, straining to hear their exchanging words.

"The thief will bother you no longer and I have retrieved all of your money."

She released a startled gasp as her heart accelerated. Did they speak of Pierino? Had Lord Sterling hired a man to kill him?

"Good, very good." Sterling said, "As part of our agreement, you may keep half of the money as arranged, so long as the man lies dead as requested." He paused a moment and than added, "You may have the other half once you have killed Ashford."

Ginelle blanched as she felt the blood drain rapidly from her face. Surely he did not mean to kill Dorian?

She pressed her ear against the door, her heart throbbing painfully against her ribcage as she strained to catch their conversation.

"She carries his child. I will not have the man suddenly at my door staking claim to his bastard or the woman."

Ginelle frowned.

He had not said daughter.

"The job will be done." Spoke the stranger. She heard a sudden shuffle and quickly abandoned the door and hastened around a corner. Her heart pounding, she peeked around the hall to watch a tall man equipped in a black cloak depart the room and disappear down the passage.

A sudden rush of anger drew her towards the door and she pushed it open. Alfred stiffened, a look of surprise crossing his expression as they caught eyes.

"Pierino is dead?"

His face hardened and his shoulders stiffened before he replied. "The man will no longer swindle my money."

"And Dorian?" she demanded, "You intend to have him killed as well?" He said nothing but remained silent confirming her fears. "You cannot!" she exclaimed, "He has nothing to do with us."

"But he has everything to do with you." Sterling said solemnly, "I will simply not abide the man showing up at my door to claim his child."

"He has that right!"

"Exactly." Sterling said coldly, slowly coming around the desk to her, his eyes boring angrily down at her, "He has that right, but I will now allow it to happen because I have gone through too much trouble in finding you to have you simply taken away so easily so I intend to avoid that scenario completely."

Ginelle jerked her chin upward, her eyes flashing as she said, "I won't let you. I'll use any means to escape if you harm him."

His expression turned livid, his cobalt eyes darkening with the emotion as he stepped towards her and she felt a chill down her spine. "There is something I failed to mention since your arrival, I attempted courtesy and kindness to win you over, even with the nonsense of siring you but it seems you've drawn it from me regardless."

Ginelle felt a sudden lump in her throat, "Are you saying you're not my father?"

He smirked, "Does this not please you?"

"But-"

"I tried to convince you otherwise, all a ploy to get you to remain here until the child was born but you are very willful, very much like Anne." He said this last remark with coldness.

He moved towards her in slow, menacing steps. "I don't u-understand." She stammered, "W-what do you mean?"

"I am getting old, far too old to marry or sire an heir before I die and considering the overwhelming amount of hatred and revenge I have for Ross and Anne's betrayal, I vowed long ago that I would somehow make them pay for what they did to me. You my dear are simply a means to retaliation. You will remain here until your child is born and once you have dispensed the babe, you will no longer be needed."

Ginelle felt her chest tightening with trepidation. She stepped away from him, her face paling beneath his hard, cobalt stare. "B-but you looked for me all this time, before my child?"

He shrugged his shoulders in a careless manner. "My plans have changed considerably. Once I learned Anne had sired a child by the very man who had betrayed my friendship, I declared I would take their child as revenge but because much time has transpired since then, and I am getting older with no heir to take on my legacy, you have solved all my problems. I shall simply take your child, after that, you'll no longer be necessary."

Ginelle felt a wave of vertigo and she stumbled beneath his blue stare. Her hands lashed out to grip something sturdy and suddenly a servant was at her side. "Miss Ginelle is not feeling well-" she heard Sterling say coldly, "-see her to her room, Thora."

Once inside her room, Ginelle wrenched away from Thora and moved to put space between them. She had never felt so alone in her life, so frightened for her child and for the man she loved. She wrapped her arms around herself and moved to stand at the window. She felt Thora watching her from behind.

"You can leave." She said callously, hurt for she had established a diminutive friendship with the girl when all along she had known her Lord's plans in stealing her child.

"Are you angry with me, mademoiselle?" Thora asked softly, her voice laced with sincerity.

Frowning, Ginelle turned away from the window to peer at the girl standing with a nonplussed expression. "Your Lord plans to steal my child, you mean to tell me that you were not aware of this?"

The girl paled at this, her audible gasp the only sound emitted in the quiet of the room. "No milady!" she cried adamantly, "I had no part in it mademoiselle, I swear it! "

Ginelle fell silent, convinced of the girl's innocence. "I am sorry, Thora." Her voice quivered as she moved to the bed and sank down. "I am just frightened. He seemed so sincere and convincing that I had not seen right through his disguise." Tears strolled down her face and she gently brushed them away.

Thora moved to her side and gently squeezed her shoulder for reassurance, "I am sorry, mademoiselle. I wish there were something I could do." she said gently.

Ginelle sniffled and shook her head, "Do not say that. Lord Sterling would likely have you killed if you were to help me in any way."

Thora stiffened at the remark, "I have never known Lord Sterling to be so cruel."

There was a sudden knock at the door, jolting both women into a start. The door opened and an older woman named Norma peeked into the room, "Girl, you are needed in the kitchen."

Thora nodded and gave Ginelle's shoulder one last reassuring squeeze before leaving the room. When the door closed behind her, she heard the lock fall into place, confirming her imprisonment once again. She felt an onslaught of tears as she lowered to the bed and closed her eyes, forcing Dorian's image to mind.

Lord Sterling had been so convincing of his pain, so sincere in simply wanting her to remain at his manor all for the sake of her mother's memory and her startling resemblance. She had been so naïve to believe even for a moment that she was that man's daughter when in actuality he had sinister plans unraveling right beneath her nose. He had killed Pierino and now he intended to kill Dorian to ensure that her child would become his beneficiary, his motives driven all for revenge.

A shudder passed through her body and she turned her face into her pillow as she released a sob. Sterling would most likely kill her once the child was born. There was much time to pass before her babe was expected but she would not take the risk in remaining at Cambridge. She had to get word to Dorian somehow and soon.

In a few days time, Ginelle had managed to gain the trust of many of the servants but luring them into her plans of escaping proved to be far more complicated for their loyalty to their Lord was unbreakable. She disguised her plans by assuming false curiosity in studying the estate, when in actuality, she was advising a way to break away from her imprisonment but Lord Sterling kept guards posted at every feasible exit.

She thought of this more carefully in her room as Thora's knock signified the afternoon meal. Since Sterling had revealed his ultimate plans for her, she had rarely left the confines of her room, insisting on putting as much distance between she and her captor to better evaluate her scheme. Sterling seemed confident enough that she would not attempt to escape for he allowed her to roam freely throughout the manor but she remained skeptical that he doubted her decision to comply.

A thought suddenly occurred to Ginelle as she watched Thora cross the room to set the evening meal down. "Are you happy here, Thora?"

The girl turned to peer at her, slightly surprised by the unexpected question. She was silent a moment before replying, "I suppose that I am, miss."

Ginelle wasn't all convinced. "How long have you lived here?"

Thora shifted nervously under Ginelle's questioning, sensing a motive to her inquisitiveness. She cleared her throat, "Um, all my life, milady."

"Do you not wish for a different life?"

Thora shook her head, "What other life is there for me, miss, but this one that I have known all my life?"

"You are content living the life of a servant?"

"I am, milady." Thora replied earnestly.

"But you are content here, at Cambridge?" she pressed.

The girl fell quiet, worrying her low lip with her teeth. Ginelle knew the girl feared of saying something wrong, something that her Lord may later find out. "I am your friend, Thora." Ginelle said gently, "Whatever it is you wish to say, than please tell me."

"Life here is not so bad." Thora started, glancing towards the door, "Tis just very lonely at times. The other servants are much older than me and I have really no one to talk too."

Ginelle studied Thora more intently, her black hair swept neatly into a plait and her dark curious eyes beheld a tiny glint of sadness that Ginelle had failed to recognize at first glance. "What if I told you that I could give you a better life?"

Puzzlement etched Thora's sudden expression. "I do not know any other life but that of servitude, miss."

"What if I told you that if you helped me escape that you could come with?"

Thora's dark eyes widened with excitement, "Really?"

Ginelle nodded eagerly, "Yes, you could come with me to Ashford, my home? I have many friends there that would be happy to meet you?"

Thora stepped forward, her joy brightening her eyes gleefully, "And I could stay there and work for you?"

"If that is what you wish."

Just as quickly as her excitement had flared, it diminished in moments. Thora dropped her head and said hopelessly, "I thank you, miss for your offer, tis very kind of you but Lord Sterling would be very angry if we were to get caught. I'm afraid I cannot risk it."

Ginelle sank with dismay onto the bed and watched Thora leave the room. She would not give up hope. One way or another she would convince Thora to help her escape.

Later that evening, Alfred Sterling made his way to the parlor room, his thoughts regarding the woman he held captive. She beheld a gentle-nature but her defiance was exceptionally astonishing, very much like his Anne.

His fists curled mercifully at his sides at the memory of his late wife. The memory of her betrayal was as painful today as it was those many years ago when a servant informed him of her infidelity. He could have killed them both for betraying him. He felt much relief in knowing that Ross was dead but he would have done anything to have his Anne back which brought him to the girl upstairs.

The resemblance to her mother was frightening but astounding. He took great pleasure in knowing he would use the girl to satisfy his motives. All that he had revealed to the girl was painfully true; he would keep the girl at Cambridge because of her resemblance to her dead mother but the child would belong to him, heir to Cambridge. It brought him a great semblance of satisfaction in knowing that he had stolen Ross and Anne's daughter and taken their grandchild as his own.

He was smiling when a servant stepped into the room informing that a visitor had arrived.

"Who is it?" he demanded, slightly piqued.

"Tis a Mister Blackburn, milord."

Ah, his grin widened, Blackburn. It was the assassin he had hired to murder Pierino and the Ashford man. "Show Blackburn in." he said anxiously, turning around to pour himself a glass of spirits.

The servant nodded and left quietly followed by a shuffling behind him as Blackburn entered the room.

Sterling lifted the glass and sipped gingerly, his smile widening as he slowly turned around. "I trust you succeeded in annihilating the Ashford threat?" his smile vanished abruptly, his fingers tightening around the glass in his hand as his eyes locked frightfully on the flintlock pistol leveled directly at his chest.

He swallowed and the brandy burned slowly down his throat as he hesitantly averted his eyes from the 9' inch iron barrel to the ice-blue eyes glaring dangerously at him.

“Good evening, Baron Sterling.” Dorian said icily, “You have something I want.”

Chapter 32

Sterling narrowed his eyes on the intruder, the hand gripping the pistol steady and evened firmly at his chest. “I could have you killed for this.” He growled, his eyes wavering nervously to the finger hovering just lightly above the trigger.

Dorian grinned smugly. “Not if I end you now.”

Sterling’s throat convulsed fearfully above the iron, “Ashford I presume?” he said a bit shakily, “Where is my man?”

Dorian smirked coldly, “Blackburn enlightened me by testing the pistol first. Let’s avoid the details. Now I’m sure you’re aware of why I’m here?”

Sterling’s nostrils flared as his face reddened angrily. “The girl is mine by birthright.”

The hand around the pistol tightened a fraction and Sterling tensed. “Do not waste my time, Sterling. You have my woman and child. I suggest you bring her to me now or I’ll simply end you now and see to finding her myself.”

Sterling remained firm, “As I’ve said, the girl is mine. You do not have the right to barge into my home making demands.”

“Are you not familiar with a Marquis of Northampton?”

Sterling stiffened his eyes hardening beneath Dorian’s icy stare. “I believe we need not further continue on this nonsense. My patience grows thin; you will produce the girl to me now.”

Sterling snorted, “You forget that I am a man of wealth and power. I’ll see that you hang for this, and if I am dead, there are others that will see it done.”

“There are other higher authorities, Baron. You are oblivious to the moment that I give you a chance to walk away with your life intact. Mayhap I should take this matter of false imprisonment to the King? You have detained a Lady without lawful authority and considering that you and I are both well acquainted with the Marquis of Northampton, who I might add is an admired colleague of the King himself, it seems the odds are against you. So what have you, Sterling?”

Sterling inhaled deeply, his eyes like granite. “And if I do not comply?”

“I will follow through on my threats and see that the King strips you of your title and lands. I think it wise you consider your options.”

Sterling cleared his throat, “If I give the girl to you, you will let the matter fall?”

Dorian nodded, “With your word that neither you nor any man you hire will seek to take what is mine again?”

Sterling stiffened as another man appeared in the parlor, this one much smaller in size but his russet eyes revealing a calculating look as they assessed Sterling solemnly. “All well, Captain?”

Neither the pistol nor the penetrating blue stare ever wavered from Sterling. “Aye, Lieutenant. You may begin searching the premises.”

“There is no need.” Sterling blurted, “She is on the second floor, third door down.”

Dorian remained as Stefan left the room in search of Ginelle. “Just to ensure her safety, I intend to marry her. There will be no need for me to explain what will happen if you have any notions of kidnapping my wife?”

Sterling nodded grimly. “I give you my word.”

Dorian took a step back from Sterling and slowly lowered the pistol. A feminine gasp penetrated the silence and he turned and felt his heart somersault against his chest as his eyes met the dewy-brown eyes of the woman he loved.

He leveled another hard stare on Sterling before crossing the room and taking Ginelle's arm firmly in one hand and began leading her towards the door.

She pulled away and said softly, "I have a small request?"

Dorian glanced at Sterling before meeting her wide, hopeful stare. "Now is not the time, mon peu l'un."

Her hand fluttered to rest lightly on his forearm as she stared up at him, "I wish to take Thora with me."

His black brows knitted together with puzzlement. "Who?"

Ginelle turned and peered into the corner where a thin silhouette hovered. Dorian lifted his head and motioned for the girl to come forward.

The girl stepped toward them, her dark head downcast as Dorian studied her a moment. "Come, girl." He ordered.

Sterling snorted with disgust as he downed another glass of brandy. "Take the half-witted wench. She is of no use to me any how." He tossed the glass across the room and stalked away, mumbling curses beneath his breath.

Ginelle's heart tightened in her chest as Thora's expression wavered by the harsh retort. She reached out and seized Thora's hand, squeezing gently as she said, "Come Thora."

The journey back to Ashford was anything but rejoicing. The four of them remained silent as the carriage transported them along the winding road back to London.

Ginelle continued to peer over at Dorian from beneath lowered lashes, her thoughts increasingly worried for he had rarely said a word or even looked at her since leaving Cambridge. She felt his anger emanating from his body as his face took on a hardened mask that revealed nothing of his emotions. She wondered than if he still believed she carried Stefan's child?

The moment she realized Dorian had come for her, she had wanted to leap into his arms and weep with delirium but her instincts warned her that he was angry and that her affections were wasted. His demeanor was distant and almost cold, his thoughts clearly withdrawn and unaware of her glancing looks.

A shudder passed through her body as she remembered there last encounter. He had been so furious and his harsh accusations had hurt deeply, but despite all that, she loved him. She bit down on her lower lip, resisting the impulse to confess all that her foolish little heart kept concealed. She had been so credulous, easily swayed into believing even for a moment that Dorian felt strongly about her.

She felt the rush of tears and quickly turned her face toward the window. She couldn't abide the thought of Dorian hating her, looking at her with accusation in his eyes. She would not consent to live with his coldness and consistent doubtfulness. She refused to torment her heart any more than what it had already suffered.

She couldn't have been more relieved when she felt the strong pull of exhaustion and gave in to the lethargy.

When next she woke, the carriage was rocking to a halt. Her eyes struggled to open but as she attempted to wake, strong arms slipped protectively around her, lifting her easily from the carriage, and her head lolled against a broad shoulder and she slipped blissfully asleep.

Ginelle awoke some time later, surprised to be abed and donned in nothing but a loose fitting chemise. As she straightened to peer around the room she was even more startled to see that she had slept in Dorian's bed. Sitting up, she pushed tousled strands of hair from her face and jerked when a shadow moved along the room.

Stiffening, she met Dorian's hooded stare regarding her quietly. He stepped towards her and she winced beneath his hardened expression and pulled the blanket tighter against her chest. His large frame tensed at this and his blue eyes darkened with contempt. Ginelle noticed the muscle tightening along his jaw as his eyes took on an unyielding gleam.

"Do you fear me now?" his terse words made her flinch not with fear but confusion as to his accosting glare. She took note that his fists were balled at his sides, and his manner bespoke his blackened mood.

She frowned, shaking her head gently. "You think I fear you?"

His solid visage flickered with confusion before hardening once more as he stepped towards her, his resolve settling as he fixed her with a doubtful stare. "Your manner bespeaks your fear of me." her confusion deepened even more for she sensed remorse along with the anger in his voice and it suddenly dawned on her, his anger was not directed towards her, but himself. He had mistaken her fear for another.

She pushed the blanket aside and arose to her feet. He watched her cross towards him, his body rigid as she stood before him, her soft eyes peering up at him with an emotion he dare not recognize. Her flaxen hair pooled over her shoulders like rivulets of moonlight, enhancing the ethereal glow of her skin, and he longed to claim her subtle kiss.

He stood motionless, unmoving as she reached tentatively between them to place her hands flat against his chest, her fingers exploring the hardened muscle beneath the tunic and he felt a sudden groan in his throat. She leaned closer and the sweet smell of heather filled his senses, tugging on the strong urges pulsating through his body.

Her eyes fluttered down and he watched the delicate movement as her feather-lashes rested gently atop high-cheekbones. "You believe I think you capable of hurting me." She said softly, drawing his attention as she lifted her head.

He inhaled deeply, his chest rising as his fists tightened and the muscle at his jaw flexed as he said, "Don't you?"

Her eyes fixated on his chest where her hands splayed wide and he noticed a distinct shudder pass through her slender shoulders. "It is not your temper that has me afraid." She paused as she lowered her head, his brows knitting together with puzzlement as she continued, "I fear your distrust in me." her voice quivered at this and she met his startled expression and added, "I fear that you do not love me as I do you." She said this with fresh tears brimming in her eyes.

Dorian was jolted into bewilderment by her words. He had expected her anger, her hatred towards him for treating her so harshly, for accusing her so cruelly, but he had not expected her love. She stood before him, her heart completely exposed and vulnerable and her eyes wide with uncertainty as to what he felt and her fear of his response as clear as light.

Unable to resist any longer, he reached up and gently took her hands in one as the other slipped affectionately around her waist, drawing her close. He smiled inwardly as he felt her swollen belly brush lightly against him, her womb carrying his child. She gasped as he leaned close, his mouth hovering above her own as he whispered lightly, "You little fool-" his lips curved into a smile as he reached up and cupped her chin gently, "-how could you not know that a day in my life without you is a lifetime of darkness."

His lips brushed the corners of her mouth and she shuddered in his arms, her hands curling in his tunic as he said, "I've loved you the moment I laid eyes on you, knew from that moment that you were mine." he captured her lips and she gasped as his arm tightened around her, her heart soaring within her chest as all her fears and doubts melted away with his fiery kiss.

He swept her into his arms and carried her to the bed. He gently placed her down and she watched as he shed his tunic, exposing the bruises and wounds that marred his chest.

Ginelle gasped as she sat upright, her eyes widening with affliction as she studied the horrid display. "What did that man do to you?"

Dorian saw fresh tears in her eyes and leaned down to cup her face in his hands, drawing her attention to him. "It is nothing."

She shook her head, attempting to pull away. "You could have died." Her voice tightened at the thought.

He settled beside her and pulled her into his lap. "The pain I suffered does not compare to the torment of not knowing where you were." He leaned forward and nestled his head between her neck and shoulder, his dark tresses tickling the underside of her chin. "I went mad not knowing where to find you, not knowing if you were being harmed and I was not there to prevent it." His arms slipped around her and tightened, crushing her affectionately against him.

"Marry me." he whispered against the crook of her neck.

"What?" she gasped, fearful she had not heard right.

He straightened and Ginelle was startled by his tender expression and the clear, crystal blue of his eyes as they peered at her with such clarifying sincerity. "I love you, ma petite. Marry me." he reached up and brushed his thumb along her lips, "I cannot abide life without you. Become my wife."

She felt an abruptness of tears and an exhilarating rush of happiness to where she was almost breathless. "Yes." She cried readily, "Yes, yes!" Dorian laughed as she flung her arms around him, collapsing atop him as they tumbled backward onto the bed, giggling.

He kissed her with such sweetness that she nearly whimpered adoringly. He lifted his head and his blue eyes moved warmly over her pausing along the swell of her belly. He reached over and gently laid his hand there, his mouth curling at the thought of many more to come.

Chapter 33

Ginelle awoke the next morning with a smile, surprised to find a white lily resting against Dorian's pillow. She laughed softly, wondering just how he managed to find a flower in the dead of winter. She cradled the sweet gesture as she arose from bed and shuffled across the room to grab her robe. Someone had already brought her breakfast and stoked the fire but neither caught her attention as a noise from outside brought her to the window.

As she pushed the drapes aside, she was startled to see Dorian down below talking to a man she had never seen before. She frowned as the two of them discussed amongst each other followed by a few occasional hand gestures that motioned towards the array of men standing off to the side. She leaned further against the window, straining to see who the other men were and recognized the laborers.

There was a tapping at her door and she bid them entry as she turned away from the window to greet Thora. "Good morning milady, did you sleep well?"

Ginelle nodded, "Yes Thora, thank you. Have you settled?"

Thora smiled, "Yes milady. Belle has kindly offered to share her quarters."

"You are happy than?" Ginelle asked.

"Very so!" Thora cried gleefully, "The servants here are very kind to me. Is there anything I might get you?"

Ginelle shook her head, hesitating to leave the window before doing so. She moved across the room and settled into the chair before the hearth taking notice that Thora lingered and appeared on the verge of saying something. "Is something amiss?" she asked, suddenly worried.

Thora was quick to shake her head, "Not at all, milady!"

Ginelle laughed than, "Than pray tell, what is it that has you frantic?"

Thora stepped towards her and dropped her head, clearing her throat as she said, "May I ask something that is bold?"

Suddenly concerned, Ginelle leaned forward, "Of course, please."

"W-what do you-" she paused, clearing her throat again, "-what do you think of Lieutenant Cummings?"

Ginelle's eyes widened, confounded as a realization struck her. She felt a smile curving her lips but resisted for Thora appeared fairly nervous, her affections clear. "He is quite a gentleman." She stated, "Why do you ask?"

Thora continued to twist her hands nervously; her dark head cast downward, avoiding Ginelle's inquisitive stare entirely. "I-I find him a-agreeable." She said modestly, her pale face blushing a deep crimson red.

Ginelle smiled, "He is very agreeable."

Thora lifted her head and smiled a timid smile. "You agree than?"

She laughed, "I think we've validated that already."

Thora giggled.

"Mayhap you should tell him so?" Ginelle suggested.

Thora stiffened, shaking her head immediately at the thought. "I couldn't possibly!"

"Lieutenant Cummings is very charming and kind; there is no harm in telling him how you feel."

Thora worried her bottom lip with her teeth as she considered this but nothing more was said on the matter as someone approached from within the hall. As Thora left the room, Dorian entered from behind, his blue eyes immediately finding Ginelle by the hearth and warming affectionately as he closed the door behind him.

"I thought to find you still abed." He leaned down and captured her lips gently teasing her bottom lip with his tongue that triggered an immediate response of arousal that trickled through her limbs like tiny flames.

He reached over and pulled the silver lid from the tray to reveal her untouched breakfast and disapproval darkened his face. "You need to eat." He ordered.

Ginelle grimaced, "Do not order me about; I am not your wife yet."

A grin touched his mouth as he peered at her, his blue eyes twinkling. He set the lid aside and reached out to pull her gently to her feet and into his embrace. "When you are my wife, fair one, you will submit to my every whim."

She felt her anger rising but as quickly as it arose; she caught the flicker of amusement dancing wickedly in his blue stare and lightly pummeled his chest. He laughed and gently seized her wrist to press butterfly kisses to her knuckles.

She resisted a smile as he released her and stepped away. She stared at his broad back a moment before asking, "Who were you talking too?"

"His name is Jon Benedict. I purchased your mare from him."

Her brow arched curiously, "Do you plan to buy from him again?"

He shook his head, "He plans to buy from me."

Suddenly remembering the laborers standing aside she gasped, "Surely you don't mean to sell your laborers to him?"

Surprised by her reaction, Dorian turned around to her. "That is exactly what I had planned to do." He frowned, "You are not pleased?"

"Pleased? Why would I be pleased?" she cried, suddenly outraged, "These are lives that you are passing back and forth like chattel."

"They are not free men by law." He said grudgingly, "They are unfortunate because of their actions." Her silence drew his attention and he studied her a moment before crossing the room to her. He leaned down on his haunches to meet her teary gaze and took her hands in his, "Why does this bother you, ma petite?"

"They are prisoners." She said sadly realizing her decision was based on the pain she endured as a child, the imprisonment she had suffered at Pierino's hands.

He reached out and cupped her chin, forcing her to meet his stare. "Yes, they are prisoners but they are prisoners because of their own judgment leading to their mistakes. They are accountable for their crimes. Benedict is a good man; he does not mistreat his laborers."

"What of your fields?" she asked, "If you do not have any laborers how do you intend to tend to your fields without help?"

"The fields will still be tended too. My men and I will see to that but aside from my plantation, there are other means of finance."

Ginelle frowned, "What do you say?"

"I plan to never part from you again, Ginelle." He said this with such severity that her heart jumped within her chest. "I do not plan to set sail again."

She gasped, "But Dorian, you have always loved to sail."

He shook his head, "It was the trade that I love but it was the trade that kept me away when Eloise died and a different trade entirely where I nearly lost you."

"But what of your vessels?" she asked earnestly.

"I have revoked my title as Captain and have relinquished the task to Cummings."

"He accepted?"

Dorian grinned, "He declined but I surmise he will come around, his heart is at sea."

Ginelle grinned, her thoughts steering towards Thora and her affections for Stefan. "Do not be so certain of yourself." She said knowingly.

A black brow arched curiously, "Do you know something that I do not, ma petite?"

She smirked and refrained from saying further. He laughed as he scooped her easily into his arms, ignoring her squeals of protest as he carried her to the bed. "I will get it out of you one way or another."

Dorian was true to his word in the coming of weeks. He maintained the household and prepped the fields despite the inclement weather. Ginelle occupied her time with what domestic chores she was allowed with a gruff Lucile looming over her shoulder along the way.

Her evenings were spent with Dorian, playing chess and reading literature. He simply lounged in the chair by the hearth, a faint smile shadowing his lips as he listened to her voice as she recited poetry. She found herself faltering over the words, unnerved by his penetrating stare that not once wavered from her face the moment she began and after several attempts of reading the same line and failing miserably; she dropped the book to her lap with a huff.

"Why are you staring at me like that?" she demanded.

His grin widened, "I am simply admiring the woman to become my wife."

She smirked, "You are insufferable."

He straightened and leaned towards her, taking her hands gently, and drawing them to his lips to kiss her fingertips. "And you are lovely." He held her hands gently in his own and studied her a moment, his blue eyes suddenly doubtful, "Are you happy?"

She sensed a sudden wariness in him, an uncertainty that clouded his blue eyes as he stared back at her. “Yes.” She said wholeheartedly, smiling as she leaned forward and kissed the brim of his nose.

A smile stretched across his lips as he reached out and pulled her into his lap and cradled her close while picking the book up he placed it firmly back into her hands, encouraging her to continue. She laughed and proceeded on to the next line.

The next day Ginelle was delighted when Ellison came to visit along with Edmund who immediately sought Dorian’s company the moment the two women cried gleefully and fell into loquacious spouts of excitement and laughter, a flow of tears and a roundabout of the room as they burst into details of the wedding to come.

Edmund slipped quickly from the room, fearful that he may lose a limb through the exchanging of embraces and twirling hems as he fled into the hall where he met Dorian.

Dorian chuckled as he slapped Edmund lightly on the back, “I was beginning to wonder if I should attempt to rescue you had you not escaped when you did.”

Edmund laughed, amused by the stream of giggles flowing from the parlor. “I escaped unscathed for the time being but eventually one of us will have to go back in there.”

Dorian’s laughter rolled easily from his throat as the two of them made there way to his study. “That is a task deemed frightful.”

Edmund settled into a chair and regarded Dorian in all seriousness. “Have you told her yet?”

Dorian shook his head as he settled across from him. “Not yet.”

“When do you plan to tell her?” Edmund asked curiously.

“In due time.” He replied, “She is delicate right now, especially in her condition, I do not want to increase any anxieties she may have.”

Edmund nodded and than asked, “Have you heard the news of Sharp?”

Dorian arched a black brow, his temper sparking at the name. “What of him?” he growled.

“He’s bankrupt.”

Dorian’s face shifted with surprise, “Sharp?”

Edmund nodded, “Evidently he is a poor gambler. He gambled away what little inheritance he had left. He’s fled London, rumor has it the winning beneficiary wasn’t satisfied with his winnings.”

Sharp was the least of his worries. He had not forgotten that Sharp had partially participated in Ginelle’s captivity but it would seem fate had other plans for the man and he was temporarily satisfied with the outcome.

Pierino’s body was discovered alongside the road, miles from Cambridge with a severed wound to his underbelly, every possession of worth on his person stolen as abruptly as the breath from his lungs. As much of a potential danger the thief had been to Ginelle, the man had not deserved such a fate and had made a mistake in swindling the Baron.

However, he thought broodingly, Victoria remained a threat. Since returning to London he had immediately began searching the streets but word of the red-head remained aloof. She would continue to be a danger to Ginelle so as long as she breathed and he vowed to assure Ginelle’s safety, even if it meant resorting to certain tactics.

Later that evening, Dorian lifted his head as the door to his study opened and Cummings entered the room. Dorian motioned Stefan to a chair across from him and grinned as his friend sauntered casually into the room, a slight smirk inadvertently tweaking the corners of his mouth as he sat down and leaned comfortably back.

Dorian arched a dark brow as he studied Stefan amusingly, “You seem in high spirits today?” he inquired, suddenly curious to his Lieutenant’s elatedness.

Stefan grinned despite himself, “I am pleased as over a particular thing.”

“This particular thing would happen to be a woman?”

Stefan’s grin widened.

“Ah, I see.” Dorian mused, smiling and than asked, “I’m sure you’re aware of why I’ve asked you here?”

Stefan nodded, “Aye and I’ve given it some thought.”

Dorian straightened, “And?”

Stefan leaned forward, “I will steer the vessels and do the trade but I am not your Captain. I shall and always remain your Lieutenant. Is that a compromise we can agree upon?”

Dorian smirked, “I suppose that can suffice.”

Stefan narrowed his eyes, suddenly suspicious. “I am surprised you did not fight me on this? What have you up your sleeve?”

His manner hardened suddenly as he straightened to his feet and said, “Victoria is in town.”

Stefan frowned, “How do you know this?”

“I have my sources.” He said and than added, “It seems she had business elsewhere.”

“So what do you plan to do?”

Dorian turned and peered at Stefan, “She is the reason I’ve asked for you today.”

Stefan arched a brow, suddenly intrigued, “I’m listening.”

Chapter 34

In the next enduring weeks, with her pregnancy progressing and restricting much of her movements, she grew easily fatigued and confined to bed a majority of time.

Accompanying her constant tiredness was a great deal of curiosity. She began to see less and less of Dorian, at first surmising that he had other affairs to manage, she simply brushed disquieting notions aside, that is until days on end of scarcely seeing him increased her skepticism.

Troubling thoughts took root, disconcerting her mind as to where he could be during his time of absence. Much time alone and spent abed had her weighing these thoughts heavily; a fleeting intuition of doubt and uncertainty clouding the base of her mind.

She was abed early one morning, awaiting a servant as her mind grew increasingly agitated and unnerved by her relentless assumptions.

She nearly jumped out of her skin when a knock resounded in the room. Ginelle waited as Lucile entered quietly, expecting her to be asleep.

"You're awake?" the housekeeper exclaimed surprisingly. "I expected you abed until midday. How are you feeling, my pet?" she asked, moving forward to examine Ginelle more closely.

"I am fine." She replied coolly. "Where is Dorian?" she watched the older woman carefully, keen to note that her dark eyes averted nervously.

Ginelle narrowed her eyes suspiciously, "Lucile, if there is something you know that I don't-I trust that you would tell me."

Lucile shifted awkwardly on her heels, almost anxiously, heightening her suspicions. “He and Lieutenant Cummings are conducting business.”

Ginelle frowned, “What sort of business? Is it plantation work? A trade?” she noticed the older woman tensing, hastening for an explanation. “Lucile, I feel that you are not entirely speaking the truth. What is going on?” she demanded.

“I cannot say, my dear. It is for the best that you not know and that you stay abed.”

“I am not ill, Lucile.” Ginelle asserted, “I am with child and I believe I have the right to know where the father of my child is? Don’t you?”

Lucile straightened her broad shoulders, releasing a heavy sigh as she met Ginelle’s penetrating stare. “Trust me, my dear; all is as it should be.”

Suspecting she wouldn’t get the answers she sought, she let the matter fall and exhaled a breath of frustration. She trusted in the older woman and knew she would not keep matters of importance from her, so what than was going on beneath her nose? She knew Dorian was up to something but what? What kept him away for such a prolonged period of time?

When Dorian returned to her that night, she feigned sleep, too angry to question his whereabouts; she decided to avoid it entirely. She listened intently as he shuffled about the darkened room, his movements more profound against the quiet as he moved from one corner to another, at one point, she thought him standing above her, peering down at her, the sound of his breathing emitting the silence.

A part of her wanted to question him, to demand an explanation for his absence, for leaving her alone for days on end without a reason to why but she feared shadowing thoughts, notions that she dare not bring to the forefront, fearing they may be true.

She felt her heart sink even deeper in her chest as his footsteps carried him away and out the room. She opened her eyes and stared around, disappointed to find she was alone.

Unable to keep them at bay any longer, she thought mayhap he no longer found her attractive? Her belly was swollen with child and she had gained a bit of weight. Did he find her unappealing? Did he not love her as he had claimed too?

Fighting tears, she sank back down and forced herself asleep.

Her anger intensified the next evening. She had been alone most of the day, aside from Thora and Belle accompanying her for a time and engaging in small conversation but after sensing her saddened and distant mood, the girls left to carry on with their tasks.

She was trying to focus on the book in her hands when a voice sounded from within the hall. Ginelle lifted her head as Ellison entered the room, surprised to see that her green eyes that usually illuminated a happiness was slightly perplexed with confliction.

Frowning, Ginelle set her book aside. "Ellison? Is something the matter?"

Ellison paced the room, not bothering to remove her cloak as her feet carried her back and forth.

Anxiety forced her heart into a frantic rhythm as she studied her friend. "What is it?" she demanded. "Would you come and sit with me?"

Ellison stopped pacing and moved to settle by her. For a moment, she was silent and Ginelle lightly gripped Ellison's shoulder. "I -" she murmured softly.

Ginelle felt her pulse accelerate anxiously. "What?"

"I am afraid to tell you. I do not know how to say it-what to make of it." She mumbled.

Ginelle shook her head, "I am not understanding, Ellison. What is wrong? Has something happened?" she squeezed her friend's shoulder, "Is it Edmund?" when silence followed she felt a sudden dryness in her throat, "Dorian?"

Ellison lifted her head, her expression torn as she said, "I saw Dorian in town, and he was escorting a woman, a woman with red hair."

Ginelle gasped as the blood drained from her face, all her fears emphasizing the amount of shock and disbelief.

She felt a violent rush of tears as she shook her head determinedly as if to convince herself that the red-headed woman was not Victoria. "No, he wouldn't-" she clamped her mouth shut realizing just how foolish it would be to dislodge the assumption.

Ellison reached out and gripped Ginelle's hand in her own, her raven curls bouncing on her shoulders as she shook her head. "As I said, I do not know what to make of it, I could be mistaken-"

"There is no mistake." She said sorely, "She is his mistress. What other purpose is there than to share his bed?" she suddenly felt cold and wanted nothing more than to seek slumber, anything to avoid the bombardment of pain.

"I'm tired." She whispered achingly.

"Do you wish for me to stay?" Ellison asked worriedly.

Ginelle shook her head, "I need to be alone."

She closed her eyes and listened as Ellison quietly left the room. For a time she laid immobile to the uncanny absence of sound as the room grew darker, signifying the approach of dusk, all the while, waiting for him to return.

Hours passed with growing anxiety. She knew Ellison would not have conjured such a lie, so what had she done? Did he find her unattractive now that her belly was swollen with child? Did he think her uncomely?

She felt her chest tightening as these thoughts scrambled through her mind. Why would he take Victoria back after what she had done? Had all his heartfelt confessions been a lie simply to lure her back to him because she was to have his child?

She wanted to scream but had not the strength to do so; instead she turned into her pillow and wept until she could do so no longer.

Ginelle was startled awake the next morning. She turned to see that the spot next to her was unstirred, meaning Dorian had never come to bed.

She pulled herself up and stiffened to see the very object of her thoughts studying her from across the room, the faint morning light playing beautifully across his handsome face. Her chest constricted with pain and anger to how he could look so strikingly handsome yet hurt her in such an unimaginable way.

She wanted to weep, wanted to scream until her lungs were aching, instead she remained silent and aloof.

"Are you well?" he asked carefully, noting her remoteness and the dark shadows beneath her eyes.

"You need not worry to my wellbeing." She replied icily.

He appeared taken aback, surprised by her reply. She watched him carefully, observing the sharp glint in his blue eyes as they assessed her intensely. "Are you angry?" he asked, certain of the answer.

She felt the insidious urge to laugh. "Angry? Why would I be?" she snapped sarcastically.

A black brow arched purposefully as he crossed the room to her and immediately she was annoyed to her body's reaction to his nearness. "Tell me what has made you angry, my sweet one?" he reached out to touch her and she jerked away.

"I'd rather you not touch me." She hissed.

"Confound it woman, what have I done?" he demanded.

She felt the tears rushing to the surface and she wanted to curse herself for her sensitive little heart. "Nothing." She said dejectedly, turning her head away to avoid his knowing stare.

He reached out and pulled her to him and despite her hurt and anger, she allowed him to hold her, loving the feel of his arms wrapped warmly around her. He placed his chin atop her head and said gently, "I am sorry that I haven't been around."

She felt her chin quiver and she clenched her eyes shut against tears. Just tell me the truth. She urged her heart heavy in her chest. Tell me you do not love her.

"Are you well enough to travel?" Ginelle jerked her head sideways, surprised to see Dorian at the door dressed in his black cloak and patent-leather boots.

She frowned, "Where are we going?"

He approached her and gently took the needle work from her hands and set it aside. She would have preferred to avoid touching him but he insisted on helping her to her feet. "There is somewhere we need to be."

Curious she asked, "Where is that?"

"I cannot say as of now. Are you well?" his blue eyes searched her face, noting the weary lines beneath her tired eyes.

She wrenched her hands from his and jerked her chin upward. "I am perfectly capable of moving about without your help." She snapped as she started around him, oblivious to the small perk of his lips as he found her haughtiness amusing.

"I am not ill." She insisted, attempting to bend over to retrieve her cloak.

Dorian grinned as he moved forward and seized it, catching her low huff of agitation as he motioned her to turn around. He wrapped her comfortably in her cloak and assisted her with her shoes before finishing.

"Where are we going?" she insisted as he led her from the room and into the hall. She was instinctively aware of his hand gripping hers and wanted to pull away but knew if she tried he wouldn't permit it.

A small, cold draft hit her face as they stepped outside. She shivered within her cloak and was momentarily comforted as Dorian's arm slipped around her waist, pulling her gently to his side for warmth.

He had a carriage waiting and helped her into the small compartment. He followed behind and seated himself next to her. She would have distanced herself but because of the coldness quickly seeping into her bones, she remained at his side.

"Can you please tell me where we're going?" she pleaded as the carriage rolled into motion.

"You will know soon enough."

She frowned as she turned to look at him, slightly unnerved by his reply and more confounded for she couldn't determine his expression.

She gritted her teeth, wanting to vent her frustration and anger. He was full of secrets. How could they ever have a life together when he revealed nothing to her?

It wasn't long before they reached their destination and the carriage came to a stop before a magnificent town house.

Confused, Ginelle stared out the window at the marvelous structure looming above, her mind more bewildered than ever. The coachman opened the carriage door and Dorian stepped out. He turned and extended a hand to her but she remained motionless.

"Where are we, Dorian?" there was fear to her voice and he sensed it.

"I am meeting a friend." He said as if to appease her worry.

"Than what reason do you have for bringing me?"

His brows furrowed as he peered at her, "What have you to fear? I would let nothing harm you, ma petite."

She worried her bottom lip as she glanced fearfully at the beautiful house. "Who are we meeting?"

"Come, Ginelle. It is cold and I wish to get you inside."

For a jarring moment, she imagined he had actually taken her to Victoria's home. Surely he wouldn't do such a thing?

Reluctantly, she placed her hand in his and he gingerly led her from the carriage. He placed his arm around her shoulders as they made their way towards the stone steps where a servant appeared at the top, awaiting them with a smile.

"Please Monsieur Ashford, come inside." The small man urged, quickly closing the door behind them and ushering them forward into a brilliant blue room with impressive pieces of porcelain scattered throughout, and plush carpet cushioning their feet as they moved to be seated onto a strikingly white sofa.

"Dorian please tell me what's going on?" Ginelle pleaded quietly.

Just as he intended to say something, a man's voice started from within the hall. Dorian stood and Ginelle followed, turning as the man entered the room.

Her eyes widened as she took an involuntary step backward.

She felt Dorian's hands on her shoulders as he said, "Ginelle, you've met Edric Collins. He is the Marquis of Northampton."

She pivoted around, baffled as she stared up at Dorian. "Why would you bring me here?"

"He is of no danger to you." Dorian said assuredly.

"But-" she glanced fearfully at Edric before back at Dorian. "He tried to steal me away?"

"Only to protect you." Edric responded quickly.

She frowned, shaking her head. "No-you knew about Pierino? You were at the banquet? You were working for him, how else would you know about me?"

He was silent as he stepped towards her and she stiffened as his eyes dropped to the locket around her neck. He pointed and said, "Because you wear her locket."

She gasped, her hand intuitively reaching for her cherished trinket. "H-how do you know that?" she whispered shockingly.

Edric said nothing but merely stepped aside as another body entered the parlor. Ginelle slowly turned away from Edric to the small, blond woman entering the room and she felt the world tilter as a jolt of shock registered one word breathlessly from her throat.

"Mother?"

Chapter 35

She felt as though the beautifully meticulous room swiveled uncontrollably as she stared in disbelief at the tiny, blond woman regarding her through a set of dark, soft eyes, eyes that amazingly mirrored her own.

"How can this be?" Ginelle breathed inaudibly, her mind struggling with incredulity and awe.

The woman addressed the two men in the room, "Gentlemen, if you would give us a moment alone?" her voice was sweet like a melody without a single strand of white-blond askew, and her layers of skirts secure of any wrinkles. She was perfectly intact; magnificently impeccable.

The men nodded and quietly left the room. The woman motioned to a white sofa with a small, gloved hand. "Please, sit down." She suggested, offering a warm smile.

Ginelle did so, not once taking her eyes off the woman as she crossed the room, her skirts swaying mildly against the heavy carpet. "Mother?" the word escaped on its own accord.

There was a quick glimmer of pain in the woman's eyes and a slight quivering of her lower lip as she said, "If only it were so."

Ginelle frowned, suddenly puzzled. "You are not Anne?"

The woman shook her head.

Ginelle's frown deepened. "You are not my mother? How is that so when you resemble her perfectly...when you resemble me?"

The woman lifted her head and smiled faintly, "I resemble her so because I am her sister, her twin Amelia."

Ginelle exhaled sharply, stunned. "That cannot be. I was never told of you, of any relatives for that matter." She shook her head as she gathered abruptly to her feet, pacing aimlessly back and forth. "This just cannot be. If you are who you say you are, then that means you are my Aunt?"

Amelia nodded.

"Why was I never told of you? Why didn't you come for me?" she demanded, suddenly hurt that she spent nearly her entire childhood as an orphan.

Amelia stood than, clasping her gloved hands in front of her as she said painfully. "Your mother made me promise not to intervene."

"I do not understand."

"My sister was forced into a marriage she deemed incompatible. Lord Sterling was a relentless man with plans and my sister was a free spirit, incapable of being subservient. Your mother confided only in me and when I learned of her pregnancy, I begged my sister to flee, for her safety and your own."

"Why?" Ginelle urged despite having met Sterling herself.

Amelia's dark eyes met hers from across the room. "Lord Sterling was incapable of producing an heir and once your mother could no longer conceal her pregnancy, he would know that the babe she carried was not his, therefore revealing her infidelity."

"Would he have harmed her?" Ginelle asked.

"He was not a violent man." Amelia said, "But he was a man accustomed to getting his way, his reputation was essential and your mother was uncertain of how he would react once he learned of her pregnancy."

"And so she fled, with my father?"

Amelia nodded, smiling gently. "Your mother told me, it just made sense to run away with him, because she loved him."

Ginelle was saddened by the thought, knowing how her father had suffered a disquieting grief after her mother had died. "What happened afterward?" she asked.

Amelia cleared her throat, "Anne and Ross attempted a life together but 'twas difficult, after all, she was a married woman, the wife of a Baron, she couldn't go far without Lord Sterling trailing behind, he refused to let her go, I truly believed he loved her despite all she had done but his thirst for vengeance was far more overpowering than his love."

She paused a moment, reliving those memories as she relayed them quietly. "I was away in Paris when I learned of your mother's death." Her disheartened words affected Ginelle deeply, realizing just how painful it must have been for her.

"Even then you did not look for me?"

"When I asked of you, I was told you had died along with your mother. I was so devastated that it had taken me a very long time to come to terms with your deaths."

"Who told you of my supposed death?"

"Sterling."

Ginelle understood than. "Only too lure you away from me?"

Amelia nodded, "Precisely."

"When did you learn the truth?"

"When I returned from Paris, I visited Cambridge to collect your mother's belongings, among her remaining items, there was one particular piece missing, her locket."

Instinctively, Ginelle reached up and touched the precious trinket beneath her cloak. "You wanted her locket?"

She nodded and said as she reached up and withdrew an identical gold locket from around her neck. "She and I had the same locket given to us at birth by our mother; on the inside are tiny portraits of the other sister."

Ginelle gasped, "You mean the picture within mine is not my mother?"

She nodded, "You carry the locket with my portrait."

"And you have hers?"

She nodded and gently unclasped the locket, revealing her sister's photo. "I returned for her locket, to have it for keepsake but when I found it missing I was surprised by this. From the day she ran Anne had always feared for your fate. She told me once that she would pass her locket to you so that I would find you if ever something became of her. I questioned your death and knew that if you were truly alive, the locket would identify you."

She paused, meeting Ginelle's attentive stare. "Eventually I was informed of your father's murder. I had an inside source relaying information, including Sterling's initial plan to find you and use you to alleviate his revenge against your parents. I feared for your safety and knew not of your whereabouts until my son, Edric came to London and heard of your debut. He came to London in search of you; I kept away, fearing that if Sterling or a man he had hired would recognize me. I did not want to chance them finding you, so I stayed hidden."

Ginelle gasped, remembering the night she had first met Edric. "He was at the banquet."

Amelia nodded, "At my bidding."

"He came to Ashford?"

"I urged him to bring you to me. I was afraid for your safety. I was worried that Sterling and his man were getting close to finding you."

"How did you meet Dorian?" she wondered suddenly.

"Monsieur Dorian came to us." She smiled, "He sought Edric to seek you. Once Lord Sterling learned of his acquaintance with us, he released you, fearing we would reveal his crimes. My son is a very powerful man, very familiar with King George and Lord Sterling holds his title above all else, he would not risk anything to jeopardize that."

Amelia paused as she stared down into her gloved palms. "I cannot make amends for abandoning you. I wish for nothing more than for us to be family again."

"I am sorry if I seemed averse. This is all so very shocking to me but I do not fault you for any of it, you were misinformed, led to believe I was dead." Ginelle quickly assured. "You did not abandon me, you have searched for me all this time." She smiled as a surge of tears rushed to the brim of her eyes. "I would like very much for us to get to know each other."

Amelia nodded and the two women stood and tightly embraced. As Ginelle pulled away, Amelia reached up and gently removed her locket. She took Ginelle's hand and placed it in her palm. "Oh I couldn't possibly-"

Amelia shook her head as her fingers closed around Ginelle's. "You are her daughter. She would want you to have it." She smiled and slowly dropped her hand.

As she and Dorian left Amelia's home, she cradled the locket around her neck, the tiny portrait within, that of her mother.

The ride back to Ashford was silent and the carriage carried an uncanny quiet. Ginelle was distinctively aware of Dorian's fixed stare but continued peering out the window in a desperate attempt to avoid him altogether.

"Are you well?" he asked suddenly, jolting her to awareness.

She nodded and proceeded to look out the window.

There was a pause. "Are you tired?" she sensed a sudden note of agitation in his voice.

She shook her head not once turning away from the window.

"Than tell me-" he growled, "-what outside that window has captivated your attention so?"

She bit down on her lower lip, resisting the impulses rushing up from her throat.

"Are you not pleased?" he asked, finally drawing her eyes towards him.

Ginelle frowned, "Pleased?"

He was perplexed by her response, "What troubles you?" his blue eyes studied her intensely. "Are you overwhelmed by the suddenness of all this?"

She was the happiest she had ever been but her happiness was overshadowed by lingering doubts.

"Do you plan to send me away?" she asked suddenly, unable to contain her emotions any longer.

He frowned, clearly taken aback. "What are you talking about?"

"Is that not why you took me to see my Aunt? Do you plan to force me from Ashford once the babe is born?"

His face darkened considerably as he leaned towards her, confounded. "Damn it woman, what are you saying?"

Ginelle felt a rush of tears as a fleeting thought of uncertainty brushed her mind. Was she wrong? "Is that not why you introduced us?"

His black brows knitted together with frustration and adamant confusion. "She is your family, Ginelle." He fell silent a moment as his blue eyes accessed her expression.

"Why would you think I would send you away?" When she did not answer, he reached out and took her hands in his own. "I thought you would be overjoyed to know you had family?" he asked, deeply puzzled by her reaction.

She gently pulled her hands from his and when she peered at him he was baffled to see tears. "I couldn't be happier." She shook her head as if to shake her mind of mindless notions and attempted a smile that didn't match the sadden gleam in her brown eyes. "I am overwhelmed by all this." She added but Dorian wasn't convinced, he sensed something deeply troubling her but she refrained from saying and his thoughts immediately shifted to other matters.

Victoria.

Did she know?

She couldn't possibly. He had been cautious all along.

He settled back into the seat, his eyes locked heavily on Ginelle as he continued to watch her. She was not telling him everything but he feared he already knew her thoughts and for that, he fell silent and they continued onward to Ashford.

The next morning Ginelle awoke to an empty bed, the space next to her clearly untouched. She felt a maddening rush of tears but refused to acknowledge the pain surrounding her heart.

The sun barely peaked the horizon and he was absent, gone to cater to his mistress. She shoved the blankets away, disgusted and enraged that he would continue to treat her so mindlessly, foolishly proclaiming his love when he secretly sought his mistress' company.

She had to know if what Ellison had seen was true. Did Dorian secretly meet with his mistress, knowing what Victoria had done to her? Did he love her?

She was driven by anger and pain, torn between disbelief and uncertainty as to what to believe. She had to find out the truth and unravel this mystery herself.

With that in mind, she dressed quickly, careful to not wake the servants as she slipped quietly through the manor. She knew once she reached town that the house would fully be aware of her absence.

With Henry's reluctant assistance, he aided her into a carriage and started towards town. Ginelle pondered her mind for places Dorian would go and could think of none other than the Eastern Harbor.

She was a bit apprehensive of going to that particular part of town, after her last encounter she feared going alone despite Pierino's certain death. She tried convincing herself that no harm would come to her so as long as she remained close to Henry whom vowed very tenaciously that she would not leave his sight.

When the carriage finally rolled into town, she was startled to find it bustling with inhabitants. She reached up and gripped her mother's locket, slightly comforted by the tiny trinket as her unease heightened.

She hadn't been aware that the carriage had stopped until Henry appeared at her side, a cold draft hitting her face uncomfortably. "We're here, Miss." He extended a hand to her and he helped her down. "Now you stay by my side or milord would surely have my head for this." His eyes moved warily around the crowd as he stood protectively at her side.

Ginelle took a few steps away from the carriage, old Henry following diligently close as her eyes flowed along the crowd. After several moments of surveying and finding nothing she started to turn away, but a flash of red in her peripheral caught her attention across the street.

She felt a sharp intake of breath at the sight that greeted her. For a moment she wanted to dislodge the image, to contemplate any other reason for Dorian being there, his arm supporting the satin-gloved hand resting lovingly in the crook of his arm, and the warm smile curling his sensual lips as he peered affectionately down at the red-haired woman clinging to his side.

She hadn't realized she had swayed on her feet until Henry steadied her. "Miss, are you alright?"

His words faded into the unknown, nothing was forefront but the couple moving along the street towards the docks. She was outraged but the heaviness on her heart overcame all the powering feelings and emotions coursing through her.

Dorian had lied to her!

The woman at his side was none other than Victoria Petroff.

Chapter 36

Hours later, Ginelle found herself sitting where she had remained since arriving back from town. She peered with an empty stare around the room, reliving those moments that made her heart ache.

The moment she heard him coming, she straightened and inhaled a deep breath, feeling a swift tightness in her chest as the door swung inward.

She noticed his hesitation, his confusion at finding the room dimly lit, and the bed neatly intact. When his eyes finally found her, sitting quietly in the chair, he slowly closed the door behind him.

"What is this?" he asked notably as his eyes accessed her frame. She had not removed her cloak or slippers.

"I am leaving." She said assuredly.

He frowned and stepped towards her. "Leaving? Where are you going?"

She stood as he stepped closer, his blue eyes piercing as he stared down at her. "Far from here." She felt her confidence swaying beneath his intense stare and struggled to say what she had practiced over and again since returning home. "Far from you."

His face darkened with a mixture of confusion and anger. "What's going on, Ginelle?"

She jerked her chin upward, determined to not waver, fighting back the tears that threatened to materialize. "I saw you." The moment she said it aloud, they came uncontrollably, laboriously wetting her face as her emotions poured out of her like a dark, black cloud containing all its rain.

"I saw you." She rasped, achingly. "How could you lie to me? How could you continue seeing her knowing what she did to me?"

She felt a sob rising and inhaled sharply, pivoting away from him, unable to look at him without feeling that merciless ache in her heart.

"Ginelle-"

She wrenched away from him as he attempted to grab her. "Do not touch me." She hissed, crossing the room to put space between them. "I'm leaving tonight. I've gathered my things. I'll have Henry assist me."

When she looked up and met his gaze, her anger intensified. He was actually smirking! Enraged, she had the sudden urge to pummel the grin right off his face. "You find my heartache amusing?" she blurted the words before forestalling them and immediately regretted it.

His smirk vanished and all sincerity softened his face. He stepped towards her and she realized she had no where to turn. He had backed her to a corner. She was determined to look elsewhere but he forced her head up and she gasped as she looked into his eyes. They were the gentlest of blue, that tender blue that bespoke his love; relayed the truth in his heart. "You are wrong, ma petite."

Her heart began to pound dramatically with his words. She shook her head as if to convince herself otherwise. "I saw you."

His mouth curled into a grin, his blue eyes twinkling as he reached up and pushed a blond strand from her face. "What did you see, ma petite?"

Her eyes narrowed heatedly. "I saw you with Victoria." Her lip quivered despite her anger, "I saw you holding her like a man who loves his woman." She attempted to pull away but he held her firm. "I'd rather we not do this. I wish to leave."

"Are you going to run like a coward?" he asked with a slight hint of humor.

Her eyes sharpened like daggers. "I am not a coward."

He laughed gently but his laughter faded as he released her. "It is your courage and defiance that has me captivated."

"Dorian-"

"Are you certain of what you saw, Ginelle?" he demanded, stepping closer until they were a breath apart.

"Yes!" she cried. "Would you have me describe it perfectly?" she shoved at his chest and he captured her wrists easily, jerking lightly until she fell against him.

She was forced to peer up at him as his mouth hovered above her own. "What you saw was all an act." He said gently, "Every gesture, every smile, every longing look-all fabricated."

Ginelle shook her head desperately, "No, you're lying-"

"'I had to make her believe. I would have never convinced her unless I devoted all my time catering to her. I had to make it seem real, that I was hopelessly and erratically in love with her-"

"I don't want to hear this!" she wrenched her hands from his and attempted to cover her ears but he pulled them back down.

"But its you, Ginelle." He captured her chin gently and lifted her tearful eyes to his. "It's you that I have fallen hopelessly for. I could love no other."

Her shoulders shuddered as she closed her eyes against the tears that streaked her face, shaking her head, refusing to believe the validity of his words.

He reached up and brushed away her tears. His hand cupped her face and his thumb adoringly caressed her cheek. "If what you say is true-" Ginelle said, "-then what did you accomplish by gaining her trust?"

His blue eyes leveled firmly on her mouth and she struggled to not encourage his kiss for she yearned for nothing more. "I had to ensure your safety." He said softly as his breath fanned her lips. "I had to make certain that no one would attempt to steal you from me again. She was all that stood between us."

Ginelle couldn't imagine Dorian harming anyone especially a woman he had once been intimate with, nor would she wish that upon anyone but she feared asking what became of Victoria.

As if sensing her thoughts, he laughed suddenly, startling her. "Your thoughts are as transparent as glass, my sweet. Surely you don't think of me such as a monster?"

She detected the humor in his voice and despite all she had thought, she felt her mouth tilting into a smile. "Perhaps a brute-" she said lightly, "-but never a monster."

Dorian laughed and captured her lips in a fevered kiss. Ginelle gave in to the fierce hunger that erupted with his fiery possession as he crushed her against him.

She broke free of his kiss, breathless as she asked, "What did you do to her?"

He was silent a moment before replying, "I convinced her that I tired of London. Knowing her taste for new and engaging things, I offered to take her to America, to begin a new life together."

Ginelle gasped, "Victoria is on a ship?"

"Let's just say when she learned that she would be traveling alone, she wasn't as delighted." His grin widened, "Lieutenant Cummings has obligingly volunteered to see her safely escorted to her new abode."

Ginelle suddenly felt a pang of remorse for Victoria.

Dorian chuckled, "Feeling guilty?"

She felt her face turn red beneath his amusing stare. "I would not wish harm upon anyone."

He shook his head, laughing softly. "No harm will come to her. Life in America will appeal to her exceptionally."

Ginelle felt a rush of tears as she stared adoringly up at him, her heart blossoming beneath his bright blue eyes. "Now what?" she whispered.

His lips curled into that sensual smile. "Now, I make you my wife."

The room was in a flurry of moving bodies and Ginelle stood amid the clamor of excitement as Thora and Belle hastened to finish the touches on her wedding gown and Fannie and Ellison worked to fasten the riot of curls atop her head.

She giggled lightly as she caught sight of Lucile's hem beneath lowered lashes as the housekeeper issued frantic orders for them to hurry.

Amidst all this, Ginelle's thoughts turned inward as she peered lovingly around the circle of women. She had gained so much in merely four years. She had family and friends, all of whom she loved deeply. And she had a man who loved her exceptionally, a man who was soon to become her husband.

She caught sight of her image in the mirror and nearly didn't recognize the woman peering back at her.

She was radiant, adorned in one of her favorite gowns, altered beautifully for her wedding day. The gown was a dove hue, perfectly embroidered with white lace, the silk skirts flowing gently over the distinct roundness of her belly. She smiled softly as she placed her hands tenderly where her babe rested, anxious for the day that she could hold her baby gingerly in her arms.

A sudden knock sounded within the room, jolting all six women. Lucile rushed to the door and opened it ajar. "Oh!" she cried, "Come in, come in!" she urged, stepping aside to allow the visitor within.

A smile spread wide on Ginelle's face as the woman entering the room extended her arms toward her. "You look lovely!" Amelia cried joyfully as the two of them embraced.

"Are you happy, my niece?" Amelia asked gently, her dark eyes roaming Ginelle's face thoughtfully.

Her smile widened, her dark eyes glimmering with tears. "Yes, very much."

Amelia reflected her niece's smile and squeezed her hands gently. "As am I."

"We must hurry!" Lucile implored and the two women laughed softly at the housekeeper's urging. Amelia squeezed Ginelle's hand once more before leaving the room and it was than Ginelle felt the swift fluttering in her belly and smiled despite her nervousness.

She was to marry.

In spite of the cold weather, they were to exchange their vows within the garden. It was specifically chosen because alongside his sister and mother, his soon-to-be-wife's fondness for the enclosure had prompted his decision in choosing it for their wedding.

Although the wintry season had destroyed the flowers, the garden at that moment was absolutely picturesque.

The sky was painted white, revealing faint lines of thick alabaster clouds. Icicles glinted like diamonds in the crystalline light, dangling from snow laden limbs; the ground at his feet was like powder as it was carried away with the wind.

A soft descent of snowflakes drifted like white blossoms from the sky and his breath caught in his throat, not from the sudden snowfall but for the woman standing before the terrace, her beauty eliciting a sharp breath from his throat.

Mine. He thought instinctively.

Ginelle felt a rush of tears as she stared at the man who had captivated her heart. He stood tall and prominent against the white backdrop. Donned alluringly in sleek black trousers, a black tailcoat layered with a white satin shirt and cravat, he was absolutely striking.

When she met his eyes, she was stunned by the expression that softened his face. His eyes were alight with emotion, a profound love radiating from his crystal blue gaze. His eyes never wavered from her and with each step that brought her closer to him, her heart beat all the more.

He reached out and took her hand in his own, drawing her forward to stand before him. And she knew as she held his hand in her own and they exchanged their vows, combining them as one, she knew she had found her place in life.

Epilogue

One year later

Ginelle laughed happily as she watched her husband duck his head to avoid the tiny hands reaching clumsily to tug at his black strands. Her eyes twinkled merrily against the morning light pouring beautifully into their room as she lounged comfortably on the bed, her eyes never straying from the two playing on the carpet.

"Cease your laughter woman!" her husband wailed as he yelped beneath another playful tug from their daughter as the one-year old grabbed another fistful of hair and pulled. "Wife!"

Ginelle pressed a fist against her mouth to keep from laughing and watched as Dorian rolled to his feet and gently plucked little Eloise Anne into his arms, his blue eyes twinkling adoringly as he cradled his daughter.

"You are as courageous as your mother, little one." He smiled as his daughter kicked her legs and giggled.

"Is that so bad?" Ginelle teased, her mouth tilting into a grin as she extended her arms to her husband.

Dorian settled onto the bed and with their daughter planted firmly in their laps, he leaned forward and captured his wife's lips.

"I wouldn't have it any other way." He said softly, kissing the brim of her nose.

Ginelle smiled and peered down at their daughter, her blue eyes twinkling and the black curls atop her little head ruffled. "Good." She said readily, peering back at her husband. "Because we're soon to have another."

His eyes widened and his mouth parted with a gasp. "You're pregnant?"

She nodded, smiling.

His mouth stretched widely into a grin and he planted another passionate kiss on his wife's lips, their daughter wiggling between them.

Dorian yelped when his daughter caught another strand of hair and tugged. He laughed heartily as he gathered his daughter and wife into his arms.

"I think it best you give me a boy so that I may fend the two of you off." He nuzzled Ginelle's neck and she giggled beneath his caress. "I love you, sweet wife."

"And I you, sweet husband."

www.ingramcontent.com/pod-product-compliance
Lightning Source LLC
Chambersburg PA
CBHW070736190726
48292CB00002B/288
9781944253431